RETURNING FROM SILENCE

MICHÈLE SARDE

Returning from Silence
Jenny's Story

Translated from the French by Rupert Swyer

SWAN ISLE PRESS

CHICAGO

Michèle Sarde is a novelist, biographer, essayist, and professor emerita at Georgetown University. She has been awarded by the Government of France the prestigious Chevalier dans l'Ordre National du Mérite and Chevalier dans l'Ordre des Arts et Lettres.

Rupert Swyer is an independent translator and journalist. He lives in Paris.

Swan Isle Press, Chicago 60628
©2022 by Swan Isle Press
©Michèle Sarde
Translation © Rupert Swyer

Printed in the United States of America
First Edition
26 25 24 23 22   1 2 3 4 5
ISBN-13: 9781736189306 (Paperback)

Originally published as *Revenir du Silence* by Michèle Sarde (Éditions Julliard, Paris, 2016)

Cover Images: ©Yannis Megas, *Souvenir, Images of the Jewish Community, Salonika 1897-1917*, Kapon, 1993
    Family Archive©Michèle Sarde

Library of Congress Cataloging-in-Publication Data
Names: Sarde, Michèle, author. | Swyer, Rupert, translator.
Title: Returning from silence : Jenny's story / Michèle Sarde; translated from the French by Rupert Swyer.
Other titles: Revenir du silence. English
Description: First edition. | Chicago : Swan Isle Press, 2022.
Identifiers: LCCN 2022014127 | ISBN 9781736189306 (paperback; alk. paper)
Subjects: LCSH: World War, 1939-1945--Jews--France--Fiction. | LCGFT: Historical fiction. | Novels.
Classification: LCC PQ2679.A677 R4813 2022 | DDC 843/.914--dc23/eng/20220401
LC record available at https://lccn.loc.gov/2022014127

Swan Isle Press gratefully acknowledges that this edition was made possible, in part, with generous support of the following:

HEMINGWAY GRANT FROM THE CULTURAL SERVICES OF THE FRENCH EMBASSY IN THE UNITED STATES

LITERARY ARTS EMERGENCY FUND: ADMINISTERED BY THE ACADEMY OF AMERICAN POETS, COMMUNITY OF LITERARY MAGAZINES & PRESSES, AND NATIONAL BOOK FOUNDATION, SUPPORTED BY THE MELLON FOUNDATION

EUROPE BAY GIVING TRUST

JIM BUDISH

KEN AND ANDREA SAFFIR

AND OTHER KIND DONORS

To Arnaud, Margaux, and Emerson.

To all those who come after us

and want to know where they come from.

For Hugo and Kimberly, who have journeyed with us.

CONTENTS

III
The Sound and the Fury

IV
The Silence

ILLUSTRATIONS

Transmission

> But for a little while some of that can be
> rescued, if only, faced with the vastness of
> all that there is and all that there ever was,
> somebody makes the decision to look back, to
> have one last look, to search for a while in the
> debris of the past and to see not only what was
> lost but what there is still to be found.
>
> —DANIEL MENDELSOHN, *THE LOST*

For a long time, I hid my name and my age. Being a woman, I could legally hide my family name behind my husband's. Later, a pseudonym gave me cover. For two centuries, this has served as a mask beneath which writers of all origins can publish. Which does writing do better? Reveal or conceal? That is a riddle I have yet to solve. Perhaps the act of rediscovering the story of my life may yield an answer.

As I began recalling my earliest years it was my childhood, not my age, that troubled me. My ill-timed and unsettled childhood began with World War Two. I was born when it was declared; I was a little over five when it ended. Those five years made all the difference, for it was during those years that my real name came to be hidden behind false papers.

Talking about my childhood meant talking about the War. It meant being endlessly on the run first from the occupier, then from the occupied. It meant owning up. Later, I realized it was not so much my childhood that was problematic as the Nazi Occupation, which had left an indelible scar on my story, a story I was forbidden to mention. For that would have entailed unwinding the entire reel; I would have had to acknowledge that my personal journey was more intimately bound up than other biographies with the broader canvas of history. In short, it would have meant disobeying my mother who was intent on keeping my identity hidden.

Still, the idea of writing one's life story is an old one. This story, my own and—my misgivings notwithstanding—my family's, had a hard time seeing the light of day. The mystery was dispelled only intermittently and invariably took me back to a single source, my mother. She had lived through two major historical upheavals in her early life: emigration and the Holocaust. Long before her own time a third upheaval had left its mark on her people's history, namely the expulsion of the Jews from Spain, transporting her ancestors, their language and their Iberian soul all the way to the Ottoman Empire.

These historical wounds scarred every succeeding generation. The most recent had seared our own, first her, then me. One drop at a time, usually with great reluctance, she passed on to me the tale of these three upheavals that had profoundly shaped her story. The most recent, above all, was haunted by two shadows that refused to fade away or to make way for normal, presentable ancestors, the kind that die in a bed.

At my request, my mother accepted to put down her recollections in her own handwriting in a 150-page exercise book, which she then handed to me, begging me to fill out the rest by asking questions. And I knew from experience the painful solitude of the blank page. On an old taperecorder we recorded a long conversation between mother and daughter. To complete this assemblage of memories, this tale—Monologue and Dialogue— which I call "Mother's Transmission," one day she took out a mysterious suitcase filled with photographs, letters, documents that corroborated what she had told me, and a family tree.

After her death I began to hunt for those of whom I knew next to nothing, conscious that it is her above all that I am exhuming and bringing back to life, from the district of the White Tower in Salonika where she was born to the small village in the Brie district of France, dozing beneath its church steeple, where she now rests. Her. My mother. The first face in my life. Behind her, other faces lost in the mist. Behind her, Moïse and Marie, who never returned. One mystery hides another, and the time machine for exploring the secrets of the past may perhaps yet reassemble the lost tribe.

In relating this quest, part history, part fiction, after much hesitation I opted for a free form mingling creative writing with family recollection. Documentary evidence attests to the veracity of History; fiction helps to humanize it and bring it to life.

I
Salonika, Oh Salonika: Born in the Orient

In the case of the Jews, every civilization was
implicated and invariably found itself in a
position of overwhelming superiority. Against
such strength and numbers, the Jews were but
a tiny band of adversaries. But these adversaries
had unusual opportunities: one prince might
persecute them, another protect them; one
economy might ruin them, another make their
fortunes; one civilization might reject them and
another welcome them with open arms.[1]

—FERNAND BRAUDEL, *THE MEDITERRANEAN*

---

1. I owe this translation to Peter Myers, May 22, 2002 [Translator].

The Great Fire

Salonika, Greece, formerly part of the Ottoman Empire. At four in the afternoon on August 5, 1917, in the heat of the siesta hour, a thirteen-month-old child named Janja was sleeping in her cradle, watched over by a prepubescent servant girl. The house was empty. Marie Benveniste, her mother, had left in a hurry for the elegant neighborhood at the other end of town, to assist her sister in her second confinement. Meanwhile, Saby Amon, her father, was at work, as always, in the family fabric store.

Suddenly, a cry went up. It sounded like a kind of roar:

"*INSENDIO! Yangin var!* Fire!"

All day, a fierce wind had blown in from the Vardar hills without dispelling the heat. It was stifling. In the western part of the town, where timber and mud-brick hovels huddled together in the Mevlané district, a woman refugee fleeing the devastation of war was grilling eggplants over a wood fire to feed her family. Suddenly, a gust of wind caught her brazier; the flame flared up and spread. Soon, the hut was a blazing torch. Within moments the whole neighborhood was ablaze. The gusting, squalling Vardarec, as the wind was called, blew the flames eastward and westward. The fire spread like a trail of gunpowder through the other neighborhoods right up to the sea, sparing a block of houses here or there, a building, a small garden or alleyway, but devouring all the rest. Soon the entire city was a huge inferno.

The fire that ravaged the town pursued its hellish course through the old port area. The fire reached the timber houses in the Jewish quarter at the foot of the White Tower, the ancient Blood Tower, which somehow escaped unscathed. But there was no water to quench it. The pipes had been diverted to feed the camps of the Allied troops commanded by General Sarrail.

The father heeded the rumor now threatening his shop:

"Saby, your house is burning down."

He raced breathlessly through the streets, entered the house, and rushed upstairs to help the young maid downstairs, threw her the baby wrapped in a sheet, grabbed his wife Marie's gold watch and the engraved silver Ottoman bowl, which the family had handed down from mother to daughter. They barely had time to step back as their house in turn vanished in the flames.

The fire hurtled on like a raging buffalo, swallowing up the shop too, from which they rescued only the ledger books. But it left the outlying districts intact. The warehouses and the home of Marie's parents, the Benvenistes, were spared. So was the Modianos' fine house on the seafront, where their second daughter, Allegra, assisted by her sister Marie, moaned, screamed for more than twenty-four hours before giving birth to another boy, thank God.

All the while, Marie had no idea her own house was burning while her child slept.

All evening, throughout that August night, all Sunday morning, the city was nothing but a vast furnace. For the inhabitants, it was everyone for themselves in their flight to the outskirts of the town, the countryside, and the fields. Fanned by the wind, the fire's destructive fury knew no bounds. The flames engulfed people's belongings thrown into boats in the port or hastily carried to the fields. Nothing could withstand the flying embers, on the water or in the city environs, as the inhabitants' remaining possessions went up in smoke.

4

That evening, the Benvenistes' home was like a transit camp. Dozens of relatives made homeless had flocked there. Women sobbed, telling dreadful tales of survivors covered in ashes, their hands blackened as they strove desperately to save their kinsfolk and their goods. Maïr and his family took stock of the situation. No victims. But the shops and storehouses were still burning, along with the merchandise. The home of Marie, Saby and their little Janja was no longer there. Other homes, other shops were in ruins. The fire had destroyed the entire area to the east of the free port, south of Saint Demetrius as far as Archiropiïtos, the Arch of Galerius and the Church of Nea Panagia.

Before the eyes of its powerless inhabitants, the Jewish town, the old city of the Romaniotes and the banished of Sefarad had turned to dust.

A few days later, the family assembled again in the home of their relatives, the Benvenistes. There was Maïr, the patriarch and his wife Oro, their daughters, Marie, the eldest, with her husband Saby Amon, and their three sons, Rafo, Pepo and Momo. All spoke the archaic Spanish of the fifteenth century, which had come to be known here as Judeo-Spanish, their language. This is the language they had grown accustomed to calling "Ladino." I can imagine what they were thinking at this moment:

"It's our town, the Jewish town, that's been destroyed," laments Maïr. "The Turks on the higher ground and the Greeks have suffered less than us. Where shall we go to pray, now? Almost all our synagogues, our oratories, our yeshivot, our libraries have been devastated."

"And the Talmud Thora," adds Saby Amon, his son-in-law. "And the schools."

"Even the buildings of our *Alliance Israélite*," points out Rafo, the eldest son.

"They've told me the community chancellery's archives have gone up in flames too. All that was left of our ancestors."

"Many of our poor have nowhere to sleep," Marie joins in. "They're camping in the wreckage, in courtyards, in the fields, in the Mosques even. We must do something."

"Some people are much worse off than we are," observes Saby. "They blew up our cousin Nissim's street with dynamite, but it didn't check the fire."

"My *Nona* told me about plenty of fires in the past, but they rebuilt the synagogues every time," now it's Grandma Oro's turn to speak.

"There'll be no rebuilding this time," the patriarch predicts. "The Greeks will never let us do it. It's only five years since they wrested their city from the Turks. Now they'll be taking ours back too."

"*Entonses, sinyor padre, kualo vamos a azer?* So, what are we going to do, then, Father?" this is Pepo, the youngest son, speaking.

"*Kualo vamos a azer, fijo? Vamos a partir.* What we're going to do, Son? We'll leave. Again. Just as our forefathers did, over four hundred years ago."

His eyes rested on the baby, who had just woken up and was looking anxiously around the family.

"For Janja and my grandchildren to come... we must *leave*... *Mos vamos a ir.* Not yet. There's a war going on. But leave we must."

Even before he pointed to her, Marie intercepted her father's glance in the direction of the baby Janja. When she married, a few years earlier, Marie imagined she was escaping enslavement to her mother, who had forced her to leave school early to handle the family's sewing. Now she had lost her home and was once more under her mother's hated yoke. Leave! The magic of her father's words enfolded her in its implied promise: they were going to leave. She would do whatever it took to ensure they did.

Maïr Benveniste, the *sinyor padre*, was deeply committed to his community, but he was right. Jewish Salonika, with its thirty-seven synagogues and eighty oratories, would not be rebuilt; Salonika, which had given refuge to those expelled from Spain and Portugal, loyalist Jews and repentant *marrano* converts. Thessaloniki, as the city was now called under the Greeks, would arise from its ashes. But the city of Maïr and his father Rafael, the city of their ancestors from Castile, Aragon, and the other provinces of Spain, would survive only in old photographs and the memory of those who had seen it.

As Oro recalled, in the past when a synagogue burned down, it would be rebuilt exactly as before and, if possible, more beautiful, where it had stood. When a house was destroyed, it grew back on the same land. The new Greek nation swept all that away. The city's land registry was reformed. The reconstruction plan entailed the expropriation of thousands of Jewish owners whose buildings and homes had been devoured by the flames. Their former neighborhoods were no longer. New housing projects sprang up in the wake of the mass expropriations, and already the old Jewish cemetery made way for homes for the Greeks from Asia Minor.

"We civilizations now know ourselves mortal," wrote the French poet Paul Valéry in *Crisis of the Spirit*. What remains of Carthage or Babylon, Nineveh or Baghdad, today? Or even the Paris of Rétif de La Bretonne? Yet their inhabitants remain the same. In Thessaloniki, however, the demise of the Ottoman Empire in 1918 brought an exchange of populations, as the Turks of Salonika made way for Greeks from Asia Minor. Two decades later, when the Nazi occupier completed the destruction of the graves in the old Jewish cemetery, driving out the dead even as they dispatched the living to extermination camps, the Jews no longer had their age-old neighbors to offer a hunk of bread and hide them in their homes as other Greeks did in Athens.

All that remains in the memory of the rare survivors of all these disasters, of whom the little Janja was one, is a handful of postcards fallen from an album titled *Thessaloniki*, which used to be sold along with another titled *Souvenir* by Mrs. Molho. She still ran the Jewish bookshop in Salonika in the 1990s. The views date from well before the sinister Alois Brunner and his SS killers completed the annihilation of the Jews of the ancient Jewish city of Maïr and his forefathers.

The disastrous Great Fire awakened an ancestral urge to resist, ancestral reflexes too. The Spanish Jews no longer belonged here in Thessaloniki. Gone was their city even before they left it. It was now in the hands of property developers and town planners. Conscription was introduced. New laws prevented the Jews from observing their faith; rumors of ritual murder resurfaced. There were accusations of a lack of patriotism, of cosmopolitanism and treason. A few years later, the city even subjected the fire's survivors to the Campbell pogrom.

As it was, Maïr no longer had a synagogue where he could rail against his God, like Solal in Albert Cohen's novel: "Oh God, God, You are, and yet, You allow this pain to exist."

For the first time since their expulsion from Spain, the Benvenistes faced a painful choice: assimilate or leave. Theirs was a milder form of the dilemma their Castilian ancestors, Don Juda Senior and Don Samuel Meïr

Benveniste had faced when they chose to flee Toledo for Salonika, more than four hundred years before.

Ancestors

On the night after the Great Fire Maïr, the patriarch, couldn't sleep. TO LEAVE? ... IR.... To go? He had spoken the word in front of his children two nights beforehand and couldn't get it out of his mind. Leave? To leave behind his town, his community, the Jewish Salonika of his ancestors, an enclave within the Ottoman town, which had only recently become Greek once more, but still a Jerusalem for the Jews. A city where people rested on Saturday, not on Friday nor on Sunday; where everyone, from lawyer to street porter, spoke the Spanish his ancestors had brought with them from Sefarad, from the Spain that had cast them out.

Four centuries later, Maïr faced a similar alternative: should he and his family stay? Or should they leave the city where his forefathers had found refuge and settled their tribe?

Should he stay, or should he go? All night long Maïr turned over the dilemma in his mind. Admittedly the decision was far less wrenching than the one that must have haunted the nights of his distant ancestors in Toledo. They faced the appalling choice of conversion or exile. Submission or resignation? For them, the Alhambra Decree was clear: it was an edict of expulsion. They could not stay loyal to both Spain and their faith. Forced to choose, the Benvenistes' forebears had made their choice.

Five years before the Great Fire Maïr, visiting the spacious cemetery where his ancestors Don Juda Senior, Don Samuel Meïr and Rabbi Rafael lay buried, already sensed that Salonika had ceased to be his city. He felt too that, even if he wanted to, he could no longer live in the manner of his father, his grandfather and their direct predecessors. Nor did he want to. Without realizing it, he was already making ready for the great departure.

Maïr knew his forebears well, from the archives of the community in which he was a leading figure. Their names were Don Juda Senior and Don Samuel Meïr Benveniste. First cousins, one a bibliophile, the other a physician. Juda Senior was born in Toledo in 1433, Samuel Meïr in the same city in 1440.

What were they thinking, wondered their distant descendant, in that terrible year for the Jews, as their ship neared the shores of the Thermaic Gulf and entered the waters of Salonika, so familiar to Maïr yet so foreign to them? Of the Castile they had left behind them in 1492, where they had been great noblemen, entitled to wear a cloak and to carry a sword by their side? Of their great-grandfather Don Abraham Benveniste, minister to King John II of Castile as well as Supreme Judge of the Jews and Court Rabbi? But Don Abraham belonged to an earlier generation before the age of persecution.

Maïr's forebears reached Salonika before the deadline banishing the Jews from Spain set by the Most Catholic King and Queen, Ferdinand of Aragon and Isabella of Castile. While so many of their brothers, cousins and sons had denied their faith, Don Juda and Don Samuel ventured forth across hostile seas, with no assurance they would find a haven. They weathered storms, overcame epidemics, avoided pirates lying in wait to slit their bellies in search of the gold coins they were rumored to have swallowed before setting sail, or hoping to sell them as slaves. Their voyage, to be repeated many times over by thousands of their fellow Jews in the decades to come, was long and perilous. But they survived.

In the port of Salonika, where Juda Senior and Samuel Meïr landed at last, these two gentlemen nevertheless came as privileged pioneers, bringing with them their households, servants, domestic animals, and their libraries. They placed their precious libraries at the disposal of the community, drawing many men of letters, until the day those repositories of knowledge vanished in another of the city's frequent fires.

Don Juda Senior. Don Samuel Meïr. Even better than their manuscripts, liable to be destroyed by fire or damaged by water, they brought with them something that death alone could take from them: their learning, their erudition, and their mastery of the sciences sacred and profane, things of benefit to the entire community. As the boat carrying the diaspora sailed the high seas, Samuel read poetry in Hebrew, while Juda Senior consulted the *Book of Splendor* from the Kabbala in Aramaic, and the philosophers of Antiquity in Greek. Both devoured their favorite work, the *Guide for the Perplexed* by

Moses Maimonides, in Arabic. For had not Maimonides dedicated it not only to his disciple but to all those facing dilemmas such as theirs?

Behind the port, the city that welcomed them was enclosed within square ramparts flanked by towers dominated by a citadel. It clung to a hillside sloping down to the sea in a tangle of greenery, dotted with plane trees and cypresses. The hospitality of the Sublime Porte was courteous, warm even. The refugees were not even required to pay a landing tax. I can imagine the two cousins muttering under their breath Sultan Bajazet II's famous jibe reportedly aimed at his adversary, the King of Spain: "How can he be wise and intelligent, this monarch who impoverishes his kingdom and enriches mine?"

Now subjects of the Ottoman Empire, the two Castilians took instruction in the Millet system, under the protection of which they were to live henceforward. Like Christians, whom Muslims respected, they were nonetheless treated as inferiors. Don Juda Benveniste and his cousin were forbidden to do any harm to Islam, to insult it or deride it. Nor could they ride a horse as in Spain, nor build a house or a synagogue taller than the mosque. They were not allowed to have any form of sexual relations with or marry a Muslim. Jews and Christians were required to step aside before Muslims in the street. Also, they had to wear clothes of a distinctive color and certain characteristic accessories. In return, Don Juda and Don Samuel enjoyed autonomy and could practice their religion as they saw fit. They had the right to live according to their laws and customs, against payment of a collective tax levied on free and valid adult males.

On this basis, Juda Senior, Samuel Meïr and their countrymen pieced together the shreds of their lost homeland and transformed the ancient Thessaloniki into a corner of Spain. There they resumed the lives they had always lived by the banks of the Tagus or the Guadalquivir. They preserved their rites, their crafts, their faith, their pleasures, and their way of life. And in their hearts, they cherished the Iberia whose joys and sorrows they had shared for centuries, yet which had so basely driven them out.

The dilemma forced on them by the Catholic Kings had unintended consequences. In their new abode, the families of Juda Senior and Samuel Meïr were Jewish, more Jewish than ever precisely because of the sacrifice they had made. But in Spain, relatives, children, parents or spouses who remained behind converted to Christianity. Their cousin Ester, for example, had journeyed with them to this unfamiliar Empire, but her husband, Haïm, had remained in Toledo, becoming a New Christian and taking the name of Miguel de Santa Maria.

Now she came to them with a novel request:

"Cousin, am I still married to my renegade husband according to our law? Can I marry your nephew Jacob without committing the sin of bigamy?"

Juda Senior, sixty years old when he came to Salonika, presided over the triumvirate that upheld the rules and now had to invent an answer to Ester's question and to many other still more unexpected and still more outlandish ones. He replied:

"Yes, Ester. Your husband is no longer one of us, so you may choose for yourself a husband from among *los muestros*, our own people."

He was later forced to revise his judgment when the *conversos* themselves, the *marranos*, were driven from Portugal and elsewhere, arrived in Ottoman lands and returned to the Jewish faith.

Don Samuel and his cousin's youth had been Castilian; their old age was Ottoman. Castile had expelled them; the Ottomans welcomed them. They built the Jerusalem of the Balkans; they kept their God and preserved their language; and they invented a city within the ancient Hellenic and Turkish city.

Four centuries later, Maïr Benveniste's youth was Ottoman. Only now, the Ottoman Empire barely existed. And Maïr sensed that his own old age would be a journey in reverse, taking him westward to the Europe from which his ancestors, Juda Senior and Samuel Meïr had been forced to flee.

Between August 5, 1917, when the fire destroyed his city, and the day of the great departure, Maïr Benveniste continued to meditate on the fate of his forefathers who had come to the city he and their descendants were about to leave. Four years later, he, the patriarch, was still taking the measure of all that his ancestors had bequeathed him. Yet here he was, preparing to leave it all behind to keep the faith with them and rebuild elsewhere.

Maïr knew what he owed those who had gone before him. He knew what they had handed down to him.

To Maïr Benveniste, Don Juda and Don Samuel had bequeathed a city, or rather a city within the city, where the persecuted of all ages had come to find refuge, and which by turns they had called the "City Mother of Israel," the "Jewish Republic," the "Land of Milk and Honey," the "Hebrew City in Exile," the "Citadel of the Sephardim."

To Maïr, Don Juda and Don Samuel had bequeathed a house in which to pray to his God, the temple for the sake of which they had left behind the thousand-year-old homeland that had ordained its destruction. Their first task on arrival in Salonika had been to provide the community with synagogues. The names of those places of worship reflected their founders' geographic and linguistic origins, names that resounded in the ears of their great-grandchildren like a roll-call of lost lands: Aragon and Castile, Majorca and Sicily, Catalonia, and Lisbon.

One of the greatest gifts Don Juda and Don Samuel had bequeathed to Maïr Benveniste was a business in cloth, a business more valuable than gold. Where the Turks were warriors, officials, and rentiers mainly, and where the Greeks were attached to their ancestral lands, transforming it with their hands, the Jews banished from Spain were artisans, craftsmen, merchants. Up until 1826, the uniforms of the Sultans' Janissaries were cut from Jewish cloth. From Toledo, Segovia and Barcelona, the exiles brought weaving techniques, tools, and machines, bringing their knowhow to the Macedonian city where they pursued trades of every kind. They were weavers, dyers, fullers, and shearers. They sorted, span, warped and starched. Maïr and his sons grew rich in this trade thanks to their wide-ranging contacts.

For to Maïr Benveniste, Don Juda and Don Samuel had bequeathed their web of business contacts throughout the ports of the Levant. Wherever the proscribed Jews had gone and settled, brothers and cousins would put down roots, forging a network of mutual trust.

Trust was what remained when all else had been lost. From Antwerp to Venice, Ferrara, Amsterdam, London, and Marseille, all the way to the Ottoman Empire, these scattered families communicated among themselves through trade and diplomacy. Wanderers they may once have been, and they were still landless, but they were travelers, dealing in goods just as invisible and as indivisible as their faith or their tongue, and binding them together was their trustworthiness in business: their word was their bond.

Above all, Don Juda and Don Samuel had bequeathed a language. The mother tongue Maïr and his children still spoke right into the twentieth century. Four centuries earlier, Juda Senior and Samuel Meïr had brought this medieval Castilian with them. So deep was it in their veins that, even mingled with local accretions, their Castilian Spanish had survived competition from the numerous rival idioms spoken in Salonika.

Waiting to welcome the two men and their tribes upon their arrival in the Ottoman port at the end of the fifteenth century were fellow Jews speaking Greek, Italian, Provençal, Catalan, Yiddish even. Coming from all over the Iberian Peninsula, their companions in misfortune strove to establish their respective languages, from Andalusian to Catalan and Galician, not to mention Portuguese. Four centuries later, everyone in Salonika, Jews and Gentiles alike, spoke the same Castilian, bastardized and enriched by local conditions—that Judeo-Spanish or Ladino, which quite simply they called *Judesmo*—"Jewish."

It was in this old Spanish tongue that little Janja babbled her first words, the language she spoke to her grandfather Maïr and her grandmother Oro. Later, it was in this language that she whispered to my father, in a corner of the room, when she wanted to keep her dreaded secrets from her own daughter—myself—when a child.

It was in his ancestral Ladino, after a sleepless night, that Maïr Benveniste made the decision to follow the example of his forebears in adversity:

"*Ya mos vamos a ir...* We're leaving."

Rafael, first in the family tree

Should we go? Should we stay? For Maïr, staying meant living the life of his father, Rafael. Out of the question!

Genealogy holds the key to the gulf separating five generations, and to the thread that binds them.

In this family tree handed down to his great-granddaughter Janja a good century later, Rafael Benveniste stands at the top. He was the last to spend his whole life in his home city. To avoid misleading the reader, only his name and that of ancestors who figure in this story figure in the family tree below. Sisters, brothers, husbands, and wives who played no part in this tale are left blank.

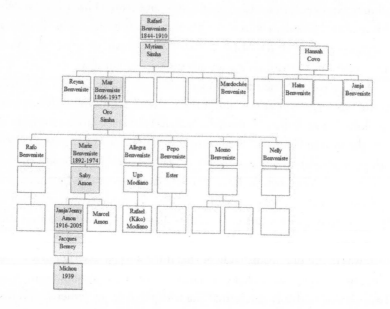

A little under four centuries separate the two Benvenistes banished by the Catholic Monarchs from their descendant, Rafael, the poor rabbi with a big family. Now, father and son, Rafael and Maïr, symbolized the radical transformations of Salonika in the space of a single generation, in terms of population, its economy, indeed its very physical appearance.

Jewish Salonika's first golden age ended with the fanaticism surrounding the apostate Messiah, Shabtai Tsevi—who ultimately converted to Islam under pressure from the Sultan. There followed a long period of decadence, as natural catastrophes—plague, cholera, hurricanes, and earthquakes—struck fear into the hearts of the community, sparing no one. Superstition and immobilism took hold in the Jewish city.

That was the prevailing atmosphere still in Salonika when Rafael Benveniste was born in 1844. He died there in 1910, seven years before the Great Fire that convinced his son Maïr to pack his bags.

Rafael was as unlike his son as he differed from their glorious forefathers. Yet he was the sole depositary of his ancestral heritage and the last person in our family to be born and die in the city. History wisely matches events to the temperaments of those who live through them or shape them. As Jewish Salonika experienced one last heyday, in the late-nineteenth, early-twentieth century, the sedentary Rafael was one of those who stayed behind, while Maïr was one of those who left while the going was good.

Salonika was the Ottoman Empire's third largest city, and it still nestled within its Byzantine ramparts. Each day at sundown the young Rafael saw the city gates being locked and barricaded. The entire southern part from the saltpans stretching beyond the White Tower was still covered in dense, game-filled woods. Within the ramparts, the family huddled in a cramped district, in a maze of narrow alleys and lanes, and he daily threaded his way through these winding backstreets, cul-de-sacs and covered passages.

Rafael knew the labyrinthine city like the back of his hand. He walked past men rushing about their business and mothers weighed down by wailing children and endless household chores, and was jostled by donkeys, cows, and chickens. The street was an annex to the home, usually built from timber or wattle and daub. People had haphazardly added their own extensions, terraces, overhangs, balconies, and belvederes where they could rest in the cooler hours, enjoying a spoonful or two of rose petal preserve.

The young Rafael bore little resemblance to his erudite and scholarly forebears, who read Maimonides in the original Arabic! While bolder students secretly consulted the impious Maimonides, who had sought to reconcile Judaism and reason, Rafael's schooling was confined to the rudiments of the Talmud Thora and a smattering of Hebrew in a Yeshiva. He and his fellows—boys only—were scrawny, sickly, dirty, dressed in rags, sometimes barefoot.

By decision of his father, he was to become a rabbi and would marry the daughter of another rabbi.

One day in 1864, at a time set by the two fathers, Maïr Benveniste the Elder entered the Yeshiva where his son was mumbling his prayers under the master's rod. The conversation probably went something like:

"*Rafael, fijo mio, tu vas a cazarte con Myriam, la fija de Jacob Simha*—Rafael, my son, you are to marry Myriam, the daughter of Jacob Simha."

"*Yo siguo su dezeo, sinyor padre*—as you wish, Father."

The fathers arranged the wedding. Myriam's father, Jacob Simha, came from a wealthy family that attended the Ashkenazi synagogue. Myriam's dowry compensated for her plain looks and rather ungainly physique. But love had no part in this transaction. Rafael's father was penniless and had to assure his son's future. As for Myriam's father, his duty was to marry his daughter, all his daughters, be they humpbacked, lame, or hideous. In that way, poor but handsome young men would be paired off with homely girls, while gorgeous but dowry-less virgins would be matched with old goats, however repulsive. There were no old maids or old bachelors: there was a mate for everyone within the community, with no need to look outside!

The young Rafael lost no time preparing for the marriage ceremony and paid a visit with beating heart to his fiancée, whom he had never met. Myriam was scarcely better-informed than her intended and was younger still. From out of nowhere, she first saw the man who would make her a mother up to ten times over (not all her offspring would survive). And they would wait patiently to take their place, marked by an empty space in the paternal home, in order to house their own children.

The wedding between Rafael and Myriam was to stretch over eight days. Eight days during which the doors of the nuptial home remained open to everyone in the town, who flocked to be sprinkled with rosewater and to say *besiman tov*. The wine flowed as dishes of rice, fish, chicken, and kebab were passed around. "*No hay boda sin pandero*—no wedding without tambourines," goes the saying. There was even a violin, a recent arrival from Smyrna.

Among the wedding gifts Myriam received was an oval silver platter with an embossed rim and a fine movable divider in the middle. This symbol of local hospitality was designed to serve rose petal preserves on the side and to present silver spoons with finely crafted handles on the other. This object, known as the "Ottoman dish," was handed down from mother to daughter, till finally it came down to me.

A decade or so after her marriage, there's a sepia photo that's lacking: that of Myriam, who had died already. Alive, she would have worn a damask *antari*, a ladies' doublet, and a *delantal*, a kind of apron, capped by a *coffia*, a headdress with a silk square at the rear, embroidered with tiny pearls. Alive, she would have ruled over her seven children, five of them boys, the last of whom finished her off. For how many long hours did she scream

as she brought the little Mardochée (Mordechai) into the world? She was carried off by a puerperal fever without leaving a sister to replace her in the marriage bed, as was the custom.

Rafael's second wife was Hannah Covo, a comelier cousin who bore him four children. The last child, her only daughter, was called Janja, who died before reaching her fifteenth year. My own mother owed her first given name to this girl who died early. Rafael was still young and could not afford to be downcast for long: he had to rule both his congregation and his household. Even before Myriam's death, the very young bridegroom had become a patriarch and justice-giver, reigning over a household rather like a tribe, inspiring a holy terror in one and all. He had eleven children to feed; there were dowries to be arranged for his three daughters; and eight sons to be provided for, including Maïr, the eldest.

On Saturdays, the Sabbath day, the young rabbi, dressed in his finery, used to go to the temple to deliver his sermon, commenting on the *parasha* or the *haftara* for the week, continuing with advice on proper behavior, charity, concord, and probity, supported by sayings from the Talmud. The synagogue would be packed with the old folk dressed in silk caftans, held in with a wide red belt and furs. In the evenings, as the sun went down, the young people would stroll about in groups, while at the third star Rafael would light the oil lamp, then utter the *Havdalah* blessing over the wine, raw coffee beans or aromatic herbs.

But as the rabbi's work alone could not feed a family, Rafael also worked in the family's ancestral cloth business. His business was concentrated in the free port, in a little square thronged by travelers stepping off the boat from Constantinople, Egypt or Europe, where people swapped political and business news. This was where he met with his colleagues, fellows, and members of the congregation. Standing in the middle of a tight circle or sitting on a low, backless stool, he sipped his coffee from tiny cups and breathed in smoke emanating from the long snaking tubes of the narghiles.

Outside the home, he shared news with the other merchants while his clerks scurried between the little square and the shops in the neighboring streets. The Stock Exchange was nearby, at Yildiz Han, and as today, fortunes were made and lost in minutes. Marseille accounted for the bulk of Salonika's trade, but Lyon, Amsterdam and London were trading partners too.

Then came the day in 1874 when Rafael was deep in conversation with Myriam's brother, the powerful Joseph Simha. I have often wondered how these men arranged the lives of their children, their womenfolk especially. Possibly something like:

"It's a deal, Rafael! My daughter's fifteen but there's no rush. She can be betrothed to your son Maïr right away, though. Oro will come with a fine dowry. My family owes it to you, since we couldn't replace Myriam... *La prove de mi ermana, bendiche sea del Dio!* My poor sister, may God bless her!"

There was no getting around it: his glorious ancestors notwithstanding, Rafael Benveniste was just a poor rabbi in the pay of his brother-in-law, Chief Rabbi Simha, a wealthy Salonika dignitary. Still, Fortune has a way of evening things up. Despite his lofty status, for his sins Joseph Simha was cursed, as his great-granddaughter Janja put it, with a "gaggle of girls" or, to put it another way, "a gaggle of dowries"—ten to be precise, from two successive marriages—and a single son, whose birth had cost Oro's mother her life.

Oro Simha, the eldest daughter from Joseph's first marriage, was a bit of a rebel, and it wasn't going to be easy to find a husband for her. After her mother's death, her father lost little time remarrying, and the young Oro was at loggerheads with her stepmother. She took her revenge by refusing point blank to go to school and ended up illiterate.

Rabbi Rafael was much luckier than his superior, since he had been blessed with eleven children, including a "string of boys." The oldest, Maïr, was not yet fourteen. He was younger than Oro. No matter! Endogamy has its rules, economic inequality too!

"*Maïr, fijko, saves, la fija del Sinyor Rubi Simha, cale que la vijites, por corteziya.* Maïr, my son, your fiancée Oro, Rabbi Simha's daughter—you need to pay her a little courtesy visit."

"*Si… sinyor padre.* But… can I bring my marbles?" replied Maïr.

Two photos suggest the gap in wealth between the two fathers. The first, a contemporary postcard taken from the *Souvenir* album shows a well-dressed young rabbi, his beard still black, who might resemble Oro's father and Janja's maternal grandfather. The second is an older photo, the only one we have of her other grandfather, Rafael Benveniste, his beard already turned white. Both men wear the striped caftan, broad belt, and pelisse. Rabbi Benveniste's headgear is black, a reserved color identifying his status as a *dhimmi*, a member of the Jewish minority. This was a distinctive though not derogatory sign. The other rabbi wears a *bonetta*, an accessory reserved exclusively for rabbis and imams, and a strip of fur to match his pelisse. Rabbis were distinguished from Christian priests by their shaven heads and their bushy beards, which covered much of their face. The first act of dissidence by Rafael's son was to shave his chin.

The Chief Rabbi's daughter was thus betrothed to the minor rabbi's son, her cousin: Joseph's daughter to Myriam's son—Oro to Maïr—leaving time for the future groom to grow up a little. In the weeks that followed, the groom-to-be would go with his pals to visit his fiancée, leaving the other kids out in the street to play. The young couple would talk, as a chaperone looked on. What did they say to each other? Relieved, the young Maïr would then race back to his marbles and his pals!

Rafael discussed family matters and politics with his brother-in-law Joseph Simha and other rabbis. Talk of equality was in the air—equality between Muslims and non-Muslims—and of freedom, not only of worship but also to choose how one dresses and to build one's own temple. But the main concern of the hour was to pay the collective tax, a major preoccupation for the community. All Rafael, Joseph and the others knew about current events and the *tanzimat*, reforms that sought to slow the decline of the Ottoman Empire, came from the newspapers, many published in Judeo-Spanish. But the ailing Empire was crumbling even as it strove to reform: a crumb for Serbia, a crumb for Greece, a crumb for Romania, and one for Bulgaria. The sick man of Europe was shrinking as the other powers fought over its remains.

Ignoring the timid changes introduced by the *tanzimat* and the winds of change blowing from the West, the minor rabbi Rafael Benveniste clung to the past, in habit and outlook. Little did he imagine that his son Maïr would end his days in Paris, the City of Light, the city to which the small but arrogant Sephardic elite living nearby aspired. Rafael's world was that of his father, his grandfather, and their forebears.

The Jews had imprinted their presence and character on Rafael's city from one end of the social scale to the other, from the powerful *Allatini* to the street porter. On the dockside, even the stevedores were Jewish. There were Jewish boatmen, donkey drivers and money changers, not to mention grain and wool merchants, engravers, rag and bone men, tinsmiths, paper boys, as well as printers, along with the dragoman[2], the lawyer, the broker, and the banker. In this melting pot everyone, even the Gentiles, be they Turks, Greeks, Armenians, Bulgarians, or Albanians, spoke Judeo-Spanish and rested on Saturdays, the only day in the week when the warehouses on the port stayed shut. But his was a city within a city. The Gentiles too plied every imaginable trade. And, as in the medieval Spain of Rafael and Joseph's ancestors, the different religions with their distinctive garb rubbed shoulders in the street, but rarely mixed.

The neighborhood where Rafael and Myriam lived, with its timber houses, was close to the water's edge and the market. The Orthodox Greeks lived in the eastern districts, from the ramparts to the Vlatadon Convent. The Turkish Muslims, meanwhile, overlooked the city from the top of the hill. Their homes were more spacious than the others, with vast courtyards. Between the two, on the hillside, stood the homes of the *deunmés*, Jewish apostates who had converted to Islam. They were sincere Muslims; some may even have been cousins of Rafael, a branch of the family having followed the heretic Messiah, Shabtai Tsevi, when he converted to Islam, two centuries earlier.

Salonika was still an Ottoman city when Rabbi Rafael Benveniste died in 1910. He spoke the old Spanish tongue and everyday Turkish, and he could read Hebrew letters. Fourteen years later, the city had become the Greek Thessaloniki, and his son Maïr had left with his tribe to live in Paris, France, on Avenue du Général-Détrie in the select 7th arrondissement. In the intervening years, his grandchildren had attended the school run by the *Alliance Israélite Universelle*, where they learned to speak French fluently and studied the works of Corneille, Racine, and Victor Hugo.

Five years before the Great Fire Maïr, visiting the spacious cemetery where his forebears Don Juda Senior, Don Samuel Meïr and Rabbi Rafael lay buried, sensed that this was no longer his city. He felt too that, even if he wanted to, he could no longer live as his father, his grandfather and their direct predecessors had. In fact, he did not want to. Without realizing it, he was already making ready for the great departure.

---

2. The name given to interpreters, translators, and official guides in the Turkish-, Arabic- and Persian-speaking countries in the Ottoman Empire [Translator].

Fathers and sons: Rafael and Maïr, ancient and modern

Maïr never forgave his father for having betrothed him, aged thirteen, to Oro, his peevish future wife. Their marriage, consummated in October 1886, was to be a lifelong one, producing six children and surviving exile. Oro was aged twenty-two and Maïr twenty when they married. They waited another four years, until the young groom was in a "settled situation," before the birth of their first child, Rafo. Luckily it was a boy! Two years later came Marie, Janja's future mother.

Maïr was determined not to be like his narrow-minded, fretful father, who was as rigid with his congregation as he was tyrannical with his sons. In all his big life-shaping decisions, Maïr took the opposite course to that of his father, starting with the boldest:

"No, *sinyor padre, yo no vo azerme rubi!* I will not become a rabbi!"

He dared to say this to his father's face, and he stood by his decision.

Rafael was part of the old world, clinging to the status quo. He kept his beard and wore his fur-trimmed caftan till the end of his life. Maïr shaved and always sported a western-style suit. Rafael lived in penury and rarely ventured beyond his neighborhood. Maïr became a prosperous businessman. He was always on the move both inside the town and beyond. He rode the brand-new tramway that served the broad coastal artery and the main road dividing the communities. Later he took the train and boat. Rafael spoke only Ladino with a sprinkling of rudimentary Hebrew. Maïr, on the other hand, attended evening classes to learn French, Italian, German, and a little English. He read *La Epoca*, a Judeo-Spanish newspaper, and *Le Journal de Salonique* in French.

Rafael was a rigorist and a moralist, the enemy of voluptuousness, whether of the table or in bed, and he led his congregation with severity, in keeping with his principles. Maïr, on the other hand, took his pleasure where he found it. He loved food and demanded the best in fine dining; he liked to entertain and was open to foreign ideas. Where the twice-married Rafael remained faithful to each of the two wives assigned him in turn by his own father and by God, Maïr was not averse to the occasional fling, with a taste for young flesh, when the opportunity arose during his numerous travels. It was even rumored he kept a mistress in Paris, the capital of debauchery in every shape and form.

Yes! Maïr Benveniste was a man with fire in his belly. He was passionate and tender with his loved ones, especially his children and grandchildren, the first of whom was Janja. But he could be cutting and cold to his wife, to his sons-in-law, and to those who crossed him.

In matters of religion, Rafael was submissive before his God, serving Him and tradition ritually, blindly, unquestioningly. His son Maïr remained pious and faithful to the beliefs for which his ancestors had suffered a thousand deaths, but he sought to modernize them. At a young age he was called to sit on the Community Council and on the Talmud Thora Committee. He contributed generously to charitable activities and worked with those responsible for levying the tax to be paid to the Sublime Porte and the community taxes, and who managed education, justice, and the budget.

At twenty-six, he helped organize the celebrations marking the four hundredth anniversary of the arrival of his ancestors, Juda Senior and Samuel Meïr, after their expulsion from Spain. The Jews of Salonika celebrated the event with pomp and fervor for the last time in 1892, little suspecting that by the time the next centenary came around the descendants of the proscribed of Sefarad would be reduced to ashes in a foreign land. And in Paris he rebuilt a temple.

The young Maïr's life choices reflected the changing face of his city. Rafael's city had undergone a thorough revolution in the space of twenty years. The walls enclosing the old town had been demolished. The seawall no longer blocked the seafront, giving way to a fine corniche and promenade where people could come to stroll. The brigand-infested roads running from the Thermaic Gulf to the Danube were but a distant memory.

When the first steamship made its appearance in 1852, the little Rafael ran to hide in the house at the sound of its strident horn. But his son Maïr was to become a regular passenger of the Ottoman Navigation Company and the French Messageries Maritimes shipping line, which sailed weekly between Salonika, Istanbul, and the Adriatic.

Long stretches of railroad now brought family members, travelers, clerks, and businessmen to Salonika from Monastir as well as Adrianople (modern-day Edirne) and Constantinople. The provincial Macedonian city slumbering behind its *mashrabiyas*[3]—historically Greek, administratively Turkish, geographically Bulgarian, and Jewish by its population—awoke to a turbulent cosmopolitanism. Ships flying many different flags lay at anchor in the harbor, while consulates from all over the world opened in the city. All of Macedonia's trade flowed through Salonika. Merchants and travelers again thronged the roads leading to the city of the Benvenistes, where for centuries they had been trodden by nothing but caravans of camels and oxcarts.

But the great, the immense new development for Rafael's son was the inauguration of the Orient Express, the railroad linking Salonika to Belgrade, and then on to Vienna in two days, and in three or four days to Berlin, Paris, and London. Maïr took to it enthusiastically, journeying "to Europe," as he put it. He'd go to Vienna to buy goods and visit a world-famous physician. He bought his wool in Manchester. He saw shows in Paris and relaxed with the *petites femmes de Paris*[4], who made a change from his glum, lumbering wife. In his mind, he was slowly distancing himself from the old Ottoman and Jewish metropolis.

Maïr's affairs prospered as these new means of communication transformed the business that had once barely sufficed for his father and his family. The Franco-Prussian war of 1870 had boosted Macedonian exports to Marseille. Maïr used Oro's dowry to build a thriving textile business with one of his brothers. Cloth was in his genes. He dealt with merchants from Constantinople and Smyrna to Aden and India. Maïr grew wealthy, bought buildings and stores, setting up his family in a fine mansion. Members of the Modiano family, later related by marriage, also resided in the same block of houses close to the Aragon Synagogue. The main street running alongside it was called *Calle de las Doblas*, "Street of Doubloons"— money street.

People felt as if they were experiencing a return—fleeting, though they

---

3. A type of projecting oriel window enclosed with carved wood latticework located on the second story of a building or higher, often lined with stained glass, commonly seen in Ottoman and Arab architecture up to the mid-20th century [Translator].

4. Euphemism for ladies of easy virtue [Translator].

could not have known it—to the golden age. Even relations among their neighbors grew warmer in the Empire's fading years. Turkish nannies minded Jewish children. The Turks would be gone soon enough, though, as Greek and Turkish populations were exchanged after the fall of the Ottoman Empire. Their neighbors, the *deunmés*, perhaps practicing their Judaism beneath their turbans, would soon be moving to Constantinople. Feast days were an occasion for exchanges of gifts with the Greeks. Soon, though, new Greeks would be arriving from Asia Minor. The Jews of Salonika disdained other Jews, especially the *Tudescos* (the Ashkenazim, who later gave as good as they got), with the arrogance borne of their noble Hispanic origins. Yet, within two decades, half of the Judeo-Hispanics had gone into exile, and the other half had been exterminated.

For now, though, the Belle Epoque was in full swing in Europe.

In Salonika too. Belly dancers, snake charmers and street musicians enlivened the promenade. Maïr never stood still. He rushed to his gambling club for a game of baccarat; he wouldn't miss it for anything. Then he'd sip his aperitif in the cool air of the Café Olympos, among elderly gentlemen in their *fez*, puffing on chicha pipes. He could choose from newspapers in Ladino and French. One of these was *L'Avenir*, published by Maïr's friend Moshe Mallah, the uncle of Beniko, Christian name Benedict and late grandfather to a future President of France.

Meanwhile, after spending the morning in the kitchens berating the maids and preparing her sons' favorite dishes, Oro would chatter with her female cousins around the stove in winter, or in the Colombo or Bechtsinar gardens, where there was a bandstand, in summertime.

Women too were experiencing a far-reaching generational shift. For just as Maïr was moving away from the world of his father Rafael, Oro too was distancing herself from that of her forebears. A postcard depicting two Jewish women seen from behind shows two generations side by side. The mother still wears an *antari* and a long headdress ending in a black velvet square decorated with pearls. The daughter is wearing a long, tighter-fitting skirt and a white long-sleeved blouse. She wears an elegant matching hat and carries a handbag. She may even be wearing high heels concealed by her skirt, as she is half a head taller than the older woman.

Souvenir de SALONICA — ... et la Fille
Souvenir of SALONICA — Two centuries meeting
Jewish - The Mother and Daughter

On a typical afternoon in the early-1900s, Oro's cousins might come to distract her with a game of cards. Their conversation would jump from one topic to another, mingling gossip with talk of the latest concert of oriental music and the play in Judeo-Spanish. Then they would lament the behavior of their offspring.

"Where are your sons?" inquires a cousin.

"Always out!" sighs Oro. "In my day, boys that age stayed home."

"It's the same with mine. Worse even because they're older. Last night my eldest went to see an operetta, *The Merry Widow*—he only likes the Viennese ones. Another went to the movies to see *Journey to the Moon*. And the youngest went cycling. Last week, none of them was home at 10 pm. I was worried sick!"

"My sons too want to spend their lives in the music hall… And at least they're boys!" adds another cousin with a ready tongue. "But the girls are the worst. Mine won't miss a single dance night. Did we ever go dancing at their age?"

"And did we study math and French like my daughter, Marie?" chips in Oro. "What's the use of an educated girl? Now she no longer respects her mother! Did I go to school? And I'm none the worse for it. The *Alliance*! The *Alliance*! That's all they ever talk about! Maïr talks of nothing else. It's alright to send Rafo there! But Marie! Who's going to sew for the family if Marie's in school? My father-in-law's on my side in this. All that instruction's not for we Orientals! But Maïr won't hear of it! Not from me, nor even from his father!"

Oro and the other women in the family were still unaware of the revolution brought about by the *Alliance Israélite Universelle*. And Maïr, whose own father Rafael had not encouraged him to go to school, sent all his children to the *Alliance* schools.

Marie Benveniste and the *Alliance*

Maïr was adamant: Rafo went to the *Alliance* school and so did Marie. The other children followed. And that was that.

It all began when Rafael was thirty and his son Maïr five and a half. On October 15, 1873, to be precise. It was a fine Wednesday morning, a red-letter day for the Jews of Salonika. David Botton, the rabbi, who also taught Hebrew at the Italian school, gathered his pupils in the schoolyard. The children lined up as usual; suddenly their teacher deviated from his normal route and headed in another direction.

One of the boys, Avramiko, never at a loss for words, remarked: "Look, the school's been moved!"

"*No, fijo, es que troquimos mozotros de scola.* No, my boy, it's we who have changed schools."

The *Alliance Israélite Universelle* had arrived: a revolution in the community. Jewish Salonika had entered the modern era. Ten days later, the keys were handed over to the new head teacher, who had just arrived from Paris.

In Rabbi Rafael's eyes, this was a scandal, a threat to the age-old Judaism; it was a devilish plot to induce the children of Moses to deny the faith their forefathers had preserved at such cost.

"Can you imagine," he thundered before his congregation, "what a nest of impiety this school is? Do they not teach that to indicate that one number is added to another it must be preceded by a *plus* sign, the sign of the cross? Sacrilege!"

God's anger was not slow to manifest itself, for shortly afterwards, in the night of February 12, 1874, a terrible fire broke out in the house of a dignitary who had been won over to these new ideas. Like the one that destroyed the town in 1917, it was spread by a fierce wind blowing down from the Vardar.

"See!" yelled Rafael, spluttering with righteous indignation. "There are nine victims! Yet more proof of the Almighty's anger!"

The *Alliance Israélite Universelle* had been founded in France in 1860 by a group of French Jewish intellectuals under the leadership of Adolphe Crémieux. It sought to defend persecuted Jews the world over and teach them the values of humanism and secularism. Liberty, Equality, Fraternity. Through its network of schools in Jewish communities, the *Alliance* taught poor students a trade and helped them learn the local language. Enough to light a bonfire under the world of Rafael and the conservatives.

The community Maïr grew up in was split. At home his father spurned this Devil-inspired institution. He watched helplessly as education underwent a radical transformation; a wind of learning was blowing, whipping up a frenzy of study and raging Francophilia. Schools mushroomed everywhere, in mid-town and on the outskirts, and French supplanted the old Spanish—the language known as *judesmo* or "Jewish."

Maïr and his friends dreamed of studying in Paris, the City of Light. Like Albert Cohen's Solal, their baggage would be carrying *"portraits of Napoleon and Racine; books by Descartes and Pascal [...]; a map of Paris; a tricolor flag and a lantern to celebrate the 14th of July."* It was too late for Maïr himself: he was unable to escape his father's sway.

But he did preserve his children from superstition. Myriam was born in 1892. In everyday life she was called Marie. That marked a first break with custom. Meanwhile, the opening of schools for girls by the *Alliance* was not the least of the upheavals roiling the community, signaling a second break with the past from which the second daughter was to benefit.

28

Maïr's transgression can be seen in this pristine photo of the class of 1903-1904 at the *Alliance Israélite Universelle* girls' school, showing Marie in her class with her fellow students.

The sepia photo shows thirty or so young girls in a kind of long black smock, buttoned at the back, against a backdrop of stylized branches. The grace of young girls in flower glows in the faces of these teenagers or pre-teens. Their thick hair falls on their shoulders. Some have a light-colored ribbon on the right in place of a hairclip. Marie, second from the left in the second row, stands bolt upright with a direct look in her eye, neither shy nor arrogant. Already she displayed that aura of calm which bespoke a firm character.

The first butt of her strong temperament was her mother Oro, the deliberate illiterate, who took a dim view of all these changes. Have you seen anything like it! Instead of staying at home and preparing to sew the family's clothes, the eldest daughter, despite her nimble fingers when the mood took her, spent hours far from her mother taking in the great moments of world history and geography, absorbing the concepts of arithmetic, geometry, physics, and chemistry.

I can imagine Oro railing: "*I mozotros? I muestra lingua? Muestra lingua i muestra fe?* And what about us? What about our language? *Maïr, kualo vas a azer con tu ija? No ay ombre de entre los muestros que va a tomarla como mujer?* Maïr, what are you going to do with our daughter? None of our men are going to want her for a wife!"

"*Calmate, Oriko.* Calm down, Oro," her husband would reply. "You know perfectly well she's receiving Jewish religious instruction in school, and she's even learning a little Hebrew."

"Does a girl need Hebrew?" whines Oro. "Do I speak Hebrew?... Do I speak Turkish? ..."

"Oro, you know the girls don't learn Turkish at the *Alliance*. It'll be useful for Rafo and Pepo though. It's just for the boys. You know I had to learn Turkish for my business and for my work on the Board. Because I wasn't able to learn it at the *Alliance*."

"'And the result," she continues, "is that no one speaks *Djudio* anymore. When I talk to my daughter, she answers in the language you all speak, at school and elsewhere—*that* language that isn't *our language!*"

That language that isn't our language: that French language symbolized the vast changes afoot in the community. For the teachers at the Alliance, French was the "idiom of enlightened people," the universal language *par excellence*.

Marie's schoolteacher made no bones about it:

"Girls, you must know that ignorance of French is a sign of ignorance, make no mistake, and knowledge of it is a sign of education. You'll be more skillful with a smoothing iron when you know French... Most of all, get rid of your accent: it grates on the ear!"

Marie wanted to know why the boys were learning Turkish but were excused sewing.

"Be glad they teach you to sew in your cursed school," grumbled her mother. "That's why I gave in to your father and why we sent you there. But you won't stay there long, trust me!"

To break down the barriers between rich and poor through education, the *Alliance* provided sewing lessons for girls to appeal to poorer parents. The girl next to Marie at school came from a poor family, and sewing lessons would equip her to become a domestic seamstress. For Oro, more comfortably off, sewing was the only advantage she could see in the *Alliance*, as Marie would thus be able to sew for the family until a husband was found. With a skill like that, an over-educated wife might be more acceptable to an ignorant husband even if she came with a scanty dowry.

Indeed, the *Alliance* was careful to avoid teaching Marie and her sisters matters suitable for the boys only, such as the subtleties of French grammar or history, especially that of ancient peoples and the peoples of Western Europe, which were of no concern to these young ladies. Still, it did insist that moral edification would emerge from the rudiments of history, which would conduce to the "necessary concord among peoples."

Thus, it was in the language of George Sand, if not with her freedom of thought, that Marie Benveniste drank in reading matter for young girls, the romantic novels of Delly, and especially *Raoul Daubry* by Zénaïde Fleuriot, her favorite bedtime read, which she ended up passing on to her daughter and granddaughter. Most of the books depicted a modest but poor young woman who, despite obstacles, wins the love of a rich and brilliant young man, like in the novels of Jane Austen. In the case of *Raoul Daubry*, the obstacle to the marriage of these young people is the girl's possessive mother. Unsurprisingly, this novel struck a chord with Marie, whose abusive mother saw in the dictatorship of sewing a means to avenge her own frustration at being illiterate.

Meantime, Marie couldn't stop Oro from removing her from her beloved school prematurely and shackling her to the Singer sewing machine from morning till night. Maïr himself gave in where Marie was concerned. But he dug in his heels for the others, Allegra, and later Pepo and Nelly. As for his eldest daughter, he harbored designs for marriage to one of his own brothers—yet another match made in endogamy!

Marie, now educated in the French and "Republican"[5] notions of the *Alliance*, drew her own conclusions when the time came. And come it did,

---

5. For the French, "Republican" refers to a nexus of values around the national motto: Liberty, Equality, Fraternity, together with loyalty to the Republic as opposed to monarchy, and a secular state that is neutral as between religions [Translator].

in 1913, when the slim, dark young woman aged just over twenty dared defy her father on a point over which in theory she had no say, an especially delicate one since it concerned the choice of a husband.

"*Sinyor padre, yo refuzo de cazarme con su ermano, el tio Asher.* Father, I refuse to marry your brother, Uncle Asher."

"How dare you?"

"I love my cousin, Saby Amon, your nephew."

"Saby?"

"Are you crazy? A penniless boy, who must support his family into the bargain! The son of my sister Reyna, with her brood of orphans on his hands?"

"I want to marry Saby. And he wants to marry me."

She slammed the door behind her.

Maïr refused to speak to his daughter in the days following this scene. He issued his orders through his wife, Oro, who passed them on.

"Tell Marie to finish all the sheets for her trousseau by Pesach. She's dawdled for too long."

Marie stood her ground. Never would she marry an uncle for whom she felt not the slightest attraction! Her cousin Sabbetaï Amon, otherwise known as Saby, on the other hand, was rather good-looking. He was the same age as Uncle Asher, eight years older than Marie. But at least, like her, he knew how painful it could be to be the eldest, fated to be sacrificed, condemned to slave away so that younger siblings could enjoy their youth unfettered.

Maïr thought things over. Saby was the son of Reyna, his sister, the widow of an Amon. No fortune, to be sure. But from a good family, originally from Constantinople, one that had left its mark in the archives of the Judeo-Spanish diaspora. At the time of the expulsion in 1492, Joseph Amon, or Hamon, one-time physician to the Muslim King of Granada, had left Andalusia for Constantinople to enter the service of the Sultan Bayezid II. His son, whose name has come down to us as Moses Hamon, achieved high status in the service of Suliman the Magnificent.

As an ancestor then, Moses Hamon, the sultan's confidant, could stand in the family portrait gallery alongside Don Juda Senior Benveniste, descendant of a minister to the King of Spain. So, Maïr reasoned, with

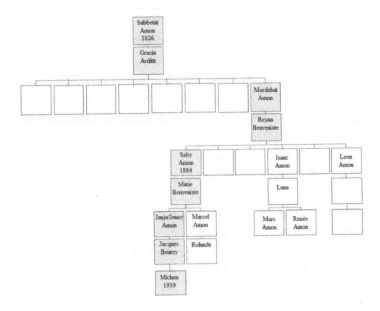

Saby things would stay in the family, since Maïr would be paying for the upkeep of his sister's son and his string of brothers, he might as well kill two birds with one stone and help his son-in-law and nephew in a single blow.

Ten years after the school photo, Marie was wedded to her penniless cousin Saby Amon without much ado. The modest nuptials took place at home, *à la turque* (*alaturca*), i.e., at local time, which differed from *à la franque* (*alafranga*)[6]. On the last day, *dia del peche*, the bride must step across a fish dish, a symbol of fertility, to general applause. Among her wedding gifts was the embossed silver Ottoman dish handed down by Oro, later passed on to her granddaughter Janja. All this happened in 1914, the year Gavrilo Princip assassinated the heir to the Austro-Hungarian throne in Sarajevo, triggering the Great War and precipitating the downfall of the Ottoman Empire.

---

6. Two time systems functioned side by side in the Ottoman Empire, à la franque or *alafranga*, and à la turque or *alaturca*. The former was associated with a form of modernity, the latter with oriental tradition. Conversion from one to the other was quite complicated. The use of Greenwich meantime spread in the wake of the Young Turk revolution of 1908 [Translator].

The young Saby might be poor, but he was steeped in Italian culture and read the *Divine Comedy* in the original Italian. He was an enthusiastic student of the history and cuisine of Sefarad, and an active member of his community. In 1921 he joined a chapter of the B'nai B'rith, the Jewish organization which had been founded in New York in the mid-nineteenth century. Yet he was undemonstrative and displayed the same unflappable calm in the face of even the gravest danger, while he left domestic chores and the education of their daughter Janja to his cousin-cum-wife. Saby was also saddled with the task of dealing with his uncle-cum-father-in-law, holder of the family's purse-strings.

At any rate, Marie was settled now! The patriarch let out a sigh of relief on the night of the wedding. That left the two younger sisters, Allegra and Nelly, though the wait was worth it, for not long afterward both married wealthy men and were able to dangle their husbands' fine mansions before the nose of Marie, their elder sister.

Allegra's mésalliance

Daughters, what a curse! Maïr was in despair as he faced a new complication. Allegra, his younger daughter, was three years younger than Marie. She should have been named for the weeping Niobe rather than the exuberant Allegra. Had Maïr and Oro named her Allegra hoping to alter her nature? She never stopped moaning from the day she was born. The Spanish *conversos* might have called her Angustias or Dolores, but the Judeo-Spanish did not use these names, despite their troubled history. The younger daughter was in an awkward position, coming after another (long-awaited) Rafael and Marie, who was tolerated because you need girls to make boys.

After Allegra, *grasias al Dio*, came two babies to be circumcised, Pepo and Momo. The youngest of them all, Nelly, born thirteen years after Allegra, was the icing on the cake and the darling of all the family. She was the only one of the three sisters to sing, recalled Janja; the other two were cry-babies.

Allegra was the awkward one. She was the only one to change her name when she emigrated to Belgium. Allegra, whom the gods had provocatively made the prettiest of the three Benveniste sisters, with her long ebony hair and her tawny Andalusian complexion. Allegra, who chafed at having to wear her elder sister's hand-me-downs as she waited for her Prince Charming.

"*Sinyor padre, Ugo Modiano.... quere cazarse con mi*! Father, Ugo Modiano... wants to marry me!"

"A Modiano! Are you out of your mind? Do you realize what he's worth, and what we're worth?"

"But he loves me."

Today's girls simply aren't what they used to be, full of ideas they get from the novels they read. Maïr could not figure it out. A Modiano—it's way beyond the reach of his second daughter. Maïr didn't like marrying above or below his station. And what about the dowry? Would it be big enough for a Modiano? an "Italian" from the top drawer of society, whereas the Benvenistes, for all their noble origins, were merely a good family, nothing fancy. For here, as elsewhere, the social and economic hierarchy gave the tribe its backbone.

An old Ladino song says it all: "*Quien puedra ser como los Modiano? I como los Nahoumim?* Who can match the Modianos? And the Nahums?"

The Nahums and Modianos ruled the roost in this late-nineteenth century Jewish Balkan city.

At the top of the tree stood the *gente alta* like them, the Allatini, the Morpurgos or the Camondos of Constantinople, an aristocracy consisting of the families from Italy, the most prestigious being those from Livorno. They had benefited from the capitulations signed by Francis I of France and Suliman the Magnificent in 1536, which guaranteed individual, religious and trading freedoms to French merchants and "protected" Ottoman subjects.

After them came the *gente buena*, a middle-class elite comprising those who had been banished from Sefarad with a glorious lineage like the Benvenistes, who had come down somewhat in society and were active in the economy.

Below that was a third category, plebeians who drew their sustenance from whatever came to hand, manual workers, the unskilled laborers, peddlers, small storekeepers, middlemen, brokers, servants—all those making a precarious living as in-betweens, who were more plentiful among the Jewish minority than among the Christian minority—for, contrary to popular prejudice, the wealth of the Jews was below average. Maïr, a community leader, often commented on this to his colleagues:

"For every Croesus preening in the public eye, can you not see the wretched masses teeming in the shadows? The Jewish neighborhoods are struggling in grinding poverty. Be charitable! Give to your brothers!"

This was a tricky situation. Maïr turned over his daughter's outburst in his mind. The Modianos were upper crust. The Benvenistes somewhere in the middle. And an Allegra Benveniste wasn't supposed to marry an Ugo Modiano.

To be sure Maïr was a local bigwig, but he was realistic. He knew that Ugo's father, Rafael, was a renowned lawyer steeped in Italian culture. Allegra's father was just a traditional merchant with no education, preoccupied with his own business and that of the community.

And the wives! the gap between them was surely insurmountable. Allegra's mother, Oro, was illiterate; Clelia, Ugo's mother, on the other hand, was a Modiano too, a musician, cultivated, and an accomplished hostess. The Modianos belonged to the cream of Salonika society.

As for his daughter's suitor, their son Ugo was a poet, and a painter too. He was a dreamer, refined, a skilled magician and fortune teller. From his childhood, his parents had promised him to an Allatini girl. But the young man kicked against the traces and turned down the heiress. Though around twenty years older than Allegra, he had noticed her at the ball following Marie's wedding in 1914. That evening, with her elder sister married off at long last, Allegra had worn a brand-new dress for only the second time in her life, a genuinely western-style gown. The lovely Allegra was radiant, yet her heart was heavy. She was truly lovelorn, and the object of her heartache was her cousin Jacob. But her passion was unrequited, and Allegra tried to starve herself to death.

That evening, at any rate, Allegra was determined to outdo her constant rival, her sister Marie, the sister who had usurped not only her dresses but also the love of a cousin. The younger sister had been champing at the bit for too long. She'd show Marie. She, Allegra, could win the heart of any heir to any of those grand *gente alta* families and reign by his side in a sumptuous seafront villa. With her Andalusian looks, that night the dusky Allegra had pinned a red rose to her corsage. The atmosphere in Salonika was electric that summer, the first of the Great War. In the midst of a heatwave, it was love at first sight as the thunder rolled in from the nearby sea. Ugo was smitten, and he never got over it. Neither did she.

The young man's father saw things otherwise and only reluctantly renounced his dream of a rich and educated Livornese daughter-in-law. Who better to understand him than Maïr? He knew his impetuous daughter only too well and remained hostile to the marriage, in his eyes a step too far up the social ladder in this highly stratified society. He too, when he learned of the affair much later, couldn't help feeling Cousin Jacob would have kept the couple inside the endogamous bubble. But Maïr was a good man and he had suffered too much from his own forced marriage. The two fathers ultimately acceded to their children's wishes. What clearer evidence that the *Alliance* had successfully instilled in them a belief in the western notion of a marriage based on inclination?

Despite the misgivings of the *sinyores padres*, Allegra and Ugo were joined together in the grand style, in a memorable wedding. They opened the ball amid brilliantly colored foreign uniforms and the ladies' shimmering gowns from Paris, London, and Vienna. Everyone danced waltzes, polkas, quadrilles, gavottes and cotillons till dawn, breaking off solely to sup from buffets laden with oriental delicacies as the champagne flowed. The newspapers reported on the dark outfit worn by Madame Clelia Modiano, who wept openly over her son's marriage, contrasting this with Madame Allatini's turquoise satin brocade dress: she, though, had kept her daughter... and her dowry.

Among the guests were the Governor-General, the Rear Admiral, European consuls, including the French Consul, local managers of western firms represented in the city, senior officials, officers from European ships in port, and members of the local business community, Greeks included.

37

Yet no one noticed that the resplendent bride, whose long tresses with reddish highlights fell to her waist, was paler than her dress. As her young groom held her tightly to him, her swollen eyes were glancing to a corner of the ballroom where the young Jacob sat with his latest flirt, now all the rage in high society.

Seventy years later Allegra waxed nostalgic as she related her honeymoon voyage to Constantinople, with boat rides in the moonlight on the Bosphorus. as the quiet waters of the Golden Horn gently rocked the young couple, utterly unaware of what lay ahead for them.

The marriage was not to be a happy one, though. At first, Allegra went to live in the Modianos' patrician villa beside the sea, with Ugo's mother, Clelia. The cultivated and capable Clelia spared her daughter-in-law nothing in the way of minor vexations as she sought to educate her in how to run a large household. Allegra overcame her aversion to food to master the art of half-Tuscan, half-Ottoman cooking to perfection; her *pasteliko* would have won her a five-star accolade.

Ugo's ardent passion did its work almost immediately, perhaps even during the honeymoon, in the shadow of Saint Sophia and the Blue Mosque. Allegra quickly became pregnant, even before her sister Marie, even though the latter had married earlier. It was a boy. It might have been Allegra's triumph, except that the child tearing her apart was stillborn.

For the first time, Allegra suffocated with pain as she held her little one. Ugo took refuge in his father's house, refusing to see anyone. They called the dead boy Andrea, in accordance with the Modiano family tree. And Allegra chose the name of Andrée for herself when she moved to the West. Andrea... Andrée, the name of mourning, the new Niobe's definitive first name. Later, she demanded the name of Allegra be expunged. For Janja and all the family's nephews, she was "Aunt Andrée."

Allegra's next child, Rafael, known as Ralph or Kiko, was born during the Great Fire of Salonika in 1917. Marked by fire from birth.

At that very moment, the same all-consuming flames were licking the cradle of baby Janja. But they spared Marie's daughter, born the previous year.

Janja is born

In the tale I am about to relate, I want none
of the characters to be inventions. My mother
is my mother.

LYDIE SALVAIRE, *PAS PLEURER* (DON'T CRY)

June 12, 1916, the day her first child was born, was not a glorious day for Marie. She so wanted a boy. A boy would have rehabilitated her in her father's eyes after her insistence on marrying her penniless cousin Saby Amon. Instead, it was a baby girl demanding her mother's breast. She had to be breastfed and Marie dutifully performed her task for two years. She needed a name. Janja was the Judeo-Spanish first name of a young aunt now deceased. But Marie also wanted her daughter to have a Western name. It so happened that her older brother Rafo, the darling of Salonika's elegant ladies, had come to visit Marie after she had given birth to relate his latest escapades. At a recent reception given by the Allied officers he had encountered a charming young girl with the delightfully British name of Jenny. It appealed to Marie who immediately adopted it for her daughter.

At home in Salonika the child would always be Janja for her grandparents, Maïr and Oro, and for Sarika, the young maid who took care of her. When she arrived on French soil, though, she became Jenny once and for all.

The milk Janja suckled so vigorously wasn't very nourishing and she stayed thin. Most of all, her scalp, covered with a wispy blonde duvet, was the despair of her mother, who dreamed of a head of flaming hair, to be sure, but abundant.

"If you want her to have lovely hair, you should cut it now," advised her sister Allegra. "It'll grow back. Blonde, but thick. Do you remember my classmate at the *Alliance*? She shaved all her daughters down to the scalp; just look at their beautiful hair! The eldest just got married to a bigwig, believe me."

So Janja's hair was shaved right off and did indeed grow back very vigorously… but very black! Time and its catastrophes were to have their way with her rather too Semitic hair, and a bleaching in the nineteen forties restored its original color. For the time being she looked like her mother and aunts. Dark and trim like them, and with piercing black eyes that sparkled with mischief and curiosity.

One thing Janja did not inherit was their gravelly Middle Eastern accent when speaking French, with a sprinkling of singsong Judeo-Spanish overtones. An accent their teachers at the *Alliance* loathed. Whatever her relatives may have felt, that inimitable accent clung to them, the indelible mark of four centuries of life in the mingled waters of the Ottoman Empire, preserving intact the melody of the old fifteenth-century Castilian amid the courtyards, terraces and gardens festooned with Greek honeysuckle.

In the meantime, it was in Ladino, in "Jewish," that this descendant of the Jews driven from Castile and Aragon, Granada and Portugal, expressed her first desires and fears. Maïr observed the awakening of his first granddaughter, and more and more he felt she was not destined to grow up in the city where his forefathers had lived and died for as far back as he could recall their names on the tombs of the old cemetery.

The child was born at a turning point in the city's history. As Maïr leaned tenderly over her cradle, he thought back to its most recent upheavals.

Eight years earlier, Maïr had welcomed the revolution brought about by the Young Turks, who had decreed that all the Empire's subjects were equal, regardless of religion. Many of his friends and relatives had enrolled in the movement. Though not especially active himself, he closely followed the strikes, demonstrations, speeches, the hymns to liberty, culminating in the proclamation of a constitutional charter. Two of his cousins enrolled in the army that set out from Salonika to dethrone the old Sultan. The dethroned sovereign was detained in the Allatinis' villa, while his successor was received beneath Elie Modiano's triumphal arch. Maïr's friend the Salonika-born lawyer Emmanuel Carasso read out the proclamation removing the aged Sultan.

Maïr and those around him were not immediately aware of having become citizens of a nation. In the old Empire, the Jews escaped compulsory military service by paying a tax. Now they would have to pay a tax with their own blood. Cousin Isaac in Constantinople had enthusiastically joined the Turkish army, but he came home traumatized by the brutality of the Turkish officers. He realized that he, a Jew, was merely a second-class citizen in a great nation.

Four years later, at the end of the First Balkan War in May 1913, Maïr ceased to be an Ottoman subject altogether. Salonika was Greek once more: the Christian Byzantine city, the Ottoman port, the Jewish Jerusalem of the Balkans, had become the Greek city of Thessaloniki.

What happened to Maïr, then? Already he was acutely aware of the dilemma that ultimately led to his emigration. For Maïr felt he was neither Greek nor Turkish. He felt himself to be a citizen of Salonika, and all his Jewish brothers in the now-dismantled former Ottoman Empire, in Bulgaria, Serbia, Egypt, and Palestine, felt likewise, viscerally bound to their place of origin and unconcerned by a rising tide of nationalism in which they had no place.

The Second Balkan War pitted the Bulgarians against the Greeks. Bulgarian troops camped within the walls of Salonika. The city was under siege. Saby later enjoyed telling his uncle and father-in-law the following story:

One of his brothers, Leon Amon, had been taken prisoner by the Bulgarians. Saby visited his younger brother in his place of captivity. The newly Greek Saby spoke to the Bulgarian sentry, an enemy:

"I want to see my brother, Leon Amon?"

"Do you speak Jewish?" asked the Bulgarian sentry, who had spotted the accent.

"Yes."

"Then you're one of ours... Go on in ... then leave ... with your brother... I'm not looking."

And so, Leon Amon from Salonika walked out of jail with his brother Saby, under the benevolent eye of their Bulgarian Sephardic "cousin."

This was something new: the country had changed people, instead of people changing countries. In the space of three weeks, Turkish and Jewish Salonika had become, or reverted to being, Greek. The rest followed from that. First, the new masters eradicated signs of the Ottoman presence, demolishing the minarets. They declared war on the fez, worn by Muslims and Jews alike. Railroad workers found wearing one were threatened with dismissal. Even before the official exchange of Greek and Turkish populations in 1923, the Muslims were already packing their bags.

The Judeo-Spanish language, the old Ladino, had had its time. Maïr Beneveniste inhabited his language as if it was his homeland and tried to take it with him into exile, clinging to the soles of his shoes, as his ancestors had done after the expulsion. The language of Victor Hugo was to prove the stronger, however.

Not only did the idiom of the city change, but also the street names. The grand Ottoman Avenue Hamidié was renamed "Union Avenue," then "Prince Constantine," and later "King Constantine," before twice becoming "National Defense," and finally "Queen Sophia." When the Greek refugees from Anatolia and the Black Sea came and replaced the Turks, rather as the Sephardi Jews had four centuries earlier, they renamed their new neighborhoods after the places they had just handed over to the Turks. Neapolis, for example, was named for Nef-Sheir in Cappadocia. Sunday was instituted as the day of rest, which meant the Jews had to work Saturdays.

What to do when one becomes a stranger in one's own city overnight? Edgar Nahum, father of the future Edgar Morin[7], remained a citizen of Salonika and traveled on a passport issued by a now-defunct community. Solal's uncles in Albert Cohen's *Solal of the Solals* invented the citizenship of Whatever; *"Why the passport of his grandfather dead these forty years? A precaution. One never knows. It's always useful to keep a passport. And anyway, is it not said that the dead shall arise again? And what was his nationality, by the way? He glanced at the passport. Ah yes, a Greek citizen? Funny. Some of the Valorous waved false passports. Nailcruncher carried the visiting card of a French actress; Salomon a dead Englishman's hunting permit; Mattathias a confessional ticket. And by the grace of God! We don't want to fatten the consulates!"*

This Hellenization, coming after four centuries of Ottoman rule, made Maïr uncomfortable. With other Jewish dignitaries, he even suggested an alternative to the Greek Thessaloniki, proposing that Salonika become a tiny autonomous State to be guaranteed by the great powers. The Young

---

7. A renowned twentieth-century French sociologist and thinker. [Translator].

Turk émigrés and *deunmé* Muslim intermediaries in Vienna gave serious consideration to the proposed internationalization of the city, prompting the ire of the Greeks. Maïr was neither a communist nor a socialist, nor was he a Zionist, or a Hellenist with Venezelos. He was an "*Alliancist*," unconditionally committed to the *Alliance Israélite Universelle*, as he showed when he left Thessaloniki/Salonika *a Francia*, for France.

The European powers, ousted when their old capitulations were abolished[8], came to the aid of their former protégés, offering assistance and passports to Jews and Muslims alike. In the space of six months, twenty-four thousand Jews changed their nationality to avoid becoming Greek. The old nostalgia for the Iberian Peninsula was rekindled, encouraged by decrees in first Portugal and then Spain enabling descendants of those who had been expelled to take up the nationality of those countries once more.

Maïr Benveniste and his sons Rafo, Pepo and Momo opted for Spanish nationality.

Saby and his brothers, the Amons, became Portuguese.

Ugo Modiano remained Italian.

The wives followed their spouses, Marie becoming Spanish, Allegra Italian, while Nelly, the youngest of the Benveniste girls, became Greek.

The family diaspora opted for the different nationalities and their attendant passports somewhat haphazardly. Once in France, Saby Amon applied for his second naturalization, his brother-in-law Pepo too. The others didn't.

In the nineteen-forties, this random selection would evolve into another, more macabre lottery, one's passport becoming one's destiny. But how could the Benvenistes have foreseen that?

The eyes of Maïr, the patriarch, glazed over as he peered into this murky, still impenetrable future. Little Janja, meanwhile, arose from her baby's cradle and stepped forth boldly to meet her own destiny, coming through the Great Fire and moving into her grandparents' fine mansion, which had been spared by the flames.

---

8. Treaties signed between the Ottoman sultans and the Christian states of Europe concerning the extraterritorial rights which the subjects of one of the signatories would enjoy while staying in the state of the other. They were abolished by the Young Turks in 1914 (Translator).

For the family lingered awhile. Even then, not all of them left. They took their time preparing to emigrate, doing so in batches. First the eldest son, then the patriarch with the others. Little Janja's cooing and giggling continued to enliven the house of *Nona* Oro. Another four years were to elapse between the Great Fire of 1917 and the departure in 1921, during which Janja metamorphosed into a cheeky little girl, insatiably curious. By then it was her turn to go into exile.

The *pazvan*

In this first photo taken in Salonika, little Janja seen perched on a stool with a big bow in her hair, seems to be framed rather than accompanied by her father and mother. While Marie has placed a hand on her daughter's shoulder to prevent her from falling, Saby, standing stiffly, his arms hanging by his side, takes no notice of either. Luckily there's *Nona*. All three were then living with her and Maïr. To be sure, Marie could not hide her disappointment at the birth of this baby. For both clans, to have a girl as one's first-born was a terrible frustration. But to have a boy and lose him, like Allegra, was to experience a divine curse in one's own flesh. By a twist of fate, August 5, 1917, a black day in the lives of victims of the Salonika fire, was a red-letter day in that of Allegra, for at last she held in her arms a living boy, Kiko.

Allegra, now the happy mother of a son, had supplanted her sister at last. Kiko, a year younger than Janja, was to be the latter's true brother. Marie often took her daughter on visits to her Modiano sister in their villa by the sea. The two children grew close, chased each other around, squabbled and held each other dear to the end of their lives. Despite her parents' dwindling warmth, as is visible in the photo, Janja did not lack for tenderness. Grandfather Maïr was fond of his granddaughter, and there would be grandsons. Oro, a stern and possessive mother, softened in the presence of this little girl, so lively and such fun.

The child was brought up by the grandparents mainly, oriental-style and with indulgence. Oro, whom Janja called *Nona*, was illiterate but a first-class cook. The girl followed her everywhere, observing her perform her domestic tasks. Three maids labored in the house from morning till night. But for her little granddaughter, *Nona* Oro was happy to put her hand to making *tajikos de almendra*, cookies normally reserved for Pesach or Passover. Sometimes though the grandmother tired of the child dogging her footsteps:

"Go ask your grandfather for a bit of *nesteaki.*"

Nesteaki, for *no esta aki*, or "I'm not here."

The child would rush off to the patriarch for some of this mysterious substance. Sometimes though she would run into her other grandmother, Reyna, sister of Maïr and mother of Saby, the poor relative who'd come to play gin rummy with her sister-in-law to keep the latter busy. As a busy community leader, Maïr had far too much to do finding accommodations for the homeless and the knotty business of the community to go handing out *neastaki*. Furious, the little girl would race from one to the other, before repairing to the kitchen, drawn by the marvelous odors emanating from the ovens where Perla and Luna toiled, and above all Sarika, who made no secret of her fondness for the only child.

Today was a big day in the kitchen and everyone was hard at work making meals for the next two weeks. Sarika would first cook eggplants before getting to work on the *berenjena asada*, which simmered for four hours. The eggplant is the queen of Hispano-Ottoman cuisine and figures in many dishes. Under the little glutton's nose, Sarika would boil a slice of beef in a little stock then add the eggplant, which had been skinned and tenderized over the stove; after that, everything would be stewed for another hour in the steam. The next step was devoted to the meatballs, one-half beef, one-half veal, egg and bread dough; the final step entailed warming the fresh tomato. Janja's eyes would water as Sarika sliced the onion, which was part of the ritual Sephardic recipe. Not garlic, though. That was good only for the Ashkenazim, whose temple was known as the *kal del ajo*, the "garlic synagogue." After being steamed for five hours, the dish would stay fresh for days.

"Janja, come here *Janum*; would you like a nice warm meatball?"

Thrilled, the child held out her tiny plate and was given a freshly fried meatball. Perla, meantime, scooped out the flamed eggplant, skinned the tomatoes, peppers and zucchini, stuffing them then sliding them into the oven for a couple of hours. A delicious odor of eggplants seared over the wood fire wafted about the kitchen before being turned into salads and stuffing for the *borekas*, known familiarly as *borekitas*, and the *pasteliko*. The raw artichoke hearts had been stripped of their leaves and the hair removed. Luna then gathered up the edible part of the leaves and gently simmered them with the hearts on a back burner, "oriental style." Sarika then went to work on the brown eggs or *uevos haminados*, the beef stew with beans or chickpeas, and on the *fijones*, or black-eyed peas and dry white beans.

By now Janja knew this wasn't the day for cookies: those were prepared mainly for feast days and guests, kept in a sweet-smelling little cupboard forbidden to the children. She had ventured there on occasion, with a wink from Sarika, filching one of those rounded cookies called *roskas*, between the figs, dates stuffed with almonds and brazil nuts, *tajilos de bimbryo*, or quince-jelly lozenges, small peeled preserved bitter oranges known as *narankitas*, and delicious marzipan.

She had to choose fast, because Oro or Marie might come upon her at any moment, and Sarika didn't want to be caught with the child in this forbidden place. So Janja avoided sticking her fingers into the jars of rose petal jelly, which stood shoulder to shoulder on the shelf with the *charope blanko*, a white marmalade made with sugar and lemon. At lunchtime, Janja knew she would refuse to eat the *mallebi*, a yogurt with a milky taste she loathed; they didn't make her eat it, but she would have to await the next feast day before being given some *sotlatch*, a kind of *crème brulée* sprinkled with cinnamon and rosewater. At dinner with her grandmother and her mother she'd be given a glass of plum syrup, dark cherries, or candied apricots, while the men drank *raki*.

When Janja didn't get to taste the dishes, she'd insist on watching their preparation. Perla and Luna would have been happy to keep the little glutton out of their skirts, but her *Nona* took a different view:

"She's got to learn... for her future husband."

Brown eggs baked for hours in onion skin, coffee grounds and many ingredients used to turn them dark and impregnate them with their aromas were a pillar of Sephardic cuisine in Salonika. The other pillar is the *pasteliko*, a large tart, and its component, the *boreka*, an individual tart. According to another Salonika-born figure, Edgar Morin, their ancestors had enjoyed these little marvels for more than a thousand years in Spain and had introduced them to Salonika, *echo de las manos benditchas de las madres* (made by the mothers' blessed hands), before subsisting as a core and a matrix, "the sole survivor in the French and gentile world of the vanished world of Sephardic Salonika"[9].

This lingering, visceral core of traditions, culinary especially, the mingling smells and tastes of our earliest childhood, are what remain when all else is gone. Later Janja, my future mother, refused to pass most of this on to me, the narrator: neither her religion, nor her history, nor her language. But she did teach me to make *borekitas*.

For the time being, though, the family's firstborn stuffed herself with delicious *borekitas* and was coddled by her three Benveniste uncles and her four Amon uncles. Her young aunt Nelly, only ten years older than herself, now studying in French at school, recounted the tales of Charles Perrault

---

9. Edgar Morin, *Vidal and his Family: From Salonika to Paris: The Story of a Sephardic Family in the Twentieth Century*, Sussex Academic Press.

to her at night before bedtime, recited the fables of La Fontaine, and declaimed Victor Hugo's *L'Enfant* to her with great dramatic effect. At the age of three, Janja could already babble in two languages, in Judeo-Spanish with her *Nona*, and in French with her aunts and her mother.

Janja listened to and remembered all her life snatches of conversation between her parents, her grandparents, the maids—who understood only "Jewish"—and her uncles and aunts. This was a time when all these young adults joyfully thronged the house in Salonika, speaking a linguistic brew of old Spanish and French, not to mention Italian, German, and English. The servants, though, Sarika, Luna, and Perla, spoke only in the old Ladino idiom. That was the language in which Sarika sang to Janja, romances and lullabies from Castile, Aragon, and Andalusia; it was the language in which she told her stories that had crossed frontiers and come down through the ages. Janja's favorite was the story of the key to the house in Spain that the fugitives had brought with them into exile.

"*Onde esta la yave ke estava en kashon? Mis nonus la trusheron kon grande dolor. De su Kaza de Espanya, de Espanya.* Where, but where is the key that was in the drawer? My forefathers brought it with such suffering, from their house in Spain, in Spain," sings Flory Jagoda, a Bosnian-Jewish-American composer and singer. The key was handed down from elder son to elder son, but one evening it fell straight into a little girl's dream and she decided to set forth across the sea in search of the missing key.

And at bedtime, in her little bedroom next to her mother's, Janja fell asleep by the soft light of an oil lamp, lulled to the sound of the *pazvan*, the watchman who walked the streets till the first light of dawn, tapping out the hours with his iron-tipped staff on granite flagstones set among the cobbles for that purpose. The number of blows increased as the night wore on, according to oriental custom, which counted the hours from sunset till dawn, and not from one meridian to the next.

Time had not changed its voice since the golden times of Castile. It had merely changed places. The Turkish or Albanian *pazvan* had replaced the Andalusian or Castilian *sereno* who lulled Spanish Jewry to sleep, awoke the craftsman eager to begin work or hurrying in search of the midwife to soothe the first pangs of a mother in labor. On the Sabbath evening, this man of all trades came to put out the lamps and light the fires on Saturday morning, which believers were forbidden to do. It was he who sounded the alarm if a fire broke out: "*Yanguin var!* Fire!" The last time, that cry failed to bring up enough water.

Yes. The eve of the great departure from Salonika so closely resembled the eve of the great departure from Toledo or Granada. The same human chime sounded out the last hours of the last night before the exodus. And four centuries of Benveniste presence slowly crumbled, its dust mingling with the ashes of the Great Fire.

The great departure

"Your son is at the station," a messenger from his eldest son Rafo Benveniste shouted out to Maïr. "Stavros is looking for him. He wants to kill him."

Rafo, twenty-eight years old, was hot-blooded. His last mistress—a salute to the city's new masters? —was a magnificent Greek woman: firm breasts, pale eyes, and long hair with reddish tints. She also had a trigger-happy husband. He had been through the Balkan Wars and the recently ended Great War. He was armed too, with a bellicose disposition.

Quickly! A suitcase was brought for the prodigal son, plus a few *borekas* just in case, and some clean linen. Quickly! The train pulled out of the station, carrying him to the West. In a few days' time Rafo would be in the capitals of pleasure and could thumb his nose at husbands at no risk to his life. Maïr spent the days and nights pondering as his son progressed westward by train, by boat and other means. Could this offer his family the occasion he'd dreamed of ever since the fire and even before, the reason why he'd been learning French in night school for years?

His daughter Marie couldn't sleep either. Rafo's flight was a sign of destiny. Her favorite brother, her big brother, was the one who would deliver her from her family jail. Marie devised a strategy and pursued it relentlessly for the next three years, her goal being to plan her own little family's great departure.

Rafo stopped first in an Italian city, where he lived for a while as a contented bachelor, along with other youngsters who had begun to flee the Greek Thessaloniki and the no-longer-Ottoman Turkey. He frequented cafés, rushed to La Scala in Milan to hear Caruso sing, and forgot his Greek muse in the arms of young Italian women whose husbands were less possessive. But another nuisance, in the shape of Benito Mussolini, was taking up deadlier arms and preparing his march on Rome. Time to move on: Rafo agreed to settle down and decamped to Paris, the City of Light, leading the way for the rest of the family. Maïr wired his eldest son the funds to open a fabric business with his nephew Rajah.

Marie was disgruntled. She had had enough of living with the rest of the family. Her husband was no longer earning enough at his father-in-law's business and wanted to strike out on his own. As soon as he set foot in the house, Marie badgered her father with incessant scenes and demands, always starting with: "*Sinyor padre, ke aga alguna koza, no puedo somportar mas!* Do something, Father, I can't stand it anymore!" And ending with: "Saby's ready, Rafo's waiting for it. He's had it up to here with that *buzdro* Rajah working with our family. *Sinyor padre*, you've got to choose between your daughter and your brother."

Maïr, who was a good man and loved his daughter, pointed out that he had already taken her side once and let her marry whom she liked. He sided with her once again. In September 1920 Saby Amon became the second member of the family to quit Salonika and go into business with his brother-in-law Rafo in a wholesale fabric business called "Benveniste et Amon." On reaching Paris, he set up the business and prepared for the arrival of his wife and daughter.

Then, on one sunny day in March 1921, Marie Benveniste and little Janja, nearly five years old, looked for the last time on the house in Venizelos Street, where they had lived for the past several years. Janja clung tightly to Sarika's hand, determined not to let go. For almost a week, Sarika and Oro had busied themselves in the kitchen preparing provisions for the little tribe to take with it on its way into exile. They'd made five days' worth of *borekitas*, lima bean balls, cheese puff pastries and pies, meat pâté, *rosketas*, hazelnut cookies, sesame crackers, and candied citrons. Oro had been up since before dawn to prepare the vital sweetmeats, her precious fresh *tajik-os de almendra*, for her granddaughter.

Then Marie and her daughter, accompanied by Maïr and Oro, Reyna, Saby's mother, the Benveniste brothers and sisters, and the Amon brothers and sister, all trooped off to the station. Like in the opening scene of *Murder on the Orient Express*, the Simplon Orient Express was awaiting its cargo of travelers with their wicker trunks. Marie had taken care to pack the precious engraved silver Ottoman platter, handed down from her grandmother Myriam. Sarika could not hold back her tears as Janja clung tightly to her hand.

Greeted by staff in the brown livery of the Company, the entire family filed through the dark teak wagons and the restaurant car, like the one in which the Armistice to end World War One had been signed three years earlier. The wagons had suffered from lack of maintenance during the war years. The restaurant car had lost its former renown from the days when its supplies didn't depend, as now, on unstable fledgling nation states. Anyway, Marie and her daughter preferred the family's provisions, which cost less. It was two years already since the Ottoman Empire had ceased to exist, and the brand-new Simplon Orient Express had been launched barely eighteenth months ago.

Janja howled when her hand was briskly prised from that of sobbing Sarika.

Soon the locomotive of the Simplon Orient Express, a magnificent train bearing the nameplate of the *Compagnie Internationale des Wagons-Lits* in French, came to life in a fracas of steam and flying sparks, bearing them to cities with mythical names, finally pausing in Lausanne, then Dijon, before reaching their ultimate destination, Paris.

Oro shed a tear as the train carried her granddaughter away, waving her big white handkerchief long after the silhouettes of Sarika and *Nona* had gradually faded, until they were just two dots on the horizon, then vanished out of sight. Janja sobbed copiously. Marie scolded her, then thought of a diversion:

"Shall we open up *Nona's* hamper?"

The *borekitas* had the better of her distress.

Each turn of the wheels carried her a little farther from Macedonia and her Jerusalem. The child gazed in fascination at the varied scenery as she went from East to West, from the Levant where the sun rises to the setting sun, conveying her to lands that lay deep in her genes, unbeknown to her.

Progress through the newly created state of Yugoslavia was slowed by work on upgrading and repairing the rail track. Yugoslav rail staff were wary, uncomfortable with their new position. After the junction at Nish, the Orient Express arrived in the Belgrade train station, and everyone got off. Janja and Marie were taken in for a few hours by relatives who had come to greet them and were curious to meet these grand cousins from Salonika on their way to the City of Light. They returned to their rail compartment, which converted from a lounge into bunk beds at night-time. Vinkovici, Ljubljana, Zagreb, Trieste… the train rumbled on relent-lessly through the night.

"*Kuanda vamos a yegar?* When do we get there?" Janja whined. She wanted to see Sarika; she wanted to see *Nona*; she wanted a story.

They passed through rugged terrain, traveling hundreds of miles on a single track. There were downpours, fierce winds, heatwaves, snowdrifts, and hailstorms. Frontiers were unstable. Country succeeded country. Customs officers and police at each border were nervous, inquisitorial at times. Strike action threatened in Italy. An Italian voice in a loudspeaker announced *Milano*. On reaching Domodossola, the train ran through the Simplon tunnel, opened in 1906, and came out at Brigue in the Swiss canton of Valais.

"*Kuando vamos a yegar?*" wailed Janja, intimidated by the long twin-gallery tunnel and astonished at Switzerland's gray skies.

"*Kuando vamos a yegar?*" came her muffled plea, though her spirits re-vived somewhat at the taste of Swiss milk chocolate, though she still want-ed her Sarika.

Suddenly, just when at last Janja had fallen asleep, the train juddered to a final halt. They'd reached the terminus. PARIS!

"We've arrived," said Marie. "And remember, from now on your name is Jenny."

Talking stones

A Francia... Three years later, in 1924, it was the turn of Maïr Benveniste to leave Salonika, traveling on his Spanish passport, with his wife Oro and their youngest daughter, Nelly. He left his two sons, Pepo and Momo, to wind up the rest of their assets. I try to imagine how, for the last time, he must have looked upon his city in the setting sun: the Bay of Salonika with, to the west, the once bustling port facing the public gardens, and to the east the White Tower beside the cemetery, *their* cemetery, where the tombstones of Rafael and Myriam, of Juda Senior and Samuel Meïr, *las piedras ke avlan*, the talking stones, stood. Maïr left behind him the young Sarika who had so adored little Janja, along with many relatives and friends, old schoolmates of Marie and her sisters, newborn babes and lovers, ancestors, and those who had died centuries ago.

Within a decade the Jewish cemetery had been broken up to make way for the extension to the university campus, in the name of the "collective will of the Macedonians," and more than a thousand corpses were transferred to another part of the cemetery. The Nazis destroyed what remained in December 1942 and after. As for the living who stayed behind in Salonika, the Benvenistes, the Amons and all the others, soon they were just names, then numbers on the manifests of transports taking them to the death camps, sinister medical experiments, and organized cruelty.

Seen against the broader canvas of history, the Jerusalem of the Balkans had been a mere parenthesis at the crossroads of two empires, a minority

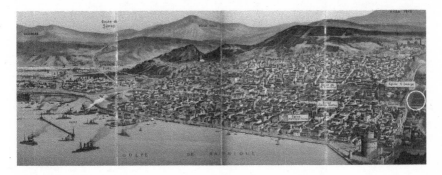

that ruled over a single city, a dream of a promised land, ending in nightmare. Today, traces of it have all but disappeared in Greek Thessaloniki, which struggles even to recall its Ottoman masters. This photo, printed during World War One, was for many decades the sole surviving evidence that the Hebrews had once flourished in this city and spoke a strange Spanish language that came to be called "Jewish."

Jenny never returned to the city of her birth, nor did Maïr or Marie. But one day I, their daughter, great-granddaughter and granddaughter, did return.

II
A Francia...
Growing up in Paris

Read no history: nothing but biography, for
that is life without theory.

—BENJAMIN DISRAELI. *CONTARINI FLEMING*

"I'm handing in my notice"

"Passengers are informed, we have arrived in Paris."

Paris, France... Janja opened her eyes wide, pricked up her ears and twitched her little Oriental nose accustomed to spicier aromas. No humidity here. On that day, March 21, 1921, a resplendent sun joyously greeted mother and daughter.

Saby Amon was waiting for them at the train station, together with Uncle Rafo. Janja was welcomed with a couple of vague kisses and a pinch and a tweak on her cheek applied with a degree of male force.

Janja and her mother were pushed into a Paris taxi, whose driver spoke French with an accent unlike the one she was accustomed to. She didn't yet know that his pronunciation was uncommon in France, for the driver was in fact a Russian prince. He too had been displaced, by the 1917 revolution in his case, and he managed his new domain, the streets of Paris, with jovial yet melancholy elegance. Janja stretched her piercing eyes as she recognized the Eiffel Tower. After passing the Invalides and the École Militaire, the Tsar's distant cousin pulled up at number 6, Rue Léon-Vaudoyer, where the upscale 7th Arrondissement meets the slightly more middle-class 15th.

"Bonjour, Madame Amon. Bonjour, Mademoiselle Jenny."

She was waiting for them in the doorway of the first-floor apartment! This was Annie, the new maid Rafo had hired for his sister Marie's family.

Annie greeted them, though with no kiss. And she ordered "Mademoiselle Jenny" to go wash her hands before sitting down for dinner and discovering her new bedroom. The apartment was a four-room former bachelor pad, not as grand as Rafo's third-floor one, but her uncle had refurnished it entirely. The entrance, dining room and Saby and Marie's bedroom looked out onto the street. At the end of a long corridor was the kitchen, then two more bedrooms. The first was intended for the future new arrivals, while the second was for Jenny... and Annie.

At bedtime, Jenny asked her mother for a story "like Sarika's," accompanied or followed by a handful of Judeo-Spanish songs.

"Out of the question!" barked Annie. "A girl of five no longer needs that kind caprice. It's unworthy of a well brought-up child."

Marie protested weakly: habit... the change....

"Out of the question! If Madame doesn't agree, I'm handing in my notice!"

Disaster loomed... Rafo raised an eyebrow. Saby lectured his wife under his breath, in Ladino. This isn't the Orient, you know. The girl's got to get used to washing, dressing, and going to sleep by herself.

Annie's way prevailed, heralding future conflicts between the mistress and the woman then known as the "child maid." She had come straight from a convent run by her aunts, who were nuns, in Vesoul, in eastern France. She was poor but knew how to behave, and it was she who would govern the household from now on.

Five minutes later, lights out. "Mademoiselle Jenny" was left on her own in the dark, in her new bedroom, whereas until now a little night light had always been left on to help her go to sleep.

"Not in the dark... Not in the dark."

Janja screamed, then sobbed for ages, calling for Sarika, then her mother and her *Nona*, who would never have stood for her being treated so, for being deprived of all the light.

But Annie stood her ground:

"It's out of the question! Madame mustn't go and comfort her in secret! If she does, I'm giving my notice!"

Annie and Uncle Corentin

"Finish your milk, Mademoiselle Jenny."

Jenny, pictured below in Paris, remembers staring vacantly at the white bowl filled with a beige liquid on which floated a thick skin, wrinkly and unappetizing.

She protested feebly:

"But... Annie! I've already eaten my *tartine*, my bread and butter."

Jenny wanted to throw up at the sight of that hefty wedge of already stale bread, weighed down by a thick layer of butter. Yet she had nibbled away at it till it was all gone, trying to think of something else... such as the eagerly awaited visit to her auntie this coming Thursday, where she would be seeing her cousins.

"Mademoiselle Jenny, finish up your milk or I'll call your uncle."

Jenny shivered. Uncle Rafo was terrifying for a little girl when angry. She knew her mother would no more stand up to her brother than she would to Annie, and that the two were in league against her. She swallowed a spoonful, not daring approach that horrid bowl with her lips.

"When I was a little girl in Vesoul, we didn't make such a song and dance! And even less with the nuns. It's only rich kids that make a fuss like that over the food the Good Lord sends us."

Jenny shut her eyes to hold back her tears, stuck out her spoon and struck the surface of the bowl. The liquid splashed out and spattered the waxed cloth. Annie leapt up.

"So now she's throwing a tantrum! Monsieur Rafo! Monsieur Rafo!"

Just then the elevator door shut. Uncle Corentin. Oh no! Not Uncle Corentin!

"Monsieur Rafo... I don't know what's got into this child. It's impossible to get her to eat her breakfast... and now she's splattered it all over the place."

"Jenny!"

When her uncle growled in his stentorian voice it was as if a pride of lions had burst roaring into the kitchen. The child shrank.

"Why won't you drink your milk?"

Jenny made so bold as to remind her uncle of her paradise lost.

"I want ... some *tajicos*, ... or even some *sotlatch*..."

How dare she? ... and in front of the French maid to boot!

"You won't go to see your auntie till you've drunk it all up, to the last drop. Do you hear? And stop sniveling! This isn't Salonika, here!"

Alas, the child knew it all too well. Sarika, her *Nona*, her *tajicos* and her *borekitas* had stayed behind in the sunlit port at the foot of the White Tower. Here in this gloomy, rain-soaked city, her mother submitted to Annie's orders; her father was bound up in his business and the affairs of the community, barely aware of his daughter's existence. Her little cousin Kiko, Allegra's son, who shared her distress and her dread of Uncle Corentin, lived far from Paris. Janja was far away. Jenny was alone.

She summoned up her courage, fought back her tears and disgust, and swallowed the bitter potion in one go, along with the cold skin on the top of the milk, which stuck to her teeth.

Annie and Rafo considered her for a moment, reassured and certain of the victory adults always win over children.

But her stomach was having none of it, the liquid wouldn't stay in her gullet, which noisily rejected it... And Jenny slowly vomited up the disgusting liquid, which came out through her mouth, her nose and all her pores, expelling the foul brew back into the bowl, which she gripped so as not to spatter the table. In horror at what she had just done, she hid her face in her filthy hands.

A grownup's anger knows no bounds when confronted with a child's defiance. That displayed by Rafo, who Jenny and Kiko called "Uncle Corentin," a reference to *Bécassine*, the comic album they enjoyed in secret, was demonstrative and oriental. Annie's anger was cold. But together they thought up a fitting punishment.

"Don't imagine you're going to get away with this so easily, you naughty little girl..."

"You'll have nothing else to eat. We know how to handle disobedient children."

Annie had learned the hard way, on the farm and in a convent.

So, three times a day for three days the bowl was there waiting for Jenny, on the table in the kitchen, Rue Léon-Vaudoyer. Rafo might have given in in the end, but not Annie. Held in even greater respect than the eldest son, the French maid was instrumental in a process of assimilation that could never have reached into the heart of everyday life in France without her. And it was by draining her cup to the dregs that the little girl from Salonika started on the road to becoming an authentic *Gauloise*, an authentic Frenchwoman. Later, she would rather make herself sick than leave something on her plate. Annie the "dragon" turned Marie and her daughter, not into native-born Frenchwomen, but into docile strivers after Frenchness of the purest kind. The Beneveniste sisters learned to cook veal blanquette and orange chocolate mousse. They kept the art of making *borekas* for themselves and their husbands, and they made them in secret on the cook's day off.

From that day on, Jenny obstinately refused to eat and had a brush with anorexia, until her grandparents arrived. Her *Nona* had left her a giggly, chubby-cheeked little girl. She found a leggy beanpole who needed lots of *borekas* to fill her out and restore color to her cheeks.

How little Jenny became truly French

Jenny's first school was Le Cours Bouchut, a fee-paying nursery school just across the street from the Amon apartment. All schools were fee-paying at that time, except for primary schools, then known as "communal" schools. Jenny was five at the start of the school year, in October 1921. She spent a year there. The school stood where several streets, César-Franck, Pérignon, Bellart and Bouchut, meet. It was a single-story timber building occupying a whole block, including Rue César-Franck, where Jenny was to live later after her marriage.

At the start of the second year, Annie, who walked Jenny to school, found a sign on the school gate saying the school was closed. All enrolled children were to go to the Lycée Victor-Duruy on the Boulevard des Invalides, with an envelope bearing their name. So little Jenny entered the junior school in first year. She was six, and her teacher was named Mademoiselle Wackeinem, a name she was unlikely to forget.

Above all though, Jenny later recalled, she gained top marks in elocution. That was thanks to Madame Fournier, her piano teacher and her great love. The lady made ends meet for herself and her husband, a Great War invalid, by giving music lessons. But Madame Fournier's true calling was elsewhere. She was an actress, a member of the prestigious *Comédie Française* troupe, and she delighted in sharing her passion with her young pupil. Marie and Saby had gone to the expense of buying their daughter a Gaveau, an upright piano that occupied a place of honor in the drawing room. Every day, after finishing her homework, Jenny would practice her scales and play her favorite pieces.

Thursday was the best day of the week, when Jenny would rise at dawn, gulp down her breakfast, and set off in the morning for her piano lesson with Madame Fournier, opposite the Bon Marché department store, accompanied by the faithful Annie, grumpy as ever. After the lesson, Jenny lunched with her teacher and the latter's son, who was the same age as her. Then Madame Fournier became Claude Riche, her stage name as a member of the troupe at the *Comédie-Française*, where she played Marivaux soubrettes and supporting roles. In *Le mariage de Figaro*, the play by Beaumarchais, Claude Riche played Chérubin, madly in love with his godmother, the Countess. The two children would spend the afternoon in a box in the theater, watching and listening to classic plays in the French repertory.

Madame Fournier took care to leave her theater program for her pupil to leaf through later, and since Jenny often saw the same play over again, she ended up knowing it by heart. She didn't understand everything, of course. But she took it in. And she memorized the French classics for life. The actress-music teacher would come to see them in the interval to hand out bread and chocolate for their tea, then went back onstage. At the end of the play, the children would walk through the wings to Madame Fournier's dressing room.

Between the ages of eight and fourteen, Jenny learned Corneille's *Le Cid* by heart, as well as works by Racine, Molière, the Romantics, and even *Le Barbier de Séville*… the whole repertory. When she had to go up before the class to recite a poem, she easily outdid her mates. Jenny still remembered her Beaumarchais after the age of eighty, "I was in love with Figaro, the young lead at the time, though I've forgotten his name. I loved the atmosphere, the costumes, the makeup."

Later, in secondary school, when the pupils were set their required reading of three classic plays, in 8th, 9th and 10th years, Molière's *Les Précieuses Ridicules*, Corneille's *Horace*, or Racine's *Britannicus*, no matter, Jenny knew them by heart, and sailed to near the top of the class.

But the greatest joys of her childhood were the arrival in Paris of her two grandmothers, one after the other.

First came:

"Jenny! Get ready, quickly. Your *Nona* Reyna—you'll have to call her 'Grandma Amon,' now—is arriving at the Gare de Lyon train station with your uncles and aunt."

Jenny hurried. A little piece of Salonika was coming to Paris. And her youthful Amon uncles were the life and soul of the party. They could even raise a smile from Annie.

Then came:

"Jenny! Get ready, quickly. Your *Nona* Oro—you'll have to call her 'Grandma Benveniste,' now—is at the station, with your grandpa and Nelly."

Now Jenny was jubilant. She was going to see her young aunt and her *Nona*. There would be news of Sarika, candies, and songs. The patriarch's arrival in 1924 eclipsed Annie's power somewhat. Rafo and Marie wouldn't dare contradict their father: he clung to tradition and had every intention of having his say in the education of the young generation.

One year later, the two other Benveniste brothers, Pepo and Momo, joined the now-reunited family. The tribe was organized under the egis of the *sinyor padre*, although Jenny was sorry not see her playmate Kiko, Allegra and Ugo having migrated with him to Brussels.

Upon arriving in Europe, the three Benveniste sisters, Marie, Allegra, and Nelly freed themselves from the Orient with a few snips of the scissors. Like other women of their time, they read *La Garçonne*[10] and cut off

---

10. A novel by Victor Margueritte, published in 1922. It describes an independent young woman living a life of sexual freedom, with both male and female partners. The book was a *succès de scandale* and a major bestseller [Translator].

their long hair, which previously fell to their waist but which their husbands alone had been permitted to admire hanging loose about the face. Allegra's hair especially, ebony black with reddish tints, covered her head with a flowing mane. Her husband Ugo never got over the change. The thoughtless hairdresser hadn't even handed over the magnificent, sacrificed locks, sweeping them away with the dust on the floor. Jenny, raised by an emancipated mother, never grew her hair long.

Between the ages of eight and fourteen, every weekend Jenny would rush over to her grandparents near the Champ de Mars, armed with her Thursday theater program. Nelly, her young aunt freshly arrived in Paris, had enrolled in the Lycée Victor-Duruy, too, though in the high school, where she was studying Racine's *Andromaque*. Jenny would never forget those Sunday treats: "I used to get into her bed early on Sunday mornings. She was revising her schoolwork. She kept forgetting most of the couplets, but I knew them off by heart. I could recite the whole play. My grandparents would take a siesta after an 'oriental' Sunday lunch. Uncle Momo was another product of the *Alliance Israélite Universelle*, and I'd go into his library, which contained the whole of the eighteenth-century theatrical repertory in fine bindings, as well as the works of Victor Hugo, Alfred de Musset, Edmond Rostand, and so on. I'd stand for hours at a time in front of my grandmother's mirror-fronted wardrobe and recite what I'd heard."

Jenny needed the outlet now, a tiny intruder having sprung up in her mother's belly in 1922, abolishing her status as an only child.

A little brother for Jenny—or boys' privileges

The arrival of a baby brother or sister is a major event in the life of a six-year-old. It was an even bigger event for Jenny's parents, indeed the goal of their life. They'd wanted a *boy* more than anything, lamenting the fact that they had a daughter only. After all, girls are useless, they cost money, will need an exorbitant dowry, and husbands must be found for them. For months, the parents trumpeted the impending birth. So certain were they it would be a boy that they didn't even envisage the alternative, nor had they considered a girl's name. Jenny was thrilled at the prospect of the baby and was almost as impatient as her parents for its arrival.

To surprise her, her father Saby picked her up at school—the only time in his life—and took her to see her mother in the clinic, with the peremptory injunction:

"Above all, not a word about a little brother to your mother!"

When Jenny entered the room, she saw her mother looking pale, as white as her pillow. And no baby! The little girl's eyes flitted in silence around the room; she pricked up her ears. Not a sound. Where could he have gone? "I was puzzled," remembers Jenny. "But I didn't dare ask. Why didn't they show me the baby? Had he been kidnapped by one of those gypsy child-snatchers... Annie used to terrify me with tales of them? But so stern was the order, I didn't dare ask and I kept my thoughts to myself."

It was Annie who spilled the beans:

"Your little brother, let's face it, is dead. Angels like him have carried him away..."

And then the "dragon," as Kiko and Jenny called her, turned away, muttering to conceal her frustration. She knew full well that the child had died without being baptized... so he would not be admitted to Limbo; best to bury him in our memories since the Good Lord had not allowed him to exist.

In fact, Annie was relieved. She hadn't wanted this baby, still didn't want it and lost no occasion to remind Marie that she might not stay if there was another child in the home: she loathed children. Jenny was close to suspecting she had cast a spell on the baby, the *mal de oyo*, the "evil eye," as *Nona* Oro called it.

Jenny learned what had happened from Annie. Her mother's labor had been long and drawn out and the pain had suddenly ceased. For want of experience, or a sign of fate perhaps, the physician had done nothing to bring on the childbirth. When the baby was born, he was blue and breathed with difficulty. He lived just four days.

"Without Annie, I would have known nothing of the circumstances," says Jenny. "I don't know if I suffered more from the loss of the baby brother or from my parents' silence. From that moment on, I knew they had no confidence in me, that I had been undeserving, since they'd hidden the truth from me, since they never even said that my little brother had existed and had left this world."

From that time on, Jenny remained curious but began hiding things herself and made a habit of not expressing her feelings unduly. When she learned, again through Annie, that her mother was expecting another baby, she showed no interest and took no part in the general outpouring of joy at Marcel's birth.

He was born on April 30, 1924. A boy, at last! Marie had struggled with the thought it might be another girl.

"I think she'd have drowned it with her own hands," says Jenny. "But all her fears vanished with the appearance of this son, whom she adored from the start. To be sure, he was a magnificent baby and an adorable little boy. Everyone went crazy over him. His uncles showered him with lavish gifts, and his presence played a big part in spurring them to want to marry and have families of their own."

The boy ought to have been called Mordechai, like his Grandfather Amon. Instead, he was called Marcel, like Proust, and like many little French boys at the time. He was such a cute child the soap maker Cadum offered my parents a lot of money to feature him in their adverts. They refused, mainly out of fear—that ancestral fear—of the evil eye. Despite her loathing of babies, Annie fell for the baby brother and was rewarded with his first smiles, while Marie strove to feed him with her own milk, which refused to flow as abundantly as it had with Janja, her first child.

"Annie remained an old spinster," as Jenny puts it bitterly, "but the only baby she really held tenderly in her arms was the little Marcel. As for me, I was the little vixen, the snitch, the one who told my parents what she was doing. We'd got off to a bad start, she and I, and things went downhill from there."

Her brother's arrival ended Jenny's childhood as the center of attention. She was eight years old. She had had the time to forge her character. Yet she never fully got over it. Her urge to assimilate in her new country sprang too from this split with her mother, Marie, coming after the break with Salonika, and her difficult relationship with her family at the time fed into this feeling. Would Jenny have understood her mother better if she herself

66

had had a son one day? The war got in the way and all she had was me, her only daughter.

"From that time on," Jenny continues, "I ceased to exist. I started getting uglier. I was only eight, but I was already fully developed. This early puberty and the arrival of my *Nona* with her Salonika cuisine made me put on weight, whereas I'd been too skinny at the time of the 'bowl of vomit.' Being too fat was an abomination for my mother, Marie. Her feminine ideal was blonde, tall, and slim, like Marlene Dietrich in *Blue Angel*. But I was none of that: I was dark, petite, and tubby. And nosy to boot. In a family bent on concealing everything I wanted to know everything."

Nineteen twenty-four was a banner year for the Benveniste family, with the arrival of the patriarch and the newborn son. A year later, Jenny was filled with excitement at her first frilly bridesmaid's dress, side by side with Kiko, who'd come straight from Brussels in his page's suit. There were two weddings in France that year. Nelly, the youngest of the three sisters, married a well-to-do young man from Salonika, while Rafo, the eldest of the boys, married an "American girl," Luce Botton. Both weddings were celebrated in the synagogue on the Rue Buffault. Two years later, Momo married one of Richard's sisters. Then in 1929 there was a grand wedding for Pepo, the youngest son, to a *Stambouli*, a girl from Constantinople. Maïr could be pleased with himself, having married off his three sons with comfortable dowries, and to lovely women—no bad thing in itself—of *buena familia*, of good families.

Destiny. The three Benveniste sons, Rafo, Pepo and Momo, experienced very different fates. Destiny. The eldest passed away quietly at the foot of Mount Popocatapetl. Destiny. The youngest grew rich and died in his elegant home in a smart Paris suburb. Destiny. The second one, Momo, was to suffer an agonizing descent into the bowels of Hell.

Lavish weddings were followed by a pendulum-like succession of births in their respective home. Tightly rationed. One boy per family. Except for Jenny, born in the Balkans, and for one last baby girl born to Momo once he was assured of a son. French fertility patterns swept through the family: where Rafael sired ten children and Maïr six, the next generation contented itself with a single child per couple in the nineteen twenties and thirties—provided it was a boy.

Then Marie, Saby, Jenny, and the three "Portuguese" family members, all Salonika-born subjects of the Ottoman Empire, took French nationality, thanks in part, perhaps, to the birth of a son on French soil. From now on Jenny's national heritage comprised the long line of French kings, and the national heroine Joan of Arc. So eagerly did she embrace her new identity that she scored a consistent ten out of ten in her French history classes.

In the latter part of the nineteen twenties, the Benvenistes were once more dancing on a volcano. Business seemed to be flourishing. The men took care of their tribe and their community. The women coped with their pregnancies and learned "Frenchness" through their domestic servants, picking up dress codes, going on slimming diets and out to tea parties. Outwardly, they were becoming like everyone else, while sticking to their own. Fifteen years later, masks fell from this faded yet tenacious Orient. Memories of it were slowly drained of color during these years of decline, as gradually people ceased to mention or even think about it. Even the old dream of a return to Sefarad was repressed, since the family was already back in the West, in a kind of time-shift, direct from Toledo to Paris.

Though privileged because prosperous, the tiny Salonika-born elite was once again an isolated, expatriate minority. The French bourgeoisie, even the Jews, cold-shouldered these *métèques*[11], if only because of their accent, never mind their French passports. For a few short years the Benvenistes achieved—or so they thought—their dream of integration with assimilation. Maïr, the patriarch, kept the family spirit alive; the nannies, meanwhile, worked unintentionally to undermine it.

Maids and mistresses: kitchen power

The scene: the Champ de Mars at the foot of the Eiffel Tower, one Thursday in the nineteen thirties.

For once, the nannies working for the Benveniste and other related families were chatting, after a family gathering in the home of Maïr and Oro,

---

11. French pejorative term for people of Mediterranean origin considered uncouth [Translator].

in Avenue du Général-Détrie. Usually, each nationality kept to itself. This time, they were all together, with a little spy at their side, who seventy years later recalled every word they spoke.

"If I ever get rich," says Nénène, "I'll never hire a nanny."

"It's practical though, getting rid of the brats," declared Geneviève, known as Vivi, while vigorously shaking the perambulator of the youngest Beneveniste cousin, a few months old at the time.

"Why bother having them... if you don't want ... to look after them?" asked Miss Papat loudly [in English], in her inimitable British accent.

As she spoke, she lashed out at her little three-year-old rascal who'd just wet his pants playing in the sandbox.

Then up spoke the *Fräulein*:

"Why leave someone else to look after the baby? If she gets it all... the first babbling, the first smile, the first kiss? We get all the best bits."

"And the sleepless nights... the whooping cough... the teething... the tantrums..."

"And on Sundays as well!" sighed Mezan. "Last Sunday, my sister Anaïs was sick, and I couldn't even take her a bowl of soup!"

"And eating [said in English] ... Eating off a tray all alone in your room.... I'd rather [said in English] eat with the rest of the staff."

The Fräulein added:

"I deliberately don't let *her* see him cuddle me when he gets out of the bath. Fifteen minutes a day, she gets. Not a minute more. And it's when *I* want."

"I avoid 'cuddles' like the plague," protested Vivi. "I grew attached once. Then I had to leave and never see them again. Thank you and goodbye."

Sigh...

Vivi speaks softly. "You know what my cousin told me... Well, you remember the Swiss girl, the one who always used to come and sit behind the merry-go-round, with the kid bawling like an ox... well, she gave him... so much of the stuff he... died."

"He died?" chorused the four nannies.

"He died," repeated Vivi, with a faint sardonic laugh that sent a chill through Jenny, pretending to be absorbed in *Little Women*. She'd already finished reading it but insisted on re-reading the final page.

"At least, I think so. Anyway, the girl was fired … without pay!"

Fräulein lowered her voice, but Jenny had sharp ears.

"I told you, you need to watch out with those doses."

Then she suddenly pulled herself up. Perhaps "cuddles" referred to something stronger.

"Miss Jenny, couldn't you fetch him his bucket? Poor little thing, he's been looking for it everywhere."

The teenager got up and did as she was bidden, as the murmur of conversation drifted out of hearing, though she thought she made out some contemptuous references to *métèques*, a word she'd often heard spoken by her schoolmates, including the other Jewish but otherwise *bona fide* French girls.

When Saby and Marie moved from Rue Léon-Vaudoyer to 5 Rue Pérignon, the domestic staff comprised a general-purpose maid, a child's maid and a maid who came in daily to do the washing. Annie, the little Levantine girl's faithful tiger nanny, was joined by Germaine, a farmer's daughter from a region west of Paris who had left her parents' big farm to work in the city. Every year, the parents slaughtered a pig and sent her sausages and pâtés, which she kept in a corner of the cupboard and ate to supplement her daily meals. She thought nothing of handing portions to little Jenny, who savored the pork sausage, traditionally forbidden in Salonika.

Maïr's other daughters and sons had introduced the reign of the uniformed nanny. The Sephardi Jews from Egypt were first to adopt this custom, and the Salonika branch followed in their footsteps, contacting the nursing agencies at the first signs of pregnancy. Coming usually from some other European country, England, Germany, Austria, or Switzerland mainly, the nannies were a status symbol. Unlike a child's maid like Annie, who was of peasant stock, a genuine nanny often came from an impoverished middle-class family and had been trained in child-minding in her country of origin. Their uniform signaled their nationality, and one could tell at a glance whether the young woman pushing the pram spoke the language of Goethe or that of Shakespeare.

"Ah no, Madame! You can't see the baby now. It's not the right time!"

A mother unable to control her impulses or who despaired at the sound of her baby crying was told by nanny to refrain from picking up baby. That was the rule. Otherwise:

"I'm handing in my notice!"

"That day," says Jenny, clenching her fist, "I swore I'd raise my baby myself."

The Benveniste family preferred French girls like Nénène or Mezan, who wore a pale blue uniform with matching headscarf, and navy-blue pinafore over a white blouse in winter. Momo, however, employed a Swiss nanny who was to play a pivotal role in the tribe's transformation. They called her "*Mademoiselle*." She was a Protestant from the Swiss Canton of Saint-Gall, and she accomplished what neither the Catholic Kings of Spain nor Suliman the Magnificent, nor even Sabbatai Tsevi, the false Messiah of Smyrna, had managed in nearly five centuries: she converted part of the family to Protestantism (though not before the patriarch's demise).

Girl talk

Jenny very nearly never studied Spanish. In Seventh Grade, pupils were asked to choose a second language: Italian or German. Jenny studied Italian for a fortnight. But the demand for Spanish was so great the school inspector called for a Spanish teacher. One morning, a lovely young Catalan woman turned up, looking nothing like the spinsters Jenny and her classmates were used to, and she got her pupils to say *para* and *parra*, *pero* and *perro*.

Jenny pronounced the words as she had been accustomed with her *Nona* and Sarika, and Mademoiselle Daran had her repeat them:

"You're making a good start, miss…."

"Amon, Jenny Amon."

Saying nothing, the teacher gazed at her with piercing eyes.

A little later, Mademoiselle Daran gave a class on the three cultures of Spain and the Catholic Kings. At the end of the class, she motioned to Jenny to stay behind.

"I see you were born in Thessaloniki. Are you descended from the Sephardim of Spain?"

"Yes, Mademoiselle."

"I see why you have no difficulty with the language of Cervantes. If you have any documents in Ladino, could you bring me them? I'm looking for *romanceros* in old Spanish."

Iberians were then rediscovering the "Spaniards without a homeland" whom they had expelled in 1492. Now they were carrying out extensive historical and literary research. Jenny brought her the Judeo-Spanish newspapers her father read, together with some poems. Mademoiselle Daran was delighted.

But Jenny lost her best friend as a result. Four times a day she and Denise Minard walked to and from the lycée, along Avenue de Saxe, Avenue de Breteuil and Saint-François-Xavier, the church opposite Victor-Duruy, entrusting her with some of her secrets. Denise invited her to tea one day and asked:

"What are those magazines you're giving our Spanish teacher?"

Her reaction to the answer was swift. Denise suddenly changed her section in mid-year, gave up Spanish and stopped walking to school with Jenny. The latter was deeply upset. She realized suddenly that, her new passport notwithstanding, her classmates did not see her as one of them.

Jenny sought solace in the Russian Orthodox girls, who livened up the schoolyard with their fierce but arcane quarrels:

"The only true Tsar is Vladimir."

"An imposter, you mean... a traitor... the true legitimate Tsar is Nicholas and I forbid you..."

"And I won't allow you..."

"Olga, Tatyana, spare us!"

Nothing could stem the torrent of Russian pouring from these teenage fanatics. Olga and Tatyana wore their long hair braided around their ears, and in the ensuing catfight each tugged with all her might at the other's hair. As for verbal battle between them, the reasons for their dispute left the French girls bewildered. All they could see was that their Russian exile classmates were in profound disagreement as to the identity of a person who would never be Tsar—but whose return might change the lives and status of their fathers. The latter would cease being taxi drivers and be restored to the titles and privileges abolished by the great proletarian revolution of 1917.

Olga, Tatyana, and Hélène were Russian but had been born or had arrived in France around that fateful year. They belonged to the great families of the Imperial circle, but their parents now were penniless, and a special committee paid for the girls' school fees, which the girls were expected to repay on reaching adulthood. Jenny became friends with Hélène Pilipenco, who never parted from her Cross of Saint George, of which her father was a Knight.

There was also a class for foreign girls, all boarders, to which neither the Russians nor Jenny, who all spoke perfect French, belonged. The foreign girls were scattered among the regular classes, sitting in at the back and listening to proceedings. Originally these foreigners had been North American, English, German, Greek, Spanish, Romanian and, after the Germans annexed Alsace and Lorraine in 1870, there were girls from Eastern France too. Then came girls from Egypt, Lebanon, and Syria, and Jewish girls from the Ottoman Empire, like Nelly Benveniste, who had retained her original Judeo-Spanish accent, or Jenny M.

Jenny M. came from Salonika and was a boarder. The school tasked Maïr Benveniste's granddaughter, Jenny Amon, with looking after her. Seventy years later the latter still remembered: "Jenny M.'s father was very rich and had married his cleaner. And their daughter was a rebel. At fifteen, she had run away with a Greek. So, they sent her as a boarder to the Lycée Victor-Duruy where I was put in charge of her. It was no picnic. I had to get her to do her homework, persuade her to see reason, listen to her outpourings. She ended up setting fire to her room. 'Jenny,' I asked, 'how could you?' 'I know,' she replied. 'I'm impossible. All Jennys are, except you.' They had to send her back to Salonika... I wonder what became of her..."

Jenny couldn't admit she'd grown fond of her namesake, with whom she had formed a close bond and who had returned, probably to a tragic fate.

That was because the daygirls from her arrondissement, like Denise Minard, or from the newly built neighborhoods adjacent to the Champs de Mars, would never mix with the daughter of a tradesman on the Rue du Sentier[12] who lived in the 15th Arrondissement, however close to the 7th.

---

12. The heart of the Paris garment district till the early 21st century, known for its large proportion of Jewish businesses [Translator].

These girls' families had links to the Army, the judicial system, the world of medicine, industry, and the colonial administration. They were the daughters of senior civil servants, physicians, governors, top Treasury and educational officials.

Jenny had to fall back on the other Jewish girls, the *Tudescas*, Ashkenazi girls her family would have looked down on in Salonika but who didn't give her the cold shoulder, girls of Polish and Russian origin, like Rose C. "She was both beautiful and an effortless star pupil. Rose was the kind of girl who'd dance till three in the morning," remembers Jenny. "She'd arrive in school at 8 am and ask around: 'Done your French essay? Give me what you've written.' And she'd turn to the next girl and say: 'Give me yours too.' Then she'd sit in a corner—she hadn't prepared anything—and she'd copy a bit from one and a bit from the other, and when we all handed in our homework, she'd come out on top. We were livid."

Later, Anna Lévy and Françoise Dreyfus joined in the race for the top marks. Jenny learned to her dismay that the Ashkenazi girls ranked above the girls from Salonika in the pecking order.

Sacrilege

The synagogue on the Rue des Victoires was packed. For once the crowd was predominantly young and female. One might have been at Notre-Dame Cathedral on First Communion Day, with nothing but girls. And our pre-teen was in a state of high excitement. The star of the ceremony might have been her, Jenny Amon, but the celebrant was Myriam Silverstein, twelve years old like herself. She was Jewish and respectful of the law and the Mosaic tradition. She was dressed in white from head to toe, as for a Christian first communion. She was celebrating her bat-mitzvah, her religious confirmation.

That day, Jenny went with her father, Saby Amon, who was already actively involved in the B'nai B'rith lodge and who frequented leading members of the Ashkenazi community.

"Papa... what does 'bat-mitzvah' mean?"

"It means 'daughter of commandment.' For boys we call it bar-mitzvah. It marks the religious coming of age. One becomes responsible for one's actions, for one's possessions, one can read the Tora in public and follow its six hundred and thirteen commandments. One can form part of a *minyan* or prayer group and enter into a marriage under Jewish law."

Jenny gazed at the stained-glass windows filtering the spring sunlight, then thought about this rite of passage these girls of her age were undergoing, radiant in their immaculate dresses. Behind her, a lady with a strong Yiddish accent commented to her neighbor:

"It's Rabbi Mordechai Kaplan who started this. His daughter was the first to do it... about six years ago."

A wave of emotion swept over Jenny and she tugged him by the sleeve of his suit.

"Papa! I want a bat-mitzvah."

"A bat-mitzvah? Are you crazy? It's not for girls, at least not where we come from!"

"But why not? Those girls are doing it..."

"They're not Oriental girls. The *Tudescos* do things differently."

"But Papa!"

"My girl, forget about it. It's not for you. I'd never allow it. And your grandfather even less."

Jenny calmed down a little. Maïr was the final authority, and she knew he truly loved her. Not like her father, Saby. So, if he too was against it! Back home, she buttonholed her mother, who hadn't attended the service. Marie took the same line:

"Jenny, it's impossible. Girls where we come from don't have bat-mitzvahs. But when you brother is old enough, we'll have a very fine one for him, you'll see, not at the Ashkenazi synagogue on Rue des Victoires, but at ours on Rue Buffault."

Jenny had never felt so left out of things, so abandoned. Why those girls? Why him? What had she done to deserve this?

The wound never healed. At first, Jenny strove to be worthy with all her being. She fasted ardently on the Day of Atonement, never letting the slightest morsel of food pass her lips.

But this time, on Yom Kippur, as always Saby Amon came home from the synagogue, where he had been since early morning in his dark suit and top hat, and now he shut himself up in his room.

"To pray," whispered Marie. "Don't disturb him, whatever you do."

And she shut herself in the kitchen.

Jenny tried to cultivate most of the virtues pleasing to God. But curiosity was her Achilles' heel, a weakness she didn't even bother to fight since her school encouraged the desire to learn. Luckily, Jenny was a curious little girl, like Alice in Wonderland. Had she not been, the Devil would have concealed some details from her story, and they would not have come down to me.

For the moment, Jenny went ahead blindly, like Bluebeard's wife about to open the door to the secret chamber. Her parents' bedroom gave onto a rather dark little passageway with a niche, now empty, that used to contain a statue in the days of previous tenants. Jenny huddled in the niche and waited. A few minutes later her mother came along on tiptoe holding a tray, then slipped into the bedroom and came out. Though small, Jenny had no difficulty peering through the keyhole.

And there she saw... she saw her father sitting quietly in front of the side table by the window, savoring with his habitual languor one of the *borekas* prepared earlier in the week for the end of the fast! This wasn't one of those primal scenes a child chances upon in her parents' bedroom. But it was a betrayal. A betrayal of the Alliance, a betrayal of the Law, perpetrated by its most eminent representative, the father figure reflected in the mirror on the big wardrobe, doubling and multiplying the imposture.

The little Jenny of the time still hadn't gotten over it seventy years later, when she recounted the vision of her father clandestinely breaking the fast, transgressing the taboo, revealed as even more naked than the emperor, in his cardinal sinfulness on the Day of Atonement, shamelessly soiling his intestines and jeopardizing the path to purification for himself and all his descendants.

"It meant he didn't believe a word he professed to believe with undisputed authority. That he, who hadn't considered me worthy to become a daughter of commandment, couldn't care less for those commandments. What counted for him was his stomach, which was starting to rumble.

What counted was his position as president of the B'nai B'rith. Everything that had prompted our expulsion, our exile, our persecutions, our emigration, the *auto da fes*, the burnings at the stake, the rejection of apostasy, everything that had led our people into its dispersals, its destructions, he... well, it meant nothing to him. So, I began to believe less. The rot had set in. I was well and truly punished for my indiscretion, for my curiosity. I never told anyone. Ever. Even my husband, Jacques, who was a pious man, observant of the rites and conventions, when I met him, when I fell in love with him, I never dared tell him early on, before we made the great leap."

Men's talk

It was at the end of one of those banquets at the home of the Benveniste parents, where they still ate after the Salonika fashion, not minding the French maids. There was Maïr, the host, Saby Amon, his son-in-law and nephew, his three sons Rafo, Pepo and Momo, and Doctor Vidal Modiano, not directly related to Ugo, a leading figure in the community and a close family friend. Young Jenny was dozing, nestling in the depths of a big armchair in the adjoining sitting room. The men were talking, half in Judeo-Spanish and half in French.

Jenny strained to listen but heard only snatches of conversation, though she understood almost everything being said. The talk was of Sephardism and the need to preserve it in the new world after the collapse of the empires. For the first time Jenny heard the name of an Austrian madman increasingly popular in next-door Germany and planning the destruction of the Jews.

"Our settlement in France, so close to Spain, must be a renaissance, a new foundation," declared Doctor Modiano. "We must organize the Sephardim and bring them together into a powerful and solid confederation so that they can regain their strength and the means to assert themselves again. Sephardism must live! It must regain its historic role in Judaism... The descendants of Ben Gabirol, Halévy and Spinoza must get back down to work."

"That's what we've done with the Community Board and the Salonika Society," said Maïr, "and now the Sephardic Religious Association."

Vidal Modiano poured himself a glass of raki and carried on forcefully:

"A Jew without a Jewish memory, without a memory of his forefathers, is a consciousness without age, a man without a past. He inhabits an empty house. He wanders aimlessly, he is lost... You remember Salonika, our city? It was a perfect image of Jewish continuity and fidelity. All those things that those banished from Spain brought with them came to be seen as sacred... When my mother bustled about the *fogarero* at the end of the Sabbath, she always said: 'You can only rekindle a fire if the ashes are still warm.' We must make haste to rekindle the ashes of Judaism!"

"Before thinking of the past, first we needed to modernize ourselves," said Pepo. "Remember: when we came here, we were 'Orientals,' 'Levantines.' We didn't speak of 'Sephardim' or 'Ladino,' which we called *judezmo*, 'Jewish.' Now, we need to make our stand as Sephardim as distinct from the Ashkenazim, and to join forces with our brothers in North Africa."

"Soon we'll be celebrating the eight hundredth anniversary of Maimonides," said Rafo. "It would be a good opportunity."

"And that of Isaac Abravanel," added Saby, "the ancestor of our B'nai B'rith president, my friend and colleague Salvatore."

"And did you know," rejoined Vidal, "that our brothers in Sarajevo have developed a 'national diaspora movement' alongside the Zionists? But here, in France, we need to do so within the framework of the Republic's institutions and in the spirit of '91[13]. Don't forget the words of Stanislas de Clermont-Tonnerre: 'We must refuse everything to the Jews as a nation and accord everything to Jews as individuals.' Here we enjoy freedoms many Jews elsewhere lack. We mustn't misuse them."

"That's why I wanted to become French," argued Saby. "Even the rabbis here have taken the Revolutionary Oath. But our fellow French Jews don't want us. They call us *métèques*."

"I agree with the call for a Universal Confederation of Sephardi Jews,"

---

13. France was the first country in continental Europe to emancipate the Jews, in 1791. The Emperor Napoleon I decreed equal rights for Jews and restored freedom of worship for them in 1806 [Translator].

said Pepo. "We supported the *Tudescos* and their *Haskalah*, their 'Enlightenment', their integration in Europe. Now it's our turn for a renaissance. But separately."

"Perhaps it's the Zionists who have it right, in the end," Saby suggested. "At least there's no Drumont or Hitler in Palestine. And Balfour supported them in 1917. His declaration was fundamentally important. I can only think of the Edict of Cyrus to compare with it in history."

"There are Arabs in Palestine. And the English will never permit the creation of a State," countered Rafo.

"That's why our first task is to come to the aid of our oppressed brothers... That's what we were doing already through the B'nai B'rith when I joined it in Salonika," said Saby. "Here, in setting up the 'France' masonic lodge with Salvatore, we've drawn in all our brothers, whether Sephardi, French or Ashkenazi, into the fight against persecution. We've fought for the Romanians, for the Russians, and now for the Germans. I hope we won't have to wait for the Americans to fight for us!"

"Yet that's where they formed your association's first lodge," Maïr pointed out, "in New York, in 1883, if my memory is right. In any case, not everyone agreed with the idea of introducing the order in France. The review, 'l'Univers israélite' was resolutely hostile. The editor claimed you were using sacred symbols reserved for worship. And especially that there's a risk of confusion with the French Freemasons, whom they call an 'anticlerical militia.'"

"It's true that, as well as being good Jews, sons of the Alliance, we're also 'laïcs'[14]," said Saby. "Salvatore replied to these attacks in an open letter. He said... I remember.... Precisely... that 'one day French Judaism will be grateful to us for having fortified, through our lodges, the universal chain of Jewry.' We even got a letter from someone called Sigismond (sic) Freud, a Viennese who's written about the theory of dreams. He said that he, who had sometimes felt like a pariah among his colleagues, had found in us a circle of cultivated and liberal men who nevertheless accepted him despite

---

14. France's Third Republic enacted the separation of Church and State in 1905. It defined the term 'Laïcité' [or secularism] thus: it 'assures the liberty of conscience' of all French citizens. A person who claims to be "laic" places loyalty to the State and the Republic above religion [Translator].

his disturbing opinions. He even added that the fact that we were Jews was one of the things motivating him, for he was one too, and he thought it not only unbecoming but absurd to deny it."

"All that's very fine, but if only we could agree among ourselves," wailed Pepo. "What a hornets' nest, with Rozanès and his '*Stambuli*,' the Levantine Jews from Smyrna, and the Association of Salonika Jews, who've been squabbling right from the beginning."

"That," Maïr interrupted, "is why we absolutely must link up with the French and join the Consistory, which is what I've done.[15] I even agreed to let Nelly marry in the Rue Buffault synagogue. Not at home, as is the Sephardi custom. If that isn't a compromise, I don't know what is! Not to mention the committee we've formed to build the synagogue. A real temple of our own, with our own oriental Sephardic rites."

"And what a success, *sinyor padre!*" exclaimed Pepo. "Thanks to you, we now have a temple worthy of us on the Rue Saint Lazare, one worthy of our new Rabbi Ovadia."

"And worthy of *chazan* Algazi," added Rafo. "Our cantor has a magnificent voice!"

Suddenly, he spotted Jenny, still slumped in her armchair.

"So, there you are! This isn't a conversation for little girls. Go to the kitchen and see if there are a few *roskitas* left over to finish off our dinner."

None of the men present had mentioned the other, already longstanding, point of discord, a true class conflict raging in the Rue Popincourt synagogue, where impoverished Jews from the East had gathered. The rich, cultivated merchants from the upscale neighborhoods and the poor Levantines in the 11th Arrondissement had come to blows, with insults and name-calling; the word "scum" had been uttered. Yet there were communists and socialists even among the better-off Levantines. But in this family the Benvenistes had no sympathy for the penniless immigrants from Smyrna, Istanbul, or even Salonika, those who were the first to be rounded up when the storm broke.

Nor had anyone noticed that Momo, the youngest of the sons and nor-

---

15. The Israelite Central Consistory of France was set up by Napoleon I in 1808 to administer Jewish worship and congregations in France [Translator].

mally the most talkative of the lot, had stayed silent throughout the discussion. No one, except Jenny, the eagle-eyed, who knew that "Mademoiselle" the Swiss governess was preaching her Protestant creed not only to the children, but to the parents also.

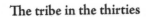

The tribe in the thirties

While he lived, the patriarch kept watch over the tribe, seen here in 1931. A model family, with the grandfather and grandmother Maïr and Oro in the center foreground, flanked by their three sons and three daughters accompanied by their spouses and their six grandsons, just one per couple. The sole exception is Jenny, then aged around fifteen, in a pale outfit behind her *Nona*. Another granddaughter was to be born later, to Momo. It was not the custom to smile at the photographer, but some of the faces here seem more relaxed than others, the patriarch for example, looking debonair, or Nelly, the youngest of his daughters, seated on his right. All the women have bobbed hair, having had their hair cut short a couple of years after the great crisis at the end of the Twenties. All except Jenny are wearing dark clothes and the men wear neckties on white shirts, some with matching pocket handkerchief.

Maïr practiced the art of being a grandfather with all the warmth of the Orient, welcoming his grandchildren every weekend, driving them himself to the pastry shop to buy them candies or cookies when their nannies confirmed they had been well-behaved. And he showered the latter with gifts and attention. For Maïr understood how things worked, and unlike his daughters, he manipulated these ladies more than they did him. He kept the tradition almost intact during his thirteen years in France.

To the end of her life, Jenny secretly recalled the Jewish festivals in her grandfather's house in Paris and could describe them in detail. Rosh Hashana and Yom Kippur, of course, "but they were 'stern' festivals, where one had to ask for God's pardon and purify oneself of all one's bad deeds during the year. Passover—Pesach—the deliverance from slavery, was really Granddad's festival. A joyous occasion!"

And Granddad Maïr was very cheerful, happy with his life; with his family, including his wife, so glum, with whom he had been betrothed at the age of thirteen and whom he had copiously cheated on; with his sons who would one day take over from him; with his daughters each of whom had produced a boy; with his grandchildren who would continue the line in centuries to come; and with a God who had chosen him, him among all the others, from among the Chosen People.

True, he had had to emigrate, shake off the habits of centuries, renounce all those small daily pleasures in the soft light of the Jerusalem of the Balkans, just as his distant ancestor had been obliged to leave friends and family behind in Toledo, Saragossa, or Granada. But the diaspora flowed in his veins. He was a child of the dispersion, able to take up the thread of life and his relationship with his God anywhere in the world, in the bosom of his tribe. And when it came to the Exodus from Egypt, the great festival of the Jews that even Jesus celebrated, he dictated everything down to the minutest detail, leaving his wife and daughters to do the work.

In the days before the festival the household took on outside help, the house was cleaned from top to bottom and the tableware kept specially for the event was washed. Jenny and her family prepared well in advance, wearing only brand-new clothes. At eight in the evening, Jenny, Marie, Saby, and Marcel would ring the bell at Granddad and Grandma's. The latter would be seated in armchairs as if on thrones, near the dinner table, which had been set already. Each new arrival went straight to Grandma and then to Granddad, greeting them with a kiss on the hand. No one was permitted to be absent, not even the family's youngest, aged four at the last Seder night in 1937. She came despite her mother's protests, objecting to all this "Jewish stuff" under the influence of "Mademoiselle."

Jenny's grandfather, who never contradicted his daughters-in-law, was insistent:

"She will come."

Jenny remembered. With precision.

Says Jenny in her *Monologue*, "The house was overflowing with flowers. The drawing room communicated with the dining room. We'd prepared a single table for around twenty-five people stretching between the two rooms. The table looked wonderful, with a tablecloth hand-embroidered by Marie, Baccarat crystal glasses, special silverware, and the ritual dishes in the middle of the table, though all I can remember is that there was celery and *kharoset*, a paste made for Pesach with raw fruit, grapes, figs and dates, which served to make a marmalade. The unleavened biscuits represented the bricks with which the enslaved Jews built the Pharaohs' fortresses. The *kharoset* represented the mortar. We'd put a spoonful of *kharoset* onto a rosemary leaf to lighten its taste.

"When everyone had arrived, we sat down to table and began the *seder*. The youngest child—which was often me, when Kiko celebrated Passover with the Modianos—kept a special piece of matzoh known as *burrito* in a clean napkin; this was a bread roll a bit like a small farmhouse bread loaf, intended for the pauper who might turn up. Apparently, he did come in Salonika, but I never saw him in Paris.

"Then the men would stand and start singing psalms and praying in Hebrew while drinking a kind of wine in a silver bowl. And it went on, and on, and on... It went on so long, I couldn't take any more... and you weren't allowed to say a word... just to listen to this incomprehensible jargon... and the maids were in the kitchen waiting to serve the meal... and the scent of good things wafted around: I had stomach cramps I was so hungry… and it just went on and on. And when at last, at last that rite was over, a special prayer was said, and the men sat down.

"And still it wasn't over, because my grandfather picked up the phone and called each of his brothers and sisters, who wished him a happy Passover… and that too took a while!

"We finally got to eat at around ten thirty in the evening! The little ones had fallen asleep on their chairs. I was ravenous. But I soon made up for lost time. There was lamb. Not leg of lamb, of course. Suckling lamb carved into lumps, with fresh peas, the first peas of the year, which they'd spent hours shelling. There was fish to start with, and other dishes it would take too long to list. Anyway, it was a big, a very big dinner accompanied by unleavened bread, matzoh, as you'd expect. For dessert, as we couldn't eat cake, my grandmothers had prepared the famous *tajicos de almendra*. Once we'd had enough to eat, tongues were loosened. The talk was lively, quick-witted, intense. There was a lot of laughter. When it was over, we were full up, it was midnight or half past midnight. It was time to leave."

Ending her reminiscence, Jenny sinks back into a contented semi-slumber, one that starts with a Pesach evening in the nineteen thirties, then leaps over the Occupation, the Extermination, the survivors, the living dead, the returnees, and the Lost, obliterating time… As if she was still on Avenue du Général-Détrie, bidding goodbye to Maïr and Oro with a full stomach and a light heart.

The captain's granddaughter

"That little slip of paper they found in the wastepaper basket; you can be sure someone had put it there!"

Mademoiselle Maurel, *professeure agrégée*[16] of history and geography, was in full flight, and her pupils were dazzled. The "Affair," almost 40 years old by now, was her pet theme. Her eyes, as she recounted it, were tinged with irony as she gazed upon the rapt faces of her best pupils in the upper

---

16. Holder of an advanced diploma qualifying a person to teach at both senior high school and university levels [Translator].

sixth form of 1933-1934: Anna Lévy, Jenny Amon and Françoise Dreyfus. Yes, Françoise Dreyfus, the Captain's granddaughter.

Seventy years later, Jenny Amon grows animated as she recalls that unforgettable lesson when Mademoiselle Maurel discussed the Dreyfus affair with the granddaughter of the man himself sitting in the class.

"We were captivated. And Françoise Dreyfus listened stock still as our teacher demonstrated that her grandfather was a traitor, an impostor, a bad Frenchman... in short, a 'dirty Jew' ... And there was I, fidgeting in my seat while the girl next to me, Suzanne Bruny from Limoges, kept hissing 'sit still! We all know her grandfather was guilty!'"

"Girls, this is the tale of a wretch with a soul so vile he betrayed his country. Instead of selling monocles or swindling people on the Stock Market like his fellows, this gangster became a staff officer. He used his position to sell his secrets to foreigners. But the leaks were soon discovered. After a few months' close surveillance, people became convinced Dreyfus, the new Judas, was guilty of the crime of treason, that he was the author of the memorandum, of the message containing State secrets communicated to the German military attaché. And that is how the Traitor was caught. Thanks to damning evidence supplied by twenty-three officers, he was found guilty unanimously. Unanimously, ladies, do you hear? And yet the court martial in its mercy spared the Traitor's life. He was not sentenced to death, but to deportation in perpetuity. On the day of his sentencing the impostor declared himself innocent and that proof of his innocence would be forthcoming within three years."

You could have heard a pin drop in Blanche Maurel's classroom, whose windows look out onto the lovely park next to what is now the Rodin Museum. Jenny Amon, Anna Lévy and Françoise Dreyfus stared at their teacher with a hint of supplication in their eyes. Suzanne Bruny, Olga Tretyakov, Blandine de la Valette and the others were hanging on their teacher's every word; the suspense kept them breathless. Mademoiselle had a fine, deep voice, and she knew how to modulate it. She would have been a successful prosecuting attorney. But in 1934 no woman held that sort of position.

"Note, young ladies, the wickedness of this impostor: 'If I handed over documents,' he ended up confessing, 'it was to obtain more important ones.'"

The tension abated for a moment. Françoise Dreyfus looked at her feet. Anna Lévy stared out of the window at a pigeon perched on a branch. Jenny Amon raised her hand impatiently, but her neighbor held her back:

"Wait, let her finish at least!"

"And that isn't all, ladies. We are not done with his black deeds. Just as Dreyfus was boarding the ship bound for Devil's Island, his henchmen stirred up a riot in an attempt to arrange his escape. They cried out furiously that he was a martyr and swore he would return triumphant to France... Well, now you're wondering whether the Traitor's prophesy came true. So, three years later, a senator called Scheurer-Kestner suddenly discovered that Dreyfus was innocent... supposedly. And whence, ladies, came this fortuitous inspiration?"

Blandine de la Croix de la Valette de Saint-Ouen d'Ernemont, to give her full aristocratic name, stretched her eyes. Jenny Amon tried but failed to catch the eye of Françoise Dreyfus. It was as if the captain's granddaughter had turned to stone. Jenny wondered if she understood what was going on.

"You can't imagine, but I'll help you. Some shady politicians, compromised in the Panama scandal and other disreputable affairs, had run to Scheurer: 'We want to believe in Dreyfus's innocence,' they said. 'But first tell us what it's all about.' The truth became clear almost immediately, bathed in a shiny metallic glitter of gold, silver, and cash. 'We have seen the light,' they all exclaimed.

"And, thus, was formed the cabal of reprobates."

A wave of indignation swept across the history class. Blanche Maurel was in a sort of trance. She took a long, deep breath. Directing her gaze over the braided hair of the White Russians Olga Tretyakov and Tatyana Feodoroff, beyond the aristocratic Blandine de la Croix de la Valette de Saint-Ouen d'Ernemont and Nicole Lesault du Pavillon, whose eyes were almost popping out, she invoked the long procession of enemies of France who had been paid to defend the criminal. First there was Mathieu Dreyfus:

"The Traitor's brother, a factory owner in Germany, opened the hostilities by publishing a letter denouncing Major Esterhazy as the true villain. But Esterhazy, ladies, as you can well imagine, was merely a pretext. The gang wanted to weaken our Army and its chiefs. And that's how these Jewish vermin battened on our generals, who were unused to dealing with this kind of enemy."

Mademoiselle Maurel fixed her gaze on Françoise Dreyfus, the captain's granddaughter, and great niece of Mathieu Dreyfus, without really seeing her. But behind Mathieu loomed another shadow, the satanic and socialist author, the father of naturalism...:

"Zola, the disgusting pornographer, whose father was a paymaster in the Foreign Legion and a wastrel, naturally joined the fray."

"Hey, Jenny," whispered the girl next to her, "what's a 'pornographer'?"

"Shut up," Jenny silenced her ignorant classmate.

She couldn't believe her ears: Emile Zola, the courageous author of *J'accuse*, a pornographer? And here was her teacher demolishing him? Yet Miss Maurel was so persuasive.

"The jury found him guilty of insulting the army, and he fled abroad to avoid spending a year in jail. Another leader was the former Colonel Picquart, the man who claimed that the memorandum was a forgery, whose place was in the penal colony too. For attempting to confound Picquart's abominable intrigues the unfortunate Colonel Henry was driven to suicide. All of France's enemies marched hand in hand with the friends of Dreyfus. The spies Schwartzkoppen and Panizzardi, all of Germany, all of England, all of Italy called relentlessly for a retrial."

The bell went, but nothing was stopping Blanche Maurel. Indeed, she gathered fresh vigor and went on:

"Young ladies, you are decent French girls, and you must understand, through this awful adventure, that the Jews are antisocial beings and extremely dangerous for the countries that have taken them in. The only existence they are suited to is that of their ancestor Isaac Laquedou, the Wandering Jew."

In a deathly silence, she set the homework for the next week, when she would be testing her pupils on the day's lesson. Without a word, Anna Lévy, Jenny Amon and Françoise Dreyfus cleared their desks. The others whispered as they followed Blanche Maurel out of the room. Mademoiselle Maurel, meanwhile, had regained her composure:

"For the rest, please see your textbook."

Jenny continues the story: "In the days following that Wednesday after-noon, when the lesson lasted from 2.30 to 4 pm, I read up about the Drey-fus affair for the next lesson. Maurel always began each lesson by testing pupils on the previous one. The following Monday, at 2.30 pm sharp, we had just finished the roll call when the door opened and the headmistress entered, accompanied by the General Inspector of Schools. We were a bit flustered, but Maurel was unfazed."

"Please carry on as if I weren't here," said the Inspector as he walked to the back of the class, while the teacher smiled at him and began her questions.

"Anna Lévy, Françoise Dreyfus and Jenny Amon, to the front of the class."

According to Jenny, a main protagonist in this scene, Miss Maurel, like all her colleagues in the presence of an inspector, was in the habit of ques-tioning her best pupils, and she did so without a qualm.

Did she realize her three model pupils shared the same religion as Cap-tain Dreyfus?

"She knew for Anna Lévy and Françoise Dreyfus," says Jenny. "I don't know if she knew for me. With a name like Amon I could have come from Brittany! She called us up because she knew we wouldn't say anything stupid."

"Mademoiselle... Lévy, can you tell the Inspector-General how the af-fair came about?"

"Yes, Mademoiselle. In September 1894, French counter espionage re-ceived a letter, or rather a memorandum found in a wastepaper basket and addressed to a German military attaché. It was undated and unsigned, and torn into several bits. According to the memorandum, confidential military documents were about to be delivered to a foreign State."

"Very good. Jenny Amon, can you tell us who the guilty person was?"

"The suspect, Mademoiselle. A suspect was identified: Captain Alfred Dreyfus, a graduate of the École Polytechnique and an artillery officer."

"You know he was from Alsace, so close to the Germans. When was he arrested? Do you know... Françoise?"

The teacher didn't dare pronounce the family name of the "Traitor's" granddaughter. The latter coolly replied:

"He was summoned on October 13, then held in secret in the Cher-che-Midi prison. On December 4th, he was tried before the first court martial. His trial opened on December 19th, in secret."

Françoise Dreyfus knew the chronology of her grandfather's story by heart and recited it unemotionally.

"You know that it was then that Major Hubert-Joseph Henry stepped in and swore on his honor, and on the crucifix, that Dreyfus was the Traitor. And then a secret file was passed to the Court. Amon! Was Dreyfus sentenced to death?"

"No, Mademoiselle. He was sentenced to be stripped publicly of his rank and deported to Devil's Island in French Guyana."

Blanche Maurel didn't dwell on Major Henry's forgery, on Colonel Picquart's investigations, nor on the discovery that Esterhazy's handwriting matched that of the memorandum. She didn't ask about Emile Zola's article in *Le Figaro* on November 25. She was in a hurry to be done with last week's lesson.

"Lévy, would you care to comment on the retrial in 1899?"

"Yes, Mademoiselle. The Court Martial in Rennes again sentenced Dreyfus to ten years in prison and a further public degradation. Then he was reprieved by President Loubet on September 19, 1899."

"Good, ladies. You may return to your seats. If the Inspector-General agrees, we'll move on to today's lesson."

But Jenny Amon was having none of it. She raised her hand to conclude, to point out that Captain Dreyfus had been rehabilitated in a ruling of the *Cour de Cassation* on July 12, 1906. But her teacher turned to the inspector:

"Miss know-it-all, I mean Mademoiselle Amon, is a good talker, but we won't be led off-topic by that red herring. I'm now going to talk to you about the revolt of the Sepoys in India, in the reign of Queen Victoria."

Jenny returned to her desk without a word. Blanche Maurel, with her fine, deep voice whisked her pupils, the Head Teacher and the Inspector-General far away from the French Army and its traitors to the British East India Company and the Great Indian Mutiny, which led to direct rule by Britain and the birth of the British Raj.

When the bell rang, everyone was absorbed in the story of Queen Victoria, Queen of England, and Empress of India. The storyteller stopped abruptly to thunderous applause.

The Inspector-General stuttered with emotion:

"Mademoiselle, ... Mademoiselle, all I can say is that these young ladies are lucky to have you for a teacher."

Blanche Maurel gained full marks for her annual inspection after talking about the Dreyfus affair in front of the inspector without once uttering the word "Jew." And it was thanks to Anna Lévy, Jenny Amon—and Françoise Dreyfus. Sometime later their teacher unhesitatingly picked Jenny Amon, one of her top pupils, to compete in the newly-created *concours général*—a national competition for the top sixth form pupils in each subject—in history. Jenny seems to remember she came in 8th in the country for history. Blanche Maurel plainly had her "good Jews" when it suited her; unless, of course, she remained oblivious till the end of her favorite pupil's oriental origins.

Jenny kept a photo of her sixth form class, and the signatures of each of her fellow pupils on the back testify that Françoise Dreyfus was well and truly there, though Jenny could no longer identify her in the picture. Harking back to that history lesson in the 1933-1934 school year, in a posh girl's *lycée* located in a former convent, one can readily imagine the young Françoise making her way back home that Wednesday, and perhaps find-

ing her grandfather Alfred there, for the ill-fated Captain lived on until 1935. Did she tell him about her day in school, and how that Pasionaria of *Action Française*[17] had questioned her about his ordeal without even mentioning his rehabilitation? Did she tell him that one of her classmates, Jenny Amon, had been ridiculed for having tentatively sought to re-establish a truth? The truth. Or did they just talk about this and that, about what was for dinner that evening, or the fine drizzle so common in Paris, or perhaps the recent Stavisky affair?

We know now from his descendants that Dreyfus himself never discussed the affair. Others did. If only they too had kept silent!

Kiko, the *enfant terrible*

The New York Stock Market crash of Thursday October 24, 1929, had many unforeseen consequences, of which Hitler's accession to power in 1933, according to chaos theory, was not the least. The tale of Kiko and Laurette figures among the collateral damage.

---

17. An extreme right-wing, virulently antisemitic movement [Translator].

At the time the Beneviste family appeared to be weathering this fresh ordeal well enough. Yet the Beneviste and Amon wholesale haberdashery had had to relocate from Rue du Mail to the less toney Rue des Jeûners in the Sentier district when the center of the garment trade migrated, ostensibly to save on costs. Coming after the Great Fire of Salonika, this was the second time adversity had forced a change of location.

"That's our last chance," said Marie with the candor of those who are ignorant of what the future holds.

The other business, the Joseph Maurice store, overseen by Maïr with his two youngest sons, had opened later. It was already located in the Sentier and did not need to move.

The one really hurt by the crisis was Ugo Modiano, Allegra's husband, in Brussels. He had the misfortune of having an artistic temperament but had married into a milieu where all that counted was money and how to make it. He was well-born, but into a now defunct society. Despite his artistic leanings and his qualifications as a lawyer, exile had left him no choice but to sell diamonds or oriental carpets. He picked the latter and went bust.

Ugo's life turned into a long tale of woes from then on. The family brought him back to France and gave him a minor job in one of the wholesale fabric stores. The man who'd dreamed of becoming a painter like Modigliano, who had been a patrician in Salonika, whom Maïr had thought too upper class for his daughter, was now the poor relative. He worked for his brothers-in-law, the butt of sarcastic comments on his lack of business flair, while his wife raged at his inability to provide for her.

Allegra, along with her son and husband, now lived in her parents' Paris apartment, her brothers having married and vacated their rooms. Oro was aging and disoriented; she took no interest in anything and pined for Salonika's White Tower again. Allegra, now Andrée, had become the head of the clan under the patriarch's oversight. She managed the domestic staff and the household, which Maïr insisted must be wide open to all his children and grandchildren. There were always people for dinner, lunch, or teatime.

Allegra's exasperation grew during the years she spent under her father's authority, burdened as she was, she said, with household tasks. She quarreled with her husband ever more frequently, and she'd spend two nights in four with her sister to evade the embraces of a husband, her lord and master, who had never been able to awaken this magnificent brunette, seemingly so ardent. She would sleep in her niece's room while the latter migrated to the drawing room sofa.

A master who cannot charm and disarm his wife was an object of contempt in this macho society.

The Bank of Tunis offered her husband a job as a manager. Allegra wailed for three days. She went on hunger strike. What? Leave her family and her beloved brothers? Never! The brothers sent Saby Amon to reason with Ugo. Hounded by the family, he finally relented.

"What you're doing is wrong. You'll be sorry," he warned.

Jenny was alone in rejoicing at this reversal of fortune that brought her beloved cousin Kiko back to Paris. She was fifteen. She leapt for joy at the news Kiko was returning to France to live with Granddad Maïr. The latter was rather less enthusiastic, for Allegra's son had gained a reputation for unruly behavior. As a little boy he had already been expelled from two successive schools in Belgium. Uncle Corentin had stepped in and found him a place as a boarder at the renowned Lycée Lakanal in Sceaux, just south of Paris. A brief respite, for Kiko was soon expelled and dispatched to a very strict boarding school in Louvain, Belgium. Now he was returning to Paris, to be with his cousin and confidante.

"He was fed up with the rows at home," says Jenny. "His mother was perpetually on the verge of hysteria, constantly wailing. His father was a nervous wreck, driven from his bedroom and weeping in an armchair. He dearly wanted his parents to divorce. But that was impossible... Why? It was legally possible in France, but... it just wasn't done in our family!"

Kiko left school in 1935-1936 and joined his mother's clan in a family store. He had already noticed one of his cousin's friends, a girl a little older than himself, who had been making eyes at him and whose name was Laura, like Petrarch's lover. For Jenny, who had met her on vacation at Saint-Lunaire, she was Laurette Moseri, her "best friend."

Says Jenny: "She came from Salonika, from a prominent Italian family. Her father, a very handsome man but without a penny, had married a large dowry—a woman with a foul temper and ugly as sin. Laurette and I had no secrets. She was two years older than I was and she'd begun thinking of boys before I did. When she was very young, she developed a crush on an aristocratic boy, René Thibaud de Beauregard. A very nice boy, a career soldier who seemed in love with Laurette, but she was Jewish, and he wasn't. Obviously when the talk turned to marriage, people changed their tune. He was never presented to the family, and little by little he dropped her.

"Meanwhile, the Moseri family had lost all its money in the Crash. They moved home, and from having been a banker, the father had to acquire a little business selling National Lottery tickets on the Avenue Wagram in Paris. Laurette was a sales assistant there. She got paid and never complained about her fate. And then I became a young woman, allowed to go out with her cousin and his pals on Sundays, to the movies or to go dancing. It was at my place that Laurette met Kiko. And it was love at first sight.

"The Moseris wanted nothing better than this marriage with a Modiano, but for the Benvenistes it was out of the question. Laurette's parents were poor now. No dosh, no wedding. Kiko had no control over his own life. His uncles had the last word and they vetoed the matter. Their sister Allegra wanted to keep her son for herself, as the family breadwinner, since her husband was incapable of bringing home the bacon. She hoped that he might one day keep them all with the aid of a fine dowry.

"In the end," says Jenny, "Aunt Andrée was left with nothing at all. Not even a son."

First love: from chrysalis to butterfly

Jenny and her tribe barely differed from the families of her classmates at the Lycée Duruy during these in-between years. For some, the 1929 crisis was merely a brief interruption in the routine of an existence punctuated by months of work or school in the off-season and long summer vacations by the sea with the whole brood. During this time, the chrysalis emerged as a butterfly, and the pudgy teenager whom Marie put on diets and forced to do sport turned into a trim young woman.

Between 1932 and 1934, Jenny successfully passed both parts of her *baccalaureate*, high school graduation exams, at the urging of Marie, who had not forgotten her own premature departure from the *Alliance* and the drudgery of sewing and darning.

"Most of my classmates didn't graduate. They left school earlier and waited demurely for a husband... But I had to retake the oral exam in September... because of my math."

Marie and family spent their summer vacation in rented villas close to their sisters and sisters-in-law at Saint-Lunaire, in Brittany.

"What did I like best, during those long vacations?" asks Jenny. "Nature, the sea, reading, long walks on the beach while I recited the poems of Machado and Victor Hugo. What did I hate most? Vacation homework, of course. Above all, though, the endless obligations invented by my mother to make up for the things she hadn't been able to do in Salonika when she was my age. From nine till eleven in the morning I had tennis, then swimming, then gymnastics, then swimming again. By then I was terribly hungry, but I was told not to eat so as not to get fat. Then it was tennis again in the afternoon; the whole family turned up to make sure I was playing well and make snide remarks. I got to loathe tennis. And I found a way out of it: I became an umpire and did it so well the others badgered me to umpire for them, which got me out of playing."

There was a change of program in the summer of 1933, when the family decided to go to Villars-sur-Ollon in the canton of Vaud, in Switzerland, while Jenny was packed off to Eastbourne, on the south coast of England, with her little cousin, Rafo's son, and his English governess. Jenny thought she was going to have fun in England, whereas Switzerland "was a bore." But July got off to a bad start.

"There was a vast pebble beach; the locals weren't particularly pleasant; the little boy made sandcastles, and 'Miss,' who was in love with Kiko, moped all the time and tramped several times a day up and down the pier saying nothing, while the object of her affections was enjoying himself with Laurette in Paris. Meanwhile, the rest of the family was having fun in the Swiss Alps."

There was an incident that her young cousin recalled and recounted later[18]. The governess had gone for a walk, leaving the child in Jenny's care

---

18. In *From Paris to Berkeley*, Guy Benveniste, Amazon 2010.

while he threw stones into the big waves breaking on the jetty. One large stone dragged the child with it into the water. Jenny stood there petrified, and a kindly Englishman dived fully clothed into the sea to fish the child out.

Marie worried her daughter was getting bored in Eastbourne and eating too much. She suggested she join them in Switzerland, at Chesières. With the governess and the boy, Jenny traveled there and had "the best vacation of my life."

They stayed in a family hotel, where a bunch of youngsters, Jews and Gentiles, was determined to have fun together. There was dancing in the evenings three times a week, and tennis tournaments. There was even a ball at the end of the championship when Jenny was awarded a prize for her umpiring.

"I won the first prize," Jenny recalls. "The prize was a huge box of Swiss chocolates, which was just what I wanted. Alas, before the end of the evening my mother turned up with no intention of congratulating me. 'Give me that box, Jenny…' 'Why, Mama?' 'Give me that box, I say. You're going to fatten yourself on candies when you've already grown enormously fat in England and Switzerland.' 'But what are you going to do with it?' 'I suggest you give it to your grandmother when we get home. We haven't bought a gift for her and I've spent too much already on your stay. *Nona* loves chocolates… And you know she'll share them with you.'

"My mother confiscated the box, with just one concession: I would be the person to offer it to my *Nona* Oro, which I did with an ill grace when I got home. My grandmother, who was much diminished from the time when she used to make me *tajicos* in the kitchen in Salonika, took the gift without fully realizing what it was, kissed me affectionately, and stuffed it in the cupboard. I didn't dare say a word. I never saw the slightest chocolate during my regular visits. I was resigned to forgetting about my prize.

"Six months later, a friend came to visit my mother and wanted to thank her for some service. She proudly handed her a slightly soiled package and on the white paper wrapping I recognized a little red ink stain made in my suitcase during the journey from Villars to Paris; I hadn't been able to remove it before giving it to my grandmother. This time I opened the box, despite my mother's feeble protests. The chocolates hadn't been touched… but they had all gone moldy!"

Luckily, Jenny was no longer thinking of chocolates. Uppermost in her thoughts was the summer's high point, the grand fancy-dress ball where she met her first love.

"His name was Pierre. Pierre Djian. He was a Sephardi, but from North Africa, and those husbands didn't have a good reputation among us, being thought too strict with their women. His family was from Constantine in Algeria but had a business in Aix-les-Bains. And he was studying weaving in Mulhouse, in eastern France. He was promised to an orphaned cousin in the care of his father and who came with a handsome dowry. He paid no attention to me at first, when I arrived from England. Then came the evening of the fancy-dress ball when I wore my first evening gown. We flirted together. Well … flirting… within the limits set by my mother. We were allowed a kiss and some petting, but 'never, ever below the waist.'

"After the ball we went up to Paulet, a nightclub built at the top of the mountain. We came down at dawn and the hotel kitchen made us an onion soup. God! It was fun! I had the impression it went on … for years."

Sixty years on, Jenny thought back to that singular night of first love when nothing could be consummated.

"Yes! A unique night… because afterward… well, he dropped me, you know! Or in a sense I got in before him. We wrote to each other during the school year when he was at Mulhouse. And he returned to Chesières in Switzerland the following summer, where we met up for three days. That revived the embers. Still above the belt. And we wrote very powerful, very romantic letters to each other, with poems… and everything… For about a month… two perhaps.

"And then he wrote me a long letter to explain that he had to obey his father who was forcing him to marry a cousin… and how he was sorry about it. I didn't write back. But a few days later, I got a phone call from Jane, an English friend who'd been part of the crowd at Chesières. I did think she sounded funny, but with her accent I was taken in. She said she was passing through Paris and asked if we could meet… She said to meet me in the gardens of Les Invalides, not far from me.

"I went and found my Pierre, in lieutenant's uniform. He was doing his military service. He apologized for having disguised his voice and resorting to subterfuge to see me. He told me again his father was a real dragon, that there were 'certain interests at stake.' He said he was in Paris for a while and that we could see each other again. I told him to meet me again the next day, between two and four pm, in the same place."

"So?"

"So... I didn't go... I hesitated. But I held out... Then I discovered he'd married her... his cousin. So, I did the right thing... Did it hurt? Yes."

Behind the old woman stood the young girl, with her tiny silhouette like the heroine of a 17th-century novel, standing erect on her high heels, the enemy of compromise, unbending in the face of the weaknesses and minor adjustments that accompany love.

"Did I find out what happened to him? Yes... he was deported[19]."

The veil has come down upon these minor miseries from before the disaster. The ones Jenny would later refer to as her "pre-war worries" the pangs of first love, money troubles, aches and pains culminating in a quiet death in one's own bed.

A gray year

"A good reputation is worth more than a golden belt" was Marie's westernized motto and she clung to it. Beneath appearances though were the harsh demands of the Orient, namely, to accumulate a dowry, for that, rather than reputation, was likelier to attract suitors for her daughter's hand.

The latter, though, cared not a jot about her mother's concerns. After her graduation year and the euphoria of first love came a gray year. It was raining in Paris, and Jenny moped as she waited, though for nothing specific. It was raining in the heart of this young woman as she coped with her first heartache. The Jenny of fall 1934 was much like many young girls of that time and since.

"Well, now you've got your *baccalaureate*, what do you want to do?" asked Marie.

"To study history."

---

19. I.e. sent to the concentration camps [Translator].

"My girl, you know as well as I do that you would have had to keep up your Latin. So, what do you intend to do?"

"OK, I'll study law."

"Law? Your father would never agree to that."

Marie knew how matters stood. She had already tried to persuade her husband who was adamant. The Law School? A den of iniquity! The Latin Quarter was worse still!

"If you want your daughter to find a husband, better teach her to cook."

Saby must have said that in Ladino. He knew he'd touched on a sore point for his wife. If Marie wanted Jenny to snare one of those rare birds, every mother's obsession, she'd better not make a blue stocking of her. The Orientals weren't Ashkenazim, still less the French Jews, who liked their girls to be bookish. If she was to marry a boy from Salonika, *first* she needed to learn to make *borekas* and the rest... how to run a household!

"*First of all*," Marie conceded, "but after that, it can't hurt if she's studied a bit. Some husbands don't fancy idiotic women."

Saby glowered.

"Alright, but on one condition: she's got to come and work in the store. At least, if she doesn't find a husband, she'll be able to do something with her hands!"

Marie and Saby knew there was one bait more powerful than all else in a suitor's eyes, namely the dowry they had been working silently to accumulate. Now time was running out, Jenny having turned eighteen. By twenty-five the manhunt would be all but over. For Christians and Jews alike, a woman still unwed at that age was on the shelf.

Jenny agreed to the compromise, working mornings in the store of Benveniste et Amon, attending law school in the afternoons.

"I wasn't thinking of becoming a lawyer. I didn't have that kind of ambition. I didn't intend to go all the way, probably just getting a bachelor's degree. Not to become a lawyer, which was unthinkable for a woman in my family, but to become a paralegal for example."

Marie loudly approved these studies she hadn't been able to pursue herself. In any case, it would be a plus on the résumé of this marriage hopeful.

So, the former star pupil at Victor-Duruy and candidate in the nation-wide *"concours general"*[20] spent the year packing and copying out invoices under her father's watchful eye, Uncle Rafo and workers in the store. She spent hours watching a desperately slow-moving clock and mentally mocking the retail customers. Most were foreigners who paid her no attention, and she got her revenge later by recounting their foibles to Kiko and Laurette on Sunday afternoons.

One morning, though, a stranger walked through the door, young, fair-haired, and rather good-looking.

"Jenny," Rafo called out, "this is Monsieur Benrey. Jacques Benrey. His father comes from Bulgaria and they run a small retail haberdashery in the Rue du Faubourg-Poissonière, you know."

Jenny didn't and couldn't care less about the little store in the Rue du Faubourg-Poissonière, not suspecting she would spend forty years of her adult life there.

"Good morning, Monsieur."

"Good morning, Mademoiselle. I've never seen you here before."

"I'm only here temporarily. I just passed my *baccalauréate* in September. I'm studying law in the afternoons."

"So, you flunked in June?" asked the stranger, tactlessly.

"Yes, because of the *concours general*[21]: I competed in history, so I didn't have time to revise the other subjects"

She took the young man's glance to convey mingled ignorance and condescendence.

Saby emerged at that moment with a bolt of cloth under his arm.

"I've got just what you wanted, a lovely velvet."

On saying goodbye to Jenny, the young man whispered in passing:

"We're setting up a youth group. Your dad can explain. You should come."

Later, walking home for lunch on Rue Pérignon as she always did with her father, usually in silence, she ventured:

"What did your customer mean, that Beu... Ben...?"

"Benrey, Jacques Benrey. Well, he and Edgar Abravanel, my President's

---

20. See p. 90 above [Translator].
21. Ibid..

son, are setting up a Sephardi youth group as part of the Religious association."

"Ah! So, he's involved with the Abravanels?"

"More than you think. He's about to become engaged to Irène, Edgar's sister... In fact, I must get to work on it!"

Jenny looked at her father curiously. She knew the community had its matchmakers, male and female, often the rabbis. She knew too that her father revered Salvatore Abravanel, Edgar's father, not only for his name—one of the most eminent among Sephardi Jews—but also for his position, having founded the French chapter of the international B'nai B'rith with Saby. Salvatore was its President, Saby the Vice President. So, it was Saby, her father, who was acting as matchmaker between the Abravanel girl and young Benrey! She'd have to tell Kiko and Laurette on Sunday. That would make a change from dull gossip about the family stores.

Later, when Marie asked her: "So, what did you think of this Jacques Benrey?," Jenny replied with a shrug:

"He's got nice eyes. But frankly I find him rather unpleasant."

A few hours later, Marie whispered to her sister Allegra over a bridge table:

"She still hasn't gotten over her lieutenant from Constantine!"

On July 14, 1935, the *Rassemblement populaire*, a left-wing political grouping, held a major unity rally in Paris calling for "Bread, peace and freedom." Jenny Amon passed her first year of law school with honors. Marie and her sisters exulted at this first success for a woman in the family, but Saby pulled a face. It would detract from the dowry. He would rather she'd flunked.

On August 19, while well-off French families vacationed, Hitler won a plebiscite to become *Reichsführer* with ninety percent of the vote. The formerly pacifist French Left now called for a firm response to the *diktats* of Hitler and Mussolini, while the nationalist Right urged appeasement.

Did Jenny notice this plebiscite, which was to wreak such havoc in her life and that of her family? Probably not. She was too busy arguing, through Marie's intercession, with her father over what she was going to do come the next academic year.

"No. No, and no again. Tell Papa I'm not going back to work at Benveniste et Amon. I want to go on studying law."

"But you're not married. You've got to work."

"I don't mind working. But not at the store."

"But where? You've no qualification, and a year of law isn't going to…"

"Mama, I've an idea. Just give me another year to train. I could study shorthand and secretarial skills in the morning at *Institut Grandjean*. I've been to see them. With a law degree, they promise to find you a job with top organizations. You just need to be able to note down speeches fast, at one hundred and eighty words a minute. And I'll be able do that. I swear I will. Please, Mama!"

Marie gave in and persuaded Saby. After all, if Jenny could earn a few pennies while waiting for Mr. Right, why not? At a time when fortunes were collapsing in a twinkling of an eye, this could be a useful insurance policy. What's more, a simple secretary wasn't going to scare off a husband. Quite the reverse.

Enter Jacques

"Who does she think she is?" thought Jacques as he closed the door on Benveniste et Amon, 1, Rue des Jeûneurs in the Sentier district.

He just had time to walk over to 65, Rue du Faubourg-Poissonnière, where his father's store was, captured for all time in a contemporary photo with its two front windows skillfully arranged by a professional window-dresser.

He ran across the Grands Boulevards, glancing briefly at the movie showing at the Rex movie theater. His mother was waiting for him with his Uncle Nissim in their apartment on the Rue Thimonnier, before going off to play poker. This was a Monday, and he was on duty at the Committee of the Sephardi Youth organization, where he had been active since its recent inception. He fumed at not having put her down her more sharply, this girl from Benveniste et Amon: these people thought they could get away with anything just because they hailed from Salonika and claimed to be the sole descendants of the banished Spanish loyalists. Nearly all the Bulgarians were Sephardi too, born and bred, and were likewise former subjects of the

Ottoman Empire; they were no less noble and had suffered no less in their efforts to preserve their language and traditions.

And she, who did she think she was, this pretentious little miss, just because she had graduated from high school? In October to boot, which meant she'd had to re-sit part of the tests, taking the oral exam! He was sorry he hadn't trotted out his own diplomas, business school included, all with excellent marks and top of his class. Jacques crossed the road without looking, drawing insults from a motorist who swerved to avoid him. He calmed down a bit. She was a slip of a girl just out of school, and he twenty-seven. Still, she wasn't like the sisters of his friends, who sometimes frequented the Sephardi Youth.

"Frumps!" he muttered, thinking of one or two of the girls who had been making eyes at him.

"No, Jenny Amon isn't a frump, pretentious though. At least she has something to say for herself," and he'd always liked smart women. We need to get girls like that into the club if we want it to take off. He'd talk to Edgar and Irène on the Youth Club board that evening.

The Sephardi Youth Club was a recent creation, founded at the behest of Chief Rabbi Ovadia, to bring young people together and teach them about their culture, which was waning in the French embrace. Elected members of the board comprised Jacques Benrey, Edgar Abravanel, Oscar Arditti, and a clutch of fun-loving fellows who put life into the dances, sports competitions, and picnics they were planning, along with other more intellectual activities. In his inaugural address, Chief Rabbi Ovadia emphasized the worldwide awakening of the Sephardi Jews:

"Communities that have lived for centuries in isolation from each other, lifeless and lacking in energy, heedless of the future and without a thought for their past splendors, are now drawing closer thanks to the Universal Confederation of Sephardi Jews and its French language mouthpiece *Le Judaïsme sépharadi*. Always remember, my dear friends," the Rabbi concluded, "that you are the soldiers of the Jewish cause... My dear friends, our great Moses said to Israel: 'This is the path of life, and this is the path of death! Thou shalt choose life!' This voice, which has never ceased to resound down the centuries, speaks to you this evening as an imperative order: 'Thou shalt choose life!'"

The Youth Club's first informal event was a dance held at an upscale venue in the Bois de Boulogne, the Pavillon Dauphine, with a free tombola and an aria from Halévy's opera *La Juive* sung in the "warm and powerful" voice of the Yugoslav-born cantor. A group photo published in *Judaïsme sépharadi* shows the first annual meeting of the Sephardi Youth Club, where Jacques Benrey was elected vice president for three years.

He was kept busy in its inaugural year. He wrote the report on the evening for the magazine and announced the board's plans for talks, sport, picnics, and a choir under José Papo. But merely getting together was not enough, in those difficult years. What was needed was to unite to "preserve the torch of Judaism under threat."

Young Oscar Arditti was one of those eager to pick up the torch. That fall, in 1935, he gave a talk on his recent visit to Palestine. This French passport-carrying "Bulgarian," who had attended the same school as Jacques Benrey in Sofia, paid tribute to the young people who tirelessly defended "this national home so dear to us all, this refuge that is the joy and hope of a whole people in exile for two thousand years." He also honored victims of all those troubles and persecutions.

He quoted Victor Hugo:

For those who die piously for their fatherland
It is right that crowds come to pray at their tomb.

A fierce controversy then broke out over the idea of Zion.

For Rabbi Ovadia:

"In the heart of every Jew slumbers the faith of a true Zionist."

For the President, Edgar Abravanel:

"It is absolutely not advisable for the Sephardi Youth Club to play an active role in the Zionist movement from the outset."

For Jacques Benrey, who wound up the meeting:

"Understanding between the Jews and the Arabs is strengthening. While this is not the place for a thorough review of relations between these two brother peoples populating the country, between these sons of Israel and the sons of Ishmael, it is clearly in the interests of both to draw closer together, understanding each other, serving and complementing each other."

On the brink of the cataclysm, these young Spanish-Oriental Jews wanted to revive their heritage in France, the "Land of Human Rights," while at the same time rebuilding a homeland with the sons of Ishmael. But a wall was about to close in around Jacques Benrey, Oscar Arditti and Edgar Abravanel, the moving spirits of the Young Sephardim, a wall that was to confine them within their community forever till the end of history, their history and that of their tribe.

A tea dance at the Pavillon Dauphine

While France and the rest of the world held their breath, barely daring to look in the direction of Nazi Germany, Marie and her sisters had but a single goal for the first girl in this generation: to find a husband for her. Marie held no end of dinner parties and spent on her daughter's outfits all she saved on her daily outgoings.

"I had seven evening gowns," recalls Jenny bitterly. "Temporarily. Later they were given to my brother's wife even though she'd found a husband already! Yet I didn't have enough money to buy myself stockings or repair my shoes. When my mother held dinner parties, she put on a fine spread, but we lived on short rations the rest of the month, eating only corn and rice."

Saby was perhaps less active in the store in 1935 than in his masonic lodge, where he was number two to Salvatore Abravanel until the latter's death, when he took over as President. All through the following year, while Jenny was in her second year of law and studied shorthand at the Grandjean school in the mornings, Saby continued to act as matchmaker between the Abravanel and Benrey families.

Jenny pestered him with questions:

"So, when are they going to announce young Benrey's engagement?"

"Not yet! ... But very soon."

"Very soon" was taking its time. Now, though, Saby had his riposte:

"If you attended the Sephardi Youth Club, you'd know more about it than I do. I backed the club's creation to bring young Sephardim together with young Ashkenazim. It's a great opportunity to meet up and have fun."

Saby knew, but wasn't saying, that the club's secret agenda was to foster marriages within the endogamous circle. The high point of the club's program was the dance, crystallizing the potential to bring the two sexes together.

Jenny was unconvinced and told her mother so in no uncertain terms.

"What on earth am I going to do there? I don't know anyone, for a start."

"That's another good reason for going. If you don't go anywhere, you won't meet anyone."

"No, definitely not. I've promised to go the movies with Laurette and Kiko on Sunday. So, I can't."

"Why can't Laurette and Kiko go with you? They could have fun too."

Jenny knew those two were perfectly fine on their own and had no desire to meet other people. But she couldn't bring herself to admit—at least not yet—that she was starting to have enough of these threesomes where she was the odd one out.

That fall, matters in Germany took a turn for the worse. The swastika was adopted in September. The Nuremberg Laws codified anti-Semitism into a monumental body of detailed legislation, stripping Jews of their citizenship and political rights, and asserting the supremacy of German blood and honor.

Did Jenny have any idea what was going on over there? Probably not.

Jenny did not take part in the parade to commemorate the Paris Commune, nor did she applaud the three women who entered Léon Blum's Socialist cabinet. Rather, one rainy day in October she went, protesting, to a tea dance given by the Sephardi Youth Club. For weeks she had resisted, but she finally yielded before her father's insistence.

"I'm ordering you, Jenny. I'm President of the lodge, your grandfather is an authority in the religious body. If even my own daughter won't cooperate…!"

Marie backed him up. This time, she didn't take her daughter's side, and Jenny felt wretched. Until Kiko spoke up:

"Go along and leave Laurette and me in peace. We want to be alone."

There was nothing for it but to go. And go she did. Which is why, on that misty fall afternoon in 1936, a twenty-year-old girl set off to meet her destiny, muttering against her father, her mother, and her cousin and her best friend who had let her down. "I can still see myself," she recalls, "coming out of the Metro station at Etoile and walking half-heartedly down the Avenue du Bois, now Avenue Foch, to get to the Pavilion Dauphine, the gathering's venue. I wondered if I was going to be alone at a table, knowing practically no one. Consequently, I was really relieved when Irène Abravanel rushed to greet me on my arrival and introduced me to everyone at her table. I truly enjoyed myself that afternoon... I was amazed myself."

"Jenny, come and meet Lucien, Lucien Lévy."

This handsome fellow was sitting at Irène's table and danced with her all the time.

Jenny cast her eye over the lively bunch, consisting of a few girls and lots of boys, when a voice behind her said:

"Miss Amon has done us a great honor... and given us much pleasure in joining us—at last. Will you grant me this waltz?"

Turning around, Jenny saw the "little fair-haired fellow," his very blue eyes twinkling mischievously. But... it was Jacques Benrey, her father's customer and Irène's "fiancé." What was going on?

The young man whirled her around in a fast-paced waltz that left her dazed. Then came a tango, a paso-doble, a rumba, a rather outdated fox-trot, and a blues. They didn't speak to begin with, careful to keep step with each other. The blues brought them together, but scarcely had Jenny sat down than another young man took her hand as the first notes of a Charleston elicited whoops of joy from *aficionados*. She danced the Charleston till she was weary and disjointed, all the while looking out for her previous partner, now dancing with Irène.

As she rested, Jacques returned to sit with her on the seat left vacant by Miss Abravanel, who looked very contented in the arms of Lucien. He talked to her about jazz, which he seemed knowledgeable about, and about the origins of the boogie-woogie that had followed on from the bolero. He talked of his idol, Louis Armstrong, of Benny Goodman and Katherine Dunham, whose modern dance performances he admired.

"And you, are you a musician?" inquired the former pupil of Madame Fournier, who used to play Chopin's waltzes so brilliantly on the piano.

"Oh, a little. I play the violin. I was even a choirboy at Mass in Bulgaria."

Jenny looked at Jacques in amazement.

"Mass? You mean Catholic Mass?"

"Yes, Catholic. I went to school with the Brothers of Saint-Jean Baptiste de la Salle in Sofia."

"How come?"

"Well, you know, people were pretty tolerant in Bulgaria. And there wasn't much choice. The *Alliance Israélite* had put up the shutters."

Jenny hadn't expected to find a former pupil of Catholic monks at the Sephardi Youth Club. She was still puzzling over it as the afternoon drew to a close and the young people lined up at the cloakroom.

"Come again... you must come again," called out Irène with surprising warmth, while Jenny felt a pang of guilt for having danced so much with Jacques Benrey.

Now he approached again.

"Mademoiselle Amon... may I call you Jenny... Would you allow me to see you home? It's safer. There's a lot of trouble around the Place de l'Étoile..."

Marie couldn't help noticing that Jenny came in with a hint of a swagger, though she didn't let on.

"So, was it that awful?"

"No. In fact, it wasn't too bad in the end..."

"That afternoon," recalls Jenny, "made me an enthusiastic member of the Youth Club. I began going there regularly, and it completely changed my opinion of Jacques Benrey."

Yet that evening our little hypocrite waited impatiently for her father, to sound him out:

"So, what's going on with the engagement you were talking about between Irène and... that Jacques Benrey?"

"My girl... engagements don't happen overnight... I'm working on it."

Jenny attended the Sephardi Youth Club's tea dances regularly, her heart throbbing more and more, now in the hope of seeing the handsome Jacques there, and in trepidation at the thought of what was going on between him and Irène Abravanel, vastly more desirable than herself, she thought.

Jenny's engagement

Jenny was not about to forget that October afternoon when she got to know the Sephardi Youth Club, and above all its attractive vice president. She didn't miss a single session in the following weeks. She prepared herself carefully, her heart pounding, terrified of learning what threatened to be ever more unbearable for her. She dared not question her father, who never again spoke of marriage between the "little Benrey" and Mademoiselle Abravanel. She dared not question the putative candidate, who continued to invite her to dance more than any other young woman. They discussed literature at length; he was even better-read than she. They had a particularly lively discussion about André Maurois' *The Weigher of Souls*. Does the soul exist? Can you measure it?

"He bases himself on the theory of MacDougall, an American physician," said Jacques. "He thought the soul had a mass of twenty-one grams. At the moment of death it escapes from the human body, which gets lighter by that amount."

Jacques was already an unconditional lover of Proust, while Jenny hadn't yet begun to read *In Search of Lost Time*. The two youngsters had devoured the first volumes of Jules Romains' *Men of Good Will* and now continued together. They discussed them for hours, but they never talked about themselves.

Still, Jenny did not have long to wait. On November 14, before the dancing began, the Club President Edgar Abravanel had something to say.

"Dear friends, I am delighted to announce the engagement of my sister Irène to..." Jenny held her breath as her heart pounded furiously... "to, need I say it, the best among us..., I mean my friend and comrade... Lucien Lévy."

There was thunderous applause and a round of congratulations. Jenny clapped vigorously. She threw herself into the arms of Irène, hugging her effusively. Then she glanced around at the fake fiancé, who was hugging the real one with unfeigned joy. No, truly, he didn't seem to be suffering.

"At that moment," whispers Jenny, still shaken by the news that had carried her away nearly sixty years before, "I knew he was for me."

What did she care of events elsewhere in the world? The reappointment of Hitler as Reich Chancellor with full powers in January 1937; the bombing of Guernica by the Condor Legion in April; Blum's resignation in June; or the attacks by the far-right *Cagoule* thugs in September of that year.

But despite the great hopes kindled in Jenny's heart, gatherings at the Sephardi Youth Club continued as before and the young man kept his counsel. Jenny grew impatient, lost sleep, and rose in the morning, eyes swollen and red. Then…

"One morning… I had to go to the market on the Place de Saxe to buy some fresh fish. As I was standing in a doorway my mother held me back."

"Come here a minute. There's something I want to ask you. There are three suitors, well, three young men lined up…"

"Lined up for what?"

"Well, who'd like… who are hoping to ask for your hand."

"Who?"

"Er, … first, there's Maurice S., that young man from Salonika, from a very good family, whom you met…"

"And then…?"

"Raoul D., a Stambouli, whose mother…"

"And the third?"

"Well, there's that little Benrey… since he's no longer going to marry Irène and…"

"Say no more… I like that one. A lot."

"Ah, right! Well… we'll see… if the opportunity arises."

"What do you mean, if the opportunity arises?"

"Jenny, calm down. We'll see with your father what can be arranged. The experience with Irène doesn't look good… We'll see. Meantime, get me a pound of mackerel and some red mullet, if there is any… Make sure they're fresh. Last time…"

Jenny was no longer listening. If she could have, she'd have answered Marie and told her loud and clear what was weighing on her heart and what was in her heart.

But in those days, one couldn't.

"In April, there was an evening dance at the Sephardi Youth Club where all the parents had been invited," says Jenny. "Monsieur and Madame Benrey were at the next table and exchanged many polite greetings with my parents. Informal negotiations were underway, and they had come to look me over. But I had no idea what was going on. Jacques invited me to dance a lot, but neither he nor my mother let on, and I continued to fret."

To be fair, the Amons had other things on their mind. On the 30ᵗʰ of that month, five days later, they celebrated Marcel's bar mitzvah in the Saint-Lazare synagogue. The entire community turned out for Marcel, the son of Maïr Benveniste's elder daughter and the only son of the new President of the B'nai B'rith. Only Jenny wasn't having fun.

Says Jenny: "My brother was dressed in white. He always looked superb and everyone in the family had eyes for him alone. But, for the first time I overheard Momo's wife telling a few others how sorry she was to be part of a religion where women counted for nothing. She had already been exposed to 'Mademoiselle's' Protestantism. I was still smarting from being unable to have a bat-mitzvah, and I had been sidelined from discussions regarding my own engagement... so I felt she had a point.

"Young people can't understand how restricted we were. I knew I had to be patient, to wait. I waited... a long time. I later learnt there had been haggling over the dowry, and then over the trousseau, and again over questions like where we were going to live, what we would live on. I was kept totally in the dark about all this. They were talking about my life, and nobody asked my opinion about anything.

"Jacques, meanwhile, didn't want to put me in the picture till the families had agreed on the size of the dowry and the rest. He was afraid it would fall through beforehand and was awaiting the outcome before asking me himself. But I knew, without really knowing, and not through him. I didn't even really know if he wanted me or whether it wasn't all being made up by the two families... Until, that is, he invited me out one evening. They were playing *Faust* at the Théâtre Montparnasse. He took me out to supper afterwards, then escorted me home. And there... he kissed me... for the first time.

"After that, it was a whirlwind... First, he proposed to me officially. Then there was a reception for the family at my place the following week, when Monsieur Benrey *père* came ceremoniously to ask my father for my hand in front of the whole family. Yes, I was relieved. But it had been such a long wait I couldn't rejoice wholeheartedly. And I was unhappy with Jacques for having taken so long to state his intentions while I was bound hand and foot. If I made the slightest move I would look like a loose woman.

Jenny demanded an explanation:

"Why did you break with Irène?"

"She had her eye on Lévy, not me! As for me, frankly I didn't really care. I didn't know you at the time. When Irène got engaged officially, my parents began badgering me to get married at last. I was introduced to all sorts of girls from Salonika, from Constantinople, Sofia, or Burgas. I turned them all down. Then Rabbi Ovadia came to see me and asked if it was the disappointment over Irène that stopped me from deciding. I told him I was delighted to see Irène married and happy. But he wouldn't drop the subject: 'Isn't there a single girl you like in the whole community?' So, I replied, 'Yes, Jenny Amon. Will you allow me to speak to her parents?' 'Yes.'"

There was no engagement party in June, just a dinner with the two families, where the young fiancée wore a printed organdy dress, very light blue with small darker flowers. Jenny remembered her dress better than she did her betrothed.

During the summer following the engagement party, summer 1937, the couple spent a few days by the sea in Dinard, in separate hotels, each with their respective mothers. The two Maries grew provisionally closer during these few days with their children. Marie Benveniste, Marie B., dark-haired and Salonika-born, proud of her origins and her family, the product of the *Alliance Israélite* and Frenchified in the extreme, looked down on her joint mother-in-law, the blonde Marie Jerusalmi from Romania, more oriental despite her Germanic *Mitteleuropa* background, who never really mastered the language and customs of France, her new home.

The two communicated in Ladino because Marie Jerusalmi, who spoke Romanian and German thanks to her schooling in Braşov, spoke no French. What did they talk about? Of their distant youth on the fringes of the Ottoman Empire? Of their own families, which took precedence over those of their husbands? Of the men they preferred to their husbands, soon relegated to the background, i.e., the brothers they adored, and even more so their only sons, the apple of their eye?

Meanwhile, the lovers made out and gazed into each other's eyes, sitting on a bench on the Clair-de-Lune promenade and discussing names for their future first-born, me.

People from Romania and elsewhere

Of the secrets Marie J. whispered in the ear of Marie B., as repeated by her to Jenny, the latter remembers only odds and ends, later rounded out as she came to learn about her mother-in-law's childhood and youth during the brief period when the young couple lived with Jacques' parents. To these recollections, dimmed with the passage of time, were added Jacques' own stories about his family as told to his wife when they still talked about the past.

Marie Jerusalmi was born in Constanta, a little Romanian port on the shores of the Black Sea, where long ago the Latin poet Ovid lamented his exile from Rome. The city was part of the Ottoman Empire practically until Marie's birth in 1882[22]. There's a photo showing Marie age seven or eight, dressed as an Ottoman girl, wearing a brick-red fez with a tassel. When her mother died, she was partly raised by her sister Esterina, whom she worshipped with filial adoration. Later, Esterina Abouaf lived in Bucharest with her sons Lionel and Mordi, and Jacques thought of them as his brothers. Marie, who had come to live in Paris with her husband in the nineteen thirties and who, according to Jenny, was incapable of buying an egg by herself in the 9th arrondissement of Paris, nevertheless made the perilous journey back across a Europe in turmoil to rejoin her sister in Bucharest.

Her love of Romania stayed with her after she left it to marry Moïse Benrey, a Bulgarian. He had fallen in love with a picture of her while traveling on business. In the picture, Marie wears Romanian national dress, her long blond hair falling to her waist. Moïse swore he would marry none but her, and he got what he wanted. The portrait of the woman who was

---

22. This region ceased to be part of the Ottoman Empire at the Congress of Berlin in 1878. Bismarck is recorded as saying of the role played by Benjamin Disraeli, the British Prime Minister and leader of the British delegation: "*Der alte Jude, Das ist der Mann*" (The old Jew, he's the man!) [Translator].

to become my grandmother has come down to me, long after her demise. Later, much later, I came into possession a lock of her hair as well.

Marie's family belonged to the Judeo-Spanish minority in Romania, lost among the Ashkenazim. Marie waxed lyrical over her native Romania, over her fellow countrymen's cheery disposition and refinement. In her telling, the Jews were not ostracized in Constanta, nor in Braşov in the Carpathians where she studied at a German boarding school, nor in Bucharest where her sister Esterina lived. Jacques' mother had wonderful memories of dances given by the Navy where elegant Romanian officers wooed her and invited her to dance. How they knew to have fun, those subjects of King Karol, who spoke a Latin tongue close to her mother tongue, Ladino! Not like the Bulgarians, those primitive, uneducated Slavs among whom she was obliged to live as a wife and raise her child.

Memory versus history. Unlike Bulgaria, Romania passed at the time for one of the most antisemitic countries in Europe, alongside Russia. Every generalization has its exceptions.

But Marie had had to leave behind her family, her beloved sister, the handsome officer who had held her in his arms on the beach of the Ma-maia casino one fine evening, when the Black Sea rippled with violet waves against the backdrop of a purple dusk, to follow a man ten years older than herself, wealthy, besotted with her, but trailing an insatiable family.

"Almost as insatiable as her own," adds Jenny. "Right up till the end, in both Romania and Bulgaria there were nieces needing dowries, nephews to be set up, studies to be financed in Germany, France and England. These mouths to feed were a source of incessant quarreling between husband and wife, pushing their respective families' claims, quarrels Jacques could have done without, darkening his childhood. Then came exile and separation from sisters and cousins."

All that remained in Paris of these two vast families when Jacques and Jenny married were a brother of Marie, Uncle Nissim, and Aunt Aseo, somewhat vaguely related.

The two Maries chattered endlessly during that vacation about their pregnancies and attendant mishaps. Marie B. had had several miscarriages, "induced," she said—for which read abortions—after the birth of her only son, Marcel. Marie J. had had eight unwanted miscarriages before the birth of her only son, Jacques.

"To begin with," Marie J. told Marie B., "each time I became pregnant in Burgas I had but a single desire, which was to go and see my sister still living in Constanta, a bit further north on the Black Sea. I had the vapors and invariably I lost the child. With my ninth pregnancy my doctor told me to stay in bed and not move till the baby was born. That's what I did, and I had the good fortune to give birth to my Jako. Unfortunately, my son wasn't born in Constanta but in Burgas, that boring provincial Bulgarian hole! And we had to wait till the end of the First World War to go and live in Sofia, still in Bulgaria, but at least it was the capital. At last! Jako went to the gymnasium[23], in French, with the Brothers of Saint-Jean-Baptiste de la Salle. He was so brilliant the teachers didn't want to let him go, and they missed him sorely!"

Jacques' mother halted here, let out a long sigh, then turned to her co-mother-in-law to ask her when and how she had left Salonika. She herself

---

23 Secondary school [Translator].

said nothing about the mysterious circumstances of her departure from Bulgaria, and no one asked her.

As for Jacques, he long kept quiet about the details of this apparently precipitate departure.

"Why?"

"A letter came."

"Who from?"

"Oh… it was anonymous… A death threat."

"For whom?"

"Er, well, my father…"

Relating all this, Jenny vaguely recalls that it had come from the *Ustasha*. But she doesn't know who they were. It wasn't the Croatian *Ustasha* who prompted the Benreys' headlong flight, as it turned out, but the Bulgarian *Comitadjis*, members of the Internal Macedonian Revolutionary Organization (IMRO), bandit-heroes of the Macedonian liberation movement who had turned into killers fighting for a lost cause. These erstwhile revolutionary anti-Ottoman independence fighters were terrorists in the service of a Greater Bulgaria in whose name they kidnapped and murdered fellow Bulgarians, Gentiles and Jews alike. They shared the widespread antisemitic prejudice, targeting prosperous Jewish merchants such as Moïse Benrey especially.

One morning, he received a numbered letter headed "Liberty or Death." His son's life would be spared in return for a large slice of his fortune. There wasn't a moment to lose.

Marie, Moïse and seventeen-year-old Jako slipped out of Sofia in the dead of night and headed for Milan. Why Milan? Because Mr. and Mrs. Benrey held Italian passports. Yet, Moïse had fought in Bulgarian uniform during the Great War, some ten years beforehand. And Jako? Jacques was still Bulgarian.

"Why?" Jenny asked her fiancé one day.

He joked:

"Because there's no divorce in Italy. Since I didn't know I was going to meet you one day, I wanted to be able to divorce if I made a poor choice."

Jenny dropped the matter. There were so many different passports in her own family, and Aunt Allegra, now Andrée, held an Italian passport too.

Jacques was a very good student in the French Catholic school in Sofia and had gone on to a secondary school in Paris specialized in business studies. There, right from week one he distinguished himself with an essay. The teacher handed back the homework and announced:

"The best essay in French was written by a foreigner. Aren't you ashamed, gentlemen?"

The foreigner was Jacques. The teacher read his essay out loud. Then a certain Henri Doueck, in the same class, went up to talk to him:

"So, it's you, the *métèque?*"

"It has to be said that Henri Doueck, scion of a Jewish family long-established in France, thought himself more French than the French," Jenny explained. "But even so, he stood with him, and Jacques the *métèque* and Henri the true Frenchman became friends."

After secondary school, Jacques passed a business exam equivalent to the *baccalauréate* and went to the École Supérieure de Commerce, to continue his business studies. He finished top of his class. He would have liked to go to HEC[24] but his father put his foot down. Enough of studying! He was against intellectuals and artists, like Jacques Canetti, another Bulgarian Sephardi, who confiscated his son's violin claiming music took his mind away from business, which was the Jews' destiny. Alas, neither Jacques Canetti, whose son Elias won the Nobel Prize for Literature, nor Jacques Benrey, had any flair for business.

Moïse Benrey had run a prosperous business in Bulgaria, but he lost practically everything on coming to Paris. Having managed a big cotton spinning firm in his country of origin, he knew nothing of the retail business to which he was now reduced. He began by choosing poorly, opening a fabric store on the rough Rue du Faubourg-Poissonnière rather than in the smart Rue Tronchet. His son wasted time trying to help him in this store. Then Jacques looked for a job.

"It wasn't easy," remarks Jenny. "He was a foreigner, people were jobless."

The Benreys had partially concealed all of this from the Amons, leading Jenny to conclude artlessly: "Luckily, my dowry must have come in handy! All the same, I had a fine marriage."

---

24. Haute École de Commerce, a top-ranked French school of management [Translator].

Jenny's wedding

Plans for the wedding advanced on the twin fronts of love and money. While the fiancés billed and cooed, the families haggled. Who pays for what? Obviously, the groom buys the engagement ring. There were lengthy negotiations over the size of the dowry, the precondition for the suitor's proposal and the official request by his father for the bride's hand. Then they wrangled over the trousseau. The Amons pretended to believe the Benreys would pay for all or part of this. To make sure, Jenny's mother chose her angle cunningly and suggested to her daughter:

"Ask Jacques if he'd rather buy white sheets or colored ones."

The very specific question arose as to the choice of embroideries, to be executed by nuns and little orphan girls in a convent.

Mortified, Jenny raised the question timidly, to which Jacques replied courteously but firmly:

"No, it's not for us to pay for that. I don't think that was the agreement."

More dead than alive, Jenny knew her parents would be furious.

"What! You've got to break it off! Immediately. It's for them to pay."

Marie got up on her high horse. After the expense of her Marcel's bar mitzvah, she had run out of money. She had to beg her father. Finally, Maïr footed the bill for a very big wedding as befitted his standing in the community.

Jenny's trousseau was made up of household linen, sheets, bath towels, pillowslips, dishcloths, tablecloths, and napkins…, plus underwear, including combinations and nightdresses and matching silk dressing gowns. For the wedding night itself, everything had to be white.

Jenny's dowry amounted to around a million old francs. Not a huge sum. Her aunts-in-law had been worth five or six million. Jenny also received numerous wedding gifts thanks to her grandfather's position in the community. Among other gifts, Marie solemnly passed on to her the engraved silver Ottoman platter, which she had brought with her on the Orient Express.

The rest of the summer was spent preparing for the wedding. This took place on October 10, 1937, in the Rue Saint-Lazare synagogue, which Maïr had helped found. The night before, Marie gave her daughter, still a virgin, some tips on how to avoid getting pregnant, and a rubber tube for injecting saltwater. After each sex act, one had to rush to the bathroom and wash in the bidet. Jenny listened distractedly to her mother's admonitions, but she kept them in mind when the time came.

On Rue Saint-Lazare, the flower-bedecked synagogue was packed. The B'nai B'rith had sent a delegation in honor of its President, Saby Amon. Chief Rabbi Ovadia was assisted by another rabbi, while José Papo directed the choir. In accordance with the bride's wishes, she was preceded by five bridesmaids and five pages, Maïr's ten grandchildren. They walked down the aisle that now connected the synagogue to the street. The ten children walked hand in hand, two by two, entering the synagogue as the first notes of music sounded out and the *chazan's* warm, powerful voice sang out.

Waiting for them under the bridal canopy, the *chuppah*, were Rabbi Ovadia, Maïr Benveniste and his wife, Reyna Amon, Maïr's sister and Saby's mother, young Marcel, already too old to be one of the pages, and the witnesses. Witnesses were reminded of their duty to watch, listen, and observe the entire ritual, especially the placing of the ring and the blessings. Theirs was an essential role: should they fail in their task that section of the ceremony would have to start all over again. Two armchairs had been set, one for the groom, the other for the bride. The children, who had rehearsed several times, formed a guard of honor.

As was the custom, the bride entered on her father's arm to the strains of Mendelssohn's *Wedding March*, followed by Jacques holding his mother's arm, and Marie Benveniste with Moïse Benrey. They walked between the children lined up on either side, the bride's long train gliding harmoniously along the floor, at a respectful distance from the groom and his mother. Marie Benveniste, from Salonika, wore a green velvet dress with matching hat and gold-encrusted, green suede handbag. Marie Jerusalmi, the Romanian, wore an embroidered black dress. Was she not about to lose her son? The groom wore a tailcoat and white tie; all the men wore top hats to cover their heads in the synagogue.

Beneath the *chuppah*, Jacques slipped the platinum wedding ring onto Jenny's finger as he uttered the ritual "For you who are consecrated to me by this ring, according to the religion of Moses and Israel." She received it wordlessly, for "it is the reception of it that is the act, it is the asymmetry that is fecund." Chief Rabbi Ovadia then read out the *ketubah*, the traditional marriage contract listing the duties of the spouse toward his wife, namely affection, upkeep and protection. He then read out passages from the Bible. He spoke in a fatherly manner to the newlyweds, exhorting them to follow in their parents' footsteps, known for their work for the cause. He pointed out that the groom, Monsieur Jacques Benrey, was a founder and one of the most active members of the Sephardi Youth Club.

Blessings were given, after which the couple received the wineglass with both hands. Holding it in their right hand they each drank a mouthful of wine. Jacques placed his *talith* over his shoulders and wrapped it around himself and his bride. Moïse Benrey then handed to him the cup, still intact but now empty, wrapped in a cloth so the shards would not fly off, and Jacques placed it on the floor and shattered it under his heel, to feel the loss of the destruction of the Temple: "If I forget thee, O Jerusalem, let my right hand forget her cunning! Let my tongue cleave to the roof of my mouth if I prefer not Jerusalem above my chief joy." The greater the number of shards, the more prosperous the couple will be. The *chazan* shook the walls of this new temple with his vibrant tenor voice.

Everyone then filed out, children first, next the newlyweds, and lastly the entire congregation. The congratulations went on "for hours," remembered Jenny, who also recalled that Allegra made her go home to fix her makeup and hair, and that she arrived two hours late at the Salle Hoche for the wedding reception, giving the signal for everyone to rush to the buffet. The couple danced a waltz, posed for the photographer, then headed for the Hôtel Claridge to spend their wedding night in the bridal suite.

Jenny never said anything about that night, though when mentioning it her expression took on a virginal sweetness, redolent of the Virgin and Child.

They had to be at the Gare de Lyon train station at eight-thirty the next morning. The lovebirds arrived breathless at three minutes to nine, to find the whole family crowding the platform with mountains of flowers. The couple leaped aboard the train, the porter throwing the suitcases after them. One of the Maries threw a big bouquet of lilies through the window. They were on cloud nine, off to Stresa, Milan, Venice, and Capri, to the Italy where the world's happy few go to spend their honeymoon, blissfully unaware that the wheel of fortune was about to turn and that in less than two years fate would turn them into outcasts.

For Jenny, the wedding was the high point of her life, an apotheosis. As the pre-war train headed for the loveliest spots in the world, places where some of her ancestors had sojourned on the road to exile, this young man and this young woman were enjoying the ecstasy of love that happens once in a lifetime, in theirs at least, culminating in my conception. They were lucky. Theirs was a marriage of love and that love never forsook them, not even when history had left its mark on them, when they could no longer speak their name nor tell their child who they were or who she was.

The patriarch takes his leave

Back from her honeymoon, Jenny returned to the synagogue on Rue Saint-Lazare, this time for a funeral. Maïr Benveniste, the patriarch, had been carried away by pneumonia at the age of seventy-one. On an icy day in December Jenny, in black from head to toe, shivered with cold and sorrow in her grandfather's temple, where many had come to mourn.

The silence was imposing as Doctor Vidal Modiano pronounced his funeral oration:

"The deceased descended from a family of eminent rabbis. His father, Rafael Benveniste, brought to their service of the Talmud a broad general culture. So Maïr Benveniste came from good stock. He too was raised in this tradition. But his true calling was for the affairs of the community. There, he worked methodically and intelligently for much of his life. In Salonika, the town of his birth, he was called upon at a young age to sit on the Community Board and on the Talmud Thora Committee. When he came to Paris in 1924, he was soon approached by the charitable organizations of the Sephardic community. There too, he brought to bear his method, intelligence, and equanimity. In Paris as in Salonika, he was the counselor, the sage to whom people came for his opinion, and to whom people listened with respect. But Maïr Benveniste was also..."

The familiar and authoritative voice of "the doctor," as the Benvenistes called him, grew more distant as Jenny realized with a shudder of regret: "never again." More than anything else, her grandfather was what remained of Salonika and four centuries under Ottoman rule. He was the conduit through whom itineraries and languages, customs and feelings had been handed down; he was the keeper of dogma and the Law.

Maïr's departure signaled the gradual dispersal of family ties. The seeds of forgetting were in place... If I forget thee, Oh Salonika, may my right hand lose her cunning! The patriarch had gone, and so had the Jerusalem of the Balkans, joining in the collective imagination the immemorial Toledo and Granada of the Benvenistes. And he was no longer there when his family came face to face with the worst disaster ever to afflict his people, even counting the expulsion from Spain and the two destructions of the Temple.

Jenny was to remember him with nostalgia when she reached the age at which he died: "I was born in Salonika, I was the eldest granddaughter, the one who shared the most memories with him, the one he could talk to in the old idiom of his forefathers, the one who could still sing the old romances of Castile. As long as he was there, I felt ... protected."

But even he could not save her from the family's dispersal, or from her later forswearing of the faith.

That day on December 21, 1937, as Jenny listened distractedly to Vidal Modiano's funeral oration for her grandfather, history was knocking at the gates. Jenny's own story kept pace with the events unfolding afar, before colliding violently with them. But there was nothing definite yet: perhaps they would be spared the final explosion. For now, nineteen thirty-seven was just another year coming to an end...

The next year began with the Anschluss and brought the infamous Munich agreement in September.

In Paris, Jenny and Jacques anxiously scanned the newspapers, though with a sense of fatalism: "It only happens to other people," doubtless reflecting the mood of the democracies. Like the United States, they waxed indignant while slamming their doors in the faces of the Reich's outcasts. For, like everyone else, Jenny and Jacques had their own worries, pre-war worries. They were yet to learn that worries come in two categories.

Pre-war worries included the housing crisis and the straitened finances of a young couple obliged for the time being to live with Moïse and Marie in their apartment on the Rue Thimonnier, in the 9th arrondissement of Paris.

Says Jenny: "My parents-in-law were loving and affectionate, and little by little I grew accustomed to their outpourings, so cruelly lacking in my own home. My mother-in-law Marie would have given me the shirt off her back; she already wanted to give me her apartment, her bedroom, her bed. Indeed, she had given me her son, no mean thing. But she was still a young woman living in the prosperous Romania of the nineteenth century, dreaming of naval balls and romantic strolls beside the Black Sea. She was used to living as part of a tribe, and the presence of her brother Nissim and Aunt Aseo, who was there every day to play poker, were barely enough for her, whereas I dreamed of having an apartment just for the two of us, with Jacques, where I wouldn't be put on show constantly before the rest of the family."

And so, Mademoiselle Maurel's top student, one-time *Concours général* candidate, high school graduate and very nearly holder of a law degree, now found herself, like her fellow young women, turning into an idle young middle-class housewife. Mornings, her mother-in-law initiated her into the secrets of Bulgarian Sephardic cuisine and its Salonika variants. Afternoons, Jenny took the bus to Rue Pérignon to see her mother and aunts. She took tea with her best friend, Laurette Moseri. The Benvenistes were trying to separate Kiko from her, so she was a bit weepy, while her beau dreamed of taking on the world... glory or death.

Evenings, the young couple met up with their friends from the Sephardi Youth Club. Among these were their future inseparable friends the Arditti brothers, the elder of whom, Oscar, had just married the fiery young Lily Alcalaï.

In Germany, meanwhile, Jews had been banned from working in the public sector, were forced to carry passports marked with a large red J, and could no longer send their children to Gentile schools.

Jacques finally found a job as a sales representative working for several firms: for Aulagne, for Blois in Angoulême, for Verboren, and for Bigot Schers in Hamburg. Jenny went with him in his Citroën, visiting farmers to sell them chemicals against mildew in potatoes and to combat disease in apples and pears. His territory covered fourteen French departments spanning the Seine-et-Marne, the Champagne region, the whole area north of Paris as far as Soissons, the Aisne department, and Epernay.

"To start with, scientists from the Institute accompanied him to explain the product. Afterward he did it alone. At one point he went into business with a Bulgarian who had invented a remedy for liver fluke, a disease found in sheep that was wreaking havoc in flocks at the time. He persuaded a Frenchman to buy the rights to the product, who then set up a company and was trying to get scientific circles to take up the invention. He even persuaded the *Jardin des Plantes* botanical gardens in Paris to conduct experiments, and within a few years they managed to cure liver fluke in sheep."

In the meantime, in Germany the Reich unleashed an unprecedented wave of violence against Jews: one hundred and ninety-one synagogues were firebombed; thousands of Jewish-owned stores were ransacked; Jews were murdered or carted off to concentration camps. Between two thousand and two thousand five hundred Jews were murdered on the occasion of *Kristallnacht*, as the event was called, a harbinger of far worse to come.

News of this night of crystal—a fine name for such a crime—spread like wildfire throughout the community in Paris. That night, Jenny prepared her contraceptive tube in the bathroom with greater care than usual. In vain, for I had decided—or was destined—to be born.

I was on my way into the world.

1939: end of a world

I cannot curse the year 1939. It was the year of my conception and birth. I was conceived shortly after *Kristallnacht*, around mid-January. Despite my mother's precautions, the tube didn't work. The fateful year was underway, and it's possible I already existed when Hitler announced in January: "The war to come will result in the destruction of the Jewish race in Europe."

In March, by which time Jenny must have known she was pregnant, Bohemia, Moravia and Slovakia had been invaded. And while Franco's troops captured Madrid and the Spanish Republican armies were surrendering, the rest of the world dithered over whom to ally with. Jenny and Jacques scoured the streets around the Avenue de Breteuil in Paris, near where Jenny's mother lived and close to her cherished alma mater, the Lycée Victor-Duruy. "Apartments for rent were advertised on the doors to buildings. We went to see the janitors who took kickbacks," she recalled.

I had been inside her belly for three months when Hitler celebrated his fiftieth birthday with a huge military parade in Berlin. With the Waffen SS leading the way, the parade featured the Luftwaffe, Panzers, heavy artillery, and the new assault guns. The newsreels showed them in the cinemas where Jacques and Jenny, then visibly pregnant, went to see Jean Renoir's *La Règle du jeu* and *La Bête humaine*[25].

---

25. Pre-war French movies, now classics [Translator].

These distractions notwithstanding, they read with unease an article titled "Why Die for Danzig" by a neo-socialist, Marcel Déat, published just after the annexation of Albania by Italy, which had invaded it without declaring war. Who would want to die to help Poland retain this thin sliver of land giving it access to the sea? Yet France was committed to coming to the aid of Poland if Germany attacked the latter. London and Paris agreed to the principle of a mutual assistance pact in the event of an attack on Poland. Reassuring. No, there would be no war. There could be no war.

At last, Jenny found a conveniently situated apartment with a most congenial concierge, Madame Chaliès. It was on Rue César-Franck, on the fifth floor, completely redecorated by Leleu, in the block that used to contain Jenny's childhood school. But the rent was high. Jenny was enthusiastic though. The drawing room and dining room windows of this fifth floor looked out onto Rue Pérignon, just opposite the Amons' apartment. There was a small balcony from which Jenny could talk to her mother, who lived on the fourth floor. Jacques dug in his heels:

"We can't go renting an apartment now. Italy's about to go to war. We too could be caught up in it in less than three days."

But on visiting the place he was bowled over. He couldn't deny his young wife. Consequently, despite the imminence of conflict and the sky-high rent, Jacques signed on the dotted line.

On July 1, I had been in my mother's womb for five months. As usual, the family rented a villa in Saint-Lunaire. Jacques and Jenny spent the month there. While they stretched out on the sandy Breton beach and took long walks, talks between France, the United Kingdom and the USSR on a mutual assistance pact went nowhere.

Kiko, meanwhile, had reluctantly broken with Laurette, yielding to his mother and family. All that remained for him was to seek glory... or die. Once an unruly child, now he had gained admission to the Saumur officer training college and had come home to celebrate his promotion to the rank of senior officer cadet.

At the end of the month, the parents-to-be returned to Paris, happy to be together in their fine apartment.

Did I shudder inside my mother at the news of the Molotov-Ribbentrop Pact on August 23? All hopes of peace died at that moment. Jacques and Jenny couldn't believe their ears. The Soviet Union had signed a non-aggression pact with Germany. Parisian cafés were abuzz with animated talk of the move from morning till night. Was Stalin playing for time by grabbing part of Poland and the Baltic countries? Or was Hitler, rather, the beneficiary of the alliance, having gained a free hand to invade Poland?

In France, people rarely focus on a given subject for more than a few hours. This was August and, thanks to the introduction of two weeks of paid annual leave, the French left to go on vacation. Unsurprisingly, the French Communists approved the Molotov-Ribbentrop Pact. The United States having voted in 1936 to become a neutral country, US citizens were evacuated aboard the steamship *Normandie*.

That day, as I completed seven months of life *in utero* and was already viable, Jacques announced to Jenny his intention to enlist as a volunteer. He had sworn to himself he would do it. All he needed now was her approval.

"But why?" I seem to hear my mother cry. "Why? You're Bulgarian. You've no reason to enlist!"

"Why? France took me in, took *us* in. I want to become French one day... like you. And I want to fight this evil, which is destroying all our people over there, the German Jews."

Jenny had no answer. She knew he was right to want to enlist, this gentle fellow who had gotten out of his military obligations in Bulgaria and was a professed pacifist. She was afraid but said nothing, agreeing to protect her unborn child while her husband went off to defend them both.

The first shots were fired on Danzig, on September 1. In Poland the world witnessed the *Blitzkrieg* for the first time, with massive attacks by tanks and planes. Germany rejected the French and British ultimatum. "These little worms won't start a world war for Danzig," said Hitler.

France ordered a general mobilization. Jacques kept his word and enlisted. His military passbook states: "Mobilized on September 3, 1939. Assigned to the 4th Infantry Regiment, 3 Company, at Sens, in the Yonne." His friend Oscar Arditti, who had been to the same Catholic school as him in Sofia, but who had French nationality, took the train for Verdun on the first day of his call up, entrusting his young wife Lily to his friends for safekeeping.

War was imminent and there was panic abroad. People were expecting Paris to be bombed. Parisians packed their bags. "The family decided to send the women and children to Saint-Lunaire," says Jenny, "and I was the first to go, being eight months' pregnant. Jacques was waiting to be called up, so he didn't come with me."

On September 3, Great Britain, France, Australia, and New Zealand declared war on Germany. Two months later, I was born in a little maternity hospital run by nuns, near Saint-Lunaire in Brittany.

There was an initial silence, which the French called the "*drôle de guerre*," the Germans the "*Sitzkrieg*," and the English the "phony war," before the sound and the fury that were to shatter the world for the next five years.

III
The Sound and the Fury

It is only by chronological narrative that one
avoids the temptation to see the past through
the obsessions of the present [...]. Chronology
is still the best way to find meaning.

—SIMON SEBAG MONTEFIORE, *JERUSALEM:*
THE BIOGRAPHY

It's war

At 11 am on September 3, 1939, after an ultimatum demanding the withdrawal of German troops from Poland, France declared war on the Third Reich.

At Saint-Lunaire, Jenny, and I inside her, listened to Édouard Daladier on an old wireless set that made the French premier's voice almost inaudible. Addressing we Frenchwomen first, and then the men of France, the last President of the Third Republic Council of Ministers declared: "We are resolved not to bow to the diktat of violence. We have taken up arms against aggression."

Jenny let out a little cry of fright which echoed down to little me, and it was then that I no doubt decided to stay inside her until I was brought out by force. I was expected on October 15 but dragged my feet till the 31st.

The war too dragged its feet. The French made a desultory attack on the Sarre region, prompting an exodus of Germans, and seized the enemies' bicycles before the tables were turned again. In the gloomy house called Isba, at Saint-Lunaire, whose windows overlooked a cemetery, a terrible wait began for times more terrible still. Jenny had arrived in Brittany ahead of the family, before September 3. Her mother Marie, her aunt Allegra with Ugo Modiano and Oro, her grandmother, then joined her. Shortly after the September mobilization, Saby hastily dropped off his own mother Reyna, dumping her like a package then returning sleepless to Paris. The panic in town and the armed soldiers pacing the train station had driven the old lady out of her mind and brought on a stroke. She reached "Isba," lay down, and passed away quietly.

Paris was put on alert after Hitler threatened to destroy it. Its population was evacuating as fast as it could. The men of the family who held a French passport, like Pepo, were conscripted. Marcel, just turned fifteen, enrolled in the Lycée Buffon, and Saby stayed behind to look after his son and mind the store. Kiko was completing his training at Saumur's Cavalry School. He was pining still for Laurette and was contemplating something drastic. His mother Allegra had no idea what was on his mind, but she never lost an opportunity to sigh, cursing the situation and her son's absence.

This was war. In the rundown summer house, made gloomier still by the dull fall weather, Allegra and her sister forbade all sweetness and pleasures, however tiny. This was war. Jenny wasn't allowed to eat candies, to listen to music, not even to read. She whiled away the time knitting. Everyone knitted, till there was no more wool.

But Jacques still hadn't been called up.

"What's your husband up to, then?" Kiko's mother angrily asked her niece.

"But... Aunt Allegra..."

"Stop calling me Allegra. You know perfectly well my name's Andrée now."

"Aunt Andrée, you and mother know perfectly well that Jacques has enlisted. It's just that he hasn't been called up yet."

"Ah! A pity! A man his age, not yet called up..."

"Kiko...hasn't gone either."

"He hasn't completed Saumur. He's much too young. But your husband, he's old enough..."

Jenny said nothing and began to get irritated.

"I'm going for a walk."

"Oh no you're not. You're not going out again, in this weather! Come and help me make lunch. Just don't touch anything. No nibbling. You're so overweight. I've never seen a pregnant woman as big as you. It's almost indecent!"

"*Ay Dio!*" Marie let out a loud cry. "Grandmother's dying!"

Everyone rushed to her side. Allegra took her pulse.

"Aunt Reyna's dying!"

She turned to her sister.

"Marie, what'll we do if she dies here? We can't bury her here. You'll have to take her back to Paris."

"Allegra... Pardon, Andrée... I heard it's forbidden to travel with a corpse."

"Exactly. You can't take her back dead. You'll have to take her back alive.

In an ambulance. You won't be allowed to take her in an ambulance if she's dead."

Marie took her mother-in-law back to Paris at the last minute. Reyna Amon, *née* Benveniste, breathed her last as she entered Paris, a few days before the birth of her great-granddaughter, me. The family owned a plot in the Jewish sector of the Pantin Cemetery, and her son Saby buried her there. The first of our war dead. She was lucky, dying in luxury, transported in an ambulance, and buried in a marked grave.

Jenny would have gone to Paris in her mother's place but dared not insist. This was October 14, a day before term. I was kicking a lot but refused to come out. I was waiting for... my father. He turned up with Marie, back from the funeral, and with Saby, who had left behind his son, his store, and his Masonic lodge.

"Jacques!"

I clearly heard Jenny's cry of joy. I was happy too that he was there for my birth, despite my nasty Aunt Allegra, sorry Andrée, who kept up her sniping. She even drove Jenny to tears a little later, telling Jenny her husband couldn't go to see her in the maternity hospital because he shouldn't go out "lest someone attack him in the street if they saw him, a young man in civilian dress."

For now, though, we were together. All three. Now the conditions were right for me to come into the world.

I am born

On the morning of October 29, it was all hands to the deck. Jenny's water was breaking. Allegra had deigned to cook that day, preparing a divine kidney-and-liver stew steeped in tomato sauce. She carefully wrapped it in a little packet and gave it to her niece, wishing her a safe delivery. Marie and Jacques left with the parturient and myself inside, having decided to finish the job and emerge into the world, taking my time about it.

Jenny had reserved a bed in the little maternity hospital run by the nuns, realizing her eminent gynecologist in the Paris clinic wouldn't be on hand when the time came to give birth. She had also reserved an individual room there for herself and her baby, with the embroidered sheets from her trousseau.

In normal times, a single midwife at the nuns' maternity hospital handled three or four childbirths weekly. The outbreak of war increased this number to fifteen a day, with no physician, the men having been mobilized. In addition to the summer holidaymakers who had stayed on, there was a large contingent of people from Alsace and Lorraine who had fled the German army, coming westward laden with baggage and pregnant women. Among them were Jews who had brought everything with them, including the heart and soul of their synagogues, and who went on living and having children.

Says Jenny: "The panic inside the maternity hospital was indescribable. There was no hygiene and no doctor to step in should a problem arise. 'Pain-free' childbirth was unknown at the time. I screamed from Sunday through Tuesday. Hospital rules required families to leave at seven in the evening. Luckily though, my mother and Jacques hid and were able to stay in the room, in the dark, for two nights. Meanwhile, I was screaming in what was pompously called the 'birthing ward,' a few yards away, with that fat woman constantly by my side, who urged me to push and push again and finally fell asleep from exhaustion while I hollered away.

"Finally, at five in the morning of October 31, you came into the world. A healthy baby of three and a half kilos, so luminous you lit up that sinister ward. You had scarcely been born when the aptly named midwife Mademoiselle Gaillard[26] placed you beside me on a gurney without cutting the umbilical cord; she didn't get rid of the placenta or change me. She didn't even offer me a drop of water. She left us there, you and me, all alone. And she went off to bed. My mother and Jacques, not daring to show themselves but reassured all the same, crept out from their hiding place. I stayed there covered in filth with my little girl in my arms until seven in the morning, when a cleaner came in. She opened all the windows without noticing me and began sweeping the floor. I called out and told her I'd just given birth. 'Ah good!' she said without looking, then went on dusting. 'It's... could you

---

26. Sturdy [Translator].

134

give me a basin? —Can't do that… You don't want to… You're just imagining things… Just let yourself go.'

"So, I let myself go. I was soaking wet but suddenly felt happy, liberated, with my child in my arms."

And that's how we met up again, Jenny and I, with me on the outside this time.

Jacques and Marie were shivering in the early morning on the deserted road, meanwhile. Suddenly, Marie plucked up her courage:

"You're not too angry with her?"

"Angry? Why on earth?"

"For only having had a girl."

Taken aback, Jacques stared at his mother-in-law:

"Quite the opposite! I wanted a girl!"

Now it was Marie's turn to look at her son-in-law in amazement. This Bulgarian really was like nobody else! For once she was willing to apologize!

Then they parted, Marie to catch the first bus of the morning back to Saint-Lunaire, while Jacques raced to break the news to his parents Moïse and Marie, who had rented a small house in the area. The other Marie clapped her hands on learning the news:

"A granddaughter! *Gracias a Dio!* My life's dream!"

Later, Jacques went to watch the sun rise over the Clair-de-Lune promenade. What was he thinking of, my father Jacques, on the morning of my birth, the war not two months old and Hitler yet to act on his dreams of liquidating the Jews in the Greater Reich? Was he weighing up the perils faced by a Jewish child born in the worst period of history for his people? Or was he simply happy to be alive, happy that his wife was alive and that together they had brought into the world a little girl so determined to live?

Sixty years later, Jenny was quite firm: "I too was glad you were a girl, because if you had been a boy, you would have been circumcised a few days after your birth… And a circumcision in a convent…!"

The idea shocks me:

"You would have had me circumcised at a time like that?"

"There was no choice. If you'd been a boy, your grandfather would have demanded it. We weren't so sure… but 'at a time like that,' as you put it, nothing had happened yet. We couldn't know! ... Anyway, I did know people ... like us... at Saint-Lunaire ... a pregnant young woman who had her baby boy shortly after me, and they held the circumcision ceremony in the hospital... We couldn't have known!"

I look at Jenny with mingled compassion and severity. "Couldn't have known!" How innocent! Of course, she could have known. One had only to look at what was going on in Germany next door: the Nuremberg Laws had been passed four years earlier, in 1935. But human beings have difficulty believing others hate them, hate them to the point of wanting to annihilate them. We don't mind being agents of hatred—we've all hated someone at some point in our lives—but to be the object of such hatred oneself is inconceivable.

The next day, Jacques went to the town hall to register me officially: Michèle (for the film star Michèle Morgan), Marie (for Marie Beneviste and Marie Jerusalmi, my two grandmothers), Reine (for Reyna Amon, née Benveniste, the great-grandmother who had just died, on the road like a genuine Sephardi in exile). Throughout my childhood, though, I was to be known as "little Michou."

I was eligible for a French passport, having been born on French soil, to a mother born in Greece who had become Portuguese when her family opted for that nationality before taking French nationality upon their arrival *a Francia*, and to a Bulgarian father whose parents held Italian passports. Both born in the now-defunct Ottoman Empire. Scant comfort at a time when even having a gentile grandfather was no protection against extermination.

Kiko dies

On May 16, 1940, senior officer cadet Ralph Modiano, Kiko for his family, the son of Allegra and Ugo, Jenny's soulmate and still passionately in love with Laurette Moseri, was killed fighting at Petites-Armoises in eastern France during an enemy bombardment. The phony war had made way for the real thing.

Meanwhile—a long "meanwhile"—Jenny had taken me in her arms and brought me back to Paris, to the dismay of the men in the family, who had been having fun in the Rue Pérignon and Rue César-Franck apartments, with their wives far away. We, Jenny and Michou, arrived at the Gare Montparnasse train station on the last day of December. Jacques had come to meet us and had organized an intimate New Year's Eve for the three of us. I have no recollection of this, but it made my genitors very happy, while I rested at last in my cradle and vigorously suckled Jenny's milk.

A fearsome cold snap swept across Europe in January 1940. The temperature dropped to 5°F in Northern France, and 8.6°F in Paris.

On February 21, a suitable site for an extermination camp was found at last and Himmler ordered it built. It was located at Auschwitz, a town of twelve thousand inhabitants lost among the marshes, but there was a railhead, a handful of factories and old Austrian Army huts used formerly by the cavalry. The significance of this news was lost on my family, women included, most of whom had stayed in Saint-Lunaire.

Moïse Benrey and Marie Jersalmi were still in Brittany; Hitler was busy in Poland. The French army chief Gamelin meanwhile sheltered the French army behind the Maginot Line, hoping to buy time to rearm. France was "biding her time." Nothing was happening, or so it seemed.

Kiko had finally been called up and sent to a garrison at Épinal. Whether due to heartache or to escape his difficulties with his family, this was his chance to be a hero. A hero—or nothing.

"I'll be back with a *Croix de Guerre*[27] or not at all," he told his cousin Jenny when on furlough. "Laurette will be proud of me."

German bombing in the night of May 9 sent my parents and me into the cellars of our building on Rue César-Franck. All I remember is the sound of a siren. I heard that many times over later, its shriek penetrating me and arousing fear whenever it sounded.

The next morning the rumor spread: the German army had invaded Belgium. The fanatical Germans, eager to serve their Führer, had concentrated their forty divisions to the south, in the Ardennes. They crashed

---

27. French military decoration [Translator].

through the forest, which the France and its allies hadn't bothered defending, crossing the River Meuse, and racing to the sea. There Kiko, serving in the "*Corps Franc*"[28], had been sent with his unit. The die was cast.

The French retreated behind the Meuse, while the Germans, with massive Luftwaffe support, crossed the river at Dinant, Monthermé and Sedan. Winston Churchill told the British people he had nothing to offer them but "blood, sweat and tears." On May 18, French radio announced the appointment of Marshal Pétain to the post of Vice-President of the Council of Ministers. The next day, France's leaders went to Notre-Dame de Paris Cathedral to pray for the salvation of France, while one half of the population fled to the other half of the country.

The exodus had begun.

It was then that Jenny tried to reach Bagnoles-de-l'Orne in Normandy with a six-month-old baby in her arms. She joined the millions of other refugees fleeing from east to west in cars, horse-drawn carts, on horseback, bicycles or on foot, dragging with them bundles, old folk, babies, suitcases, and assorted furniture, traipsing they knew not where in an unholy muddle and chaos—like their government, which fled to Bordeaux on June 14, or like Jenny, who found refuge in a cousin's home.

Jenny never forgot that episode, though far worse was to come. As she says in her *Monologue*: "From Bagnoles, we saw all the civilians fleeing the German advance; first came the Belgians, who were in transit with fine cars filled with children, trunks, chests, and furniture. Then came the inhabitants of northern France, panic-stricken and hunted down in never-ending flight. And us! And me and my daughter, cut off from my husband. He was alone in Paris; there was no point hoping for any news from him. Trains chock full of passengers ground to a halt. People were machine-gunned on the roads; cars were abandoned when they ran out of gas or rendered useless by the bombing."

Jenny was escorted by her brother Marcel, then in full "teen delirium" says his sister, obsessed with rumors of a fifth column infiltrated by enemy

---

28. Special squad of French Army volunteers carrying out reconnaissance and hit-and run-attacks. Forerunners of the commandos [Translator].

spies. She reached Bagnoles-de-l'Orne with her kid brother and me, her daughter, in tow. I liked this young sixteen-year-old uncle who pulled faces at me and talked to me at length, Jenny told me later. I also learned that he told a lot of tall tales which my parents didn't believe.

Jenny looked around for somewhere for the rest of her family to stay. And so the tribe ended up in Bagnoles. First Allegra and Ugo with Oro. Then later Marie and Saby.

That was when the French troops and the British Expeditionary Force were battling one against four in the Dunkirk pocket. A French infantry division was sacrificed to enable the British to rebuild their reserves. The Battle of France was over.

Ralph Modiano, aka Kiko, was killed on May 16, fighting for France and Laurette. Born the day of the Great Fire of Salonika, he was just twenty-three years old. The whole family was crammed into our tiny lodgings at Bagnoles-de-l'Orne. A delegation from the town hall turned up one morning in early June to announce to Allegra and Ugo the death of Kiko, their son, senior officer cadet in the 93rd divisional reconnaissance group. His death was mentioned in the dispatches of his army corps.

Marie had already heard the news from Paris. The Army knew the Modiano's address on Avenue du Général-Détrie, and two soldiers had been sent to announce the awful news. Finding no one there, they notified the concierge, who informed Marie, then still in the capital. She arrived at Bagnoles in a distressed state just as the town hall officials were knocking on the door. Before leaving Paris, she had telephoned Doctor Cazès, the family physician, also from Salonika.

"It's appalling... what if Allegra tries to kill herself?"

Appalling. Kiko's mother screamed as if she had been stabbed in the stomach, while Ugo, his father, collapsed onto a chair, speechless. Allegra screamed, then moaned for hours as Marie mopped her brow with a damp cloth. "Afterward," her niece recalls, "she said nothing, neither eating nor sleeping for days on end, while Ugo, grief-stricken, remained in a heap, inconsolable. If they'd shown him greater understanding...," broods Jenny seventy years after the event. "If they had accepted Laurette, Kiko wouldn't have rushed off to Belgium to join Corap's army and be one of the first soldiers to get himself killed in the Battle of France."

Kiko was dead. The atmosphere lay heavy over the tiny house in Bagnoles. Everyone spoke in hushed tones and all available clothes were dyed black; no one even dared swap rumors and news of the war.

Kiko was dead. Jenny tried to think of nothing, feeding her daughter, mechanically performing household chores, and taking turns to console the prostrate mother. Marcel, the imaginative extravert teenager, did his best to keep out of sight of his Aunt Allegra. Anyway, she couldn't bear to see him, the spitting image of Kiko at the same age. He vanished from dawn till dusk, returning to eat, mingling with other wild-eyed, tousled teenagers like himself, whose sole topics of conversation were music and fighting the enemy. What was he up to, young Marcel, who passed the first part of his *baccalaureate* in 1940?

Kiko was dead. No one, not even his mother, paid any attention just then to this impetuous young rebel now experiencing his first enthusiasms. Kiko's death on the field of honor was the family's first in time of war. There are honorable deaths that warrant our tears. Kiko's was one of those. Then there are the others, deaths not spoken of, over which people remain dry-eyed and of which we cannot, can never speak. Laurette's was one of those, in deportation. She was classified "Missing." As was her mother. And her younger brother.

Kiko wasn't there to wait for her. Or to weep for her.

Summer 1940

June 12 was Jenny's birthday.

Apparently, I, Michou, was very agitated that night and cried a lot. I had a good excuse: my first tooth was coming through. Jenny, who hadn't slept for several nights, changed my diaper in grief, thinking of Kiko, whom she would never see again, and of her husband, of whom she was without news. The sound of voices drew her to the window. It was one of those groups of refugees, haggard, weary, ill-kempt, and ill-shaven, she'd grown used to see passing by. Suddenly, against all odds, she recognized a voice. She grabbed her baby and rushed into the arms of her husband, who ran to greet her.

140

Leaving the now-deserted Paris hadn't been easy. Jacques remembered that his car, kept in a garage since the outbreak of war, might still be serviceable thanks to the ministrations of Basile, a White Russian who worked as a janitor and mechanic in return for a consideration. With a pair of cousins traveling with him and a friend picked up on the outskirts of Paris, they had found some gasoline at the last filling station still open, after several hours wait. In Chartres, they spent the night in the open, on the main square. It was raining so hard that night the German planes could not drop their bombs. They made up for it the next day, flattening Chartres. But Jacques was here now, safe and in good health, and once again we were all together again and happy.

I'm told my gums were still sore, though I have no recollection of it.

Lying together on the ground at night in the open air to escape the tiny over-crowded room, Jacques and Jenny listened as people muttered about suspected fifth-columnists, spies working for the Germans in what was still France. Jacques whispered to his wife news of friends and relatives scattered hither and thither. Their great friend Oscar Arditti, one of the first to be mobilized, was alive but a prisoner in a Stalag. We learned later that he had been captured in the afternoon of June 8, on the Ailette canal near Soissons. His wife, brave Lily, moved heaven and earth to get him released.

The car was a jalopy but priceless at times like these. Inside were more hidden riches. Jacques had piled everything he could onto the roof and in the trunk. He had no idea how long he'd be away from home, without work. Perhaps they could sell something. He'd brought with him the silver platters and the most valuable or lightest of the abundant wedding gifts his wife, as the daughter of Saby Amon and granddaughter of Maïr Benveniste, had received three years earlier.

Jacques was worried for his parents, Moïse and Marie, who had been in Dinard since summer 1939. He had to find them. Two days earlier, on June 10, Italy had declared war on France and the United Kingdom. What would happen to Moïse and Marie, who held Italian nationality and were now enemies of France?

Jacques and Jenny set out by car for Dinard, where Moïse and Marie welcomed them with tears, hugs. There were probably *borekas* too; I missed out on those, being breastfed at the time. They hadn't seen me for ages and said I'd grown a lot.

"You were just a baby," says Jenny, "but already you looked so much like your grandmother Marie that Moïse was astonished. There was something special between you and her: I was almost jealous."

Jacques and Jenny were given leave to do the cooking, but the house had just a single room, which they shared with Moïse, Marie and myself. Re-energized, my parents slept soundly, having parked the car on the town square and putting off the job of unloading it till the next day.

That was a mistake! When they reached the spot in the morning, the car had vanished. Gone was their baggage, their bundles and silver platters! Even Jenny's suit and hat had gone. In its place they found a very official document stating that the vehicle had been requisitioned by the French air force for the use of airmen making their way to England. Later, the French government bureaucratically reimbursed the car at the going rate, though with no compensation for the silver dishes, gold-plated coffee spoons or the suit and hat. This was war! Jacques and Jenny could only hope the airmen reached England safely. And I can only hope they swelled the ranks of those who joined De Gaulle when he arrived in London shortly afterward.

That same day, June 14, German troops marched into Paris, which had been declared an open city. The wolves had entered the fold. Some Parisians committed suicide. Otto Abetz was named the representative of the Wilhelmstrasse in Paris. Two days later, Philippe Pétain, the "hero of Verdun," became Head of the French Government. On June 17 he made his famous speech, which Jenny, Jacques, Moïse and Marie listened to on their landlord's wireless set, raging at their powerlessness as fear churned their stomachs: "It is with a heavy heart that I tell you today that we must stop fighting," quavered Marshal Pétain.

Next day, they were glued to the wireless once again. But the voice, and more importantly its tone, were different: "Whatever happens, the flame of French resistance must not and shall not die. Tomorrow I shall broadcast again from London. Today we are crushed by the sheer weight of mechanized force hurled against us, but we can still look to a future in which even greater mechanized force will bring us victory. The destiny of the world is at stake."

This speech by De Gaulle was "extraordinary" and calmed their nerves, says Jenny. But Nazi Germany and France signed an armistice that Saturday, June 22, symbolically in the same old railcar as the one used to sign the November 1918 Armistice, a harsh reminder of the defeat France had just suffered.

The Germans fanned out across France, but the two families were temporarily reunited. Saby and Marie Amon rented a small house near Saint-Enogat where there was room for the five of them. Says Jenny: "What was to become of us and how long was this going to last? We had time enough to reflect over and over during that long summer of 1940, with its magnificent June and July weather. Weather such as no one had seen for years. In fact, it made the German advance through France easier. In three weeks, Germany had laid our country low. We went to the beach but didn't bathe. The sea belonged lock, stock and barrel to our occupiers. They were handsome, those first Wehrmacht soldiers. Young, energetic, tall blond Aryans, the answer to Hitler's dreams; they couldn't believe how easily they had rolled through France, while their dive bombers picked off the fleeing civilians.

"On July 9, '40, the Chamber of Deputies, which had voted for Blum and the Popular Front, with its important social reforms in '36, backed the Government motion sealing the death of the Third Republic. The next day, Marshal Pétain was granted full powers by the Parliament meeting in Vichy. And on July 16, a decree stripped recently naturalized Jews of their French nationality.

"The decree didn't apply to our family, as we had taken French nationality in the mid-twenties. Hitler's victorious Germany occupied two-thirds of France up to a line running from Bordeaux in the southwest to Besançon in the east. German customs posts were set up along this demarcation line and no one could get through without an *Ausweis*, a pass delivered by the German *Kommandatur*. Posters were put up at this arbitrary frontier prohibiting Jews living in the south, in the Free Zone, from entering the Occupied Zone. We were there already, but we had run out of money and everything we owned was in Paris.

"Finally, the trains restarted in mid-August, and we were able to get back home. We took the boat from Saint-Enogat to Saint-Malo, where the trains now stopped. The city we returned to was no longer the Paris we had known. Everything was ruled by German time. The clocks were set to Central European time, i.e., two hours behind the sun. We were treated to daily parades of enemy troops, one down the Champs-Elysées, the other along the Rue de Rivoli.

"We tried to get back to normal. Jacques used to represent a German chemical maker whose business had been interrupted by the war. He re-opened Moïse's little fabric store, Moïse having come back from Brittany with Marie, his wife. Business boomed at first. All you had to do was find the goods. German soldiers were rationed at home, so they leaped to buy the cloth and send it home to their wives in Germany. We built up our stock in anticipation of the ghastly future that lay ahead.

"France was paying three hundred thousand francs a day for the Germans' upkeep. They were flush with cash and paid well. To send my little girl to sleep in the evenings, I sang her the 'Ballad of dead ladies[29],' which I updated in keeping with the times: 'The cream white like the lily/ The bacon pink with its dark-brown rind/ Our good local cheese / The potatoes from our plots / And the rabbits from our heath / Murdered by our occupier / Where are you off to, Sovereign Queen?/ But where are the snows of yester-year? / Prince, ask not when / In which week all doth flee, nor in which year / All shall go to our sister Germaine / But whither go the snows of yesteryear?'"

Throughout this period Jenny's family lived a normal life as Parisians under enemy occupation. Many declared those enemies to be "more than well-behaved." The German soldiers in the Metro thought I looked "cute," a blonde child in the arms of an Aryan-looking father.

---

29. A poem by the medieval French poet François Villon [Translator]:
    "Tell me now in what hidden way is
    Lady Flora the lovely Roman?
    Where's Hipparchia, and where Thais,
    Neither of them the fairer woman?
    Where is Echo, beheld of no man,
    Heard only on river and mere --
    She whose beauty was more than human?...
    But where are the snows of yester-year?"

"*Schön, Schön,*" commented one to his comrade while slipping a candy into my hand.

I wailed, it seems, when Jenny snatched the enemy's sticky sweetmeat away. There's a studio photo of my father and mother enveloping me with their twin gaze. In hindsight, I see their attitude as a fierce determination to protect their child to their dying breath.

But, taken up with their "normal" concerns now that they were back from the exodus, Jacques and Jenny were heedless of what was brewing up against them, the "abnormals." During the summer, laws were drafted against foreigners, politely called "undesirables." The Marchandeau decree prohibiting racist propaganda, issued in April 1939, was repealed. Henceforward the sluicegates of antisemitic hatred were opened wide, setting the scene for what was to come next.

During that same spring-summer of 1940, the Nazi Hans Frank, Governor-General of Poland, laughed that he hadn't yet managed to kill all the lice and all the Jews and addressed his dear comrades thus: "I must ask you to rid yourselves of all feelings of pity. We must destroy the Jews."

On becoming pariahs

"We were so pleased to be back home after the nightmarish exodus. Everyone was. Well, all French people, I mean," Jenny's tone softens. "Anyway, summer was drawing to an end and the school year was starting.

Obviously, food was getting short, but despite the lines and restrictions, cloth could be used as a means of exchange, so we were no worse off than ordinary folk, except..."

"Except?" I ask.

"Except that in September a German Executive Order, and in October a decision by the Prefect of Police, ordered all citizens of the Jewish faith, having more than two Jewish grandparents, to register. So, we went and registered.

"You went to register yourselves, us, as Jews? Without thinking something was amiss?"

"Well, no. Why should we? And we had *nothing, nothing*, you hear, to be ashamed of! Everyone went. Respectable people who'd done nothing wrong. The Avenue Victoria was jam-packed. Everyone was eager to obey, to show they complied with the law. Every member of our two families went, including my parents-in-law, Moïse and Marie, who had just re-turned to Paris. We were recorded in a registry, with a file card for each of us, blue for me because I was French, and orange or beige for your fa-ther, who was Bulgarian. Later, they printed the word JEW on our identity cards, in red letters on a beige card."

"How could you?"

"How could we? But we didn't know, we couldn't imagine! And we were threatened with serious trouble if we didn't obey."

Eminent people set the tone for Jacques and Jenny. The celebrated phi-losopher Henri Bergson, though gravely ill, made it a point of honor to come down to the Passy police precinct in bathrobe and slippers to have himself registered as a Jew. Colonel Brisac performed his duty in military uniform.

I tried to imagine what they could have said to each other in those long lines, patiently waiting to register and damn themselves in the process. What sort of small talk did they share?

"So, you're here too! Fancy that! Who'd have thought it...!"

More probably there was silence. This was the start of the silence that betokens dignity. A dignity that was still theirs.

"Name? First name? Domicile? Occupation? Nationality?"

All these records were methodically sorted into four sub-files.

But, while Jenny, Jacques and the others were striving to live like everyone else, in the foolish hope of being spared, the trap was closing about them.

At the beginning of October, Marie sent the pre-arranged signal from her fourth-floor balcony looking out onto the Rue Bouchut, which our fifth-floor balcony overlooked also. It was a white sheet, like the sails of ships bearing news. Jenny rushed breathless to her mother's, on the other side of the street.

"What's going on?"

"What's going on," echoed Marie, "is that the Council of Ministers has just approved a statute on the Jews. Like in Germany. And it applies to all of us in the Occupied Zone."

"Which means?"

"Which means that we have been 'barred,' it says, from political life, from the judiciary, from the diplomatic service, from the administration, the educational system, the press, and entertainment... from the civil service, the State, the Army."

"Which means Kiko... couldn't have been in the Army! And he wouldn't be dead?"

"My poor girl! Kiko died for nothing. Look what Doriot[30] writes in that rag Saby just brought in a while ago: 'At last, the Jews have been driven out of the civil service and their access to other occupations is regulated,' putting an end to their 'insinuating and ultimately putrefying influence.'"

Discouraged, Jenny put down the rag whose title was *Le Cri du people*[31].

"But what... what are we going to do?"

"Saby says the statute promises not to affect people or goods."

"Are you kidding? Look what they've done in Germany!"

"France isn't Germany!"

"For now... But Drumont[32] was there before Hitler!"

---

30. Jacques Doriot, journalist and politician. Initially a communist but became a leading French fascist and collaborator during the war [Translator].

31. Literally "The people's shout," a fascist daily published during the occupation [Translator].

32. Edouard Drumont. French journalist and political figure, born 1844, died 1917. Founder of the National Antisemitic League of France [Translator].

Jenny was onto something in doubting her father's indomitable optimism, even though he was well-informed through the B'nai B'rith chapter. Aryanization measures soon overturned the promise contained in the first statute. A second statute made these measures tougher still, now covering the southern, so-called Free Zone, as well. A circular stipulated that "in most cases, grandparents' membership of the Jewish religion will be deemed the best presumption. In the presence of Jews detached from the practice of their religion, useful evidence may be found in the appearance of certain surnames, in the choice of registered first names and in the fact of having ancestors buried in a Jewish cemetery."

For the Germans, the enemy was the Jew, deemed to be "subhuman." For the French, the enemy was the foreigner, the undesirable. The Germans wanted to eliminate "subhumans." The French wanted to be rid of "undesirables." The common solution had a name: deportation to the East. As and when the "undesirables" were driven away, destined for physical elimination, the Germans worked to transform as many French Jews as possible into undesirables ripe for deportation. Hitler bombarded Pétain with incessant demands to denaturalize Jews to which the latter acceded, with some reluctance, it must be said. The question was to poison relations between the German and the French governments till the end, and it helped determine the fate of my family and myself.

This fate began taking shape in the stark simplicity of a handful of equations:

The Vichy government wanted to be rid of foreigners. Jacques was Bulgarian. He was already slated for exclusion from the French community, deprivation of ration coupons and near instant arrest.

The Nazis wanted to be rid of the Jews, whoever they were. Jenny was French but naturalized in 1924, so she was walking a thin line.

I was born on French soil but the daughter of those two. For the time being I was just one year old and unaffected by these measures. Not yet. Ultimately though, my fate was in the balance.

Moïse and Marie were Italian. They were enemies. Then they became allies when Italy entered the war on the German side. But as Jews they were the enemies of everyone. They had no idea what awaited them. Nobody knew at this stage.

To flee one needed money and contacts. The United States had slammed shut its doors. The English had barred entry to Palestine. That left Latin America, which Judeo-Spanish Jews could reach via Spain and Portugal: the governments of Franco and Salazar were more accommodating, some of their consuls especially. Some family members escaped via that route.

The process of Aryanization commenced in October 1940. All Jewish-owned businesses had to announce their origin. From then on, Moïse and Jacques were obliged to display the ignominious yellow poster on their little fabric store on Rue du Faubourg-Poissonnière. Four thousand six hundred posters were put up on "accursed" businesses in early-December. At first, native-born French Jews tried to set themselves apart, announcing the fact with no little fanfare. A prominent hosiery on the Rue du Temple, near the Place de la République, bore the yellow sign "Jewish-owned Business." Above it, a large cardboard white sign surrounded by a blue and red circle read: "Business founded in 1909 by Maurice Lévy, who died for France at Douaumont[33] in 1916. Business taken over by his son, a veteran of 1939-1940, decorated with the War Medal and mentioned in dispatches." Another Jewish proprietor displayed in his store front the Medal of Saint Helena won by his forebear, a veteran of Napoleon's campaigns.

Very soon, the yellow cardboard sign was replaced by a large red sign announcing: "Under the management of an Aryan commissioner-manager appointed pursuant to the German decree of October 18, 1940." Honors from another age no longer adorned the disgraced storefronts. Eight days after the decree, Pétain met Hitler at Montoire and announced that France would henceforward collaborate officially with Germany.

Up till then our lives had been no different from those of other Frenchmen and women. I was a baby who, like so many others, had set out on the road to exodus with her mother and uncle, ending up far from anywhere. Returning to Paris, my parents had moved back into their apartment and went back to earning their living. We were privileged.

In the ensuing months we became pariahs.

---

33. In the Battle of Verdun.

Fit for... Aryanization!

Jacques and Moïse were dispossessed of their little fabric store, their liveli-hood, at the beginning of 1941.

Nineteen forty-one was a ghastly year! It made manifest the widening gulf between the French and the Jews! It wasn't the worst of those dark years. But it was the first. Acts of violence followed upon each other at a seemingly leisurely, yet deliberate bureaucratic pace normally associated with less urgent legal questions or minor regulations.

There was one piece of good news for the former members of the Sep-hardi Youth. After eight months in captivity, Oscar Arditti, their favorite friend, had succeeded in escaping from the Stalag, aided by his wife Lily. How had she done it?

"Oh," says Jenny, "it was quite a saga. Lily told me about it when we went hunting for food, usually followed by whispered conversations at her place or mine. There wasn't much to eat, but we had plenty to say. Oscar was the shrewdest and smartest man I'd ever known; he managed to escape the barbed wire of his Stalag by getting himself recruited as an interpreter and car mechanic at Beauraing, in Belgium, then as a railroad worker in Charleville."

"How did you find out about that?"

"He communicated with Lily through Thérèse, a girl in Charleville who was rooming in the building where Oscar and four other prisoners of war were housed alongside German rail workers."

"Was she the one who wrote the letters?"

"No, he did that, in his handwriting, which his wife would recognize. But he signed with the girl's name. They had a code, a distinctive sign they'd agreed on before the war, a signature ending with a curl signifying 'a true and certified document.' Otherwise, it would be just a normal signa-ture with no special sign."

"And that's how they planned the escape?"

"Yes. That's how Oscar asked Lily to get him some civilian clothes, the ones railroad workers wore at the time: caps, berets, pullovers, vests, and city pants to pass unnoticed. And she got them to him."

"Did he have accomplices?"

"The man guarding him was from the Sudetenland and didn't much like the Germans. At one point they were ordered to distribute anthracite pellets brought by rail cars to various German units. Oscar got himself the job of driver. He suggested to his guard that they sell part of the coal to poor French people and share the profit. He arranged his escape and that of four companions with the paid help of the Sudeten guard."

And so, on January 18, 1941, Oscar Arditti and four fellow escapees arrived at the Gare du Nord in Paris thanks to their Sudeten guard, who pocketed the money and vanished.

Lily was waiting for him at her brother's place on the Rue de Rivoli. She spent the night at Jacques and Jenny's place, a good thing too, because at seven the next morning the Gestapo turned up at her apartment, only to find it empty, of course. Oscar and Lily embraced quickly. Jacques hugged his old friend from Sofia. There was no time to lose. Lily figured out a hiding place, or rather a hideout, until she found some way to cross into the Free Zone.

"Oscar was a kind of Ulysses," Jenny reflects. "Twice he returned to his Ithaca. But the first time, his captivity was almost... benign. We all thought we were in a bad way in 1941, but of the black hole awaiting us we had no idea."

Around that time, Benrey et Fils, the store selling silken goods, woolens, and hosiery where Moïse and Jacques made their living to support their families, was handed over to a French "provisional administrator," a figure who came to acquire disproportionate importance in this first year of the plundering of the Jews. He would decide if a business was to be sold or liquidated, if it deserved to be Aryanized or not, i.e., transformed into a respectable, native business.

The Benreys' administrator's name was Charles Quantin, appointed in February. In a letter dated June 17 of that year he reported that he had verified the accounts of Benrey et Fils and was freezing the firm's bank account at Crédit Commercial de France. He also stated the nationalities of the two partners, Moïse Benrey, Jewish and Italian, and Jacques Benrey, Jewish and Bulgarian "by choice," in a letter to *Monsieur le président du service de contrôle des administrateurs provisoires*, the official overseeing the work of the provisional administrators.

This mention of their nationalities was devastating news. Italian Jews were a special case in the early days of the war and the German occupation. The Italians, allies of Vichy and the Germans, as indeed the Spaniards, Portuguese, Turks, and nationals of other neutral countries, began to worry about their interests once their citizens' property became liable to Aryanization. To prevent this property from falling under the control of the Vichy government, they arranged for it to be put in the hands of Italian administrators reporting to the Italian consulates. The task of untangling this mess fell to Xavier Vallat, the new Commissioner-General for Jewish Questions, appointed in March.

In spring 1941 Charles Quantin, the French provisional administrator, was relieved of his duties by the top brass in the administration of the *Militärbefehlshaber*, the military governor in France, and Moïse Benrey's store, being owned by an Italian, was placed in the hands of an Italian administrator. During the handover, the Frenchman took an inventory of the stock and concluded: "this firm is well-run and does continuous and regular business. It is the only firm of its kind in the area, serving a retail clientele. I consider," he concluded, "that it would be worthwhile continuing in business and Aryanizing it."

The principle was clear and effective: for a property belonging to an Italian there had to be an Italian provisional administrator. And for a firm well-run by a Jew, there had to be an Aryanization procedure.

Relations with the Italian administrator Signor Giuffrida were not bad, it seems, since Moïse Benrey still went to his store every day. Jacques gave up, on the other hand. But he did continue as distributor of anti-parasite treatments for the *Groupement interprofessionnel de répartition de produits indispensables à l'agriculture*, a farm products marketing consortium, especially for a firm in Angoulême run by a certain Monsieur Blois. Meantime, like so many Jewish storekeepers banned from working in their own stores, he wandered the streets of Paris dejectedly, whiling away his idleness meeting friends wherever he could, since they were barred from everywhere.

It was from his clandestine hideout in the 9th Arrondissement of Paris that in September 1941 Oscar Arditti, about to leave for Marseille and always first with the latest news, told him about the French decrees promulgated pursuant to the German ones. Oscar also told him about the second (French) statute on the Jews.

"The French statute is even more drastic than the German one," commented Oscar bitterly.

"You mean the statute dictated to the French by the occupier," replied Jacques, who rejected the notion that this France that had opened its arms to them could be the cause of such misery. The France of which the Ashkenazim used to say: "Happy as God in France."

"Jacques, wake up! It's the French who are stoking the fires. And watch out. We met in Sofia. We went to the same school. But at least I've got a French passport, whereas you've stayed Bulgarian. That makes you an undesirable!"

"We're both 'Aryano-Latin Sephardites of Israelite Faith,'" remarked Jacques with irony. "That's how our religious association came to sign the memorandum it submitted to the Commissioner for Jewish Questions. And at the same time, it contacted Franco's government to get it to accept us back into Spain—which had kicked us out long before the Germans."

"Listen to me, Jacques. I learned a lot during my captivity, talking to the people around me. Hitler isn't only making war on the English and the Soviets, now. He's making war on the Jews. And that's his priority. He wants not just to win the war but to wipe us out too. He's mad, Jacques. Utterly mad! Take your family and clear out of here."

"Clear out? But where to?"

"Anywhere! I'm heading for the Free Zone. At least there's no census there."

"But the Allies? The Russians?"

"They won't lift a finger for us. Not till *their* victory. I repeat. For Hitler, the Allies are just the puppets of the Jews, 'our puppets.' You'll see, this is just the beginning!"

Jenny confirms this in her *Monologue*: "Indeed, it was just the beginning. The decrees and orders rained down on us. We had become second-class citizens, then third-class, then we ceased to be citizens. Finally, we'd ceased to be humans.

"I and my daughter were entitled to food coupons. Not Jacques, being Bulgarian. But very soon all that counted for nothing when the roundups began. The worst of the worst were the roundups. We never knew when it would be our turn. Most of us were completely in the dark, even after the event. But my father Saby generally knew through the B'nai B'rith, and with each new roundup Marie would hang out her sheet, which we got to loathe, on her balcony, calling out 'Hou, hou.'

"There were three big roundups that year and three times the fated signal would go up on Rue Bouchut. The first was on May 14. It was called the 'Green ticket roundup' because the victims had been sent a green document ordering them to show up, accompanied by a member of their family, for a 'review of their situation.'

"That was for stateless Jews, who had already fled Germany and Poland. Just the men. We couldn't imagine that someday they'd come for the women and children."

The recollection was eloquent. They were stateless. They were men, not women or children. They were the "others."

But two major events, ones that revived the hopes of Jenny and her family, sparked a wave of Resistance attacks, which in turn triggered roundups in reprisal. On June 22, Hitler attempted the gamble that had destroyed the Emperor Napoleon. He invaded the Soviet Union. This move prompted France's young communists to enter the underground struggle. An attack on a German officer threw more than four thousand two hundred Jews into the camp at Drancy. A minority of these, Jews with French nationality, were arrested in the 11th Arrondissement of Paris.

On December 7, 1941, Hitler's ally Japan attacked the United States at Pearl Harbor, bringing America into the war against the Axis. Further Resistance attacks were a pretext for a third roundup in December. This time seven hundred and sixty-nine French Jews were picked up, including members of the "elite," prominent members of the community, who were sent to the camp at Compiègne, along with three hundred prisoners from Drancy. Eighty hostages were shot, including fifty-three Jews.

By now the pawns were in position on the Apocalyptic chessboard. Humanity held its breath, blind to the physical elimination of an entire people now ramping up in the East.

On October 31, 1941, I was two. My grandmother, Marie the Romanian, whom I called *Nonamali* because I couldn't yet pronounce the *r*, had made dinner in her apartment. She had procured some flour and eggs on the black market. She made ersatz *borekas* with ersatz cheese, and a kind of ersatz *sotlatch*. I have no recollection of this birthday, but Jenny told me about it with damp eyes and a husky voice.

That day, *Nonamali* and her brother Nissim were worried for their sister Esterina in Bucharest. There had been no news of her for weeks.

That day, Moïse quarreled with Aldo Giuffrida, the store's provisional administrator who decided everything and ordered him around.

That day, Jacques was still mulling over his friend Oscar's urging to "Get out of here!," while Jenny cursed the young terrorists who were provoking the shooting of hostages. She was unaware that one of those "terrorists" was sitting among us.

That day, this little family, ours, was still together in the apartment at 2, Rue Thimonnier, in the 9th Arrondissement of Paris.

Terrorist or resister

The doorbell rang on the fourth-floor apartment, Rue Pérignon, on Saturday afternoon, January 10, 1942. It was the French police.

Jenny, Jacques and Michou had come for the afternoon to celebrate what people soon no longer dared call "Shabbos" with Marie and Saby. I was two and a bit, so I have no direct memory of the event. My uncle Marcel was seventeen and a half and was in the upper sixth at the Lycée Buffon. Keeping out of trouble, or so we thought.

Since the entry of the Soviet Union into the war, the Germans were hunting down young communist terrorists in the Occupied Zone. There had been attacks on German officers in August. In October too. Since then, there had been a spate of yellow and red posters announcing the execution of hostages in reprisal against "foreign" spies and terrorists. But this did not concern the Amon-Benveniste family, protected by its French nationality.

Marie had little reason to worry when she heard the doorbell ring, until she saw her son Marcel in handcuffs, flanked by two policemen.

"Madame Amon? Criminal Police."

"What's it about?"

"Your son has just been arrested at school. We'd like to search his room."

"There must be some mistake, Officer! See for yourself."

Marie was convinced Marcel was innocent; he was just a teenager; a child, practically. Still, he was Jewish. "The question of his Jewish identity didn't come up," says Jenny.

While the family huddled in deathly silence, the policemen searched the bedroom, opening and emptying drawers, prodding the mattress... but overlooking the wood-fired stove, stuffed with flyers. That was the first stroke of luck.

The youngster looked on expressionless. Passing by his sister he whispered:

"Get Marc to let Rolande know."

Rolande? Jenny had no idea who she was. But Marc Amon and his sister Renée, the children of one of Saby's brothers, were Marcel's favorite cousins and he was always holed up at their place.

Marcel left with the French police in an unmarked car. His mother and her sister Andrée raced around all the Paris prisons searching for him. They finally learned he was at the *Santé*, but when they reached that prison, they were told he'd been moved to Fresnes because he was a minor.

According to the public records, "On the orders of the Occupation authorities," Marcel had indeed been taken to the General Intelligence Division at Police Headquarters, where he had been held for a few days, then to the *Santé*, and then to Fresnes. He was indicted for "participation in the constitution of a National Front committee" among the students, and for "clandestine communist propaganda."

According to the document dated February 14, 1942, written the day after his release, "in the course of his interrogation by the police superintendent," Marcel Amon stated that "he abstained from all political activity on account of his Israelite origin." Indicted for violation of the September 26, 1939, decree, on February 12, 1942, he was ordered to be released provisionally. Finally, on February 13, 1942, the day of his release, he signed the following statement: "I the undersigned Amon, Marcel, declare that I disapprove of clandestine communist action in all its forms. I freely undertake on my honor not to engage in future, whether directly or through a third party, in any form of communist activity."

"The second stroke of luck," says Jenny, "is that he was still a minor."

Pierre Daix[34], who had already reached his majority, was handed over to the Germans. He went from the *Santé* prison to the one at Clairvaux before being deported to the concentration camp at Mauthausen. Conditions at Fresnes were less harsh, but it was freezing cold that January. The prison governor allowed Marcel to be sent a sleeping bag and authorized his parents to visit him in his own office. Marcel was also allowed a lawyer and trial.

Marie didn't sleep for six weeks. The case was under investigation by an examining magistrate, and in mid-February the lawyers had high hopes of being able to extricate the two youngsters from the claws of the penitentiary system.

"At last, we were told he was going to be released, that we should pick him up at the *Conciergerie*[35]. We took the first metro, my mother and I, and we turned up at the prison. Robert Canou's mother was there too. The three of us waited for hours for the promised release, among prostitutes who had been arrested during the night. Neither of the two came out. There was a rumor they were going to be placed in a halfway house in Poissy. We phoned the lawyer who came and told us to go home."

Dejected, Marie and Jenny did so, and at three in the afternoon received a phone call from Marcel, who was at the Pasteur metro station:

"Jenny, come and get me. I'm crawling with lice. I can't come home like this."

His sister went to fetch him and ran him a hot bath.

According to Jenny, my young uncle enjoyed a third stroke of good fortune: not only the prison governor at Fresnes but also the judge investigating the case harbored "sympathy," she says, for the budding Resistance and its young "terrorists."

One senses an element of a rancor on the subject of Marcel's "baraka"[36] compared to Kiko's tragic lack of it. But who was he in reality, this Marcel

---

34. Later a leading communist journalist and art critic, friend and biographer of Pablo Picasso [Translator].

35. The medieval fortress on the *Île de la Cité* in the heart of Paris that housed the headquarters of the French Criminal Police [Translator].

36. A word commonly used in French to signify good fortune, derived from Eastern religions, signifying "indwelling spiritual force" and "divine gift" [Translator].

Amon, the younger brother who kept overshadowing Jenny, the apple of Marie's eye, son of the elder son of the Amons and of the elder daughter of the Benvenistes, and whose bar mitzvah had been a highlight in the life of the family in the 1930s? Jenny's portrait of him is incomplete. All that remains are bits and pieces of the eccentric biography of a boy who was the icon of my childhood, mysteriously Janus-faced, hero and impostor.

In his sister's telling, he had a rebel's temperament, a subversive who obeyed no one, an impetuous hothead, she says. Idolized by his mother. His early adolescence coincided with the outbreak of war. He was courageous, with a courage "bordering on reckless," says Jenny. Above all he loved practical jokes, making up details to embellish a tawdry or trivial reality. His parents, born Oriental Jews, had leaped several centuries in a single generation: he thought them rigid and conventional, but he never tackled them head-on. He preferred to conceal things likely to upset them, serving up tall stories to reassure them. In return, the young man flouted every convention and got himself into all kinds of scrapes in a time of violence and excess, an age well-suited to characters like his.

For he really was a child of his time, young Marcel, so like Cocteau's *enfants terribles* or the characters in Sartre's plays. His Jessica was called Rolande L., a very pretty brunette with green eyes and a wasp waist. She came from a middle-class Catholic family against whose standards she rebelled. Marcel and Rolande in 1940 were like Bonnie and Clyde in Paris, fearless lovers who attended banned demonstrations, kissed on park benches in full sight of the Germans and maybe planted bombs on rails and machine-gunned officers in field gray uniform.

He had met Rolande at his cousins,' Marc and Renée Amon. But he never breathed a word of her existence to his close family. And Jenny was still in the dark as to who this young woman was when she went to warn the cousins.

What she did know was that her kid brother was an ardent music lover and that he "composed" music. Marcel and his brother-in-law Jacques, the violinist from Sofia, shared this passion. They were unconditional admirers of Yehudi Menuhin and before the war they went to hear Charles Munch conduct at the Opera.

Marcel imposed a change of vocabulary in the family.

"Let's stop saying 'Jewish,'" he suggested. "Let's say 'musicians.' It sounds better."

So, Jenny went to tell Cousin Marc to warn Rolande, of whom she knew nothing. And she certainly did not know that Marc too was deeply involved with the *Éclaireurs Israélites* de France, a Jewish scouting group that was also a form of resistance.

There had to be some way to get this *enfant terrible* to safety in the Free Zone. In the spring, the Rue Pérignon building's concierge, the trusty Monsieur Charles, was given instructions and cash to escort the young resister across the demarcation line via Jarnac, a town on the border between the two zones, where he had a contact.

"So, Monsieur Charles, you've taken him to Lyon, where he's now in a safe place?"

"They've both reached safety, Monsieur Amon, your son... and Mademoiselle Rolande."

Yet another surprise out of the blue for Saby and Marie. "Mademoiselle Rolande" was not part of the travel plan. The young lady's family took it even worse and threatened to sue the cheeky fellow's father—a Jew into the bargain! —for abduction of a minor, if the girl wasn't returned forthwith to her home in the Occupied Zone. Marcel and his Rolande crossed the line before completing his high school graduation. He never did graduate.

In a fourth stroke of luck for Marie's favorite child, he knew nothing of the fate of his fellow pupils. Those high school kids were shot by firing squad less than two years later.

Buffon's way: the Five, the Seven, and the arms of wrath

For Marcel and the other students at the Lycée Buffon, it all began in fall 1940, during a class run by a very determined teacher. In the summer already, Raymond Burgard had festooned German barracks with banners proclaiming, "Long live de Gaulle." On September 20 he founded a resistance group and newspaper, *Valmy*, with some friends. Burgard, a Christian and humanist intellectual, came from Alsace and had joined a left-leaning Catholic movement, *Jeune République*, Young Republic, before the war. In his classes and in his newspaper the teacher called on the French to "rattle their chains, not to become a people of running dogs, not to lick the boots of the Prussians." Pupils flocked to him, his own students and those in other classes, drawn by word of mouth. Among them were Marcel Amon and the "Five": Lucien Legros, Pierre Benoît, Pierre Grelot, Jacques Baudry and Jean-Marie Arthus.

This subversive, fledgling resistance took the form of heckling teachers suspected of Vichy sympathies—Marcel and his friends were quick to pounce—or slipping a leaflet into a book as they leafed through it in the Gibert bookstore. More than anyone else, Marcel went handing out National Front leaflets everywhere in the Latin Quarter, in cafés even. While a comrade threw them into the Café Cluny, starting on the upper floor, the Benoit brothers threw theirs out from the platform at the back of a bus going down the Boulevard Saint-Michel. Marcel rode around on a bicycle creating a diversion.

The first acts of sabotage were being committed around this time: phone and telegraph lines were cut and occupying army equipment was destroyed. Many more direct attacks on the occupier followed.

On May 11, 1941, Marcel, Rolande, Marc Amon and their Lycée Buffon companions stood before the statue of Joan of Arc, on the Place des Pyramides. Raymond Burgard, the schoolteacher, struck up the *Marseillaise*, which had been banned by the occupier. The youngsters joined in, under the noses of the Germans.

The Communist Party launched the National Front, to which Marcel Amon made no secret of his membership, on May 27, 1941, as a "National front for the independence of France" and appealed to "all who wish to act in France," to the exclusion of "capitulators and traitors," against "national oppression."

But it was above all after the German invasion of the Soviet Union in the summer of 1941 that the French young communists organized to harass the occupier. Another demonstration took place on August 13 in the République district of Paris. The flag bearer was none other than Pierre Daix, and its organizer was Pierre George, who came to be known as Colonel Fabien. The French police called in the Germans, who opened fire and arrested demonstrators. Two, including one nicknamed Titi, were condemned to death, and executed on August 19 in the Bois de Verrières, a suburb south of Paris.

Fabien, the demonstration's organizer, was aged twenty. He was a veteran of the International Brigades in Spain and feared nothing. He swore revenge. On the morning of August 21, 1941, he was standing on the platform of the Barbès metro station with three comrades to protect him. One of them told Marcel the details:

"At that moment, a young officer wearing a cap and navy-blue outfit stepped onto the platform. Fabien told me: 'That's the one that's going to pay.' The train entered the station, and the first-class car came to stop in front of us. The officer boarded straight away, and Fabien shot him in the back with two 6.35 mm bullets. Fabien rushed for the exit. 'Titi's been avenged!' was all he shouted."

It was still possible to demonstrate. On November 8, Marcel took part in a demonstration of high school boys and girls against the arrest of a communist professor.

Three days later, he answered the call of General de Gaulle in London inviting the French to place flowers on the Tomb of the Unknown Soldier. Many responded, and within the crowd the rallying cry "Buffon, we're here!" was heard.

This time, the French police began their repression, backed up shortly by the German army. Twelve Lycée Buffon students were arrested, including Marcel's companion Pierre Daix, who was sentenced to his first spell in the Santé prison. Among demonstrators or prisoners released were the members of the Group of Five, a Jewish metalworker from Salonika who was the first to shoot German officers, on Rue Lafayette. Tony Bloncourt was there too, a member of the "Group of Seven," young resisters from the 11th Arrondissement of Paris. Marcel's file mentions Bloncourt as a "recently-arrested terrorist," to whom Daix had allegedly supplied "false identity papers."

In December, some of Marcel's teachers at Buffon, Lévy, Dreyfus, and Cahen were dismissed from the school. An Irishman whom Raymond Burgard had recruited to his resistance network narrowly escaped arrest by the Gestapo. His name was Samuel Beckett, future Nobel laureate. That winter, the high school students, including Marcel, formed a federation.

Pierre Benoit recruited Pierre Grelot. Lucien Legros recruited Jean-Marie Arthus. All four joined the National Front, of which Jacques Baudry was an active member.

Marcel and his coconspirator Robert Canou narrowly escaped being caught in the net, having been arrested in January 1942.

Tony Bloncourt and the Group of Seven were less fortunate. On March 4, 1942, two months after Marcel Amon's release, a mockery of a public trial opened in a room at the Chamber of Deputies: "Seven red terrorists were tried before the Paris Council of War." The Prosecutor held them responsible for the executions of hostages ordered by the German Commander in Chief. The seven youngsters were condemned to death as "gunmen and for having taken part in repeated and concerted acts of violence against the German army and its members." The accusation was signed by the Commander in Chief of Greater Paris.

Marcel had already made his way to the Free Zone when his friends from the Group of Five went underground following the Gestapo's arrest of their teacher Raymond Burgard, in April 1942. Sentenced by a German court, Burgard was later beheaded with an ax in a prison courtyard in Cologne.

The Five turned to armed struggle. They shot a German officer on Quai Malaquais in Paris, attacked another on Rue de Vaugirard, and threw a grenade onto guests at a reception aboard a launch on the River Seine. Four of them were turned in and sentenced to forced labor for life, while the last of them, Pierre Benoit, fought on alone, carrying out numerous acts of sabotage against the railroad and aerodromes, before being caught and handed over to the Gestapo. The Five were tried before a Luftwaffe court in October and sentenced to death for "participation in attacks on the German army."

Of the five youngsters, Lucien Gros was doubtless closest to Marcel. He was the same age, had a passion for poetry and painting, and above all was an excellent pianist. It was he, probably, who had introduced Marcel to music and played the pieces Marcel "composed."

None was allowed a farewell visit. They were dragged from their cells at dawn and left for the execution site at Issy-les-Moulineaux with a song on their lips. There they were shot between five and eleven in the morning of February 8, 1943.

Each wrote a farewell letter before leaving to be executed. Lucien Legros wrote: "My darling parents, my darling brother, I'm going to be shot with my comrades. We are going to die with a smile on our lips because it is for a fine ideal. At this moment I feel I've lived a full life... Rebuild a lovely family... I received your splendid parcel on Thursday. I ate like a king. I've thought long and hard over these last four months. My examination of my conscience is positive. I am fully satisfied. Hello to everyone, my family and friends, I clasp you one last time to my heart[37]." Lucien Legros wasn't even twenty on the day of his execution.

The youngest of them, Jean-Marie Arthus, whose mother was dead already, wrote to his father: "My darling father, I don't know if you expected to see me again... We heard today that this was the end. So, goodbye! I know this is a very heavy blow for you but, I hope you will have the strength and that you will go on living, confident in the future. Go on working. Do it for me, go on with the books you wanted to write, think that I die as a Frenchman, for my homeland. I embrace you. Farewell, my darling father[38]." Jean-Marie Arthus was still not eighteen on the day he was shot. He looks so boyish on the last photo taken of him.

Slightly denting the impression left by these heroic deaths, reports of their interrogation casts them in a slightly less flattering light. Asked who gave the orders and who followed them, Jacques Baudry accused Pierre Grelot, who accused Pierre Benoit. But who can blame a kid who cracks under torture? This merely shows things weren't that simple, and that goodness is a fragile thing.

The poet Paul Éluard was a friend of Lucien Legros' family. He wrote this short piece in homage to the five young Lycée Buffon students executed:

The night before his death
Was the shortest of his life
The thought he still lived
Boiled the blood in his veins
[...]

---

37. "Lettre de Lucien Legros," in *La vie à en mourir, Lettres de fusillés 1941-1944* (Letter from Lucien Legros, in *Dying to Live*, Letters from the executed 1941-1944), éditions Tallandier, 2003.

38. "Lettre de Jean-Marie Arthus," *ibid.*

In the depths of this horror
He started to smile
He had not ONE friend
But millions upon millions
And the day dawned for him.[39]

Destiny: the oldest of the Five was twenty-one on the day of his execution. Had they lived till the moment I write this sentence, Pierre Benoit and Jean-Marie Arthus wouldn't even be ninety years old, with a whole life behind them. Destiny: Marcel Amon, meanwhile, crossed the demarcation line, traveled to Grenoble, joining up with his resistance network and heading for the Vercors and the *maquisards*.

Spring Breeze

Marie did not hang her sheet over the balcony of the apartment facing ours in January 1942. For good reason. The Final Solution had just been decided in great secrecy at the conference on the Wannsee. The whole vocabulary of the killing machine was pushed into the shadows, to be supplanted by euphemisms. The planned annihilation of the Jews was dubbed "Operation Spring Breeze," "deportation to the East" became "Population Resettlement"; "Shower" meant "gas chamber."

More than five thousand people were dying already in the Warsaw ghetto. Places of suffering and death were springing up with barely murmured names such as Belzec, Chelmno, Sobibor, Treblinka, Auschwitz, Birkenau... Gas, Zyklon B was being used to exterminate people in trucks and purpose-built chambers. Jews were being massacred by the dozen, shortly by the hundreds of thousands, in the Russian territories occupied by the Wehrmacht.

Jacques and Jenny still had no inkling of what was going on.

In March 1942 Saby heard that a convoy of Jews deported from the

---

39. This translation from the French is due to Denis Holler and R. Howard Bloch, *A New History of French Literature*, Harvard University Press.

Drancy and Compiègne camps had left France for Auschwitz. There were many French Jews among them, a point that was missed on Saby. Destination "unknown." He heard something about salt mines in Poland or forced labor camps in Germany. He went home, wolfed down the rutabaga, their daily staple. And said nothing to his wife.

That spring 1942, a handful of men held the lives of Jenny, Jacques, me, and millions of others, in their hands. Pierre Laval returned to the Vichy government. In June, Adolf Eichmann came to Paris to demand the deportation of *all* Jews in France. Vichy clung to its "nationals" but sought to get rid of the "undesirables," the foreigners in both zones, by shipping them eastward. The Nazis needed the French police to arrest the Jews. It was a win-win situation. The French authorities loaned their police to do the dirty work. In return, the Germans left the French Jews alone, for the time being.

They quarreled over figures and quotas involving human material. They bargained, they haggled. Heydrich reckoned the Jewish people numbered a total of eleven million. He wanted to make them disappear. All of them. But how? Theodore Dannecker, Heydrich's representative in Paris, wanted a hundred thousand—for the time being. France gave him forty thousand over three months. Even then, they had to raise the age of women eligible for deportation from forty to forty-five to fill the quota. These haggling tradesmen were trafficking in human lives. They had to keep up their numbers. But to deport more people they had to count them. And what better way than to brand them?

From June 7, 1942, onward, all Jews, French, stateless and foreign whose country of origin required them to wear the sign of shame, were obliged to wear the yellow star in the Occupied Zone. All Jews aged over six were ordered to sew onto their clothes a six-pointed star the size of the palm of a hand, with a dark edge. The star had to be made of yellow cloth and bear the inscription "Jew" in black letters. It had to be worn visibly on the left-hand side of the chest. The star did not come free. Jews had to hand over one textile coupon for three stars at the police precinct.

Jenny was French. She sewed it on her clothes.

Jacques was Bulgarian. He didn't have to for the time being.

I was under six. I was to serve as camouflage. Jenny no longer went out without holding me in her arms to hide her mark of infamy.

In France, our fate hung in the balance in July 1942.

Jacques and Jenny were allowed to do their shopping only between 3 and 4 in the afternoon, when there was nothing left in the stores.

They could no longer listen to the radio, not even the occupier's radio. They missed the BBC and its "French talking to the French" through the voice of Pierre Dac, with his rhyming punchline: "*Radio Paris ment. Radio Paris est allemand*" (Radio Paris lies. Radio Paris is German).

They were barred from going to movies or the theater. But Jenny and Jacques no longer wanted to go to the movies. What was the point if it was just to see the antisemitic "*Le Péril Juif*" (the Jewish peril) or "*Le Juif Süss*," which had a long run in the movie theaters?

Had they not been complete pariahs, they could have gone to hear public concerts given by the Germans once or twice a week in the Jardins de Luxembourg, or in the Jardin de Paris on the Champs-Élysées. But Jacques and Jenny didn't want to, now that the *Compagnie du chemin de fer métropolitain* railroad company relegated them to the last car of the subway, renamed the "synagogue." They no longer took the Metro if they could avoid it. Their telephone was cut off. They were forbidden to use the public callboxes. Barred from restaurants, cafés, cinemas, theaters, concerts, the music hall, swimming pools, beaches, museums too. No longer allowed to visit a chateau, an exhibition, or a historical monument. Racecourses, parks, campgrounds, and sports arenas were off-limits too.

I wasn't allowed to play in public gardens or, if old enough, to borrow a book from the public library.

In mid-June 1942, the Vichy government finalized the timetable for the deportation of foreign Jews: first the provinces in the northern Occupied Zone, then Greater Paris, finally the south, Free Zone. The Nazis looked farther ahead: they wanted all the Jews in France. Otherwise, today's France would become tomorrow's Poland. The thought shook Pétain, who caved in, and then did so again.

On the evening of July 15, a white rag appeared in the window of Marie's and Saby's apartment. Saby had seen a pamphlet in Yiddish urging those concerned, Germans, Austrians, Poles, Czechs, Russians, and stateless persons, to resist by all available means, to bar their doors, call for help, fight the police. They had nothing to lose. They were exhorted to save their lives, to flee if need be.

"It concerns recent immigrants," averred Jenny. "Not us?"

"No, not us," Marie concurred.

"They'd better keep their men out of sight!"

That's what they did. The fathers went into hiding, leaving their wives and children. The French police, finding the fathers gone, took the mothers and children. Those rounded up were held first in the police precincts, schools and garages dubbed "primary rallying centers," then at the *Vélodrome d'Hiver*[40] for families. The hell that was the Vel d'Hiv lasted till July 22, a week.

What did Saby and Marie know of this tragedy? If they did know, they said nothing. Jenny cannot recall any further details. Whatever really happened at the Vel d'Hiv, she didn't find out at first. Nor did she want to know. She closed her ears to reports—if any.

Yet rumors travel. At the speed of light. They permeated snatches of conversation, slipped into the gaps of the unspoken, conveyed between the whisperings of total strangers yet who instinctively recognize each other as the expiatory victims of the upcoming batch.

Did Jenny hear these reports that surfaced fifty years later, taking the place of my pen just as I try to enfold within these few lines the abomination of that year, 1942?

Take Hélène Berr, for example, then working for her advanced degree in English literature, five years younger than Jenny. In her diary for Saturday July 18, she wrote: "...Some of the children they took had to be dragged along the floor. In Montmartre there were so many arrests that the streets were jammed. Faubourg Saint-Denis has nearly been emptied. Mothers have been separated from their children... In Mademoiselle Monsaingeon's neighborhood, a whole family, the father, the mother and five children, gassed themselves to escape the roundup. One woman threw herself out of a window"[41].

---

40. The winter cycle racetrack, which became a notorious holding center for arrested Jews before they were sent to concentration camps [Translator].

41. Excerpt translated by David Bellos, Weinstein Books, New York, 2008

There was Jacques Bielinski, for example. In an article in the paper *L'Univers israélite* he noted that at the same time, nearly four thousand Jewish children were on their way to the Loiret department, some still accompanied by their parents, others alone. They arrived at the Vel d'Hiv "a terrified look in their eyes, faces drawn, aged, well-dressed little girls, and little children from the working-class 20th Arrondissement, cherubs of sixteen months and little eight-year-old men."

Did Jenny want to know that on the last day of July and in early-August, mothers were brutally separated from their children and deported, that little children were not allowed to leave in the same convoys as their parents but were held in the camp to await the children's trains? That, at the end of August, practically no one remained in the camps at Pithiviers and Beaune-la-Rolande? That the parents were taken to Auschwitz at the beginning of August? That in a few days, their heads shaven and after being searched thoroughly and brutally, small children too were sent to an "unknown destination"? All alone? That a certain Édith Thomas, archivist, journalist and resistant, described such a convoy passing: "At the head, a wagon carrying French gendarmes and German soldiers. Then came the cattle wagons. Sealed. The scrawny arms of children clutched the bars. A hand hanging outside waved like a leaf in a storm. When the train slowed, voices cried out: 'Mama!' No one answered save the squeal of axles."

A deported person by the name of Georges Kohn jotted down a single word in his notebook at Drancy: "Pity." Pity, that overworked word, saved none of these little ones deported that summer, 1942. Not one returned.

I, Michou, did not understand till much later what all that signified. It signified that children like me, perhaps not even aged three, were torn from their parents and thrown into cattle-wagons that took them to slaughterhouses. Only a chance birth in Brittany and a little booklet called a "passport," obtained by my grandfather twenty years beforehand, separated me—*provisionally*—from the fate of those children in the Vel d'Hiv.

For Jenny, that "provisionally" was to determine her survival strategies from then on.

In the other camp, that of the Vichy French leadership, a bureaucratic dilemma arose: what to do with the children if the parents are rounded up?

What to do with these little undesirables not included by the Germans in the first convoys deporting their parents? What to do with me should my father, and then my mother and the rest, be taken away? Snatching children from their parents in public looks bad, and the authorities feared the impact on opinion of searing scenes of separation.

During the evacuation of Jewish families from the Free Zone, Laval told Dannecker:

"Take the children aged under sixteen!"

"And what about Jewish children still in the Occupied Zone?"

"I'm not interested!"

Eichmann agreed over the phone, then by telex, to "the deportation of stateless Jewish children in suitable proportions."

From that time on convoys of children rolled eastward, to general indifference or ignorance.

Did Laval have any better idea than Jenny of what "unknown destination" meant? He gave his answer in an interview with the Protestant theologian Pastor Boegner, which the latter relates thus: "What could I obtain from a man who had been led by the Germans to believe—or who pretended to believe—that the Jews taken from France were going to Southern Poland to till land for the Jewish State, which Germany claimed it wanted to create? I spoke to him of massacre, he answered gardening."

Some Catholics understood straightaway, though. The first time Madame Troublé, who lived on the fourth floor at 8, Rue César-Franck, the apartment below us, saw Jenny in the elevator wearing her yellow star, she told her:

"If they come for you, put the child on the mat outside our service entrance."

Among these thousands of children from all over Europe about to be massacred, whose names are now listed in a darkened room in the Yad Vashem museum, I recall that of my first "fiancé." Or rather it was Jenny who recalled his face and passed it on to me. He was five, and I two.

"He was determined to marry you," remembers Jenny, "but on condition his mother taught you to cook, because he adored *borekas*."

He was deported with his mother in 1943. Gassed, very swiftly I hope, my little fiancé who so loved *borekitas*. You never had an adult's face and

Jenny—in an unwonted memory lapse—couldn't remember your name. No matter, it's you, among the millions of others, of whom I wish to sing.

In those troubled times I still lived in the apartment on Rue César-Franck with my father and mother. I'd no idea how lucky I was. The leaflet in Yiddish passed around before the Vel d'Hiv roundup concluded: "Every free and living Jew is a victory over our enemy; he must not, he does not have the right, he shall not permit our extermination."

At the end of the summer of 1942, I was still alive.

Rounding up Bulgarians

September 14, 1942. Two French policemen turned up at number 8 Rue César-Franck accompanied by Madame Chaliès, the concierge, to arrest "the Bulgarian Jew Benrey." They rang and rang again. The door stayed shut. With good reason: there was no one there.

"They won't get away that easily. We'll be back tomorrow."

Says Jenny: "For us, we knew the game was up the day the French police came for Jacques." By some incredible miracle we'd been warned they were coming for the Bulgarians.

"The night before, we'd heard dreadful rumors they were rounding up foreign Jews. But which? They were making arrests by nationality. At the Vel d'Hiv, they'd mainly taken the stateless people and the Poles. We were completely cut off: no radio or telephone. And there was the curfew. No way out.

"Now it so happened that my aunt Nelly, who'd kept her Greek nationality, still had her telephone. And Aunt Eda too. Don't ask me who Aunt Eda was but bless her! Aunt Eda's son had heard that they were going to arrest the Bulgarians the next day and she cast around for who was Bulgarian among the people she knew. Most of the Bulgarian Jews were Judeo-Spanish cousins. She thought of Jacques. She called Nelly around seven in the evening, in the middle of the curfew. Nelly lived near the Champ-de-Mars. She'd rather not send out her son, barely in his teens, to sound the alert and risk arrest himself. But the boy insisted: 'I've got to warn Cousin Jacques. It won't take long on my bike.'

"He jumped on his bicycle and raced over to his aunt Marie on the Rue

Pérignon, and just had time to tell her: 'They're coming for the Bulgarians tomorrow,' then rushed off again.

"Marie went to her window, put up her white sheet and called out 'Hou hou.'

"You were sleeping, so I woke you, took you in my arms, covering up the star. And all three of us crossed the road to sleep at my parents' place. We told the concierge Madame Chaliès where we were going. I can tell you, we didn't sleep a wink that night.

"Next morning, at seven, Madame Chaliès came across to the Rue Pérignon to tell us 'They came!'"

"We were more dead than alive, and we were discussing what to do when there came another ring on the doorbell. It was Madame Chaliès again, this time with Jacques' boss from Angoulême, Monsieur Blois. Jacques had continued working for him, and they had arranged to meet that morning to talk business. The concierge mistook him for another policeman at first. Understanding who he was, she took him across the street. Robert Blois was a truly good man and a bigwig in the city of Angoulême. He was head of two chemical and phosphate plants in Limoges, Union Française and SFEC. Jacques was the sales representative for an array of crop treatments: vine mildew treatments in Dordogne, Bordeaux mixture in Sarlat, and Dauby fertilizer in Normandy. Surprised at first, he quickly grasped the situation. 'I'll fix things. I'm going straight back to Angoulême. Meanwhile, go into hiding right away. You can't stay here.'

"Jacques went to hide in the Avenue de Breteuil, in a hideout someone else had used. That person had stayed with us then gone to the Free Zone in the south of France, leaving us the keys. There was no electricity or water, but Marie brought Jacques food and drink, taking care to cover her tracks. He holed up there for several days.

"As for me, I went back to the apartment with you, my baby daughter, in the evening... to save what I could ... Yes, back into the lion's den! But we weren't in much danger: we were French after all! Then Annie, Annie the fearsome nanny of my childhood, came to sleep at the apartment to give me courage. And together we put the place in order.

"The police rang the doorbell at dawn... I jumped out of my bed putting on my bathrobe: you didn't have to wear the star on that... and I screamed through the door as if it was my husband coming home from a pub crawl. I screamed, 'Liar…, bastard… Aren't you ashamed to be coming home at this time? And in front of your child! I'm not opening… and it isn't the first time… I'll never forgive you… You hear? Never! And don't ever think of coming back, you…'

"I kept up the performance for quite some time. Until they threatened above my yelling to break down the door, and I decided to open it. 'Calm down, Madame. Can you tell us where your husband is?' I carried on as before. I didn't know where he was. With his floozy, of course. And then I started up again… till they gave up.

"The policeman was French through and through, with globular fisheyes. His colleague by his side wore a dark raincoat, ice cold. Good Madame Chaliès had insisted on accompanying them.

"As they went back downstairs, she asked them: 'But why do you want to arrest these nice people? What have they done to you?' The policeman with the globular eyes looked at her and said: 'If you like these people, tell them we'll take *everything* they've got, and we'll take them *all.*'

"I slept another two or three nights there. Meanwhile, Monsieur Blois' employee, Monsieur Giraud, brought us two genuine forged identity cards in the names of Bourinet, Fernand and Bourinet, Germaine."

"And what about me?"

"You? You were Bourinet, Michèle, our daughter. But you weren't mentioned on the ID cards because the real Bourinets didn't have a daughter. I tried to teach you your new name, but you persisted in calling yourself Michèle Benrey. And you shouted it out, which nearly got us caught once. Jacques left straightaway for Angoulême with Monsieur Giraud. He didn't even have time to kiss his parents goodbye."

Jenny thought that by sitting in her apartment she could protect it from being sealed up, and that our previous French nationality, hers and mine, would shield us from arrest. True, it was better to be French than Bulgarian at the time. That was soon to change. It was changing already. But news traveled at the speed of a dead star, not that of light, though falling behind with the news could cost you more than your life.

"Then one evening," Jenny resumes, "things were going really badly and there were rumors that a big roundup was planned for the following morning, so you and I slept in the maid's room[42] on the Rue Pérignon. You wanted to go to the bathroom, which was dangerous as people could hear everything. I took fright and decided to go and join my husband with our false papers, since I couldn't travel under my real name and with my yellow star.

"Before that, I informed my parents-in-law, who still lived on Rue Thimonnier, on the other side of town. They rushed over on the eve of our departure. They were so eager to hug their granddaughter, to see you once more... As if they had ... a foreboding...

"*Nonamali* never stopped stroking you and bouncing you on her knees. Then suddenly she removed her engagement ring from her finger, with a little diamond; she always wore it. 'That's for Michou. I want it to be for Michou.' 'But she's too young. And in any case, you may need it.'

"She looked at Moïse, who agreed. 'Take it, Jenny. It'll be for Michou. We both want this.'

---

42. Maids' rooms, or *chambres de bonne* in French, were situated on the top floor of buildings. They were usually very spartan, with a toilet and washing facilities at the end of the corridor [Translator].

"What happened to the ring? Honestly, I've no idea. Lost! Or sold... I had to drag you away from them. My mother-in-law was sobbing. Even Moïse was weeping softly. I was in no better shape. But I had to take things in hand."

The next day, the faithful Madame Chaliès, and the counterfeit Michèle and Germaine Bourinet got ready to take the train for Angoulême. Jenny left her yellow star behind in Paris, not needed in the Free Zone. It was her first step outside the bounds of the law. Not wearing the star could have gotten her arrested immediately, but the forged papers would protect her. Jenny piled up a few personal belongings she didn't want to lose or sell—photos, letters, and documents, along with her school reports from the Lycée Victor-Duruy, including Blanche Maurel's comments on her—and the embossed silver platter from Salonika. She put them in Madame Chaliès' two maids' rooms on the eighth floor, Rue César-Franck, and left the rest in the apartment for the Germans and their French collaborators to pick over, trusting them to her guardian angel.

As soon as Jenny had turned her back on the place, the apartment was sealed up. Jenny, Jacques and Michou thus became "hunted beasts," in the words of a 1942 police report. Under a government order issued at the end of 1941, Jews and non-Jews lodging them had to register at the police precinct within twenty-four hours. For French citizens to have Jews living with one was to risk reprisals. There was no going home now. Still, even when on the run, Jacques and Jenny went on paying their rent. Even when they had no more money to pay for new hiding places.

There were no empty seats in the train, so the two women made the journey standing, Madame Chaliès holding me in her arms. When they reached the station at Angoulême, Jenny got out on one side, Madame Chaliès and me on the other. They had arranged that if Jenny was arrested Madame Chaliès would take the train back with me. No one asked for their papers and they met up outside the train station. Jenny hugged Sophie Chaliès warmly, and the latter went to the waiting room hoping to board the night train.

Destiny. History records that on that day, September 14, 1942, the French police rounded up a little over two hundred Jews with Bulgarian nationality, along with Latvian, Lithuanian, Estonian, Yugoslav and Dutch

Jews. If Jacques had been caught that day or the following day by the two French policemen come to fetch him, he would have been deported two days later, on September 16, and gassed in Auschwitz on the 18th, together with the other two hundred and eight who had had no Aunt Eda to forewarn them.

One live child for a dead hare ...

"No one was waiting for us at the Angoulême train station, so we two made our way to Rue de Bellegarde where Monsieur Blois had his office," Jenny continues. "My suitcase was very heavy, so I asked you to walk. You were nearly three. You didn't mind a little bit of a climb. I didn't want to take the bus because of the risk of having to show our papers. It was almost closing time when we arrived, but luckily Monsieur Giraud, Monsieur Blois' righthand man, was still there. He was amazed to see us. It wasn't planned, and the arrival of a woman and child complicated things. He called Jacques right away. We rushed to embrace. Once again, we were all together. Alive!"

A very ancient memory—I cannot say whether it was real or a later construct—wells up within me at the mention of this last episode recounted by Jenny: a Neptune-like figure with a salt-and-pepper beard, a pagan divinity with the cheerfulness of Santa Claus, who threw me in the air and caught me with a loud laugh. Was Monsieur Giraud that amiable giant who played with me?

While I dream of Giraud, Jenny talks about that other divinity in the form of a little round woman, with a wart and a hair growing from it at the corner of her mouth, namely Madame Chaliès, another "native-born" Frenchwoman who never for a moment hesitated to risk her own life for us, even though under no threat herself. "She came from the Auvergne," says Jenny. "Or more precisely from the Cantal, a charcoal burner and the wife of a *bougnat*[43]. They'd had a daughter called Lucie who'd died. They were inconsolable. Yes, they were devout Catholics, but above all generous

---

43. Small coal merchants who migrated from the *Massif Central* (including the Cantal district) and settled in Paris. They opened cafés that also sold coal and firewood [Translator].

people…. And they truly loved us. She told Jacques one day: 'Your wife is a pearl. A pearl!'

"Things were pretty bad in Angoulême. But we were together. We stayed in the house of a woman, a friend of Robert Blois. The room we slept in had been requisitioned by the Germans. They were out on maneuvers for the time being, but they could return at any moment. We had to act fast. This was still October 10, 1942. We celebrated our wedding anniversary by eating rabbit in the little restaurant next door. Rabbit! Rabbit stew on October 10, 1942!"

Lost in her gourmet musings, Jenny savored again her rabbit—which may have been a cat—eaten at a time when the Germans could have burst into her room at any moment. However trivial or futile it may seem, that tenth of October 1942 could be summed up in the imaginary diary of Jenny and Jacques Benrey as: "It's our wedding anniversary and we ate rabbit stew." Perhaps the key to that fixation on a rabbit lies in the following episode, featuring a rabbit once again—or rather a hare that was to save our lives.

Did Jacques and Jenny have any notion of their good fortune, thanks to the kindness of the freemason Robert Blois? He had helped more than one clandestine traveler across the demarcation line, graciously and free of charge at a time when professional smugglers were lining their pockets, and the price of a crossing had skyrocketed since the summer. Failure or betrayal spelled disaster. Shortly before, four hundred and forty men, women, children, and elderly people had been arrested trying to cross the line and sent directly from Poitiers to Drancy, and from there to a "destination unknown."

"It took Monsieur Blois three weeks to prepare the forged papers," Jenny recalled. "He knew the mayor of Écuras, who signed them. Écuras lay within the blessed Free Zone on the other side of the Vienne River. The real Bourinets from the Charente, who had been born in the little village, were supposed to be visiting land they owned near Écuras. And here we were, the false Bourinets, on our way in the wood-gas powered car that belonged to our benefactor, Robert Blois—a black Hotchkiss with a white hood. At La Rochefoucauld, the first frontier post separated in two by the line, the German sentry examined our *Ausweis*. Robert Blois, who had a business in Limoges, held out his renewable white one, and we presented ours, which was yellow, good for one journey. The German was suspicious. He peered inside the car. And then he spied a little girl of barely three sitting on my lap. 'Nein! The child... not on the papers!'

"Blois insisted, but to no avail! We had to go back from where we came, our hearts in our boots. But Robert Blois, a keen hunter on his family estate at Pontaroux and permit-holder for the Forest of La Braconne, didn't give up easily. 'I know another sentry who loves game. I'll promise him a rabbit or a hare. He loves that'.

"The Polish soldier at Chazelles was a normal human being with a solid appetite, and he took the bait. So, we crossed with you into the Southern Zone, which wasn't controlled by the Reich and the Nazis but by Pétain's government. Throughout the short trip, Monsieur Blois chatted affably to soothe our anxieties, explaining how this arbitrary demarcation line cut some farms, some fields even, in two. The line cut through the village of La Rochefoucauld, separating it from its own town hall. The cemetery of Chazelles, meanwhile, was in the Free Zone. A family of farmers in Bouëx, whom he knew well, also guided clandestine travelers across their land, which straddled the two zones, handing them over to an uncle who was mayor of a nearby village.

"Once we'd got to the other side of the line, we hugged Monsieur Blois, unable to express the depths of our gratitude. He joked about it, telling us about other crossings. He used to hide his lady passengers' silk stockings in the gas generator's filter. The last time he'd crossed, he'd hidden gold jewelry and *louis*[44] in the heater. Everything had melted by the time they arrived."

Jenny falls silent. Now I realize the full extent of the circle of solidarity needed to save me, a little girl: Aunt Eda and her son; Aunt Nelly and her son; the concierge Sophie Chaliès; the peasant woman from Auvergne; Annie, the Amon family home help in the nineteen thirties; Messieurs Blois and Giraud, prominent citizens of Angoulême; their friend the landlady in Angoulême; the mayor of Écuras; and the real Bourinets. And what about the German-Polish sentry with a taste for game, the two French

---

44. *Louis d'or*, gold coins [Translator].

policemen who perhaps pretended to believe Jenny's spiel and who turned a blind eye by not arresting us? And how about Madame Troublé, the lady on the fourth floor who taught children their catechism and said she would adopt me if necessary?

What will go down in history is that the demarcation line, that "gaping wound made across the country" in the words of De Gaulle, cut France into more than one zone, separated by this frontier stretching for one thousand two hundred kilometers between Spanish territory and the north-east of the country. Twenty kilometers east of Angoulême, the line ran through the Forest of La Braconne, sure to be filled with game, cutting the Charente department from north to south, with a total of fourteen German-manned checkpoints. Of these fourteen, we failed to make the crossing at La Rochefoucauld, but succeeded at Chazelles.

Destiny. Jenny never learned that in the night of October 8 or 9, as she rested with her husband and daughter in the requisitioned room, another four hundred and twenty-two foreign Jews were arrested in the Dordogne and the occupied portion of the Charente; that they were assembled in a nursery school, that they left for Drancy on October 15, and were deported eastward in sealed railcars on November 4 and 6.

On a more personal level, history will record that, thanks to a hunter's promise, a living child—me—was exchanged for a dead hare from the Forest of La Braconne. That this child crossed the line separating the Occupied Zone from the Free Zone, and thus came closer to another chance of survival. More than any other boundary, the route traced by the demarcation line was haphazard. No less arbitrary was the crossing of it, but to it I owe my survival.

The near arrest of my father and our arrival in the Free Zone introduced Jenny and Jacques to the life of concealment that was to be theirs from now on. By ridding herself of her yellow star and becoming Germaine Bourinet, my mother took her first step toward the world of dissembling and silence. Like their pursuers, Jenny and Jacques began turning everything on its head, even their vocabulary, adopting young Marcel's joke and calling themselves "musicians," a disguise so in tune with the times.

In recounting this story, I have adopted the same stratagem: in my telling, the adventure in the Forest of La Braconne could have ended tragically.

But instead, it becomes a joyous outing of "musicians" bound for an "unknown destination," blown along by a "spring breeze."

Operation Anton: The Free Zone has had its day

"What a relief," sighs Jenny, "to have crossed that dreadful line at last and to land in a place with no yellow stars! Monsieur Blois left us in a small train station in the late-afternoon, with a little choo-choo to take us to Limoges. We climbed aboard, thrilled to be in the Free Zone, and we reached Limoges. There we were to take a train for Spain, right at the Portbou frontier, with a change at Toulouse. The station at Limoges was chock-full of people and we sat down on our suitcases. The train must have steamed in at around three in the morning, filled to bursting, and we had to fight to board it. We managed and even found a seat, then two. This was a 'normal' train, with people going on vacation. It seemed extraordinary to us. People going on vacation! You slept as one man."

It's odd, that "You slept as one man," a familiar expression in the France of the time, tossed out by Jenny to her now adult child. It cast me back to my earliest memories of night trains in my mother's arms, so tightly held that a sense of security prevails, in these shreds of memory, over the ambient fear my mother strove to protect me from. Yet I can still hear the rumbling of the train, the roar of the locomotive, the stops in small unlit towns, the stationmasters with their Southwestern accents... "Brive-la-Gaillarde... Three minutes stop."

At that very moment and along the same rails ran ghoulish convoys of sealed wagons filled with deportees, heading in the opposite direction from the "vacation" trains we were traveling in, yet which were bound to catch up with us—myself or other people—some other night, some other day.

Jenny, meanwhile, had already jumped onto the platform. "We reached Toulouse around seven or eight in the morning," she says. "There, we took another train to Marseille in the afternoon. We'd been traveling for twenty-four hours. But it didn't matter, we were safe and in the Free Zone!

"Once we reached Marseille, we gathered up our suitcases and walked directly to Clément S.'s house to keep out of sight. He was the one who had hidden Jacques after the roundup of Bulgarians in Paris. We had his address. We were warmly welcomed when we got there, and they took us to their place in a higgledy-piggledy rundown house in La Valentine, a village on the outskirts of Marseille. The main thing, though, was that they didn't register us with the police.

"We had embarked on a new existence, one of danger-filled wandering, so different from our former life, which hadn't been all that adventurous. We had no idea how long this might last or if we would come out alive. But we thought only of the present and how lucky we were to have crossed that infernal frontier. For a few days, everything seemed lovely: the sun, the Mediterranean, the friends we'd met up with again.

"Because we weren't alone in Marseille. In addition to our hosts, we found our friends Oscar and Lily Arditti again, and Léon, the younger brother, not to mention the surviving members of the Sephardi Youth Club, with whom we used to party not so long ago, though it seemed like centuries. Then there was the Marseille branch of the Benvenistes, the family of Haïm, Maïr's brother, and that auntie who used to celebrate my birthday when I was little. They couldn't get over what had happened to us: 'Come on, Jacques, why did they come for you? What had you done?' 'Nothing. I assure you. I *haven't done a thing.*' They couldn't believe they were coming to arrest men who'd done nothing and were sending them to camps where we didn't know the half of what was going on. 'Oh, come on, Jacques. You can tell us. You must have done something?' 'No! I repeat. *Nothing!*' They just could not come to terms with the idea of people being arrested merely for being Jewish.

"But they were deaf and blind!" Jenny explodes. "When the Germans began the roundups in the Free Zone, then they saw the light. They'd had to get their identity cards stamped with the mark of infamy! They too had fallen into the well. Like us in the northern zone, when we'd had to get ourselves registered in '40. But where could they go, now? And as for us, where could we find a refuge?"

For, on November 11, 1942, less than a month after the false Bourinets crossed the demarcation line, the Germans launched Operation Anton. Before seven in the morning, Wehrmacht units crossed the demarcation line without encountering the slightest resistance. The German army and its Italian allies invaded the Free Zone and abolished any distinction between the two zones. Even the fiction of the so-called Free Zone had ceased to exist.

The next day, the Germans occupied Marseille and requisitioned schools, barracks, telephone exchanges, sports arenas, and the grand hotels. The Vieux-Port (haunted by the ghosts of Marcel Pagnol's heroes Marius, Fanny, and César), was turned into a German enclave. The Gestapo torturers took up residence on the misnamed Rue Paradis, while the Wehrmacht set up its headquarters in the Grand Hotel de Noailles on the Canebière avenue, where German tanks now paraded up and down.

In mid-December, Jacques and Jenny were in Oscar and Lily Arditti's apartment.

In Jenny's recollection, the mood was somber: "Did you see Laval's latest decree?" asked Oscar. "It says: All persons of the Jewish race are required to present themselves within a period of one month at the police precinct of their place of residence or, failing that, at the gendarmerie bureau, to have the word 'Jew' stamped on the identity card of which they are holders or on the equivalent document, and on their personal food ration card."

"It's very specific," added Lily bitterly. The cursed word had to be "stamped in red ink, superimposed or diagonally with the aid of a damp stamp bearing characters one centimeter high."

"We're all in the same boat this time," said Jenny, "French and foreign alike. I'm glad I didn't go to the gendarmerie to fill out the registry form when I arrived in Marseille."

"And you, Jacques, you're still Bulgarian. In any case, if you'd registered, you'd be heading for a holding camp, and eventual deportation," added Oscar.

"But this time, I've understood," Jacques replied. "Don't expect me to go and get them to stamp 'Jew' on my identity card!"

"And in any case, we've sent the genuine-forged papers in the name of Bourinet back to Monsieur Blois, in empty food tins," commented Jenny.

"So you've no papers now?" Lily asked. "No identity card, nor rationing card? We'll see what we can do for you."

No papers, no work, nowhere to live, no life. It was social death. Civil death. Death from hunger. Waiting for death, period.

But people did show solidarity. A few days later, Momo and his wife, who had taken refuge in Lyon and who still had their Spanish nationality, sent forged identity papers, albeit not as safe as those in the name of Bourinet from Écuras. These papers are still in Jenny's files, made out in their real names. Except that Jacques Benrey is registered as born in Bourges instead of Burgas, and Jenny Amon in Salon-de-Provence instead of Salonika. Nice places to be born, nice and French: that changes everything. No rubber stamp of infamy on these perfect forgeries.

Our friends the Ardittis came up with forged, unstamped ration cards. But there were only two. For the two French nationals, Jenny and myself. Nothing for Jacques the Bulgarian. His life hung on a thread since his missed arrest in September 1942. He was still alive. More than anywhere else, ration cards were a key to survival in Marseille, as food was cruelly lacking. There was no farmland anywhere near the city, and meat and fish from elsewhere no longer entered the Occupied Zone.

The Marseille Benvenistes looked for somewhere for the Benreys to live. "With their help," Jenny explains, "we'd found shelter with a Greek-Italian family. There were three generations of women, Catholics of Italian origin. The son-in-law, father and husband, Monsieur Papazoglou was Greek, and he'd been interned with other foreigners in the camp at Gurs. He imported exotic produce and was accused of being a black marketeer. The women agreed to take us in undeclared, in return for a hefty sum. We shared the kitchen and the toilet with them, and occupied two rooms, a bedroom, and a dining room.

"It would have been fine if the Germans hadn't been around. But cohabiting with people who could chuck you out or report you at any moment was terrifying. All it took was an incident or a misunderstanding. The slightest detail. And life is filled with minor details. We had to eat in the shared kitchen either before or after them and use the toilet when they didn't need to.

"There was the Italian grandmother, a good woman and a good cook, who taught me to make loads of dishes out of nothing. There was her daughter, who'd married the Greek, Monsieur Papazoglou. And then the granddaughter, seventeen or eighteen, a beautiful girl who cared about nothing but clothes. Her older sister had gone off to Egypt with husband

and child, a little girl exactly your age. You reminded them of this little girl and that's why they took us in. The grandmother especially... She adored you. But I had to make you understand, it was vital that she go on adoring you till the end."

I try to reconstruct this scene, of which no trace remains in my memory. A little girl of three and a half who needs to understand that the safety of three people hangs on her smiles, her hugs, her docility, just being nice.

Now it was the turn of our haven in Marseille to be targeted. On January 16, 1943, Adolf Hitler himself ordered the destruction of the old town, calling it the "cancer of Europe." The general order for operation "Sultan" went out two days later in a circular—a circular issued by the French authorities.

Once again. We were looking into a black hole. What were our chances of survival?

Roundup in Marseille

There were monster roundups in Marseille in early-winter 1943. Homeless people and vagrants, prostitutes and their pimps, dealers and escaped convicts, cosmopolitans and "people of no faith"[45] were picked up. The roundups concerned anyone found without a ration card, undocumented foreigners, expellees, and "all persons not engaged in legal work for more than one month." Above all, they rounded up Jews. All the Jews. With no regard to nationality, gender or age, Israelites[46] from Marseille along with refugees like us from the Occupied Zone.

"The nighttime roundups were the worst. We'd identified a hideout in the garden," Jenny recalls. "The winter of '43 was terrible. It was freezing inside the unheated house, and you caught a bad flu, running a high fever. We took turns to sit by your bed, unable to sleep a wink. We heard foot-

---

45. "*Gens sans aveu*" in the French. A relic of the Middle Ages referring to people whom no lord had recognized as a vassal. By extension, rootless people [Translator].

46. A commonly used euphemism for "Jew" in French at the time, and until the 1960s or 70s [Translator].

steps, doors being knocked down, orders to surrender, cries and screams shattered the night.

"At three or four in the morning, *they* came looking for the people next door, a few yards away. Old Madame Papazoglou decided you couldn't go out into the garden in that weather, and that she would pass you off as her granddaughter if they came. Jacques went out alone. It was starting to snow, which hampered the police search.

"The house was in the suburbs of Marseille, just where *they* would assemble before heading off in all directions. At that time, it wasn't the Germans. It was the French. And it went on relentlessly for at least a week."

The old Marseille was in everyone's sights. And it wasn't just Hitler and Himmler. The French writer Lucien Rebatet wrote about "that bastard populace, that oily vulgarity." While another writer, Louis Gillet, talked of a "worm-eaten hell, a sort of charnel-house of decomposition ... These neighborhoods abandoned to the rabble, to poverty, to shame! How can we void them of their pus and regenerate them?"

Simple: wipe them out.

"Don't go out without your papers," warned the newspaper *Le Petit Marseillais* on January 5, 1943. "Don't go out without your ration card," it added on the 27th of the same month.

The storm burst on January 22. The day before, the city's inhabitants looked on as twelve thousand gendarmes poured in from Toulouse, Lyon, Nancy, Paris even, since local policemen might harbor sympathy for their neighbors. French and German riot police cordoned off the neighborhoods. Any Jew they encountered was mercilessly rounded up. Buildings were combed meticulously; locksmiths were requisitioned to open the doors of people feigning absence. A wave of arrests, particularly near train stations, and especially of anyone who produced stamped identity papers, signaled the start of the operation.

Then the roundups grew in intensity, especially at night, seeking out ever more people. They continued without let-up day and night until January 27. Evacuation of the area north of the Vieux-Port began on January 24. In twenty-four hours, the district was surrounded, and the historic cradle of the city was razed to the ground. Then it was the turn of the city-center business districts, Rue Sénac, Rue de l'Académie, Rue Saint-Saëns and Rue Pisançon, where Marseille's Jewish families lived.

The day after, the area around the train station was sealed off and large-scale arrests followed. The following day, the police occupied whole neighborhoods. Also on the 27th, there were savage roundups in the movie theaters and outlying neighborhoods. It was the largest roundup in France after that of the Vel d'Hiv.

No pity for the Jews. "Our soldiers have been dying of hunger at Stalingrad for eight days now," said a German officer. "These Jews don't need to eat."

According to Raymond Raoul Lambert, a friend of the Ardittis, passengers who had come to Marseille for the day with no change of clothing or overcoat, veterans, girls, the sick, the elderly on medications, a man with a serious lung disease, a released prisoner, the wife of a blind deportee with her husband's food ration card, the widow of an artillery captain killed in the war: all were piled into cattle-wagons without seating, without water and without food, and with no chamber pot or bucket. Whole families who had lived in Marseille for generations, fathers with seven or eight children… around one thousand five hundred people, were brutally treated by the Germans and the French riot police.

Who cared for the fate of the Jews in a martyred city, in a martyred country? Starting on February 1, 1943, the Germans blew up one thousand five hundred buildings. With each explosion, the bells of the ancient Abbey of Saint-Victor on the other side of the Vieux-Port rang out their sinister message. As if in echo, the parish priest, who had barricaded himself inside the Church of Saint-Laurent, tolled the knell without interruption for the seventeen days during which his parish was systematically destroyed. The Vichy government created a Militia to hunt down more efficiently the men evading STO[47], and of course the Jews. Their methods

---

47. The *Service du travail obligatoire* (STO) or compulsory labor service in Germany was introduced in 1942. By the end of the war, more than a million Frenchmen had been forced to work in Germany. To avoid it, many young French joined the Resistance, becoming *maquisards*. Penalties for evasion were severe [Translator].

included anonymous denunciations, torture, roundups, summary and arbitrary executions, and massacres.

"As for us," says Jenny, "we lived precariously, or rather we subsisted, hiding out in a fine house, while I went out alone in search of something to eat. We had to buy on the black market, which involved additional coming and going, at the risk of getting arrested in the endless waiting lines or in the tram. It nearly happened several times. I was stopped on a tram one Sunday. The fright of my life! But I had my forged papers with my real name. They saw nothing amiss... Another time, I was able to get off just as they were getting on. I had to walk all over town to avoid them.... The black market wasn't only far away and dangerous, it was expensive too. Our reserves were dwindling fast."

Some of the thousands of "gentile" detainees were released. Not the Jews. It seems half of the non-Jews deported to the German camps perished. But there were no survivors among the Jews. This time, the stamped card had done its job: even French Jews with everything in order were arrested, like all the others.

Jacques and Jenny could congratulate themselves on not having registered in the Free Zone.

Destiny. Operation Sultan caught seven hundred and eighty-two Jews, but not us. Most of those arrested left via Arenc train station for the camp at Compiègne, then for the extermination camps: Sobibor, Maidenek, Auschwitz.

"Roundups and searches were our daily lot," Jenny recalls. "But we'd learned to live from day to day. Your father and you never went out. The neighbors would have spotted you. I was less obtrusive because there were lots of women in that family.

"So we didn't go out? Ever?"

"Never. Only on the worst nights, Jacques camouflaged himself in the garden in case *they* entered the house."

"And how long did that go on for?"

"About five months."

"Five months? Without going out?"

"Without going out!"

And so, belatedly, this is how I learned about my childhood from Jenny's mouth, a succession of lessons punctuating the itinerary of my survival with absurd anecdotes: a birth in drafty Brittany; a failed arrest disguised as a comedy, in Paris, when I was aged between three and four; a trade with a dead animal on the demarcation line; five months' captivity in a house in Marseille.

But I was *with* my Dad... Compare that fate with Juliette, who was interned in the camp at Gurs aged five; or with Monika, who spent these same months in Warsaw, hiding motionless under a sewing table; or with my little nameless fiancé, now just a fistful of dust; compared to all those children still traveling in sealed railcars... compared with all those little children, I was one of the lucky ones.

The demarcation line had been turned in on itself, aligning the unoccupied with the Occupied Zone within the frontiers of France. The best way to grasp this new situation, both historic and personal, is to think of a Moebius strip. The strip is a paradoxical, symbolic figure, a ribbon without end, turned in upon itself, where one surface becomes the other. You can make one by half-twisting the ribbon, then sticking the ends together. The engraver Escher envisioned enclosed insects buzzing infinitely within these seamless meandering pathways. If we think of this ribbon as the territory of France, when the Nazi High Command decided to extend the Occupied Zone to the whole of France, it turned all those people who had been so eager to cross into the Free Zone into insects trapped and buzzing around within a never-ending ellipse. The whole of France, like Europe, had become an escape-proof prison. Thus, along with millions of others we, Jenny, Jacques, and me, Michou, were suddenly locked within a country from which the only way out was by rail, leading to the death camps.

Dispersal...

At the end of that dreadful winter of 1943, we were half-way through the Occupation. But nobody knew that. Oscar Arditti had told Jacques: there are two wars. Against the Allies and against we Jews. The first was at a tipping point after the Allied landing in North Africa and the Soviet victory at Stalingrad. Occasionally, from far away came a parcel from Marie and

Saby, or a censored letter from Moïse. Jacques and Jenny had only a vague notion of how the rest of the family was faring. They received two visits in March: Marcel arrived from Grenoble, while Marie's brother Momo and his wife came from Lyon.

"Hello there, big sister! Hi there, my favorite niece! How you've grown since the last time I saw you!"

Marcel had put on weight and was no longer the skinny teenager from his Lycée Buffon days.

"You know I'm three and half, Uncle!"

"Quite a little girl, I must say! Jenny, don't tell the parents, but Rolande is with me in Grenoble… And there's work. You've heard of the *STO*?" he said, lowering his voice. "It's hit several of our comrades. They won't go, of course. I've already gone underground. We're resolute, in Grenoble."

The STO, instituted by the Vichy government, forcibly sent all young men to work in Germany. Those who refused to go left home and enrolled in one or another of the different underground movements and took to the *maquis*. The Resistance took many forms. There was the Secret Army, the Armed Forces Resistance Organization, the National Front, the *Francs-tireurs et partisans français* (snipers and partisans), *Main-d'œuvre immigrée* (immigrant laborers), *Résistance-Fer* (a railworkers' resistance movement), and so on. Marcel and his companions had come to swell the ranks of the army of the shadows, as it was known.

A few days later, Momo and his wife turned up. With his Spanish passport, Momo continued to work and travel. He had passed through Paris and brought news of all the family. All four visitors told how the family was getting on, starting with the oldest member, Oro. A place had been found for her in a clinic, where she had died in her bed of natural causes, like her sister-in-law Reina. Quite an achievement given the circumstances.

Of all the children of Oro and Maïr Benveniste, now laid to rest in his sector of the cemetery in the Paris suburb of Pantin, only Rafo had succeeded in escaping from France, thanks to his Spanish passport. From France to Spain to Portugal; from Portugal to Mexico. Pepo, the youngest, who was French, refused with Ester to abandon the Paris house they loved in the Auteuil district. Momo and his wife, like Nelly and her husband, were living in Lyon. But all their young children, who had converted to

Protestantism under the influence of "Mademoiselle," were at a boarding school in Chambon-sur-Lignon. The principal there, Pastor André Trocmé, gained fame for having saved many Jews under the occupation[48].

Two of Saby Amon's brothers had held onto their Portuguese passports and were living safely in Lisbon.

Marie Benveniste and Saby Amon, who had been French like Jenny since 1924, had been left untroubled despite Saby's community involvement. They made ready to leave the capital and join Marcel in the Isère region.

That left the "Italians," Allegra and Ugo Modiano, and Jacques' parents, Moïse Benrey and Marie Jerusalmi.

"The Modianos and your parents, Jacques," Momo reported in Ladino lest someone was listening, "took the train repatriating Italian citizens. I went with them to the station. Frankly, Italy has stood by its people."

"I'd known ever since '41 that the Italian consul in Paris had secured the release of the Italian Jews from Drancy," said Jacques, "... despite Rome's opposition. Above all, he obtained a waiver for Italian Jews from the obligation to wear the yellow star. My parents didn't have to wear it."

"When they came to arrest you, Jacques, in September '42, neither your parents nor Allegra and Ugo were in danger in France," Momo explained. "They were still protected by their Italian nationality. And the Consul General told Röthke that the anti-Jewish measures did not apply to Italian Jews without the consent of the Italian consulates. It seems even Mussolini had begun to distance himself from his ally regarding the latter's anti-Jewish policies. Around two months previously, Count Ciano[49] had warned the Germans that the Italian Jews from France and other countries would be repatriated. And that's what happened. The Italian government arranged for one or more trains to bring its Israelite citizens back home with the consent of the Gestapo and the Vichy government, which were happy to be rid of them. I saw Monsieur and Madame Benrey leave. I even have a letter for you from them."

---

48. The Protestant Pastor André Trocmé and his wife, together with the surrounding community, helped to shelter and save thousands of Jewish children during the occupation. Chambon-sur-Lignon and the surrounding villages were declared "Righteous among the nations" by the Yad Vashem Institute in Jerusalem in 1990 [Translator].

49. Mussolini's son-in-law and foreign minister of Italy 1936-1943.

Jacques heaved a sigh of relief on learning that his father and mother had left Nazi France, even if it was only to return to Mussolini's Italy, of which they were nationals.

"And aunt Allegra, I mean Andrée, how was she?" asked Jenny.

"They're poorly, both of them... Such a loss! One never gets over that. But a stay in Parma will do them good. Your parents, Jacques, opted to go to Milan, where they know people... But on the subject of the Italians, we have a proposal for you."

It was an offer they couldn't refuse. Momo owned a little apartment in Nice that Rafo and his family had left empty when setting out on their epic journey to Spain, then on to Portugal and Mexico. If Jacques and Jenny wanted to leave Marseille, the apartment in Nice was theirs.

By now the Benreys, Jerusalmis, Benvenistes and Amons were no longer a family rooted in a single location, Paris. Now they were pariahs, part of a tribe of nomads whose haphazard assortment of nationalities decided not only their identity, but also their very existence and survival. The die was not fully cast at that point in time, nor had all the cards been dealt. But the wheel of fortune was turning, pointing now this way, then that. Why him? Why not her? Why the two of them? They are of the same blood. Ours. But a passport, a scrap of paper, a wretched document that might be a forgery; but the choice of one region, village, or town rather than another was about to divide the living from the dead, without rhyme or reason.

When Momo and his wife left Marseille in early-spring 1943, they had boosted Jenny and Jacques' morale completely. One event that was to prove vital for them had passed by unnoticed in December 1942, just before the terrible weeks in Marseille. The city of Nice passed into Italian hands. A haven on the Riviera, and a refuge for the persecuted from everywhere, the outcasts and the dispossessed.

A dove from the Ark

Two episodes escaped Jenny's silence throughout the long post-war decades during which she censored the events that had turned her and her fellow-Jews into sub-humans: the first was our stay in Nice in 1943, the second the heroic moment in the Vercors.

I barely remember the train journey from Marseille to Nice. I assume it was trouble-free. My first memories date from the time in Nice. I was aged between three and a half and four. That's when I discovered the sea. I never even saw it in Marseille, having never left the house.

"We moved into the little apartment with a balcony in the Musicians' sector—genuine musicians—a stone's throw from the Promenade des Anglais, on Rue Rossini," Jenny recalls that detail. "It was early spring. The building was fairly isolated, surrounded by vacant lots planted with vegetable patches. The months we spent there were radiant, though we were fearful for the future, and the money was running through our fingers as we were barred from working.

"How different from Marseille! Even the sun was more luminous. We were surrounded by roses, rhododendrons, and mimosa. The place smelled of lavender, jasmine and orange blossom, and life, which had been so hard in Marseille, was perfectly easy in Nice. You could get anything you wanted if you could pay. The Italian occupiers were so gentle and kind, it took our breath away. They weren't antisemitic like the French, and they let the poor people who'd been arrested go free. Their officers were splendid; all the women looked at them with a glint in their eyes."

History confirms Jenny's surprising enthusiasm. When the Germans occupied the southern zone in November 1942, their Italian allies too came to occupy a broader swath of French territory: Haute-Savoie, Savoie, the Drôme, the Hautes-Alpes, the Basses-Alpes, the Var, the Alpes-Maritimes, a large slice of the Isère and the Vaucluse, a small portion of the Ain, Corsica, and the Principality of Monaco all came under their sway. But the Italian Fascists did not make war on the Jews like the Nazis, nor were they submissive like the French police. To be sure, Mussolini's motives mirrored those of the Germans. He wanted to annex part of the French departments he had occupied. Jews in the Italian-occupied areas benefited from the political rivalry that grew up between the French and Italians.

Suddenly, though, jackboots were heard pounding on the Promenade... Germans? That's the fear. No, just an Italian regiment marching past with martial step and fixed bayonets. Their friend Jacques Franck welcomed Jenny and Jacques to Nice with a reassuring:

"You're in the Jews' paradise, here."

Another friend later regretted making a stupid joke about the cockerel feathers adorning the Italians' caps. With hindsight, he thought they represented "a dove from the Ark."

Says Jenny: "With the Italians, there were no more stamped identity cards, no conscription into the occupier's labor force. Refugees were issued resident's permits placing them under Italian protection. We even saw the *carabinieri* intervening to stop the French police making arrests. Obviously, refugees flocked there. And inside this promised land there arose a center for the fabrication of forged papers and a refugee-aid committee. There were any number of rescue operations, and the rest.

"Just after we arrived at the beginning of March Ribbentrop sent Mussolini an ultimatum ordering him to choose between standing aside as the French police acted, getting the Italian police to do the work, or leaving it to the SS and the French police. Mussolini opted for the second. So, the Italian police took over from the army and steered Jews into the hinterland where Jewish organizations took them in hand. They even posted *carabinieri* inside the synagogue on the Boulevard du Dubouchage to prevent the French police from getting near."

History confirms Jenny's version of events. There really were two sides in the south of France that spring 1943. There were the Italian occupiers who tolerated Jewish refugees on the one hand, and their Nazi allies and the French collaborators on the other. The former freed those whom the latter had arrested. All through my childhood and early youth Jenny would intersperse her conversation with fleeting allusions to this situation, yet her listeners never realized their full import: "Nice? Did you say Nice? It's the most pleasant city in France. Quite unlike Marseille!"

Jenny and Jacques were far from alone in this Eldorado. The whole of the Sephardi Youth "crowd," plus others brought together here by their youth and persecution, were waiting for them in Nice. Betty Alcalaï and her husband Jacques Franck were there, as were Yolande and André Prévost, AKA Doudou, who wasn't Jewish, Léon and Simone, Oscar and Lily who had left Marseilles beforehand, and others besides.

Lazing around one summer's day in Nice, they were all stretched out on the pebble beach trading memories. Of Bulgaria first of all. Like Jacques, Oscar and Léon had been to the Catholic school on Pirot Street in Sofia. They used to make fun of gentle Brother Flavien, who ran his French classes with a velvet touch, as they listened to him reciting rambling poetry for them. Their father, Salomon Arditti, was a cloth merchant like Moïse Benrey. The two families had known each other and used to spend summers together in the Arditti's spacious house at Varna, or at Mamaia in Romania, where both Salomon Arditti and Marie Jerusalmi were born.

France had long been part of their DNA as well.

"Citizens of France since the dawn of time," Léon joked, ironically.

At seventeen, Oscar had been the first to make the journey. He went off to study at the textile school in Roubaix. Then the younger brother Léon became a boarder at the prestigious Lycée Louis-le-Grand, studying furiously for his *baccalaureate* even as the Führer thundered ever more vehemently before the fanatical Germanic crowds. Léon, who was five years younger than Oscar, was called up in 1939. In the fighting in May 1940, he was forced back with his unit. He evaded capture and was demobilized when the Armistice was signed.

Oscar Arditti and Lily Alcalaï had known each other as children in Bulgaria but had fallen in love in France in 1936. They were pillars of the Sephardi Youth Club, where Oscar had given a widely noted talk on Palestine. Their engagement and then marriage had been reported solemnly in *Le Judaïsme Sépharadi*. Oscar had then left for the front, was captured, and escaped. It was in his small apartment on the Rue de Rivoli that he had seen Jacques again and talked to him about the Nazis' "other" war.

Returning from captivity, still waiting to cross the demarcation line, Lily proudly announced:

"I'm expecting."

Oscar was taken aback at first. A baby, at this time? Keeping it was out of the question. He didn't feel up to raising a child in these circumstances. But Lily insisted, and a baby girl was born in the Free Zone, at one thirty in the morning of January 31, qualifying the family to receive rationing cards for the entire month. A priceless boon that paradoxically made Claudine, my future playmate, a wanted war baby.

All these happenings came flooding back in detail as the "crowd" recollected them, as they lay on the beach during that brief instant of calm.

"It's nice here," commented Oscar with a hint of anxiety, "though I'd have preferred my sister Ida and her children, Jako and Ninon, to have stayed behind in Bulgaria with my parents."

"Since she's divorced, it was better for her to be here with us," was Lily's response.

"Bringing them with her? No way! We're better off dispersed."

"Dispersed means separated," said Lily. "Surely we're better off together?"

"For a Jew to land up in France in August 39," joined in Jacques Franck, "it wasn't the wisest thing to do... But remember, Bulgaria has joined the Axis and is allied with the Nazis, and probably has racial laws like them. Oh well... who's coming for a dip with me? Come on kids, coming for a swim?"

The children were Jako, thirteen, Ninon, nine, Jean-Pierre and Jean-Michel, five, and me, nearly four. Baby Claudine was sleeping in a basket.

"We're building a castle with the pebbles," shouted out Jean-Pierre, hard at work on his rickety keep, surrounded by his helpers, Jean-Michel and myself.

The women were in less of a hurry to go for a swim and stayed behind with the children. There were Jenny and Betty, Lily, and Ida. They drew closer together and whispered among themselves in Judeo-Spanish, sharing distant memories. Commonplace memories of times by the sea, bursts of laughter, jokes in Ladino, songs in Bulgarian, breathless discussions in French of history, poetry, the hunt for food during shortages, under the debonair eyes of the Italian officers in their uniforms, while the waves of the Mediterranean gently lapped the pebbles.

Few traces remain of the balmy days of that Italian interlude, with few anecdotes to relate. It was as if everyone was catching their breath before tragedy struck once more, in ever stronger waves, ever closer to swallowing them up. Springtime in Nice, 1943! An unforgettable vacation on the edge of the volcano. Every member of the "crowd" sported a suntan. They played tennis and invited each round for a "cheap Sephardi" meal. Under the admiring gaze of his young brother Léon, Oscar regaled the others with details of his escape as planned from afar by Lily. They giggled a lot while sharing private jokes about "musicians."

Jacques was fair-haired and blue-eyed like his mother and father. He so resembled an enemy officer that a passerby took him for one and spoke to him in German. It was a language he spoke perfectly, having idled in the spa resorts of the late-Weimar Republic in his gilded youth. Oscar, a true Frenchman, though with a dusky complexion and black, frizzy hair, like the rest of the "crowd," Jew and Gentile alike, guffawed at the mistaken identity.

They were still alive. They were young. Aged from eighteen to thirty-five. We were still alive, aged from one to thirteen. Sitting on the pebble beach. All through the spring and then in the dying days of summer. Not for long.

An angel named Donati

Fate took a fresh turn on September 8, 1943. Summer brought in its wake the rout of the Germans and Italians in Tunisia, the Allied landings in Sicily, and above all the fall of Mussolini in the night of July 24-25, dismissed from office by the Grand Council of Fascism and imprisoned by the King. Badoglio set up his government in a climate of all-pervading uncertainty. Saby Amon and Marie Benveniste had just left Paris for the Italian zone. They stopped over for a few days in Nice, then journeyed to the Isère to join Marcel. There they snatched their son away from young Rolande and sent the latter back to her family. The region then passed from the Italians to the Germans, whereupon everyone went up to Villard-de-Lans in the heart of the Vercors mountains, still beyond the Germans' reach.

From there, Marie sent out uncharacteristically reassuring, enthusiastic even, letters. In high school Marcel had shown a keen interest in music, encouraged by Lucien Legros, one of the five Lycée Buffon students who had been executed. Now Marie reported that Marcel had done a lot of composing during his time in Grenoble. The first recording of his works performed by the eminent pianist Jean Doyen had just been released. Obviously, one wouldn't find the record in a tiny village in the Vercors. Perhaps Jenny could find a copy in Nice? She scoured every store in the city, but to no avail. The masterpiece hadn't found its way there.

Other letters from Villard-de-Lans followed, ever more fulsome. Not only had the disk been released and performed by one of the most celebrated pianists of the time, but the greatest musicians, Charles Munch and even Ernest Ansermet, had personally written enthusiastic letters of praise. Marie was bursting with pride. She had forgotten the war, the dearth of food, the sword of Damocles hanging over their heads. She even passed on one of these letters, on headed notepaper from the Basler Gesellschaft. Signed by Ansermet, the letter began "Dear Maestro," calling the young man a "musicologist of genius."

Her sister showed the letter to one of the "crowd's" merry men, who happened to be learned and an artist himself. He handed it back with an ironic smirk.

"I can't imagine a great musician talking like that! It's got forgery written all over it!"

But Jenny and Jacques had other worries. Their initial joy had given way to growing concerns in the Italian zone. What would happen if the troops evacuated the haven they had helped carve out? In the night of July 28-29, 1943, a German motorized division drove into Nice and was housed in a nearby barracks! An ill omen!

While the "crowd" wavered between panic and enjoying their last moments on the edge of the abyss, an Italian Jew was scurrying between Nice and the Vatican in a bid to rescue those caught in the zone before it was too late. The aptly named Angelo Donati, with the help of a French Capuchin, Father Marie-Benoît, was hoping to enlist the aid of the American and British representatives at the Vatican to charter boats with a view to shipping thousands of Jews out to Africa via Italy. The Italians began assembling their troops and Jews flooded into Nice from all over the zone.

History relates that the French authorities in the Alpes-Maritimes changed around this time. The tone too: "Henceforward, I will not permit any arbitrary action against the Jews, even those in an irregular or illegal situation," wrote the new Prefect. "I will not leave to the Italians the noble privilege of being the sole heirs to the tradition of tolerance and humanity that belongs to France."

The Germans did not like this one bit. Commander Knochen waxed indignant: "The Italian troops and the Jewish population get on extremely well together. The Italians live in Jewish homes, get invited by the Jews with the latter paying for them!"

The German response was horrific.

The Duce's arrest triggered a race against time between the Italians and the Germans. While Angelo Donati and Father Marie-Benoît were working to get the Jews to safety, Röthke devised a strategy to hunt down men, women, and children alike. He planned to start with the rich and influential Jews, arresting the Jews from allied and friendly countries. French Jews were to suffer the same fate as the rest. There were to be no exceptions, no quarter given.

At nine in the morning on September 8, 1943, Donati had one last conversation with the British and American diplomats putting the finishing touches to his rescue plan. That same day, at half past six in the evening, General Eisenhower's headquarters announced *prematurely* that an armistice had been signed with Italy on September 3.

The net was tightening. In Nice and the rest of the zone the Italian forces collapsed, sowing panic among the Jews. The Italians fled their former allies in disarray. They hid under train seats and abandoned everything, weapons, and all, to the Nazis.

"Despite our own fears, we pitied these poor Italian soldiers who had been so kind to us. We knew what lay in wait for the enemies of the Nazis. We gave them civilian clothes, money, food, whenever possible, and shelter. They no longer had any commanders. It was utter confusion," says Jenny.

A woman's last glance, a Jewish woman's, at an Italian uniform. One last look with a glint in the eye, for already history was lurching forward once more and the new occupiers would be eager to lay hands on their designated victims. In two days, the Italians vanished from Nice, to be replaced by the Nazis and their henchmen. The dove flew from the Ark to other climes, abandoning the "Jews' paradise" to darkness and the specter of the camps.

Brunner, the genius of evil

The Arditti family was arrested on December 13.

Aloïs Brunner had already been at work in Nice two months earlier, beginning September 10. This man, whose sinister reputation went before him, had come to round up Jews. He had just demonstrated his prowess in Salonika, where all that remained of the Benvenistes, the Amons and their relatives had been wiped out, deported in a matter of weeks to Treblinka and Sobibor, and chiefly to Birkenau. Brunner had done his worst in Vienna, Berlin, and Drancy, leaving a trail of violence and annihilation in his wake.

The roundups began forthwith. In Nice, they struck in the night of September 8-9, even before the military occupation of the zone. The next day the Gestapo and the Wehrmacht took up position, aided by the French police and under the leadership of Aloïs Brunner, a pure evil genius. He set up his assembly center in the Hotel Excelsior, near where Jacques and Jenny were living. His men secured the services of professional informers and physiognomists who scoured far and wide for likely faces. Their specialty? Recognizing Jews in the street. That's what they were paid for, earning a hundred, a thousand, and even five thousand francs a head. In doubtful cases, men were ordered to drop their pants to the ankles. Circumcision was a surer sign than a rubber stamp. These commandos blocked off streets at both ends trapping everyone within them. In all, one thousand eight hundred and twenty Jews were deported from Nice between September 18 and December 15. Those who escaped went into hiding.

"For us, that was the end of swimming, tennis or strolling!" Jenny recalls. "Anyway, the seafront was barred to us. The Germans had walled-off the streets leading to it. They built a wall, like the Atlantic Wall, and the local residents were evacuated. We cowered at home. We were terrified of informers. Terrified of the merest identity check. Betty and Jacques Franck, the parents of your friend Jean-Pierre, barely escaped a round up in their building. A French Jew was arrested in their place."

On December 12, 1943, Oscar and Lily gathered their friends in the apartment where they were living with their baby, their brother and brother-in-law Léon, their sister and sister-in-law Ida and her two children, Jako and Ninon. Their father, Salomon Arditti, aged sixty-four, and his wife occupied a room with a local man, a French captain who was the uncle of their friend Maguy. The Ardittis had gone their separate ways so as not to tempt the devil. That day someone they knew was there too, the daughter of a colonel Oscar had met in the *Stalag*. She was Jewish too. Above all, she possessed an "exceptional" gift of clairvoyance according to Oscar. All the shutters in the apartment were closed as the "crowd" spent the afternoon trying to foretell their futures, each one more uncertain than the other. An afternoon of conjecture, guessing, anticipation and omens. The female sphinx, who was no Cassandra, did all she could to reassure everyone. She predicted that Oscar, Lily, Léon and Ida would come through. Jenny too, "though with some tribulations."

The next day, on December 13, the Arditti family, minus the parents, was gathered in the little apartment. Léon, Oscar and Lily and their daughter Claudine were there, as were Ida and her children Jako and Ninon. Their friend Maguy, daughter of the captain housing the aging parents, had come to visit them.

The doorbell rang. Persistently.

Ida opened it. Before her stood three men in long leather raincoats.

"German police! Your papers!"

The men from the Gestapo scrutinized the documents in deathly silence. They looked up when they came to Maguy's identity card. Not Jewish.

"Come with us," said the chief to the other five, in near-perfect French.

As he did so, his eyes fell upon the two little girls sitting quietly on the sofa, baby Claudine and Ninon, eight.

Maguy stepped forward and pointed to the two children:

"They're my god-children… I'm in charge of them. I'll take care of them."

She spoke with resolve. The German hesitated for a moment. But he had caught five people in his net already, not to mention the father, who had got everyone into this mess as it turned out.

"Alright! Let's get going!"

Ida rushed to her daughter. She kissed her. Hugged her fiercely, unable to let go. Maguy saw the Gestapo agents growing impatient. So, she grabbed the baby in one arm. Her free hand caught that of Ninon and ordered her to come with her. Then she quickly vanished down the stairs with both children, followed by the Gestapo and the little group. Two black Citroën sedans were waiting in the street. Jako and Ida got into the first, Oscar, Lily, and Léon into the second.

The Hotel Excelsior was a few blocks away, in a district ironically called *Les Musiciens*. Two SS stood guard at the entrance to the white and ochre building. The group went through narrow corridors and found themselves in a second-floor room with no furniture but packed with bedding. Oscar, his brother, nephew, and his sister saw their father, Salomon Arditti, sitting there, head in hands.

"It's my fault. I was caught up in a raid in the market and my papers still bore the apartment's address. I hadn't had time to put it right. It's my fault you were caught!"

Over the next two days each was interrogated in turn:

"Do you admit to being Jewish, or do I have to order you to drop your pants?"

A couple of days later, it was Lily's turn to be bought before the Gestapo. She began by stating:

"I'm not Jewish but Christian. I'm a Maronite born in Beirut."

"Prove it!"

"I left my birth certificate in Lebanon."

How did she manage? They grilled her for hours. She never wavered. Now the SS wanted her niece, Ninon, whom they'd let slip away with Maguy.

"Where is she?"

"I've no idea."

"Tell us where she is, and we'll let you go."

"I just don't know."

Minutes seemed like hours, and hours like minutes. Unspeakable violence took place in full view. Mentally, Lily counted the time needed for Maguy to get old Madame Arditti out of her room and bring her to safety with Ninon and the baby, her baby.

Finally, she blurted out whatever came into her head, and they believed her:

"She's... in the girls' high school in... Montpellier."

Did they really believe her? Had they wearied of hunting the sworn enemy of the Reich, eight-year-old Ninon? No, she'd stood her ground, bold, audacious Lily. And Brunner's men ended up letting her go.

Lily was returned to the hotel bedroom-cum-prison-cell, where she threw herself into Oscar's arms.

"They're letting me go!"

She swiftly emptied the contents of her inside pocket into her husband's jacket. Their last savings!

"Go then, go quickly," said Oscar.

Lily hugged each of them long and fiercely, the grandfather, Ida, Léon and young Jako, with his childlike eyes, then left without turning back.

The next morning, Lily and Betty were standing on the street corner, gazing at the group of fifteen or so people leaving the Hotel Excelsior on their way to the station, marching four abreast and flanked by SS troops wearing helmets and armed with submachine guns.

"*Los... Los... Schnell...* Fast... Faster!"

Passersby didn't even bother to glance at the unfortunates walking toward their destruction, weighed down by their heavy suitcases. There were Salomon Arditti, the father, Oscar, Léon, Ida, and Jako, now a gangling outsize teenager of just fourteen years old. Their eyes met with unbearable intensity—in a city that looked on blindly, indifferent to where they were heading. Destination: *the unknown*. Now they were farther away. One could hear their footsteps fading away in the Musicians' quarter. A wan December sun lit the silent scene.

And that was it. Lily took shelter with her brother, then very quickly left with Ninon, baby Claudine and her grandmother for the Saône-et-Loire department, where they went into hiding. Lily or Betty passed on the details to Jenny in haste, panicked at the thought of further raids. Like the one in March that picked up Simone Jacob, better known today as Simone Veil[50], and her entire family. As the Gentile Maguy had done when she could, Christians and Jews worked in the shadows to snatch little children

---

50. Simone Veil was deported with her family to Auschwitz at the age of 16. She survived to become the Minister of Health in 1974 and the first President of the European Parliament in 1979 [Translator].

from the claws of the SS. The Jewish founders of the Marcel Network, Moussa and Odette Abadi, helped by Bishop Paul Rémond of Nice, the Swedish Consul and local families, between them saved the lives of five hundred and twenty-five children bound for the gas chambers.

Without realizing it, being aged only four at the time, I was daily rubbing shoulders with appalling tragedies. All I can recall of that cruel winter of 1943-1944 is a patchy memory, revived by Jenny's account, the memory of Christmas, my first Christmas as a conscious being; it must have been so hard to bear for the adults around me. Yet they summoned the spirit to give me a real little French girl's Christmas. Like everyone my age, according to Jenny I couldn't get to sleep, aching to see Santa Claus, but I did regale my parents with my daily concerto of nursery rhymes Jenny had taught me, and the songs she loved such as "*Tout va très bien, madame la marquise*"[51] by two "musicians" Paul Misraki and Ray Ventura. I knew them by heart and used to sing them as a childish lullaby for my parents, who found it harder to sleep than I did. On the morning of the 25th, in the little sun-filled dining room I found waiting for me a doll's cradle that Jenny had somehow unearthed for me. She had wrapped it in pink muslin with pink flowers, cut from some old drapes.

I rushed toward it, noticed a worn-out doll sleeping soundly in the magical cradle and cried out:

"You can see it's come from heaven!"

That sparked a round of hilarious laughter, a burst of laughter—incomprehensible to me at the time—that must have come as a relief for my parents in those times of terror and was to resound in Jenny's ears, and later mine, till this day.

There was no tree, but there were Christmas garlands still visible in a photograph. It shows us, my pal Jean-Pierre Franck and myself, sitting on the steps of a kind of porch, with the garlands on our knees. We are also both wearing winter overcoats, and my hair is quite long with bangs on the top of my head. The image is totally misleading, portraying a fleeting,

---

51. An evergreen comic French song in which a butler sarcastically informs an aristocratic lady that "Everything is fine," except that her mare has died, the castle has burned down, her husband is dead, etc., but that 'Apart from that, everything is perfectly fine...' [Translator].

exceptional normality where abnormality was the rule! It was just this kind of distortion of reality that contributed to all those systems of denial after the war, Jenny's and mine included.

Yet the imposture had been revealed in December 1942; the unknown destination was now known. Great Britain, the United Stated, the Soviet Union and the National Committee of Fighting France in London announced to the world that the Jews of Europe were being exterminated. This was indeed that "other" war. They were concentrating on the first, focused on military victory over the Third Reich. Oscar, Léon and the millions of "musicians" had no option but to await the Allied victory; no alternative but to *keep going*.

The maestro of Fleur des Alpes

At the end of February, a censored letter from Marie reached Nice. In veiled terms she urged Jenny to join them in the Alps, where they were "quietly" enjoying the pure mountain air and the grazing cows in the meadows. Jacques and Jenny had run out of money. They decided to brave the perils of the journey, knowing the dangers of an identity check since they were no longer protected by their forged papers. The first train took us to Marseille, of bitter memory. We had to wait five hours in the station in a state of agonizing tension. Then we took the night train for Grenoble, where I slept as usual curled up in my mother's arms. It was very cold in Grenoble, but Marie had taken the morning bus from the mountain to come to greet us. There followed a day's wait to complete our voyage, taking the evening bus to Villard-de Lans, nestling in the Vercors massif. The war wasn't over, but Jacques and Jenny could breathe a sigh of relief. They had come through another trial.

Says Jenny: "When we arrived at Fleur des Alpes, a little apartment house at the edge of the village, on the road to Corrençon, the first thing Marie proudly displayed in the tiny two-room apartment she shared with Marcel and Saby was a wardrobe filled with musical scores, recordings and musical accessories, and a phonograph. 'Play them your composition,' Marie ordered Marcel.

"We all sat down and listened in silence. My mother didn't care that we had been traveling forty-eight hours and were cold and hungry. She listened in a kind of ecstasy. She who had been dry-eyed all her life had tears in her eyes. Marcel looked a little embarrassed. He looked away while Marie was enraptured.

"In fact, Marcel and his friends from occupied Grenoble, fleeing the STO compulsory labor draft, had joined the '*Plan Montagnards*' and the *maquis*. For almost three years by then, Pierre Dalloz and Jean Prévost had been planning to turn the area into a Trojan horse for airborne commandos. Marcel had gone up to Villard-de-Lans, a mountain village and popular pre-war ski resort, which had been relatively untroubled by the Italian occupiers. The Germans didn't leave a garrison when they invaded the zone, because they couldn't occupy every little bit of territory. And then, the villages were very high up, at more than fifteen hundred meters' altitude. There was just one bus serving Grenoble. It left in the morning and came back in the evening. The Resistance established itself in this quiet corner of France, in this mountain fastness. The farmers were scattered, and one could easily find refuge in the farms. With all its neighboring villages, the Vercors *maquis* was cut off from the rest of France but was in contact with London and Algiers.

"We didn't see many Germans, which of course attracted Jewish refugees. They lived there with forged papers and false names. It was pretty funny to hear Mr. Dubois and Mrs. Dupont speaking in a thick Russian, Polish or German accent as soon as they opened their mouth. To be sure, black Citroëns came by from time to time to pick up 'foreigners' whom we'd never see again. But that didn't happen often, and news didn't travel much by word of mouth because no one trusted anyone.

"It was hard not to notice that the apartment to the right of us harbored the Janovskis, who whispered in Yiddish. There was a Czech couple in the apartment on the left. They listened a lot to the British radio, and we could hear them through the thin partition walls. Fleur des Alpes had two floors with six apartments, plus maids' rooms in the attic, which were rented furnished. There had been a Polish school for wartime exiles on the ground floor. The Papos, another family of 'musicians,' lived on the first floor, as did the landlady, Mademoiselle C., an old maid, who was a spirited lady. She

204

had a man friend who looked like a little old man with a cap. He would disappear for weeks on end, then come back, and twice a week he'd come to eat a fondue with her. Sometimes they came for coffee in our apartment. All we talked about was the weather. We thought they must be on the side of the Germans... But okay.

"We moved about as little as possible. There was a steep walk up to the village. I did the 'official' shopping with my father, Saby, using our milk and bread coupons, and we waited in endless lines outside the half-empty stores. The pharmacy was owned by a woman from Brittany, Madame Ravalec. People whispered that her husband, a Jewish physician, was a Resistance leader. The two spinsters who ran the tobacco store also helped those without papers, both Jews and members of the Resistance, exchanging tobacco rations for cigarettes, which we could then take to the neighboring farms and trade for food. My parents, Marie and Saby, played bridge in the afternoon with their friends the Alfandaris, the Rovanous, and the Bienenfelds. They all knew Marcel, the great musician, pride of the family, and young Violette Alfandari was truly smitten with him.

"For lunch, I'd go to the bus stop in the middle of the valley. There was a little inn where they served white bread accompanied by the English radio, turned on full blast. Then I'd go up the other side with my bags, which were heavier and heavier. It was a red-letter day when Jacques came with me. We took the four o'clock bus back, with flour, seven or eight liters of milk, cheese, and some good butter covered with rose motifs stamped on it. Once, I even managed to get hold of a rabbit in exchange for children's clothes. I gave everything to my mother, and we didn't get the best bits. It was Jacques who kneaded the dough for bread with Marie, but she paid for the flour and Marcel gobbled up the result."

As Jenny speaks, suddenly a personal memory pops into the flow of those I manage to extract from my mother's recollections. I'm very hungry. I was always very hungry during that time of privations. This exasperated Marie, who preferred to keep the good things for the family artist. The barking of the dogs at each farm entrance scared me. This time, we enter a vast kitchen where we hear a child crying. The farmer's wife is feeding her son, about my age. With my eyes, I devour the delicious boiled egg as the yolk smears across the little boy's cheek, before he regurgitates the rest.

I'm aghast. He pushes away the delicious spoonful and the white bread soldiers. The farmer's wife turns around, sees what I'm thinking and, angry with her child for refusing to eat, she points Jenny toward a half-dozen eggs with some feathers still clinging to them:

"That kid's driving me crazy! Take them for your girl, since he doesn't want them."

Jenny doesn't need telling twice. Nor do I at dinner that evening, while my uncle grabs half the booty for himself.

"Our apartment was cramped," Jenny recalls. "There was just one wardrobe, and it was full, so there was nowhere to put a single handkerchief. Every day, we had to rummage in the trunk for a pair of shorts or knickers. Before we came, Marcel slept in the room with the wardrobe, and Marie and Saby in the other. You slept in a little bed with your grandmother. And we four slept in the other room. After a few weeks, we managed to rent a little room in the attic on the fourth floor. But Marcel wanted it, while leaving his things downstairs, so we were camping all the time, except when my brother went off to the *maquis*."

Another wave of memories comes to me. It is midday, breakfast time for my idol, who has been "composing" till late into the night. It's my job to bring him up his thick slices of bread made by his mother and his bowl of ersatz coffee with steaming hot milk.

"Be careful," was Marie's warning. I knock on the door.

"Come in, turnip flower!"

"Hello, Uncle. Did you sleep well?"

Marcel is the only person who has ever called me turnip flower, and to this day I have never discovered whether turnips have flowers or if the nickname was affectionate or snide. No matter! I was performing an important mission, feeding a prodigy.

Jenny's tone, on the other hand, grows bitter when recounting this: it's not so much the promiscuity as what she sees as Marie's wickedness and her blindness. The day after our arrival, Marie showed her daughter the abundant mail received from Charles Munch, Marcel's master, or so he claimed, which arrived very regularly and was gradually filling the wardrobe. Nor was that all. Huge sums, worthy of his opus, were said to be piling up in the name of Marcel Amon at the Basler Gesellschaft, a bank in Switzerland. He'd go and fetch the money straight after the war and repay his parents a hundred times what they'd spent on him.

Ever since his childhood, Marcel had told tall tales to make himself look good in the eyes of his mother, too inclined to idealize him. And his sister, who had been overshadowed by his arrival, had sought in vain to unmask him.

Jenny tried to convey her suspicions to Marie:

"Don't you think it's a bit, well, bizarre? Our musicologist friend says a great musician would never write like that to a beginner."

Her mother was indignant:

"A beginner? Have you no ear, you who've studied piano since you were a child? But you've never acknowledged your brother's worth! And you'd rather listen to your friends than to your own family!"

"But... Mama!"

"That's enough! Another word and you're out!"

Jenny left it at that. She had no choice, considering she was lucky to have this place. But she and Jacques, who thought the same, turned themselves into detectives, eager to pierce the mystery. They noticed a similarity between the typeface used in the Swiss maestro's correspondence and that on the envelopes Marcel received from Rolande, who had a typewriter and never wrote by hand.

The young man's motives were plain: in exchange for glory and prestige among the High Society of Villard-de-Lans (the Alfandaris, the Bienen-felds, the Rovanous and other exotic names best left unspoken), not to mention the fortune accumulating in his name in Switzerland, he was left in peace to enjoy his mother's bread and preserves.

The arrival of our little family undermined this delicate arrangement. I have no recollection of the time I asked my grandmother for another slice of white bread. But it is seared into the memory of Jenny. Marie, she tells me, refused point blank:

"You've had quite enough to eat as it is, Michou... Anyway, if you want to grow to be a beautiful girl, tall and slim like the models, you'll have to stop stuffing yourself."

Ten minutes later, Marcel asked for a slice, which his mother handed him without a word.

"Why did you refuse to give it to my daughter," protested Jenny.

"I make the bread for my son, and for no one else!"

Mother and grandmother glared at each other with hatred in their eyes. Not for the last time. From now on, it was war between Marie and her daughter. Between Jenny and her mother.

The day after that memorable occasion, Marie climbed the stairs to clean up the master's mess while the latter had gone to join his comrades in the mountains. Behind the wardrobe, under the bed, she discovered a large pile of canned food, stolen at night from her store of reserves. They were half-open, half-eaten. There were rotting sardines that could have supplemented many of our meager meals, which usually consisted of a few salad leaves with a bit of salt. She dared not reveal the dirty secret publicly, but echoes of the "bawling out," as Marcel put it, did come to the ears of Jacques, who was reading quietly in the next-door room.

Says Jenny: "Three days later, as if by magic, a new letter arrived from Switzerland. This time from Ernest Ansermet, legendary conductor of the *Orchestre Suisse Romande*. Like all foreign mail, it had been opened by customs and censored, then closed with a strip of sticky tape obscuring the stamp. It was indeed a Swiss stamp, but it had been postmarked in 1943 and this was 1944. I spotted it straight away. But Marie riposted: 'The Post Office got it wrong!'

"This time, the letter went way beyond the bounds of credibility. It began: 'Maestro, you are not a maestro but a genius,' and went on in the same vein: 'You will become, you are already the greatest musicographer (sic) of our time.'

"Marie shot a look of triumph in the direction of the rest of the family and ran to show the letter to her neighbors. We heard cries of bravo, rejoicings, and congratulations."

Jenny and Jacques said nothing. Anyway, they had other concerns.

Those crucial months of spring 1944 passed in an atmosphere of relative calm externally, but a domestic storm was raging. The war, meanwhile, was rising to a bitter climax. The Allies were advancing up the Italian peninsula, sustaining heavy losses at Monte Cassino. Something momentous was brewing... was imminent. But what?

"Les sanglots longs...."[52]

"*... des violons bercent mon cœur d'une langueur monotone.*" (The long sobs of autumn violins lull my heart with a languorous monotone).

"We heard that one ages ago," said Marcel.

"No, not so long ago," replied Jenny. "It's the opening line of Verlaine's poem."

"Yes," said Jacques. "It's Verlaine, and it goes on "*... blessent mon Cœur d'une langueur monotone.*'" (Lay waste my heart...).

"Not at all," rejoined Marcel. "It's not 'lay waste,' but 'lull.' And it's not the poem, it's a song by Charles Trenet!"

All three were glued to the radio in the evening of June 5. They had gone for a walk with me up to the Col Vert during the day, though I remember nothing. On their way back into Villard in the evening they passed a house with open windows. The official "German" radio was on and talking about the "siege of Rome." Back at Fleur des Alpes, the Czech neighbors announced the great news: the Allies had taken Rome the day before and declared it an "open city."

Since 9 pm, the English radio had been broadcasting personal messages non-stop.

"It was unbelievable," exclaims Jenny. "There had never been so many!"

"*Le chamois des Alpes bondit...*" (The mountain goat is leaping).

"I bet it's for tomorrow," wagered Marcel.

"Not yet," Jacques tempered. "They aren't ready yet!"

"I bet you it's for tomorrow morning," Marcel insisted.

"Nothing's going to happen tomorrow," repeated Jacques. "But I'd love to be wrong. I'll bet you twenty francs, if you like."

"I'm going to bed," was Marcel's response. "OK then, twenty francs!"

Jacques and Jenny had trouble sleeping. At around six thirty, Jenny heard vague crackling from an English radio station coming from the Czech couple's room, though she couldn't make out what was being said. Minutes later, she distinctly heard the long-awaited word: LANDING.

---

52. The opening words of *Chanson d'automne*, a well-known poem by Paul Verlaine, were used to signal to the French Resistance the start of Operation Overlord [Translator].

"Jacques! Wake up… I think this is it… should we wake the parents?"

They rushed to the wireless in Marie and Saby's room.

"Tuning in to London was practically impossible," Jenny recalls. "The Germans were extraordinarily good at jamming broadcasts! All the Vichy radio would say was that a handful of boats had come close to the coast and been driven away. The coast? Which coast? Provence? The Pas-de-Calais? Finally, the airwaves calmed down. Then came two words: 'landings' and 'Normandy.' Then Jacques, still in his pajamas, climbed up to Marcel's floor and hammered on the locked door, not daring to say anything in the staircase because of Mademoiselle C."

"I owe you twenty francs…"

Marcel's sleepy voice returned:

"Stop bothering me! Let me sleep."

Then he cried out:

"What?"

Marcel raced downstairs, four at a time. His sister Jenny does not say how the five adults gave vent to their joy. All she will say is: "And that was the start of a big party!" To celebrate the event, or to prepare for the storm? I was still asleep, and nothing remains in my four-and-a-half-year old's memory.

Still, this was the 6th of June 1944. The Allies had stormed the beaches of Normandy and breached the Atlantic Wall.

At noon, the whole family gathered around the sacred wireless set, listening intently to the words of De Gaulle: "*The battle has begun, and France will fight it with fury. For the sons of France, whoever they may be, wherever they may be, the simple and sacred duty is to fight the enemy with every means in their power.*"

The tenants of every stripe at Fleur des Alpes exulted. Was this the beginning of the end of their Calvary? For a few weeks, the men up in the Vercors believed the Allies, the professional French Army, the French government embodied by De Gaulle, and the *maquis* leaders were pulling together. At that moment, on June 6, 1944, Jacques, Marcel and all the "musicians" in Fleur des Alpes clenched their fists as they heard these words. These people who had been so humiliated, these sub-humans the Nazis wanted to slaughter, were ready to die as free men.

Marcel didn't hang around, ignoring Marie's pleas.

"My comrades are waiting. This time, we're going to fight."

The *Plan Montagnards* got underway in the mountain forest. Prematurely, however: the Allied commanders had no plans to support it, and the projected landings in the South of France ignored it.

Three days later, on June 9, 1944, Jenny set out to buy some food in Autrans.

Says Jenny says: "Jacques didn't come with me, as things were turning nasty. I boarded the bus at the same time as two young fellows who stood up near the driver: 'Ladies and gentlemen, we represent Free France. Show us your papers, please!'

"You could feel the silence as we took out our papers, keeping our thoughts to ourselves. This time it was not for the Gestapo or for the Militia or the Vichy police but for the representatives of the Resistance. I couldn't get over it. I couldn't believe it. Then we arrived at Méaudre, where I began going from farm to farm, filling my bags with provisions.

"Ahead of me, I saw two young men going into and coming out of the same farms, carrying no provisions. 'It's the Resistance,' a farmer's wife told me. 'They've come to enroll our boys.' Then, as I was leaving a farm, one of them turned and spoke to me: 'It's a shame to see you so weighed down. Would you let us carry your bags to the bus?'"

Jenny didn't wait to be asked again. Fifty years later, she beams as she speaks of it: "They were so charming! And good-looking too, which was a bonus. It was such a long time since I had met such well-mannered strangers.

"A little later, other men got into the bus and announced to the passengers: 'We are the Free Republic of the Vercors. Now the Allies have landed in Normandy, the French Resistance takes up the flame. We invite all those who can to join us.' Reactions in the bus were mixed. Meanwhile, I was beside myself with joy."

The Vercors became a little corner of Free France, where the French flag flew, and people sang *La Marseillaise*. The occupiers had banned the French national anthem. Singing it could cost you your life. The young people on the plateau went off with light hearts to deliver France from the Nazi yoke, ignoring the order to rein in guerilla activity issued by General Koenig on June 10. Among their ranks figured the maestro of Fleur des

211

Alpes, Marcel Amon. The same Huillier buses that ran from Villard-de-Lans to Grenoble and back were now requisitioned by the Resistance and ferried the young recruits to their assembly points on the farms.

The massif was well-guarded, like an impregnable fortress. Marcel had disappeared into the depths of the mountain along with his companions. His mother fretted, waiting for news which, as his sister put it: "naturally never came, the *maquis* having no postal service, nor any other kind of service for that matter."

According to Jenny after the war, the two charming young men who carried Jenny's bags, and who for her embodied the Free Republic of Vercors, were called Simon, and possibly Pierre, Nora[53], though the latter was only thirteen at the time and could not recall the incident when questioned later. The day after they carried Jenny's provisions while out recruiting fighters of the Free Republic of the Vercors, a detachment of the 1st Battalion of the 4th Regiment of *Panzergrenadier der Führer*, part of the *Das Reich Panzerdivision* of the *Waffen SS*, massacred the entire population, six hundred and forty-two men, women, and children, of Oradour-sur-Glane, a little village in Haute-Vienne department. The war wasn't over. Neither in the Vercors nor anywhere else.

The Free Republic of the Vercors: an islet in enemy territory

Did Marcel take part in the battle of Saint-Nizier, as he later told his doubting sister? History, as consigned in the archives of the National Association of Pioneers and Volunteers of the Vercors, confirms that "Marcel Amon, born in Paris on April 30, 1924, unmarried, joined the *Compagnie Philippe* on June 9, 1944." Four days later, Marcel Amon was indeed on the battlefield.

The respite was short-lived. Legend has it that it was the "tricolor," the French national flag flying over the village of Saint-Nizier, visible from the

---

53. The first was later a top civil servant who played a key role in the modernization of post-war France, the latter became an eminent French historian, author of *Realms of Memory* (Columbia University Press) [Translator].

valley, that attracted the Germans' attention. Saint-Nizier was the most accessible village in the massif. From Grenoble, where a curfew from 8 pm had been reinstated and where communication with the plateau was cut off, General Karl Pflaum launched an offensive to test the *maquis'* capacity for resistance. The battle of Saint-Nizier took place from June 13 to 15, that of Écouges on June 21. Contrary to legend, though, it was not the unfurling of the French flag over Saint-Nizier that triggered the German offensive, which had been decided well beforehand.

This is what Jenny, who stayed in Villard-de-Lans, recalls of the battle raging a few kilometers away. "What happened? Intrigued by the absence of buses coming in from the different villages and the mountain, the Germans in Grenoble decided to see what was going on. A German company set out on the road to Villard-de-Lans and trapped *maquisards* in a little village, the first mountain bastion, called Saint-Nizier, about twenty kilometers distant. The fighting was very fierce. There were many dead among the *maquisards*: they were young and inexperienced, with no heavy weapons, and they weren't wearing the distinctive red-white-and-blue armbands worn by the French Forces of the Interior. Anyway, organization was poor throughout the battle of the Vercors. There were too few parachute drops from London and Algiers and those that came were ill-coordinated, with a terrible shortage of heavy arms and airplanes, and seasoned troops to handle them.

"Down in Villard-de-Lans, meanwhile, we had no idea what was happening on our doorstep to our sons, brothers and husbands. The battle of Saint-Nizier took place in mid-June. Not in our wildest dreams did we imagine Marcel was taking part. One fine day, a detachment of Germans in battledress, some of them Polish fighting in the German army—by force or otherwise— arrived in town and stayed in Villard-de-Lans for two or three days, officially for a 'breath of fresh air.' We were unlucky to have them billeted downstairs in our house, in the disused former Polish girls' school. Finally, they left, and we were able to breathe again.

"Then, Marcel arrived 'on furlough,' full of his own importance. He told us about his battle of Saint-Nizier, before going off back into the mountains."

Jenny now lets Marcel recount the events. "On the first day, we gathered on the plateau at Saint-Nizier. As you know, it's a little village clinging to the Moucherotte, and when you come up from Grenoble it's a good way into the Vercors massif. That's where we were attacked first. We could clearly hear explosions—dull but regular. In late afternoon, as the firing grew less frequent, we saw thick smoke rising from the hills.

"Our sentry spotted the first Germans coming. They were coming up by a road called the Route de la Tour sans Venin. By then it was too late. At least four hundred enemy troops quickly occupied the plateau. I was afraid then. In the center of the very thinly spread-out line our company was holding, our machine gunners were on the point of letting rip and putting us all in danger. We had run out of mortar bombs, there was no more ammunition for our submachine guns, nothing for the rocket launchers that had been holding the enemy at bay behind a verge on the road less than twenty meters away. All we could do was try to attack with hand grenades when Chabal's section arrived; they'd been sent to reinforce us by Goderville, who was manning the heavy machine gun himself.

"I can still see them racing up from the river, leaping from their trucks singing La Marseillaise and charging with bullets flying all around. We lost men, but we managed to push the Germans back, harassing them with our Gammon grenades. By evening, we were worn out, but overjoyed to celebrate our first victory over the enemy despite our exhaustion!

"The day after next, the big guns started firing again. The enemy had brought up reinforcements and renewed their attack with artillery support. By the end of a day of hell, it felt like the whole mountain was in flames. Saint-Nizier was ablaze. The Germans had shelled the village and burned it down."

What Marcel does not say is that the battle of Saint-Nizier had cost the resisters their access to Grenoble and Villard-de-Lans. The Republic of the Vercors was now confined to the southern Vercors and the area around the village of Méaudre. It was proclaimed officially, with a military ceremony. The motto "Liberty, Equality, Fraternity" replaced the Vichy motto "Work, Family, Fatherland." The first piece of French soil to be liberated in a country still under occupation established its capital in Saint-Martin-en-Vercors, a few dozen houses amid gently sloping hills with scattered farms, overshadowed by the Roche Rousse. "Free France," with its four thousand novice maquis fighters, measured fifty kilometers long by fifteen wide. Marcel Amon paraded with his comrades. Like them, he now wore the red-white-and-blue armband bearing the Cross of Lorraine[54], a leather jerkin, plus-four pants, hobnailed boots, and a beret worn at a tilt. Like some of them, he carried a home-made submachine gun slung over his shoulder.

His path crossed that of real French soldiers in the uniform of the *Chasseurs Alpins* mountain troops, with a navy-blue cloak and an over-large beret known as a "tart" flattened down over one ear. The French flag hung from the windows of the liberated town. Wallposters proclaimed "People of the Vercors, it is here that the Republic has just been reborn. You can be proud!"

Like the others, Marcel underwent rifle drill, shooting at portraits of Hitler and Pétain for target practice. Senior officers took up their quarters in the Villa Bellon on the outskirts of the village. Relations were tense between the career officers and the volunteers of the interior who wanted to turn the *maquisards* into a regular army. As for the *Corps Francs*[55], they wanted nothing to do with those who had "dropped their pants in '40 and now wanted to come and play at tin soldiers."

Marcel took part in the everyday life of this "islet in enemy territory," as another eyewitness, his comrade the future historian Marc Ferro, put it. Did he, as the latter did, "weep for joy" at the sight of the Republic's posters and flags flying from the public monuments? In any case, he strolled about the streets of the little capital, amidst the banners, the red-white-and-blue sashes, the blue uniforms of the *Chasseurs Alpins*, the red *chechia* headdress of the Senegalese troops, the *fleur-de-lys* pennants of the armored troops, the gendarmes' *képis*, and the Crosses of Lorraine.

This slice of freedom lasted thirty-six days. François Huet, the military chief of the *maquis*, decided to incorporate his men into reformed military units. The *maquisards* became uniformed soldiers in the regular army, properly registered in the Army lists. This explains what happened next and the consequences for Jacques and Marcel. But who cared right now?

---

54. A cross with two horizontal bars, the emblem of General de Gaulle and the Free French (Translator).

55. The *Corps Francs de Libération*, a paramilitary resistance group [Translator].

They stopped being terrorist thugs and became fighting soldiers. Fighters for freedom.

July 14, 1944: the Vassieux trap

At the beginning of July, Jacques too left for the *maquis* with the other volunteers. The Resistance had been informed that a German division was heading for the Vercors. It asked all able-bodied men to join the *maquis*. A youngster came to Fleur des Alpes to recruit.

Jenny protested feebly, but Jacques was inflexible:

"Remember what Oscar said," he remonstrated. "There are two wars. If I join the *maquis* I'll be fighting for the Allies, and for our own people also, *los muestros*. It's a way to save our lives and uphold our honor. And if you want me to take French nationality one day, this is the way to do it."

"So, he left me and set out for the unknown. I was a bundle of nerves as I watched him walk away in civilian dress with his package in his hand. After that, no news! During the early part of July, the only men still in Fleur des Alpes and in the rest of the village were aged over sixty, my father Saby included," Jenny remembers.

French and English officers were parachuted onto the plateau in the night of July 6. This was a special mission in anticipation of some big event, still under wraps. But rumors were flying around.

"We're expecting reinforcements from North Africa," one of Marcel's comrades told him.

"Nothing of the kind," another chimed in. "It's General de Gaulle himself."

Everything was happening in Vassieux-en-Vercors, a village with a hundred or so houses, lying at the end of an open valley flanked by two wooded hills. A truly natural aerodrome. The Commander of the Vercors ordered a landing strip to be laid out for the US Army Air Corps cargo planes. This strip of land, a kilometer long by one hundred and fifty meters wide, was known as the "pencil sharpener." The Goderville Company was sent as reinforcements to level the land, push back rocks and stones, fill in the ditches and cut down bushes. The men slept in barns.

On the appointed day, on Bastille Day, the National Resistance Council called for a "Fighting 14th of July." The *maquisards* had been waiting on the landing strip since dawn. It was a glorious day with a clear blue sky. There was high excitement in anticipation of friendly reinforcements. Suddenly, waves of bombers dropped hundreds of parachutes bearing containers. The Allied planes, their wings sporting the double white star, flew very low across the plateau. Like a single man, the *maquisards* uttered a cry of joy. Their shouting grew louder still when the blue, red and white parachutes—in honor of France's July 14th celebration—opened under the bellies of the Flying Fortresses and floated down toward them. The men rushed forward to where the parachutes and their eight hundred and sixty containers had fallen, then dragged them into the forest after cutting the ropes. There were tons of weapons and munitions... but no help in the shape of men.

Suddenly, German bombers! The Allied planes had barely disappeared when they roared in, dive-bombing, and strafing the parachute drop area and parade ground. Impossible to collect the containers! All afternoon the enemy rained bombs on the villages on the plateau, destroying everything, farms, people, and animals. Shrapnel shells reduced the wheat to stubble. Saint-Martin and Corrençon were hit at the same time as Vassieux, where houses burned and villagers were mown down at random, dead, and wounded alike.

The men of the Vercors were caught like rats in a trap.

What Marcel and Jacques did not know was that conflicting messages had been sowing confusion throughout the little fortress the young *maquisards* had thought impregnable. Before the landing, Chavant, the civilian chief in the Vercors, had obtained written approval of the *Plan Montagnard* from De Gaulle's Provisional Government. On June 6, messages from London recommended undertaking all possible action to hamper German troop movements. The Vercors leadership decided to mobilize the reserves and lock down the zone. It was then, just as two or three thousand volunteers flocked in, Jacques among them, that General Koenig's counter-orders arrived; they had been drafted on June 10 and issued on the 17th, recommending that they avoid large concentrations.

This timing difference in the receipt of orders explains the tragic misunderstanding that trapped the *maquisards* in an unequal fight. With little support from the Allies and the French Army, forced to rely on their good will alone, the resisters were unable to avoid the predictable disaster. Later, each camp blamed the other for the failure.

That same July 14 in Villard-de-Lans, Saby, Marie, Jenny, and myself sat down to a very special lunch. Jenny had obtained a choice cut from a farmer's wife, one she thought she'd never eat again in her life: saddle of lamb. Marie passed the slices around on plates as they listened to the dull roar of the first bombs falling on Corrençon. She got up, taking her daughter and myself with her, but a sign from Saby ordered her to close the shutters and sit down again, while he chewed religiously.

For years, I thought I had no clear childhood memory before that of August 1944, when German soldiers came looking for Marcel. But this one did come back to me when Jenny described that July 14 scene, with the muffled thud of exploding shells, sometimes drawing near, our dumbfounded silence, sitting motionless, to the point where no one had any appetite for that fine piece of lamb with its crispy skin and pink flesh inside; our only thought was to flee, hide in the cellar, under the bed, while the patriarch sitting in the shadow stopped us from moving as his mandibles chewed relentlessly, heedless of the bombs—without a thought for his son in the *maquis*, who might be right underneath them—concentrating solely on his near-sacred activity. For Jenny, the scene prompted memories of the sacrilege that had undermined her childhood faith, while I associate it with the law of the Grandfather, with the categorical taboo: Be Not Afraid.

This memory, consequently, comes before what I had till then thought to be my first and the matrix for all others, including the later arrest of my uncle. Till then, I had no conscious timeline for this prehistory of my memory. But there was no way the bombs falling on Corrençon could not have been heard at Fleur des Alpes, which stood precisely on the road leading to that village.

"For us, in Villard-de-Lans, it was hell," Jenny goes on. "Marie went around with clenched teeth, thinking of Marcel. I couldn't sleep at night, thinking of Jacques. Only Saby, with his characteristic optimism and indifference, continued his daily walks and ate with a hearty appetite when there was something to eat. Because food was running very short now, I could no longer go to Méaudre and Autrans, there being no transport.

Nothing was coming up from Grenoble either, where communication had been cut off too. I got into the habit of going to Les Pouteilles, where there were three farms, and the people were very kind. I made friends with one of the farmer's daughters, and their produce helped us survive. Les Pouteilles was about five kilometers from Villard, so I could walk there."

Meanwhile, Marcel and Jacques took part in the battle lost on July 21, when the Vercors stronghold was sacrificed to the enemy. It was at that moment that I included in my evening concerto a song that Jenny had sung to me ever so softly, making me swear to sing it low, because of Mademoiselle C. That song went: "*Ami, entends-tu le vol noir des corbeaux sur nos plaines? Ami, entends-tu les cris sourds du pays qu'on enchaîne ? [...] c'est nous qui brisons les barreaux des prisons pour nos frères [...] Ami, si tu tombes, un ami sort de l'ombre à ta place...*" (Friend, do you hear the dark flight of the crows over our plains? Friend, do you hear the cries of our country in chains?... It is we who smash the bars of prisons for our brothers; Friend, if you fall a friend from the shadows will take your place) [56].

The *Chant des Partisans* became part of our personal folklore, on a par with the *Marseillaise*. The entire month of July 1944 was so intense, with Jacques caught up in the torment of the Vercors and Jenny in German-occupied Villard, that the two letters from Moïse and Marie sent from Italy passed unnoticed.

Last news from Argegno

Jacques had had little news of his parents since our arrival in Nice. In March 1943, they had boarded one of the two trains repatriating three hundred or so Italian Jews from France. The list had been drawn up from the registers of the Italian consulate and embassies with the help of the Gestapo and the Vichy Prefect of Police. Ever since reports of the destruc-

---

56. The *Chant des Partisans* (music by Anna Marly, French lyrics by Joseph Kessel and Maurice Druon) was the most popular song of the Free French and French Resistance during World War II. It was performed by a Russian *émigrée* Anna Marly, broadcast by the BBC and adopted by the *maquis*. Members of the Resistance and other French people sang it softly to avoid provoking German ire [Translator].

tion of the Jews of Europe had begun to spread in official circles in 1942, Mussolini's government, though allied with the Germans, had proposed an alternative to Italian citizens—and to Italians only—in some European countries: either return to the country whose passport they held, or stay in German hands. Volunteers flocked from all over, from Paris to Sofia and elsewhere.

The train taking Moïse and Marie Benrey, as well as Ugo and Allegra Modiano, left the Gare de Lyon in Paris and stopped in Lyon, where people could board but not get off. It went directly to Bardonecchia, an open town, in the Italian Alps. There, passengers were told to choose a precise destination in Italy. Jacques' parents opted for Milan, where they had lived after fleeing Bulgaria in 1924. Ugo and Allegra chose Parma, where the Modianos had relatives. In Milan, Moïse and Marie stayed in a little hotel that declared them as Jewish residents. Marie still had some jewelry which they hoped would tide them over till the end of the war, now seemingly in sight since the landings in North Africa and the victory at Stalingrad.

Mussolini had been disavowed by the Grand Council of Fascism, and he was arrested on the King's orders on July 24, 1943. A few days later, the Allies landed in Sicily. The Benreys and their friends hailed the event, especially Ézéquiel Tagger and his wife Victoria Hasson, old acquaintances from Bulgaria who had been repatriated from Sofia in a train like the one that had brought the Benreys here.

The bombing of Milan in August of the same year prompted many of the city's inhabitants to flee. Time to leave once more. Like other Jews, Moïse, Marie, Ézéquiel and Victoria were not allowed to go to one of the big tourist resorts. And, like everyone else, they had to register wherever they went in order to obtain ration cards.

"I've got an idea," said Ézéquiel to Moïse. "I know a remote little village on the shores of Lake Como. It's called Argegno. It's close to the Swiss frontier, so we might be able to cross it. Our friends the Aravs are ready to come with us."

The Benreys, the Taggers and the Aravs, three Sephardi Bulgarian couples aged between sixty and eighty, set out for Argegno between the month of August and the capitulation of Italy on September 3. They settled into the Albergo Argegno, a modest inn on the lake shore facing the landing stage.

Barely had they arrived when the situation turned irremediably for the worse, as it did for Jacques and Jenny in Nice at the same moment.

On September 11 the Germans entered Como.

On September 12 the Nazis freed Mussolini.

On September 23 the Republic of Salo was proclaimed, with Mussolini at its head.

A few months later, on June 8, 1944, Marie sat down on the terrace of the Albergo Argegno, looking out onto the landing stage where the *vaporettos* tied up, dipped her pen in the ink obligingly supplied by the innkeeper, Signor Rosati, and turned her thoughts to her brother Nissim Jerusalmi who had stayed behind in Paris, in their apartment on Rue Thimonnier. She wrote in Ladino, but this is what she said:

"Mi kerido Ermano, *my dear brother,*

You can't imagine the joy I felt in my heart when I received your kind letter. I was so afraid you wouldn't reply to mine. As for us, thank God, we are well. But we miss our family and above all the children infinitely. Thank God, I still receive good letters and good news from them, and they were very pleased to hear that you too were well. If only the war could end and we could see each other as we used to, I would begin cooking those borekitas *the way I used to! You write that you are entering your seventieth year, may it be happy and peaceful for you. God willing, we will all be together again, next year. My husband celebrated his seventy-ninth birthday. May we all be together again, at last!*

You write that you are alone: be happy that you are, for many would be delighted to be quietly in their homes. May God keep you in good health, and us too.

You cannot imagine how sad I felt at the death of our poor Esterina. She who so keenly wished that the war would end so that she could see her children. We have no news of how Lionel and his brother are doing. If I had their address, I would write to them for news of the rest of the family... Please say hello to our concierge, Madame Triboulet, and tell her how much I miss her. I still think of the good times I spent in her lodging. Please also say hello to her daughter and her husband. Say hello to all my friends. Do not leave me without news, continue writing to me to assure me you are in good health.

I have nothing else to write, other than to greet you; I clasp you in my arms,

Tu kerida Ermana, Marie"

In a short paragraph signed Moïse:

"*Dear brother-in-law,*

I have received your postcard whose contents I read with pleasure. We are pleased to hear that you are in good health, and I can tell you that we are too. Thank you for the news you write about our store, only you do not say if the Administrator Monsieur Giuffrida has taken the goods away and if he has the keys. Have my insurance premiums been paid on time so as not to let the insurance in Berlin lapse?

Te saludo con toda estima—my greetings and respect."

Nissim Jerusalmi added a comment in Judeo-Spanish on the letter, which reached him at Rue Thimonnier where he came secretly to pick up mail from the concierge, Madame Triboulet, having found a way to transfer it to Jacques in Villard-de-Lans: *"Le respondi.* Replied to him on July 10, 1944." Then:

"Sent a postcard to Moïse on Wednesday July 12, 1944.

"Wrote to Marie a second reply to this letter on Monday July 24, 1944.

"Sent a postcard to Marie on Monday August 6, 1944.

"Sent a postcard to Marie on August 15, 1944."

The Benreys' final letter from Argegno in Italy to their son Jacques and their daughter-in-law Jenny is dated July 14, 1944, the day Corrençon was bombed and the day we ate a slice of saddle of lamb under the watchful gaze of Saby and behind closed shutters. The first part of the letter was written by Moïse in French:

> *"Argegno, July 14, 1944*
>
> *My darlings,*
>
> *We are hoping still for your news, which we await impatiently. I can tell you that on our side we are still in good health. We have had a few days of rain, then the weather turned fine. We are very happy with the pensione. So, do not worry about us, on the contrary, it is we who need news from you to be reassured.*
>
> *In your last letter, you wrote that* kerido Marcel *gave* kerida Michou *a ring which delighted her. I can imagine the pleasure she must have felt, only please take care to remove the ring when it begins to tighten on her finger, because afterward it is very difficult to take off, and even dangerous at her age. We hope you still have the one we wanted her to have.*
>
> *We have received a card from your uncle saying that he is in good health.*
>
> *I kiss you as I love you. Our best wishes to Monsieur and Madame Amon.*
>
> *Moïse Benrey"*

argemo 14 juillet 1944

nos grands chéris.
nous sommes toujour à l'attende de
vos nouvelles que nous attendons
avec impatience.
Je vous informe de notre part
que nous sommes toujour en
bonne santé, nous avons eu
quelques jours dela pluie, et
le temp a changé au beau
et la penssione nous somme
très content, donc n'ayez aucun
souci pour nous, au contraire
c'est nous que nous avons
besoin de vos nouvelles pour
être tranquille
Dans votre dernière lettre vous
nous avez ecris que choi Marcel

From Marie, in Ladino:

"*My dear children,*
I too send kisses and hug you in my arms. Kisses for my dear little Michou.

Saludo a ti, la muy kerida Jenny, besos—Greetings to you, my dearest Jenny, and kisses,

Marie"

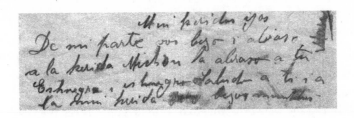

Two things stand out in the outlook on life my grandmother and grandfather bequeathed me before vanishing into the mountain of ashes blown away by a terrible storm: a yearning to make *borekitas* once more for those Marie loved, and Moïse's concern for his granddaughter's finger. Seventy years later, as I touch these two letters unearthed from that summer of 1944 with the same, now elderly, finger, and translate them as well as I can, I enter them in the profit and loss columns of my own process of remembrance.

Fleur des Alpes under the Germans

Exactly one week to the day after Marie Jerusalmi dipped her Ladino pen in Italian ink, the dream of the little Republic of the Vercors flickered and died. The Germans came up from Grenoble and entered Villard-de-Lans, where they paraded slowly then took the Corrençon road, heading for the massif and the men up there. The German division made a show of force and terror before the eyes of the petrified villagers, one Jenny would never forget:

"We'd been under curfew in our homes for twenty-four hours, starting in the morning, without even being allowed to open our windows, and they announced that the Germans were going to check everyone's papers. The village was packed with 'musicians.' At Fleur des Alpes, there were nothing but Jews! I was in Marcel's room in the attic, and I'd put you to bed so that you wouldn't move. The villagers had deserted the streets of Villard. I could feel my heart pounding, but I couldn't think what to do to stop it. All day long I saw that German army rolling past with its guns, tanks, airplanes, everything in camouflage, even its field kitchens. From my window on the fourth floor, I had the impression it was the trees that were marching past in perfect order, going up to the mountain and our wretched *maquisards*. Because they'd come to fight. That Friday July 21, 1944, was the day the great battle of the Vercors began.

"We 'musicians' were expecting to be rounded up. I'd even prepared our bundle in anticipation. But it was harvest time. The local farmers were also blocked by the curfew, so they went to see the Mayor of Villard and begged him to explain to the Germans that they absolutely had to go to work in the fields, otherwise the wheat would be lost. So, the mayor and the priest went off to make their request to the German commander, a certain Schultz, who said to them: 'Alright for the harvest. But it's full of Jews in your parish and your village!' And the priest and mayor chorused: 'Not a single one. We can guarantee it!' 'Alright then, no round up. But on your honor and on your lives, you guarantee there's not a single Jew in Villard-de-Lans. If we find just one, you'll both be shot.' The priest swore. The mayor swore. And we were spared.

"The next day, on July 22, we were ordered to hand over all radios and all bicycles in our possession, on pain of death. We were thus deprived of news. The last we were able to glean was the German generals' plot against Hitler, which failed, alas. So, July 21 simultaneously saw the battle of the Vercors and the failure of the plot against Hitler, which led to the liquidation of several generals, including Field Marshal Rommel, who was forced to take poison to escape the firing squad and spare his family. All we knew of either of these two major events was vague hearsay, whispered by word of mouth.

"Marie and Saby's bridge partners, who lived in Côte 2000, contrived however to keep a wireless set and camouflaged it in with the firewood stored in the cellar, where they'd made a little hole. Every evening, when the BBC came on the air, the radio was taken from its hiding place and friends and neighbors gathered round to listen, giving rise to rumors true and false, reaching Fleur des Alpes and beyond.

"But when it came to the battle of the Vercors, after the Germans' triumphant march past our windows, there was utter silence. We understood there was fighting going on, but no one knew where; chiefly though, we had no idea where our loved ones were. The army had blocked every way out of the village, and we were under practically permanent curfew. Fear gripped us through every pore, we couldn't eat a thing—anyway there was nothing to eat! —still less get a wink of sleep. And we had to stop you moaning when you were hungry and wanted to get out of the bed you were kept in for hours on end, while outside we heard the clatter of jackboots and soldiers singing.

"Finally, after a few days, we knew there had been fighting and that the enemy had won. Where were our men? What was happening to them? Imagine our heavy hearts as we listened to the whispered account of a supposedly well-informed but unnamed person encountered in a 'musician's' home in Villard-de-Lans! Yes, the battle had been lost. Yes. They were hanging up men on butchers' hooks. Yes. There were massacres, rapes, atrocities.

"Returning home in tears that day I ran into Madame Papo, who lived on the second floor at Fleur des Alpes. She grabbed me by the arm and whispered: 'I've heard news. Come in. I'll tell you everything.'"

The Battle of Vercors: an unequal struggle

When he joined the *maquis* Jacques was inducted into the 3rd Company of the 6th Battalion of *Chasseurs Alpins* mountain infantry, commanded by Captain Goderville, a *nom de guerre* taken from his father's native village. In civilian life his name was Jean Prévost, a graduate of the élite École Normale Supérieure and a specialist in the nineteenth-century writer Stendhal. He had already distinguished himself in the Battle of the Vercors.

The company was garrisoned in a farm called Herbouilly, near Valchevrière, deep in the mountain. Jacques received initial weapons training and an introduction to military life. The raw recruit was given a uniform, and despite being thirty-six years old and having no experience, he was sent right away to the most exposed spots, in his uniform and armed with a submachine gun. That was how he set out for battle on the *Pas de l'Âne* and the *Pas de la Sambue* mountain passes where, with two or three hundred other lightly armed men, he helped hold the crest dominating the Corrençon Valley.

On July 21, the entire plateau was surrounded by two German divisions, which Jenny, Marie, and Saby had heard and seen marching through Villard-de-Lans, just in front of Fleur des Alpes. The *maquisards* were outnumbered six-to-one. But they were confident. They were expecting reinforcements. Like Napoleon at Waterloo.

The Germans began by trying to control the passes leading through the cliff-face. The *maquisards* holding these narrow gaps were ready to fight to the death and resisted fiercely. The eight men dug in at the *Pas de l'Aiguille* pass were mown down by machine-gun fire and grenades. One by one, the other passes fell into enemy hands, at Corrençon on the 21st, then the Sambue pass. That is where Jacques and the other mountain infantrymen were. They held out heroically for two days. Then one of the leaders, Chabal, was mortally wounded at Valchevrière on July 23. Before dying, he threw his notebook containing the names of the men in his company over the cliff, saving them from later arrest.

But the decisive moment came in the center of the Vercors, and it came from the sky. In the night of the 21st, *maquisards* and civilians labored to prepare a landing strip near Vassieux for Allied parachutists, the aim being to catch the enemy from behind to coincide with the landings in Provence. At last, forty gliders arrived overhead, towed by powered aircraft. On the ground, everyone was overjoyed. The planes came in from the south, suggesting they had come from Algiers.

In fact, it was a ruse. Suddenly, black Luftwaffe crosses came into view. "The *Boches*!"

The Free French realized their mistake.

There was a clatter of machine-gun fire, but too late. A glider was hit, and crash landed. But all the others landed safely. Troops leaped out. The *maquisards* were chopped down even before they could open fire. Altogether, five hundred enemy troops landed on the field. A specially trained and equipped unit brought in from Strasbourg. They fanned out and occupied the village of Vassieux and the nearby hamlets of La Mure and Le Château. Their heavy arms quickly silenced the machine guns. There ensued a massacre of every living being in their path. Counterattacks by members of the Resistance in the evenings of July 21 and 22 came to naught.

The battle swung this way and that, with attempted counterattacks, dispersal, breathless flight through the forests, regrouping, and fresh attacks. Bullets whistled, shaving the heads of the young maquisards. Some crouched behind the rare machine guns, firing on the gliders, then slumping forward, dead. A very young man, his torso bared, rushed toward the Germans, pistol in hand, leaped into the air, then fell heavily into the grass.

They had been hoping all available units would come to their aid. All they got was the enemy. On July 23, after two days' relentless fighting, the Germans broke through onto the plateau. These were Luftwaffe parachutists, many of them Eastern European legionaries. By noon, it was over. The Battle of Vassieux was lost. The last passes fell, and Die was occupied.

Between July 20 and 21, Chavant, the civilian head of the Vercors telegrammed to Allied commanders: "Population's morale excellent but will quickly turn against you if you do not take immediate steps, and we will agree with them in saying that the people in London and Algiers have totally misunderstood our position and will be seen as criminals and cowards. Repeat: criminals and cowards."

For three days in the village of Vassieux and outlying areas, the Germans executed the order they had received: "Destroy everything." They treated the civilians with the utmost savagery: women, children, the old, the sick. Vassieux was a heap of dead bodies, a field of ruins. Victims were machine-gunned without distinction, their bodies thrown into the flames. Marcel Janovski, a neighbor of Fleur des Alpes, witnessed the tragedy and told of a little girl, Arlette Blanc, lying across the bodies of her parents, murdered by the Germans. For five days and five nights, the child cried out, begging for water.

"The *Boches* walked past her, jeered and went on drinking and partying."

Vassieux is a sacred spot in the tale of the rebirth of Free France, later designated a *Compagnon de la Libération*[57] by General de Gaulle.

In despair, the commander of the Vercors gave the order to disperse into the *maquis*. Some took refuge in the forests or the mountain heights, avoiding roads and crossing points. Everyone was advised to become "nomads," i.e., to go their separate ways and scatter across the plateau, to vanish into the landscape, leaving the enemy master of the battlefield.

---

57. The highest rank in the Order of the Liberation created by De Gaulle [Translator].

Commander Goderville told his men:

"All is lost. Now we're going to get out of here, because if we stick around they're going to slaughter us. Get back into civvies!"

The men looked at each other. They were up in the mountain, in the middle of nowhere, with nothing to eat or drink.

Jacques didn't know what to do. He had long kept his suit in his kitbag. But it had become so cumbersome, and he was so exhausted he had gotten rid of it.

"Oh God! I've thrown away all my civilian clothes!"

Just then, a fellow next to him gave him a look:

"Hey, are these yours?"

By chance, his comrade had picked up the abandoned clothes and kept them.

Jacques took off his uniform and donned his civilian suit. The men set off in all directions. Some tried to reach another Resistance hotspot, others tried to return home.

"Where are you from?" Captain Goderville asked a shepherd.

"Villard-de-Lans... Les Pouteilles farm."

"Les Pouteilles! That's where my wife gets her food!" Jacques exclaimed.

The captain turned to the shepherd and said:

"Take Benrey with you. If he stays by himself, he'll get lost and he'll be dead."

Goderville, or rather Jean Prévost, liked Jacques. They discussed literature together, Stendhal of course, and Montaigne's *Essays*, which the commander always kept with him, and Proust, favorite reading for Jacques, who later gave a copy of *In Search of Lost Time* to his daughter on her fourteenth birthday. Jean Prévost had a Jewish wife and a little daughter. He saved Jacques' life, but not his own. He was killed a few days later trying to reach the *maquis* in the Isère. Emerging from the Engins gorge on August 1, 1944, he came upon a German patrol and was shot. He had been a friend of Antoine de Saint-Exupéry, whose aircraft had disappeared just the day before. Commander Huet, unaware of Goderville's death, sent him the following message: "I know what you did in the fight at Corrençon. Congratulations. It was unfortunately such an unequal struggle."

Meanwhile, Jacques was making his way across the Mountain with the shepherd from Les Pouteilles. For three days they trudged, half-dead from thirst, till they reached the spring at Herbenouze, where the animals went to drink. There, the muddy, brackish water tasted wonderfully refreshing, and they ate wild strawberries. It took them another two days to reach Les Pouteilles, hiding from the Germans and seeking short-cuts through the woods. The shepherd signaled their presence, but the two men remained in the forest. Farms sheltering *maquisards* were pitilessly burned to the ground and their inhabitants murdered. Ignoring the curfew, the farmer's daughter walked the five kilometers from the farm to Villard-de-Lans. It was she who was on the second floor of Fleur des Alpes when Madame Papo asked Jenny to follow her:

"Your husband's alive... come and fetch him."

"I would have climbed Mont-Blanc..."

"Your husband's alive...!"

"Alive?"

"I was thinking, 'This is it, she's going to tell me something's happened to Jacques.'"

Jenny never forgot that moment. Sixty years later, she recalls it down to the last detail.

"Those words," she repeats, "I heard them in Madame Papo's apartment, from the farmer's daughter. She'd become a friend and had walked ten kilometers there and back, despite the curfew. She wanted to reassure me and let me know that Jacques, by some extraordinary miracle and after no end of troubles, had landed up in her farm, Les Pouteilles, in the company of a shepherd from his unit. These good people, like all the farmers in the area, had given them food, but they hadn't given them shelter because of the danger to everyone. Jacques asked them what had happened, fearing we might have been carried off to the camps in the East. 'Don't you worry! I know your wife well. She was here not long ago with your little girl. They're alive and well.'

"I was so happy! I never thanked Heaven as much as I did that day. The next morning, wearing a very creased peasant dress, beneath which I'd concealed a shirt and civilian pants in my knickers, along with shaving things, and carrying my empty milk cans, I walked past the Germans who were blockading all the roads. I just told them I was going to fetch some food.

"It was a risky undertaking! The mountain was teeming with soldiers, 'Mongols,' as they were known, who hunted down fleeing *maquisards*. Some, it was said, raped young women found walking alone on deserted tracks. Nothing happened to me—I would have climbed the Mont-Blanc—and I fell into Jacques' arms in a corner of the forest. He was unrecognizable, emaciated, filthy, his pants and jacket in tatters. His hair had grown long and was falling over his face. After all those days of fighting and fleeing he and his brother in misfortune looked like hobos or hermits. They were dying of thirst because the farmer who had brought them some ham to eat had brought nothing to drink. Who cared? We were so happy to be alive and together!

"From him, I heard about the scale of the disaster, how he had fought alongside Goderville in the Battle of the Pas de l'Âne pass, and how the Allies had let the Resistance down. Jacques thought he had seen Marcel in the thick of the battle, but there had been so many dead! So, we were still unsure as to the fate of my brother and all our friends.

"I made my decision on the way back to Villard-de-Lans, with my full milk cans, under the eyes of the Germans. I'd go next day to fetch Jacques at Les Pouteilles, and I'd try to bring him back home. Early the next morning, I took my milk cans and set out for Les Pouteilles despite my mother's opposition: she claimed there were Senegalese troops on the roads raping all the girls. But I was not to be deterred. I wanted to go and fetch my husband, and I met no Senegalese. I came back with Jacques in civilian clothes, fresh-shaven, chatting gaily as if we were just returning from a morning walk in the mountain splendor. The 'others,' the Germans, let us through. Jacques climbed the four floors to the little attic room at Fleur des Alpes and collapsed onto the bed. I took off his boots, which he'd been wearing for days and stank unbearably. I undressed him. He slept without waking for three days, and for long after.

"The day before, we'd been thrilled and relieved to learn that Marcel, who'd been fighting in the *Compagnie Philippe*, was safe, and that he too was at Les Pouteilles. He'd been in the 12th *Chasseurs Alpins* infantry battalion, under Battalion commander Philippe Ullmann. They had been holding the Rencurel, Presles and Choranche area, with the Coulmes forest between the Isère and Drôme rivers. The mayor and priest had gone from house to house telling everyone to 'bring the men home.'

"In the afternoon of the same day, my mother, Marie, followed my example and went to fetch her son, not fearing the Senegalese who, unlike the 'Mongols,' were part of the French army. Other *maquisards* were coming home on foot, in dribs and drabs. You could tell them from their outfits, which were either too short or too long, which they'd got from farmers, having discarded their uniforms. Like us, members of their family helped them home. Our friend and neighbor Marcel Janovski, who'd survived the Vassieux massacre, also made it home. Then we jealously keep our men out of sight in our homes.

"It was a ghastly time. For three weeks following July 21, we and the people on the plateau suffered the terrible revenge of the Germans, murdering, executing hostages, raping, torturing, burning, looting. They were scouring the woods, taking no prisoners. Any man caught was tortured and shot on the spot as a terrorist. *Maquisards* captured by the Germans suffered endless torment. Some were found hanging by their feet, their heads buried in anthills. Alongside the SS and the 'Mongols,' there were the Bavarian and Austrian reservists from the 157th Division of the Wehrmacht, aided by the French militia in some cases, as on July 6 at Beauvoir-en-Royans."

The *maquis* hospital was installed in a cave called La Luire between July 22 and 27. But on the 27th a patrol of German mountain infantry discovered (had an informer given them away?) some thirty-odd wounded there, including four Wehrmacht soldiers of Polish origin who had been taken prisoner, plus seven nurses, three doctors and a chaplain. The seriously-wounded were summarily dispatched, while the less badly-wounded were murdered the next day. Two of the doctors were transferred to Grenoble, where they too were executed.

Jenny saw them passing beneath her window at Fleur des Alpes, along with the nurses, en route for Ravensbrück; one of them never returned.

"I'll never get that memory of the seven women in handcuffs out of my head!" Jenny sighs.

233

Emotionless, the Germans let the *maquisards* return home. They had their lists. They bided their time. But they forbade the mayor and the priest to go into the mountain in search of the tortured men's corpses, now rotting in the summer sun.

Who was responsible for the Vercors tragedy, General Koenig? Commander Huet, alias Hervieux, the military commander in the Vercors? Colonel Constans in Algiers? De Gaulle? The Allies? Internal divisions? Inexperience? Shortage of weapons? It's up to the historians to decide whether this was a case of betrayal or abandonment. Whatever the case, Jacques, Marcel and their comrades, the nameless foot soldiers, many of whom never came back, did their duty, and received no reward.

Jacques never complained, though. As he saw it, the harsh experience of the Vercors, with its moments of glory and camaraderie, was just a stroll, a bit trying, compared with all the rest.

Monsieur Bienenfeld, or the "musicians" bridge game

"I can tell you, my friends," Monsieur Bienenfeld was holding forth, "I really thought my last hour had come. In my mind, I said goodbye to my dear wife, Ada. I said goodbye to my dear sons, Nicha and Michel. I said goodbye to little Jojo, my sister-in-law's nephew, whom God had sent us via a Red Cross convoy. I closed my eyes, expecting to be sent eastward to Poland, where my ancestors had already suffered so many pogroms."

"And then?"

You could have heard a pin drop in the room where Saby, Marie and their fellow players and friends had gathered for a game of bridge.

Monsieur Bienenfeld paused and enjoyed the attention, as all eyes were on him. He cleared his voice, which was loud, and continued in perfect French, accent notwithstanding:

"And then... And then... I handed over my card with the cursed yellow stamp to the Boches and waited for my final hour."

"And then?"

They were all eager to hear the story, though they already knew how it ended. In the days that followed the sacrifice of the stronghold and the return of the surviving *maquisards*, the village of Villard-de-Lans was calm once more. Jacques and Marcel were still resting from the extreme ordeal of the battle. Marie and Saby had left them to sleep as they hastened over to the other side of the village at Côte 2000, in search of news of their bridge partners. That August afternoon in 1944, the assembled friends included the Alfandaris, the Rovanous and the Bienenfelds, a blend of Judeo-Spanish, Romanians and Poles. Persecution had brushed aside their ritual and theological differences: today they were all "musicians."

In fact, though, Monsieur Bienenfeld was never really a "musician" like the rest because he lacked forged papers. His story is a reverse illustration of the precautionary principle. Monsieur Bienenfeld, as his bridge partners called him under their breath, was scarcely inconspicuous. His thick Yiddish accent betrayed him the moment opened his mouth. Yet despite this, he had never tried to obtain forged papers. Admittedly, that wouldn't have been easy in remote mountain village like Villard-de-Lans. One had to know "someone" important, like a sympathetic police chief. And the Bienenfelds had never left Villard, where they had taken refuge since the start of the war, while not many Germans had been seen in this area, initially unoccupied, then occupied by the Italians, and finally left to its own devices.

As a result, Marc and Ada Bienenfeld had lived a quiet life there with their two grown-up sons, Nicha and Michel. Not far away lived their brother and sister-in-law David, Esther, and the latter's nephew, Georges Peretz, baptized Perec[58] but nicknamed Jojo. Jojo was a boy of eight at the time. He had been sent here from Paris by his mother two years beforehand. He was a boarder at the Turenne school in Villard, but he spent his vacations with his uncle and aunt. Like Marcel and all the other young men, Nicha and Michel had joined the *maquis* after the Normandy landings in June. All the while, Marc Bienenfeld had not given a thought to the inconvenient stamp on his identity card. That explains why, when General Karl Pflaum's divisions invaded the village, the mayor and priest

---

58. Georges Perec later a renowned author of numerous publications, including *W, or the Memory of Childhood*, (London: Harvill, 1988) and *Ellis Island and the People of America* (New York: New Press, 1995). [Translator].

could honestly swear on their lives that there wasn't a single yellow stamp in the whole of Villard-de-Lans.

That awful morning of July 21, Monsieur Bienenfeld resolved to flee into the heart of the plateau. And there he remained, hiding in the woods for days on end. Finally, at the end of his tether, utterly lost and finding no food, he decided to return home, regardless of the danger. Suddenly, turning a corner he ran into a German patrol, which took him to headquarters for their superior to determine his fate. The latter was away, so they kept him... a long time.

That was where, more dead than alive, with his Jewish identity card—all he had on him—he thought his last hour had come.

The chief finally returned, in a foul mood: "Papers!" And Monsieur Bienenfeld held out his document, hands shaking.

"And then?" chorused the other six bridge partners in unison.

"And then..." Monsieur Bienenfeld dragged out the suspense, milking the effect, "without looking at me, the guy grabs my ID and, without bothering to open it up, tears it into little bits and chucks to the other end of the room, screaming: 'They're all forged, these papers... Get the hell out of here!' So, I picked up the pieces of paper and ran off, without waiting for an explanation! I went back into hiding in the Forest of Lente, not far from the La Luire cave where the field hospital was. There, I met some *maquisards* making their way back to Villard, and I came back with them."

The six "musicians" paused to take in their friend Bienenfeld's incredible story. Then, Madame Rovanou, the wife of the doctor who came to treat us in secret, spoke up:

"It's like for me, two years ago. Villard was still in the Free Zone. I had my yellow stamp on my identity card. The French gendarmes came to arrest me and took me to Grenoble with other foreign Jews."

"And then?"

"And then, they let me go... Because I was Romanian. They weren't picking up Romanians at the time. All the others were deported, all of them."

"And what did you do then?" asked Marie.

"Ah, well, yes. I had my papers forged, and my Romanian parents' stamped papers. I used bleach."

Madame Rovanou gave no details. She didn't explain how, despite having run out of money and with her warm heart, she had decided to take in Jewish children as boarders. How she had also sheltered "little" eighteen-year-old boys, claiming they were fifteen to avoid them being taken away for compulsory labor. Did someone turn her in? She never talked about the hours she had spent standing in the barracks courtyard, in the sun and without food, with her companions in misfortune.

That afternoon, the "musicians" wanted nothing more than to gasp at these anecdotes, still fresh and not yet part of history, and to rejoice at the way their two bridge partners had escaped the Nazis without even having to hide. All around them, those children who had been spared played, among them little Dominique Rovanou, who as an adult became my friend; Michel Drach, Angèle's young boarder and future movie director, who wouldn't be parted from his squirrel; perhaps also Jojo Perec, who later immortalized his encounter with *maquisards* in need of food and supplies in *W, or the Memory of Childhood*.

Perhaps Jacques and his Goderville comrades, or Marcel and those in Philippe Company, were among the famished, bearded young men little Georges and his pals were ordered to hand over their meager teatime treat to, without fully understanding why.

Their fate was about to be sealed when Jenny burst into the bridge party at Côte 2000, yelling at Marie:

"Marcel!... Marcel's been arrested!"

My first childhood memory

Marcel's arrest… My first childhood memory, the first in a sense of an "official" and legitimate memory in my eyes—because I have never forgotten it since that day on August 7, 1944. For I can now put a date on it. It was morning. I was playing with other children outside Fleur des Alpes. And I precisely recall the bouquet I was gathering. I'd picked bluebells, buttercups, daisies, and poppies, which I clasped carefully so that those ever so delicate petals would not come off their stalks. I was concentrating on my bouquet when, from far off, I heard the characteristic crunch of our ogres' jackboots.

At what moment in my childhood did I identify the enemy and grasp the danger he represented? I was born with the war and the hunt for Jews. When did I begin to feel afraid? Was it the day after the botched arrest of my father in September 1942, when those two French policemen came ringing the doorbell of our apartment on the Rue César-Franck at dawn? Was it when the German sentry refused to let me cross the demarcation line with my parents? I wasn't three at the time. Was it during the round-ups in Marseille, in January 1943, when the terrified screams of neighbors who'd been caught mingled with the bellowing of Germans carrying out their orders? Was it in December of the same year, in Nice in the grip of Brunner and his men, brutally driving their victims to the Hotel Excelsior, before dispatching the mother of Ninon and her brother Jako to the train bound for Drancy and onward in sealed railcars to Birkenau? But I was only four, and the only memory I have of that Christmas month was the cradle wrapped in pink muslin, with its cute sleeping doll.

One can never be sure where memory is concerned. But timelines can help. Just before that singular day in summer 1944, there was the lunch on July 14 while bombs were falling, and the singing of our enemies marching past our windows on the 21st. Not really coherent memories, just bits and pieces, hazy; I could not have localized or identified them before I began my research.

I remember nothing of my father's and my young uncle's return to the welcoming rooms of Fleur des Alpes a few days earlier. But that morning of August 7, 1944, is as clear in my memory as the day my own son was born. I could tell you the color of the sky, the summery light of a fine morning, the dazzling hues of my wildflowers, and the sound, at first muffled, then louder and louder, of fourteen jackboots hammering the sloping road to Corrençon, awakening a terror that has haunted my nightmares ever since.

In a flash, I dropped my bunch of flowers and rushed to the stairs in Fleur des Alpes. I raced up them two at a time, as fast as my little legs could mount the steps, which seemed so high, barely stopping to pick myself up before racing up to the second floor. I had to pause a moment on the first-floor landing. The ogres were on my heels. Their footsteps were drawing near. I grabbed the handle of the door on the right to catch my breath. I held on with all my strength, thinking they couldn't snatch me away from behind because I was holding on so tightly—me, a little girl not yet five, against these Nazi giants.

Then I continued upward to the second floor. I reached the landing in a twinkling of an eye, then hammered frenziedly on the heavy wooden door, on the other side of which were Jenny, Jacques, my uncle Marcel, and Marcel Janowski, who'd come around for a visit.

"Papa! Germans!"

The door opened quickly, then closed. I barely had time to see my father get out his paper and the neighbor slide under the bed when already a call came through the door:

"Open up! German police!"

I sat down cross-legged, my favorite position. And from my few centimeters above the floor, I lifted my head in the direction of these goliaths scarcely able to fit through the door. There were seven of them. Seven members of the German military police carrying submachine guns, bursting into the tiny apartment.

"Amon, Marcel? Papers! ..."

My uncle drew the documents from his pocket.

"Get your things and come with us!"

They didn't even glance at my father, who trembled as he waited his turn. Marcel calmly packed some clothes and left with them.

As for Jenny, she hurried to the other end of the village to warn her parents and their friends, who ceased forthwith from chortling over Monsieur Bienenfeld's story. Marie broke down, and all three went back to Fleur des Alpes in distress. No, the war wasn't over. German reprisals against the surviving Villard *maquisards* were only just beginning.

Marcel was the first to be arrested because his name began with A. Others, young and not so young, were apprehended in their homes. All night, the German army marched to the tune of its famous warrior song, while never ceasing to hunt down the *maquisards*. No one could sleep a wink. Early next morning we learned that around seventy or eighty men had been picked up and taken to the old school, now a prison. It stood next to the Hotel Splendid, where the *Kommandandtur* had set up its headquarters. All these people were members of the *Compagnie Philippe*, like Marcel. The Germans knew their names, and all had been arrested.

From this it was deduced that the Germans had a list of the company's members that included the *maquisards'* real names in alphabetical order. The French considered them to be members of the regular army. For the Germans, they were mere terrorists: they would have been better off keeping just their *noms de guerre* as resisters.

"Why did the Germans have the identities of the *Compagnie Philippe* and not the others?" Jenny wonders still. "There was rumored to be a traitor. There were so many informers, voluntary or under torture! In any case, the youngsters arrested with Marcel all belonged to the same company. Jacques and Goderville's men were left in peace. Most of the men lived in Villard-de-Lans. In some of the farms where young men had hidden in the woods, the Germans had politely asked the inhabitants to hand over their sons, saying they had nothing worse in store than being sent to work in Germany. Elsewhere, they threatened to burn down the farm, eliciting this distressing confession to the priest, Abbé Vincent, from a father who had given up his son: "What can I do, Father? It takes a century to build up a farm and only twenty years for a boy to grow up to be a useful worker!"

"Suspicions of an informer were never proven, but the whole story of the Vercors is steeped in suspicion. In addition to the normal sources, the Gestapo and the Militia, there was also the SD, the military intelligence, which was highly effective; there were informers, willing and unwilling; confessions extracted under torture; reports of gossip; recklessness; carelessness; cowardice; personal hatreds and jealousy."

For Jenny, and even more for Marie, the long wait and deathly anguish began all over again. They brought food to their prisoner in the school building every day. The guards were fairly easygoing, one a Bavarian who perhaps had a few things on his conscience, and a Pole who'd been forcibly conscripted. They too listened to the English radio and knew they were fighting a losing battle. The game was up. The prisoners were interrogated daily in turn by Major Schultz.

The youngsters agreed among themselves to say they were students who had come up to Villard-de-Lans in their vacations to get away from the bombing of their towns after D-Day. Some of the older ones were released. Then came Marcel's turn to be interrogated one morning.

In the afternoon, Marie asked the sentry in her halting German why her son hadn't been released while others had.

"Just go to the *Kommandandtur* to ask them why! *Gehen Sie… Gehen Sie zur Kommandandtur ! Los !* Go on… Go on…"

"Shall we go?" asked Marie.

"Yes, let's," replied Jenny.

The *Kommandantur* was next door. Jenny trembled but went in head held high.

The Executed of the Cours Berriat[59]

"Madame, your son is not eighteen years old. He's twenty. He is not a student. He is a dangerous terrorist who's mainly concerned to evade compulsory labor in Germany. We're going to kill all terrorists. The first thing they deserve is a bullet in the head."

The two women had gone into the lobby of the Hotel Splendid. It was teatime. All was quiet in the *Kommandantur*. Officers were sitting at round tables, drinking fruit juice or beer, and eating biscuits. The women were greeted cordially, almost. They were ushered to a table. Major Schultz joined them immediately and uttered these brutal words politely, with the utmost refinement.

Marie blenched. She didn't need to muster her faltering German. Major Schultz spoke perfect French with a faint, barely detectable accent. She responded with a gesture.

"I know, I know. You're his mother. And the young lady with you is not a friend but his sister. I too have a mother, and a sister… You see, Madame, I've interrogated your son. He's a charming fellow. A genuine musician. I talked music with him, German music, which I love above all in the world… Beethoven… Bach… Handel…Haydn… Wagner… Above all Beethoven… I must tell you, Madame, that I'm a conductor in civilian life. Yes. A conductor in Leipzig… I've read his letters. The ones found in his pockets when we searched him. Munch! Ansermet! The greatest

---

59. A broad street in Grenoble [Translator].

musicologists! All praise him! Music! It's greater than war, music. War is a horrible thing. But music..."

The German Major paused. As if the notes of a symphony lingered in his ears, then:

"Yes. A horrible thing! Alright... We're not going to destroy them, these young people! I'd like to pardon them and send them to work on the railroad in Grenoble. As for your son... I can't let them shoot a boy who could one day become one of the glories of his country."

"Major Schultz got up," says Jenny, "and gave us a kind of military salute as he showed us the way out, leaving us dumbstruck. We got out as fast as we could, my mother—Marie—and myself. If I hadn't been there myself, I would never have believed it. Actually, no one did. That episode, and the ones that followed, were dreamlike.

"The next day, we thought English radio had gone mad. We had nothing to go on but hearsay since we no longer had a wireless. All we knew was that there had been a flurry of cryptic messages repeated over and over, such as 'The huntsman is hungry... Nancy's got a stiff neck... Don't knock the cripple over... No horseplay in the morning... Sherry is a Spanish wine...' Operation Dragoon had just begun on the night of August 14-15, 1944." Another Allied landing. In Provence, this time. With seven French divisions under General de Lattre de Tassigny.

"In Villard-de-Lans, we were back to waiting. With a lump in our throat. Torn between joy at hearing of this new landing and fears for Marcel and the others still being held in the school. And we couldn't leave the village as it was barricaded at either end.

"Then, out of the blue on August 21, Marcel, our young *maquisard* and a Jew!, was released into the village square in Villard with a safe-conduct allowing him to go outdoors during the curfew. The conductor from Leipzig had spared the composer-genius. Along with another fellow. As for the rest of the prisoners, there were only twenty-one left."

Jenny pauses. There is a slight tremor in her voice, but she carries on: "The major told their families that they'd be working on the railroad in Grenoble... which was being bombed, but, well... there was a chance they'd survive. They were locked up in the prison in Grenoble. Then we had no more news of them. We thought they'd been sent to work in Germany.

And then... and then... a mass burial site was found with their corpses. Inside Grenoble itself, in the Cours Berriat. All dead. All twenty-one. No, just twenty. Young Gilbert Soroquère was spared because he had been alone in a cell whereas the others had been two in a cell. That odd number had saved him. He'd been overlooked. The others were executed by firing squad. In Grenoble. They'd been taken from the truck, one by one, and executed. There's a monument to them now: 'Les fusillés du cours Berriat,' the Executed of the Cours Berriat. I returned there after the war and shed the tears I'd held back at the time.

"As for Marcel, he'd had the luck of the devil. His prank had saved his life. 'I can't let them shoot a boy who could one day become one of the glories of his country.' Major Schultz, or rather the Leipzig conductor, had kept his word. For him, music took precedence over war. Then war had returned to the fore, and he had ordered the execution of twenty-one 20-year-old boys: I knew all of them and used to call them by their first names."

For years, like Jenny, I thought Major Schultz had pardoned Marcel because he had believed in his genius and had condemned the other twenty, because in his eyes or ears they had none. We know now, thanks to the work of local historians, that these young prisoners in Grenoble were not intended for the firing squad. They had been taken from their cells on August 14 and put into a truck, quite possibly bound for the village. That same day, at 11.50 in the morning, two German soldiers had just been shot in the Cours Berriat. No one claimed credit for the attack, quite possibly the FTP-MOI[60], or a criminal shoot-out involving the militia.

Baying for reprisals, the Germans decided to shoot hostages. Fate pointed its finger at the twenty *maquisards* from the *Compagnie Philippe*. The men being held in the Bonne barracks were executed late in the afternoon, on the corner of Cours Berriat and Rue Ampère, near the bridge over the Drac River. The first four were brutally pushed out of the truck and machine-gunned. The others watched in horror as their comrades

---

60. *Franc tireurs et partisans-Main-d'oeuvre immigrée* (Sharpshooters and partisans—Immigrant workers), a celebrated Communist resistance group made up mainly of immigrant workers, many of them Jewish. Most were rounded up and executed [Translator].

were slaughtered, knowing they were next. Each was murdered in turn, one after the other, in groups of three or four.

Twenty corpses, each aged twenty, lay on the sidewalk at the corner of the Cours and the street.

Doubts linger as to the circumstances: were these young men taken from their cells to be shot, or were they simply crossing the road at the wrong moment? Were they machine-gunned three at a time, four at a time, or all together, like birds? Had she known, Jenny would have appreciated this finding that potentially absolves Major Schultz of responsibility for the shooting.

On the evening of that famous Monday August 21, Marcel made a point of thanking the Polish and Bavarian guards who had wanted him released. Marie insisted:

"You can't go back alone. Your sister will go with you."

For the third time during the war, Marcel's sister confronted her adversary. The first time was in the prison at Fresnes, then at the *Kommandantur* in Villard, and finally in the tent of the last occupiers.

Says Jenny: "It was eleven in the evening. The two of us set out at night into the mountain, with no light, without really knowing where we were going. These low-ranking soldiers weren't living in the Hotel Splendid like the officers. They were bivouacking under a huge tent in the middle of nowhere, where it was completely dark. Marcel showed the sentry his safe-conduct. The sentry lifted a tent flap and I found myself, the only one of my kind, facing these dozens of men.

"No one can imagine what it was like. Almost pitch black! There were perhaps two hundred, three hundred guys, not saying a word, with tiny candles flickering around them. Of course, they mustn't be seen. They could have been bombed. So, Marcel thanked his Pole and his Bavarian. Then I pulled him by the sleeve to cut matters short. It was a scene I'll never forget. Really, it was like a hallucination. All these silent men, motionless, in that twilight atmosphere, with those little lights, like candles in a church. And there was I, the only woman facing them.

"We went out into the night. Next day they had gone, leaving behind them the corpses of seven hundred French. On Tuesday August 22, there wasn't a German to be seen in Villard-de-Lans. They had moved out without a sound, like shadows. They had cleared out in silence, with no marching band, no singing. Leaving us free!

"For us, the war was over."

A local author wrote these lines in memory of the twenty Executed of the Cours Berriat, Marcel's unfortunate companions:

"Torn from the blinding darkness of your cells, You gazed upon the flight of the dragonflies that cried for joy in the mint and thyme. All seemed oblivious to discord and hate. Nature exhaled a balmy breath. Love danced in the morn. An ethereal veil slipped over the fields. You were lined up, standing, facing the mountains from whence took flight the breeze of liberty. Birds circled in the cloudless sky, no doubt accompanying your soul, as summer poured in, on its ultimate journey!"

Destiny! The Executed of the Lycée Buffon. The Executed of the Cours Berriat... They had perished. Yet still Marcel lived.

Liberation..., and a Jewish godfather

Tuesday August 22, 1944. As if by magic, the enemy had vanished, though no one had seen them leave. The barriers blocking access to the town were gone. All was quiet. The town square in Villard-de-Lans was deserted. At Fleur des Alpes, Marcel, free once more, slept late.

Jacques and Jenny walked out into that lovely dawn of peace. Suddenly, climbing the steep path leading to the square, Jenny felt a presence behind her. She spun round: another soldier!

Jacques shuddered, then:

"He's an American! Jenny... An A-me-ri-can!"

An American... AT LAST!

"I was beside myself!" recalls Jenny. "I rushed to embrace him!" Suddenly, people thronged the square. They were shouting for joy, weeping, dancing. Our liberators had arrived. Everyone wanted to talk to them, touch them, kiss them, thank them.

"A woman approached the first soldier I'd seen, begging him, in English at first, 'Please, *monsieur*... would you agree to be godfather to a newborn child?'

"'I'd like... I'd love to... but I'm Jewish—*Juif!*'

"'Never mind, the baby is too!' came the reply.

"And the next day, August 23," says Jenny, "we all held a party for the baby and its American godfather, both Jewish. And for the rest of humankind.

"On our way home from the celebrations, we ran into Mademoiselle C., our landlady. I asked about her friend who sometimes came to share a *fondue* with her. We distrusted him: we thought he looked like a '*collabo.*' He hadn't been able to come up from Grenoble, she said, because the buses weren't running. We thought he must have fled with his friends the Germans. But a few days later Mademoiselle C., whom we also suspected, invited us in for a cup of coffee 'to celebrate the Liberation.' We all poured into her dining room—all of the building's tenants, the Janovskis, the Czechs, the Papos, well, all the 'musicians' in Fleur des Alpes. There was a ring at the door. It opened to reveal an impressive English officer resplendent in his uniform. It was 'him.' The man we'd taken for a *collabo*, a traitor... and all the rest. He'd been a British agent all along, passing information back to England. And she was a brave resister, doubtless a liaison agent. We were thunderstruck at the thought of having lived with them cheek by jowl, unawares. It was just one surprise after another. We were so thrilled."

The grownups were so distracted during those troubled times that they often ignored me, a mere child, bewildered at everything going on but seizing every opportunity for a fresh escapade, like the Comtesse de Ségur's child heroine Sophie. Left to my own devices in the Fleur des Alpes residence, I decided to shorten the dress on my old doll from the days in Nice, hunted for a pair of scissors and spied a box of matches that, thought I, ought to raise the hemline. My uncle came upon me perched on a stool over the gas cooker, catching the little arsonist and the tools of her trade in a nick of time.

"You know what happened to the son of your great-aunt's friend Stella?[61] He played with matches while his mother was out. He was so badly burnt he died. Promise me you'll never do that again and I won't tell your parents."

---

61. Stella's nephew, Patrick Modiano, won the Nobel Prize for Literature in 2014 [Translator].

It wasn't the first time Marcel and I had shared a secret. I never betrayed him. Nor did he me.

Jenny was unaware that the war wasn't over for everyone. The mayor and the priest went with some youngsters to look for the bodies of the dead and those who'd been tortured on the mountainside. Jacques looked on as the remains of his comrades were brought back, as the lorries brimming with corpses passed beneath the windows of Fleur des Alpes, which had seen so much already.

But other momentous events briefly overshadowed these atrocities. The Battle of Paris took place between August 19 and 25. On the 25th, General de Gaulle gave his famous speech at the Hôtel de Ville: "Paris outraged! Paris broken! Paris martyred! But Paris liberated!"[62] and refused to proclaim a new Republic. "Vichy was and remains null and void." Paris LIBERATED! Women and men wept and laughed all at once. Women and men were bursting with joy, embracing strangers, hugging each other. They sang as they walked. They strolled aimlessly, singing, carrying lanterns, waving to the soldiers in their tanks.

The recent landings in the South of France had been successful. Grenoble had been liberated within seven days instead of the sixty initially planned. Our family awaited the return of the buses from Grenoble before departing from Villard, which it did on the first of September. Before that, Jenny took a step she had vowed all through the war she would take, if she survived. She had her hair shade lightened to the blonde she had been as a little girl in Salonika, before Marie cut off her hair. And there's a photo to immortalize the occasion.

The person to attempt this experiment, relatively untried at the time, was the hairdresser in Villard. She made a mess of things the first time around and Jenny came out a carrot red. Further attempts turned the Sephardic woman into an Aryan, with a hairdo in keeping with the fashion of the times, a Venetian blonde with hair falling in long, supple waves. Privations and mountain walking had kept her fresh-looking and slim, with a trim figure. The war had not aged Jenny, who was only 28 in the summer

---

62. An oft-repeated quotation from De Gaulle's speech on the Liberation of Paris, familiar to all French people since the end of World War Two [Translator].

of the Liberation. The adrenaline rush needed to remain true to herself was still at work, despite the new hair color. The revelations and disillusionments of the postwar period were to end all that, and her looks faded prematurely thereafter.

Says Jenny: "So, on September 1, 1944, we left behind that gorgeous scenery where we had known such torment. I had had a raging toothache for several days, and the first thing I did on arriving in Grenoble was to track down a dentist, who extracted all my wisdom teeth. The town had been bombed and there was rubble everywhere. We found somewhere to live, all six of us, in two tiny rooms in ruins, eating whatever we could as we had practically run out of money, and anyway it was impossible to find food.

"But the atmosphere in town was amazing. Everywhere we saw American soldiers escorting long lines of German prisoners with their hands on their heads. Jacques and Marcel had sorted things out with the Army, which paid them a small sum for their part in the Battle of the Vercors. In the Cours Berriat, on the spot where Marcel's comrades had been shot, six French militiamen were sentenced to death and executed on August 24 or September 2, urged on by a rabid crowd that then squabbled atrociously over the corpses. Six boys aged between 14 and 18. The *epuration*[63] had begun.

"On Rosh Hashana we went to the synagogue, which was filled with Jewish US Army men and their officers, looking superb in their uniforms, wearing their *tallit*, their prayer shawls. Human beings at last, and no longer hunted prey! We prayed for our loved ones, for our friends the Ardittis, who had been deported; for Moïse and Marie, Jacques' parents, who we knew were still in danger of the Nazis in Italy; for Pepo and his wife Ester, whose arrest we had heard about just before the Normandy landings and the fighting in the Vercors in June. We prayed for the conflict to end, for the war was still going on in much of the world not so far away. We prayed for peace. We prayed for ourselves, for our daughter, for our unsettled future, still not fully realizing what we had been spared.

"In Grenoble as elsewhere, the hunt was on for *collabos*, the Free French (the FFI) were rounding up members of the *milices* (militia members); women had their heads shaved for sleeping with the enemy; a wave of summary justice with its nastiness, its excesses and abuses. We didn't condemn it, because we'd suffered too much, and we wanted to make these bastards pay. We were in Grenoble for around fifteen days. Then we took the train to Lyon, where Momo and his wife, who had sheltered Marie and Saby, were waiting for us. We stayed with Jacques and Michou in a little half-ruined hotel and waited for the first Paris-bound train. Marcel, with all the enthusiasm of a twenty-year-old, had got himself sent on a mission from the Vercors and wasted no time hitching a lift to the capital to meet up with Rolande, still his great love. He was the first to tread the streets of Paris once more and to check that no one was occupying his parents' apartment or ours.

"The long-awaited day arrived at last, one of the most longed-for days in our lives, when we were able to take the train home. It was on September 28, the 28th of September 1944! The journey wasn't without danger. Many bridges had been destroyed and the train had to make several detours to avoid them. The Germans were on the run, but they hadn't all gone, and there was always the possibility a bomb might fall on the train.

---

63. Literally "cleansing" [Translator].

September 28 was the day of Yom Kippur. We decided to fast—the fact that we had practically nothing to eat helped—and we left what little we had for Michou, who had a hearty appetite."

What Jenny did not know yet was that September 1944 was the month of last times. It was the last time she would pray in a synagogue and the last time she would fast on Yom Kippur. The time for settling scores with others, with herself, with God, was drawing near. The Jenny who set foot in the Gare de Lyon on September 28, 1944, was no longer the Jenny who had left it for Angoulême in September 1942. Two years... Two centuries... Two millennia... Things were coming to a head, and Jacques and Jenny were absorbed in the intensity of these once-in-a-lifetime moments.

As for me, Michou, I was there with them, though my memory needs some maternal jogging to complete the picture, to know our train left at dawn but reached Paris late in the night. That we caught the last Metro. That we hired a porter who followed us with our bags. That the Metro stopped at La Motte-Picquet-Grenelle but not at Ségur, our subway station, which was still closed. That we covered the rest of the way on foot, so excited we couldn't utter a word.

Number 8, Rue César-Franck hadn't changed, and on arrival we awoke Madame Chaliès, Marcel having warned her of our homecoming. She hugged us warmly and lent us a pair of scissors to break the seals that had been placed on our door. Luckily, Jacques and Jenny had made a point of paying their rent promptly throughout the war, via their guardian angel. She also loaned us a candle, the electricity having been cut ages ago, so that we toured our apartment by the flickering light of a candle.

Much was missing.

"But it was a close call," says Jenny. Suddenly she cried out: "The Ottoman dish!"

The silver dish had accompanied them all the way from Salonika. Now tarnished, it was there, miraculously, waiting to be filled with rose petal jam, amid the tied parcels strewn all over the place, especially on the ceruse oak dining table. But the best items in Jacques' stamp collection had gone, along with other valuables, including embroidered tablecloths, linen, and even rare books.

The French inspectors had helped themselves, but the enemy too had removed a sizable chunk. Doctor Modiano, a family friend and an important figure in the Sephardic community, had spent the war at Dufayel, a big department store, putting looted Jewish possessions into packing cases bound for Germany. He had even found himself packing up his own furniture, one day.

"You did find an old doll in a corner," Jenny concluded. "You wouldn't let go of it after that. We made your bed and you fell asleep straight away, clasping the doll to your heart. Then we too went to bed, half dead from hunger, fatigue, and emotion.

"But we were alive!"

IV
The Silence

It is in that silence that the war is present still,
that it seeps in through the sand, the wind.

—MARGUERITE DURAS, *MEMOIR OF PAIN*

That is what I say, that is what I write and
that alone is what can be found in the words
I trace, and in the lines drawn by these words,
and in the blanks left by the spaces between
these lines […] never, as I endlessly rake over
them, will I find anything but the last echo
of words spoken yet absent in writing, the
scandal of their silence and of my silence: I
do not know whether I have anything to say,
I know that I am saying nothing. I write: I
write because we lived together, because I was
one amongst them, a shadow amongst their
shadows, a body close to their bodies. I write
because they left in me their indelible mark,
whose trace is writing. Their memory is dead
in writing; writing is the memory of their
death and the assertion of my life.

—GEORGES PEREC, *W, OR THE MEMORY
OF CHILDHOOD*

Joy

The joy was short-lived. Still, Jenny does not hold back on the details, giving form to a moment of happiness she refuses to forget.

"The next morning," she continues, pensive, "Madame Chaliès, to whom I remain everlastingly grateful, brought us a tray with a proper breakfast... real coffee... with milk... white bread... butter and jam. A feast! At midday, she invited us round to her concierge's lodging. She had prepared roast veal... genuine veal. We couldn't believe our taste buds. We were in Paris, in our apartment. We were eating white bread and roast veal. We were drinking coffee... Drancy... it had been shut down and was now a distant nightmare... And there was no early morning ring on the doorbell... No sound of jackboots... The first thing I did, after that meal fit for a king, was to scrub down my kitchen, while Jacques raced off to the store... We were on Cloud Nine.

"You... As soon as you spotted the doll, you were happy. It wasn't a child's doll like the Christmas one in Nice, two years before. It was one of those decorative dolls dressed like a noblewoman, the kind one puts on a daybed, a wedding gift from 1937, centuries ago. You went to sleep with it; for months you wouldn't be parted from that symbol of the *Ancien Régime*.

"The euphoria lasted until the year-end festivities. We were entering 1945. For the first New Year's Eve following the Liberation—we tended to forget that the war wasn't over yet—we decided to hold a big party with our re-found friends. Other than those who had been deported, the 'crowd' had got together again in Paris. We cruelly missed the Ardittis. Lily knew her husband and his family were in Auschwitz—she had even sent them parcels—but what was Auschwitz? Nobody knew. Lily preferred to sit this one out. Should we have waited till the end of the war? The deportees' return? How right we were not to put it off!

"The crowd had decided to hold the party at our place as ours was the biggest apartment. We were expecting maybe up to thirty people, and given the food shortages, we'd divided up the job of getting the food and drink. Jacques and I were in charge of getting the *foie gras*. Because it was horribly expensive, it didn't require ration coupons, like all luxury goods. We found a store selling cold cuts on Boulevard Montparnasse. The others resorted to the black market and whatever came to hand. They muddled through. Jacques Franck knew a fellow who knew a guy who worked in champagne, and he came back from Rheims with a case of the stuff. Robert Béhar brought the oysters. Marcel Janovski the poultry. The women made salads. It was the women who did the cooking in those days; some of them were cake-baking artists.

"The Francks had a woman friend, a dentist who'd been treating the English and the Americans. She was supposed to bring along some Allied airmen, young and not-so-young. We were dead keen to invite these representatives of the people who'd liberated us. We met them for a drink in a bar, shortly before the end of the year. And we'd bought tickets for an operetta at the ABC theater. You'd have thought it was pre-war all over again. For three months we thought of nothing but our party, despite the gathering worries.

"That's because December was ice-cold. And the Führer launched his Ardennes offensive on the 16th. A sharp reminder that peace was still some way off. The young British and American airmen we'd been hoping to invite cried off. They'd gone to get themselves shot to pieces in the Ardennes, to stop the enemy from breaking through and recapturing Paris.

"So, we looked around for some other Allied soldiers. We absolutely had to have some for our Liberation party. We found a very nice Englishman who came in the afternoon of the 31st to lend us a hand. For want of any other talent, he sliced up bread tirelessly. At the last minute, we dug up some Americans to replace the original bunch...

"At last, the great day arrived. We'd decorated the apartment with flowery garlands and brought all the dinner services that had escaped the enemy's attentions. After the theater and the operetta that reminded us of pre-war life, we all made it back to Rue César-Franck, where we began playing charades. The big thing right then was to sing 'When shall we be married?,' which your father had learned. We dressed up Jacques as a girl with one of my dresses and a wig, and we put make-up on him. Jacques Franck, all six foot three of him, played a gaucho, wearing boots belonging to his son Jean-Pierre, your pal from Nice. He pulled your old wooden horse around with a string. And they sang. Jacques was so well made-up no one recognized him. People were asking: 'Who's the girl?'

"The new Americans were burly rednecks from the West. Real hillbillies. They downed gallons of champagne. They were uncouth. After that, it was a real business to get them to touch a mouthful of *foie gras*! We helped them out on that one. Finally, they fell asleep during our 'show.' They obviously didn't get it."

"What was I doing while all this was going on?" I inquire.

"You were sleeping in your room, with Marcel watching over you. We'd paid him to babysit while we went to the ABC, and we came home on foot because the Metro had closed. Then he partied with us when we got back. He even woke you up so you could hear the song."

A memory awakens in turn in my slumbering memory of 1944, and its memorable ending after all:

"Come on! Turnip top! Enough sleeping! Happy '45! Come and listen to your favorite song!"

I knew the beginning and the end of the song only. Here's how it began:

"When shall we two marry, we two marry, we two marry? When shall we two marry? My darling cowboy?"

The rest wasn't meant for little girls:

"They call me the Texas killer. The only crime I haven't yet done is to be a strangler. But that could happen yet, it all depends on you and on your answer..."

And it ended:

"Let's do it another year, some other year, another year. Let's do it another year, my darling cowboy."

I opened one eye and saw a fat girl singing with a crackling voice, and a ridiculous big fellow astride my hobby horse. I went back to bed. It wasn't the first time I'd thought grown-ups were very, very strange.

But nothing was going to spoil Jenny's fun: "We partied and sang till the first Metro. It was the First of January 1945. No need to ask what we wished for, with every fiber, for that year. And finally, it came! Peace."

The party had been short-lived indeed.

Noah's mantle

"And what became of Mademoiselle Maurel?"

During that winter of 1945, as everyone tried to pick up the threads of their lives, Jenny ran into Mademoiselle Wackeinem, her elementary school teacher, who still taught nursery school, on the Boulevard des Invalides. She invited her for tea in her apartment, "with whatever came to hand." The conversation turned naturally on the only possible topic, the Occupation and its outcomes, each more catastrophic than the last. Mademoiselle Wackeinem was one of those teachers who had resisted. A high school is a microcosm, holding up a mirror to what is going on everywhere, with its traitors, its victims, its martyrs, and all those men and women who lived through those tormented times without batting an eyelid.

"Blanche Maurel? Oh! A real Odyssey!" the teacher replied. "It's worth telling. From the start of the phony war, your teacher picked her side. She made no secret of her sympathy for the enemy; some of her pupils were the daughters of French army officers, and they were indignant. They began to turn their backs on her, even in her own class. One of them told me she had violently attacked England in a class on Garibaldi. There was an incident even. Coming out of her history class she found herself surrounded by her pupils who were putting on their coats in a confined space; it was the end of class on a Wednesday. One of the girls tripped her up and she fell to the floor, breaking her arm. They couldn't identify the girl responsible for this 'mishap,' and the head teacher, Madame Kantzer, was in no hurry to find out.

"Blanche Maurel finished the semester in plaster. And six months later she was transferred to Beaugency, an annex to the Boys' High School in Orleans. She was backed by Xavier Vallat, who was then an extreme-right member of the National Assembly."

"Xavier Vallat! The Commissioner for Jewish Questions?"

"Future [Commissioner]! He wasn't appointed till '41, after the Armistice."

"And what did she do after the Armistice?"

"In '40-'41, she was back at Duruy, in a position of strength. The former head teacher had been fired, being married to a Jew. And from that point on Blanche ruled over her colleagues and everyone. I remember she got one of my old pupils, Rosemarie, expelled for passing a note to a classmate expressing her belief in the defeat of the Nazis and in our liberation. Not to mention the Jewish girls and members of the Resistance!"

"How was it for you, then?"

"Well, starting in November 1940, we each received a questionnaire where we had to state if the Statute of the Jews applied to us. Our colleague Myriam Lévy, who taught physics and chemistry in 'Philo 2,' said goodbye to her class. It was in January 1941, I recall. A former pupil of hers told me about it. Madame Lévy came in, went to her desk, but she wasn't her usual self. After a silence she announced to her pupils that that afternoon was to be her last chemistry class because she was affected by Vichy's antisemitic law. Then she cried as she taught her last class in an emotional silence."

"And how did your colleagues in general react to these measures?"

"In different ways. I had a friend in a provincial secondary school who was banished from his classroom along with another Jewish teacher in a climate of general indifference. Nobody, during their degrading walk through the schoolyard, lifted a finger or said a word, except for one, a math teacher who shouted out: 'We can't just let them go like that!' and who walked with them to the gate."

"We had the same experience," said Jenny. "But we were lucky, as there was always someone to hold out their hand to us."

"Yes, you were lucky," continued the schoolmistress. "Which wasn't the case for our young French literature teacher Renée—another Lévy, Jewish—who was a resister in the *Musée de l'Homme* group and later in the Hector network[64]. She was arrested in '41. Or my friend Madeleine Michelis, who wasn't Jewish but who worked with the Resistance to help escaped prisoners along with Allied parachutists and airmen. She was arrested a

---

64. The Hector-STATIONER network was a resistance network set up in France by Hector Buckmaster, head of Section F of the British Special Operations Executive [Translator].

year ago, in February '44. Or Marguerite Aron. You must have known her: she taught literature here. She was aged seventy-one. She'd converted to Catholicism a long time ago. She applied for admission to the Dominican Third Order and had retired to her house near the Abbey of Solesmes. The Gestapo arrested her on January 26, 1944, as she was leaving morning mass. When she gave her age, they told her, 'We take them up to eighty'. And she wasn't the only one from [Victor] Duruy!"

Mademoiselle Wackeinem's voice faltered, and tears welled up in the eyes of both women as she recounted this unbearable roll-call.

"Here... I've just been sent this," she went on, holding out a sheet of paper to 'Dear Mademoiselle, I write to you as a former pupil of the Lycée Victor-Duruy during the tragic years of the German occupation. In our class there were Liliane Kreizer and Georgette Braunstein, both of the Jewish faith. At Commencement in fall 1942, we were sixteen. Liliane was arrested with her mother, then sent to Drancy. Georgette was seventeen. She was arrested with her father and mother in January 1944 and deported.'"

"And Mademoiselle Maurel during that time? Did she still teach at the lycée?" asked Jenny, trying to pull herself together.

"No. She became a prominent collaborator. In spring '42, Laval gave her a mission on the staff of Abel Bonnard, who'd been appointed Minister of Education and Youth."

"And... what did she do there?"

"Oh! There's lots of rumors. It's said she went with the Germans and French to occupy the premises of the Grand Orient of France[65] and drove out the members. It's said she monitored university lectures. And the rest.... She was tried before the *Commission d'épuration*[66] and suspended from her post last September."

"She wasn't arrested?"

"Yes, in October. They sent her to Fresnes prison. She's just been released on parole... for medical reasons. Oh! She'll get by every time... But

---

65. The oldest and largest Masonic organization in continental Europe [Translator].

66. An ad hoc court set up after the Liberation to purge elements convicted of collaboration with the Germans [Translator].

the others, little Georgette, or Liliane, who were in my nursery school class, will they come back? So, you know, all those independent gangs of armed youngsters who went around rounding up the *collabos* and executing them without any kind of trial, well, despite the excesses, I wasn't too unhappy about it."

"It won't bring the others back," said Jenny. "And there have been so many mistakes. I hope the courts will do better than just beat up on the scapegoats."

"Yes," said Mademoiselle Wackeinem. "One must hope so."

That same month of February 1945, the writer Robert Brasillach was sentenced to death and executed for having advocated collaborationism, denunciation, and incitement to murder during the Occupation.

Contrary to the popular saying, revenge is a dish best served hot, preferably scalding. Even at that temperature it tastes and smells too much of bile. Once it has cooled down, it emits a stench of vomit and blood. Not my favorite dish. Nor was it that of Jenny and Jacques after all they had endured.

Hatred flared up even before the Normandy landings. People called revenge "punishments." Their targets? Ten thousand people in France, according to historians, including the six young members of the Militia who had paid for the Executed of the Cours Berriat, who paid for the hostages, who paid for the presumed resisters.

"But if hatred answers hatred, how will hatred end?" asks a Shinto proverb. I too have experienced my childish period of hatred and revenge. It found expression in a recurring dream in which I stand at the window of a building, throwing German soldiers out of it one by one, lining up to be defenestrated by my little child's arms. They are the spitting image of the giants who came to arrest Marcel at Fleur des Alpes.

National humiliation found its scapegoats in that half of the population that simultaneously embodies submission and betrayal: women. As is well-known, women suspected of having slept with the occupier were stripped and exhibited in public with their heads shaved, while the rabid crowd hurled abuse at them, giving vent to their basest instincts and their impotent rage. Jenny and Jacques had looked on, impassive, in Grenoble. But in the longer term these scenes brought neither relief nor consolation, nor vengeance. What took place before their eyes concerned neither Jacques and Jenny nor those they were waiting for, still less those who had looked upon the Gorgon or who never came back.

The avengers who wrongfully perpetrated these scenes were never indicted. But then punishment came only slowly and unevenly for some of those who had snatched small children from their parents, rounded up the old and sick, and sent whole families to the gas chambers. Many were never punished at all.

The Republic and its institutions were finally restored, hand in hand with an ill-assured system of justice. The verdicts handed down by the official courts were often inconsistent. Many innocent people were convicted while others got off scot-free. Three out of four judges had served the collaborationist State. Sentences were mild. The punishment of "national degradation" put lives and careers on hold temporarily, but no more; likewise, convictions for "intelligence with the enemy."

"They shot Brasillach," Jenny recalls. "But nothing happened to Céline[67], who'd written 'I am the number one enemy of the Jews' in 1937."

"He was sentenced to a year in jail, which he spent in a prison in Denmark. But it's true, he was amnestied in the end and allowed to return to France."

I spared Jenny the line peddled by my comrades from the days of May 1968, who argue that Céline's genius exonerated him from all blame, and still more from any kind of punishment. As for Blanche Maurel, she got off lightly, as Mademoiselle Wackeinem predicted. At the end of 1945 her case appeared to be closed; the court dismissed it out of hand and didn't refer it to the "Civic Chamber."

But that wasn't the end of it. In the winter of 1946, she was preparing her defense and asked to be sent the glowing inspection report dating from 1936 written by the Jewish inspector Jules Isaac. Ironically, Isaac, who had been fired under Vichy's Jewish Statute and whose wife and daughter had

---

67. Louis-Ferdinand Céline is widely-regarded as one of the great French novelists of the 20th century. Sentenced *in absentia* after the war for his virulently antisemitic writings and sympathies for the Nazi occupation of France, he was arrested and imprisoned in Denmark, dying in France in 1961. [Translator].

been murdered in the camps, wrote a book after the war titled *L'Ensei-gnement du mépris*[68], condemning the kind of lessons Mademoiselle, the one-time schoolmistress turned star professor in the nineteen thirties, had dispensed to generations of young "republican" girls, Jenny Amon and Françoise Dreyfus included.

Future generations can look up Blanche Maurel's file at the French Na-tional Archives. The file shows how, by dint of successive appeals, Jenny's brilliant teacher fought to secure the lifting of the minor penalties inflicted on her. Let the reader judge: for four years, from 1947 through 1951, she received no pension! Mademoiselle Maurel appealed and appealed relent-lessly to recover that portion of her pension, taking the case to the Paris Administrative Court and right up to the Council of State.

Blanche Maurel died of natural causes. Her colleague Renée Lévy was sent to the La Santé Prison, transferred to Germany with her comrades, also victims of the German NN (*Nacht und Nebel*, Night and Fog) decree, then disappeared without trace. She was guillotined in Cologne on August 31, 1943, at the age of thirty-seven. Madeleine Michelis died under torture, without talking, in Paris on February 15, 1944, aged thirty-one. Marguerite Aron was deported from Drancy to Auschwitz on February 10, 1944. She was gassed three days later. Liliane and her mother were part of a convoy sent to Auschwitz, where they arrived on September 16, 1942, and were sent to the gas chambers two days later. Georgette, her father, and mother left for Auschwitz in a convoy of one thousand two hundred and fourteen deportees that included, among others, one hundred and eighty-four chil-dren aged under eighteen, and fourteen people aged over eighty. Also in the convoy was a mother with her seven children, aged from two to fifteen.

There were others besides who are no longer remembered. For "Noah's cloak cast upon the army of shadows," as another of Mademoiselle Wackei-nem's former pupils puts it, "is woven from sturdy threads." Yet in that win-ter of 1945, people knew nothing of all this; they did not want to know.

In that winter of 1945, like millions of Jewish families Jacques, Jenny and Michou waited. They were waiting for the return of the deportees.

---

68. Literally: Teaching contempt [Translator].

Waiting...

They came back on April 18, 1945. The two brothers, Oscar and Léon Arditti. The rest of the family—Salomon, Ida and Jako—had gone up in the black smoke of Auschwitz.

I clearly remember the day and can still hear Jenny's voice returning from the market in the Avenue de Saxe, shrieking: "They're back! They're back! Oh my God! They're back! I'm going to make them a rice pudding!"

Rice pudding was Oscar Arditti's favorite dish, apparently. I've no idea how the waif-like skeleton returning from the Night was able to digest Jenny's culinary masterpiece. Nor even if he ever saw it.

"It was later, when the first accounts surfaced little by little, that the waiting began," wrote Marguerite Duras in *Memoir of Pain*. Indeed, we had been waiting for them since January 1945. Tirelessly, we awaited the return of the deportees. The vast, indistinct mass of those who had evaporated into the fog became individuals once more, resumed a human face, a name. Jacques was waiting for Moïse Benrey and Marie Jerusalmi, his mother and father. Lily was waiting for her husband Oscar Arditti and her father-in-law Salomon, Léon her brother-in-law, Ida her sister-in-law, and her nephew little Jako. People began bringing out photographs. Far-off prisoners' numbers, of which we still knew nothing, gradually became identities again. We awaited them all without distinction, Jews and Aryans, Pariahs and Gentiles, French and Foreigners. Desirables and Undesirables. No one knew that an implacable hierarchy ruled the death camps, separating sub-humans from the other deportees.

April arrived. The Allied armies launched their attack on Germany. The Red Army pursued its victorious march in the South. The US Air Force and the RAF had blasted away the city of Dresden in February. The Allies were advancing on all fronts. Germany was being pushed back within its borders. The Rhine was crossed. "Berlin is in flames; it will burn down to its roots"[69]. Marguerite Donnadieu, not yet Duras, was in Paris. She too was waiting for her husband Robert Antelme, not Jewish but a resister. In her journal, published under the title *Memoir of Pain*, she describes the

---

69. Marguerite Duras, *ibid*.

Paris night that spring; Paris was brilliant, Place Saint-Germain illuminat-ed, Les Deux Magots[70] crowded, as were all the little restaurants. "But, for me the well-lit city has lost all meaning except for this: it signifies death, signifies tomorrow without them. There is nothing present in this city ex-cept for we who wait. For us, it is the one they will not see."[71]

Those not awaiting deportees waited for peace, which took its time coming. Hitler wavered; he wanted to capitulate, though with the An-glo-Americans only, not yet Stalin. But the Red Army was surging for-ward. All that remained to defend Berlin were "thirty suicide battalions." At last, the Führer shot himself in the head, in his bunker. People thought that was the end. Was it?

They were to find out very soon...

But who knew what had really happened? As late as August 1944, Mar-guerite Duras was able to write that she did not know, that she was pure of all knowledge of what had been going on in Germany since 1933, that she was still in the prehistory of humanity.

On April 28, 1945, on the very day Hitler preferred his pistol, fearing poison wouldn't work, she wrote that she knew. She knew that "seven mil-lion Jews have been exterminated, transported in cattle-wagons and then gassed in gas chambers built for that purpose." She looked for equivalent events elsewhere, at other epochs. "We are astounded. How can anyone still be German? [...]. Some will stay dazzled, incurable. One of the world's most civilized nations, the capital of music for all time, has just murdered eleven million human beings methodically, perfectly, a State industry"[72].

The figures quoted by Duras are inexact. And her references to the camps incomplete. People knew about Buchenwald at the time, with its well-or-ganized committees of Communist political prisoners. They knew about Bergen-Belsen, liberated by British troops, with movie theater newsreels showing walking skeletons, not yet identified as Jews. We hadn't heard of Birkenau. Marguerite Duras hadn't heard of Auschwitz, where Salomon, Ida and Jako had been exterminated; she hadn't heard of Monowitz, where

---

70. The famous literary café in post-war Saint-Germain des Près [Translator].

71. Marguerite Duras, *ibid.*

72. Marguerite Duras, *ibid.*

Oscar and Léon Arditti had been tormented from winter 1943 through spring 1945, not far from Primo Levi.

Nor did Jenny know. Not yet. She prepared a rice pudding with special care for her friend Oscar, who had been rounded up in Nice in December 1943, and for his younger brother Léon, who was only twenty-seven the day he was arrested. She knew nothing of Jako's whereabouts. Not yet.

Jacques didn't know either. But he had been thinking about it, endlessly, ever since our return to Paris following its liberation. He was thinking of his beloved mother, Marie Jerusalmi. And of his father Moïse, of whom he was the only son, with whom he'd got on well despite the occasional disagreement. He was viscerally attached to both. He had had no news of them throughout these turbulent months. But he hoped. He hoped—the word hardly does justice—*ardently* that he would see them again one day soon, as he was to be reunited with the Arditti brothers from Bulgaria, his friends in the Sephardi Youth "crowd," among whom he used to flirt with the girls and play young bachelor pranks. He hoped that Marie would once more prepare the *borekitas* she cooked so well, as Jenny was doing right then in the Rue César-Franck kitchen, waiting for the milk to boil.

The Returnees

The Ardittis arrived at the Gare d'Orsay train station, where Marguerite was waiting for Robert Antelme, on April 18, 1945. There were other reception centers for deportees: the Rex movie theater on the Grands Boulevards, the Reuilly barracks, and the Molitor swimming pool. And above all the Hotel Lutétia, which had been the German headquarters under the Occupation and was then requisitioned at the time of the Liberation.

Of the sixty-six thousand people deported from France for one reason or another, including forty-two thousand for acts of resistance, twenty-three thousand returned. But, of the seventy-five thousand Jews deported, the so-called "racial" deportees, barely two thousand five hundred survived. At this time, even Jewish associations made no distinction between the various categories in terms of how they had suffered. But the reception they were given was not the same: Denise Jacob, a resistant, was welcomed as a heroine; yet French society now saw her sister Simone (later Simone Veil), a "racial" deportee, as a victim.

On April 18, 1945, Lily Arditti had just heard from Jacques Franck. "They" are alive. "They" are at the Gare d'Orsay.

"Everyone? Are they all there?" asked Jenny, who'd been told by the same friend.

"I don't know. I was only told about two people, two brothers. Oscar and Léon probably."

The Arditti brothers had been liberated from the Dora camp by the Americans and flown back to Le Bourget airport. As they disembarked from the plane, they were greeted by a guard of honor with two ranks of soldiers presenting arms. Then they were ushered into a reception center in the main terminal, where they were given food and drink.

"Where do you live? Where's your family? Whom should we notify? Where do you want to go?"

They were in a daze, speechless. They had come from another world. They were being asked for an address in this world. Suddenly, Oscar recalled the Francks' phone number. Were they still alive? In their apartment? With a telephone? And were they in touch with Lily, little Claudine, and their mother?

The answer was Yes. Yes to everything.

They scarcely dared believe it and climbed with other returnees into a truck taking them to the Gare d'Orsay. The train station had been turned into a reception center for prisoners of war and subsequently for the first deportees.

Further questions, further lines and still more questions awaited them on arrival.

"Name? Age? Date of birth? Place of birth? Where have you come from? Which camps were you in?"

They spied a friendly face in the crowd. It was Jacques Franck, and he had hired a bicycle taxi.

"Lily wanted to come, but I told her not to. Everyone in the family's okay. I'm taking you to your new lodgings."

Between their joy at being back home and the gravity of the news they brought with them, Oscar and Léon could not contain their emotion.

Soon, though, they came face to face with an old lady, their mother—their father's wife, their sister's mother, their nephew's grandmother.

"JAKO? Léon, tell me... is he here? And IDA? IDA... Oh my God! YOUR FATHER? Oscar, I beg you. Tell me... tell us... the truth!"

A few days later, Marie called Jenny from her balcony on Rue Pérignon. Someone had told her to go to the Hotel Lutétia, where the deportees were being sent, to try to find Marie's brother Pepo and his wife, of whom they still had no news.

"Will you come with me, Jenny?" Marie asked.

"I'll come with you, but Jacques has to go and work in the store."

What Jenny did not say was that she feared how the experience would affect Jacques. He'd been severely run down and dejected at the rumors of the death camps these last weeks. In any case, his own parents had vanished in Italy and were not among the potential Returnees at the Hotel Lutétia.

Like hundreds of others, Marie and Jenny stood outside the Hotel Lutétia and began to wait, and hope. They grew uneasily accustomed to seeing striped "pajamas" shuffling through the gilded lobby, carrying a little bundle containing their sole treasure: a lump of sugar, a rag, a cup, a little blanket. Little by little they learned what came next: registration formalities and an interview, before being issued with a repatriated person's card.

Returnees complained to them about these interrogations. Endless. Meticulous. Their purpose was to detect false deportees, infiltration by former *collabos*, and even former SS members. Genuine returnees pointed out imposters who slipped in dressed in striped pajamas.

All was bedlam and confusion in this chaos.

"A total mess," a Boy Scout volunteer commented to them, a scene he'd never forget.

On Boulevard Raspail, the chestnut trees were in blossom; spring had arrived, bathing the freshly liberated capital. But they didn't notice, neither Marie nor Jenny in the lobby, nor the crowd pressing anxiously against the barricades surrounding the Lutétia, the strain showing on their faces as they brandished photos with placards bearing the names of their lost ones.

Many friends and relatives turned up in the morning before going to work, then returned in the evening. There were peak hours during this waiting without end. For no one knew anything specific yet. There were whisperings. Details of atrocities no one dared believe. Suddenly a convoy of buses arrived and came to a halt. Their cargo of ghostlike skeletons disembarked. The Returnees walked through this mass of peering eyes, seeking to identify or recognize a once-loved face behind these disfigured creatures.

Intimidated at first, Marie and Jenny finished by questioning deportees, showing them their placards with the names and photos of Pepo and his wife Ester. But no one could identify them; no one had seen them.

They questioned former deportees about themselves. One, five feet four tall, weighed eighty-three pounds.

"My name is Charles Palant. I'm Jewish, a former Auschwitz pajama, and survivor of the Death March. I arrived at the Gare de l'Est train station at dawn, in a convoy of repatriated people. I and the others were greeted by a band playing the *Marseillaise* and a military detachment to honor us. They lined us up in ranks on the platform, starting with the deportees—racial and political together—then the POWs, and finally the compulsory labor service workers. In order of suffering."

"I'm Joseph Bialot, an Auschwitz survivor too. I'm a Polish Jew from Belleville[73]. I was deported aged eighteen, liberated by the Red Army and repatriated here, the Lutétia."

"My name is Léopold Rabinovitch, a former member of the FTP-MOI."

The Returnees read glimmers of hope in the eyes of the waiting survivors[74]. They heard names and questions. They gazed at the pictures they were shown. But the photos on show were those of normal human beings, with flesh on their cheeks, and hair. All they knew were sub-men and sub-women, serial numbers, bags of bones and shaved heads.

The Returnees saw hands clutching them by the sleeve, eager to KNOW, and they understood those crazy hopes, not daring to shatter them. They were offered food, a jacket or a pair of pants, a bed, and a room. But they no longer knew what it was to eat a meal or sleep between sheets. They preferred to keep going, searching for their relatives. Their relatives? Where?

---

73. Then a working-class district of Paris [Translator].

74. Here, the word "returnee" refers to someone returning from the camps; "survivor" to Jews who remained in France and were not deported; "lost" to those who never returned from the camps [Translator].

Their homes had been taken over or looted. Or worse: nothing had changed. But it was deserted. The concierge was there to greet them as if nothing had happened, to hand back their keys, the mail even. Sometimes, in an empty apartment from which a whole family had been snatched away, the table was still laid.

Others did find their nearest and dearest, or not all of them. The worst—and there is always something worse—was having to answer their questions, their nameless fears. They dared not, could not say what it had really been like: Auschwitz, Birkenau, Treblinka. They couldn't take the risk; they could not answer. They felt a rising sense of suspicion. If they had survived, they must have been *Kapos* at least. They were guilty, waiting to be unmasked. It was such a small leap from suspicion to hatred.

No one could understand that they could not tell others what their loved ones had endured, how they had died. The truth? Tell them the truth? Impossible! It would amount to killing them slowly again. A lingering death. The most fearsome of tortures: watching the death of loved ones. How to explain to a daughter how and when her mother had died? How could she imagine her own mother undressing, then running the gauntlet to the gas chamber?

How to explain to Salomon Arditti's wife, to Ida's mother, to Jako's grandmother when, and above all how, they had fed the crematoria of Auschwitz-Birkenau?

The deportees' homecoming! It should have been a time for rejoicing, a moment of liberation. Yet it was one of the most painful episodes of the Apocalypse: for the Returnees, who were now mere shadows; for the Survivors, who had experienced neither the roundups nor the camps.

Today, I know on which day the Returnees Oscar and Léon Arditti came home. They had been Jacques' fellow pupils at the Catholic school in Sofia, my parents' best friends, the people with whom they'd shared engagements and weddings as members of the Sephardi Youth in the nineteen thirties, those they'd met up with in Marseille and Nice in 1943, those they'd known to have been rounded up and deported to a destination whose name no one knew nor recognized.

I know now that on April 17, 1945, they were still at Dora, having left Auschwitz in January.

I know now that it was probably on the 18ᵗʰ of April 1945 that Jenny made her celebrated rice pudding for their homecoming. She must have brought it with her carefully, still tepid, covered by a white cloth. Then there's another date, an evening, the Ardittis had assembled the entire crowd, all those who had still been partying in Nice on the eve of their arrest, eighteen months earlier. All those who had solemnly listened to the fortune teller's extravagant predictions.

I don't know exactly what night it was that the two brothers invited their friends around to "celebrate" their return home and tell them what they had endured. I know Jenny never forgot that night: "Oscar and Léon, the two brothers talked all night. They told us everything, or almost. In the morning, they swore it was the first and last time. What had happened would cease to be. It had to be forgotten."

I long regretted not daring to ask Jenny what the Returnees Oscar and Léon Arditti had passed on to their friends, the Survivors, that night in April 1945, about the torment they had endured and about the Lost, those who had not had the luck to come back like them. After that night, the Arditti brothers too fell silent. For decades.

Then, Oscar decided to record his two captivities in a still-unpublished manuscript. After which, Léon in turn decided to come out from the darkness. He wrote, and published, their story, under the title *The Will to Live: 2 Brothers in Auschwitz*[75]. Today, it's a book everyone can read. One person's tale! One among six million. It is not that of Primo Levi. Not that of Aharon Appelfeld. Not that of Elie Wiesel. For each has told it in his own way. Each a unique and different tragedy. Each survival is a question of chance, or a miracle. Each liberation an epic or a saga.

More than sixty years had passed when I discovered Léon's book. We were in a different century. Oscar was dead. Léon opened the door for me to Bluebeard's chamber. Thanks to him, I was able to paint a picture of what my father must have heard on that night in April 1945, when Marie Benveniste, her brothers and sisters were still hoping that Ester and Pepo, that other deportees were on their way home; when he, Jacques, was hoping for the return of his father Moïse Benrey and his mother Marie

---

75. *The Will to Live: 2 Brothers in Auschwitz*, Léon Arditti, Schreiber Publishing, 1996.

Jerusalmi, from a destination no one doubted any longer. Doubts were morphing into terror.

Anguish... *En tierras ajenas yo me vo murir*

"*En tierras ajenas yo me vo murir...* In foreign lands shall I go to die...." Thus sang the Judeo-Hispanics on the frozen soil of Auschwitz I, Monowitz and Birkenau.

For song alone or poems can do justice to an evocation of the House of the Dead, like that of Oscar accompanying Léon's tale:

> In those times, All those, like me
> Or like Jesus,
> Descendants of Zion's line,
> Were
> Hated
> By the Nazis.
> Persecuted,
> Imprisoned,
> Deported.

To read them is to enter the Temple, the Temple they wanted to open for their friends and relatives on that May night in 1945. Not to close it, as Jenny thought, but to reopen it for all one day, and for all time. To read them is to draw near to the sacred source that dictated to Oscar and Léon the words whereby they summoned me to follow them on this Voyage from which they returned.

Jenny had last seen the Arditti family when she left the Hotel Excelsior in Nice. Lily and her sister-in-law had seen them passing by on the street corner: old Monsieur Arditti the patriarch; Oscar and Léon, his two sons; his daughter Ida and his grandson Jako, the gangling teenager aged only fourteen. Their eyes had met one last time with dreadful intensity; then she'd heard their footsteps fading as they disappeared into the district known as *Les Musiciens*. A pale December sun illuminated that tragic, silent scene in 1943.

A few days, a few hours, a century later, the same people reached the ramp at Auschwitz-Birkenau.

Writes Léon: Between their arrest in Nice and that ramp there had been...

... the third-class railcar to Paris from which the three young men could have jumped through the window, which wasn't barred, but they didn't because of their father and his weak legs, and out of consideration for their sister, not the nimblest...

... the arrival at the Gare de Lyon train station, where ordinary passengers quietly went about their no less ordinary business...

... the bus awaiting the future deportees...

... Drancy, the detention center, the antechamber to Hell...

... the first night when, scarcely having arrived, they heard their names in the roll-call for the next convoy... they, the most recent arrivals, were being sent away...

... the convoy... thrown into freight cars with "40 humans, 8 horses" printed in white letters... no platform, no steps up... they hoisted their father, old Monsieur Arditti, up the three-foot gap between the ground and the railcar... the door slid shut and was bolted from outside.... a German soldier handed in a large gray metal pail to serve as a sole latrine for all onboard... before the slit window an SS soldier fired a machine-gun burst to warn that everyone in the car would be shot at the slightest attempt to escape...

... the journey—can we call an ordeal like that a "journey"?... the floor trembled... the train jerked forward... nights... hours... days... an age.

Auschwitz. The arrival at Auschwitz-Birkenau...

"A brutal whiteness... snow everywhere. Green and gray silhouettes. A few buildings, a tangle of rails and then those skeleton-thin men wearing some improbable garb: a kind of gray pajama with blue stripes. We jump three feet onto the platform, leaving all our baggage to be looted." 'Men to one side. Women to the other.' We all bump into each other, pushing and shoving, a fevered crowd gripped with waves of panic, like sheep, harassed by howling dogs.

"Suddenly a face pops up: Léon Baruch."

In this "pajama" busying itself with stacking a pile of suitcases, Léon recognizes a Sephardi who quickly whispers in Ladino:

"Don't get into one of those trucks over there, whatever you do… It's death. They go straight to the gas chamber…"

Léon was horrified. He spotted his father clambering with great difficulty into one of the trucks… bound for the forbidden destination. Ida had vanished with the women and children into other trucks now starting up.

Oscar, Léon and Jako were rooted to the spot, "all three unable to weep, beyond pain."

Never again, never again will they see their father or their mother.

> Auschwitz: death flowed there like lava,
> I saw walking to the crematorium,
> Morning, noon, and night,
> Innocents in thousands:
> Men, women, children.
> Without a sob, without a cry:
> Dumbfounded, stunned, surprised[76].

There were three survivors from this first selection: Oscar, Léon and Jako. They were sent to the Monowitz labor camp.

The sequence of degradation is well-known: undressing, shaving, disinfection, shower, dispossession of one's last personal items (wedding ring, rings, medals), serial number tattooed on arm, striped pajama, disgusting soup, roll-call in Arctic cold, extenuating work to the death, blows with whips, a thousand humiliations and harassments, selection of the weakest, hangings. The banality of atrocity deliberately intended to dehumanize, then exterminate.

"We didn't see much of the SS," says Léon. "They were up in the watchtowers and guarded the entrance. That's all. The prisoners themselves ran the camp. It was a devilishly efficient system! Those in charge of oppressing these soon-to-be-dead were soon to be dead themselves. The more merciless and cruel they were, the longer they kept their job: the longer they stayed alive." These were the *Kapos*.

The common criminals wore green triangles. Red triangles designated

---

76. *Ibid.*

the political prisoners. The *Kapos* were recruited from their ranks. They ran the camp and reigned over the wearers of yellow stars, the sub-humans, the Jews.

There was a subtle hierarchy even among the tattoos, with the number telling "all": the date of entry to the camp, the number of the convoy, nationality. Numbers between 30,000 and 80,000 were always treated with respect: there were only a few hundred remaining, the rare survivors of the Polish ghettos.

Numbers 11,600 through 11,700 were the Greeks from Salonika, who spoke the Ladino the Arditti brothers knew. The Italian Primo Levi arrived in the same camp a month after Oscar and Léon. His attention was immediately drawn to these people from Salonika. He noted that the Greek Jews formed a coherent and educated group, their wisdom a blend of all Mediterranean traditions. He noted their contribution to the international jargon of the *Lager*, the camp: thanks to them, everyone knew that *la caravana* meant "chow" and that *la comedera es buena* meant "the food's good." He emphasized their national solidarity, their disgust at any form of gratuitous brutality, their exceptional sense of dignity.

Oscar, Léon and Jako found themselves at Buna, a plant manufacturing synthetic rubber that was part of the IG Farben group, which the Germans were then building. They possessed just one thing. But it was critical. They were together and so they would remain. The two brothers had but a single, simple obsession: *survival*. "We must think of nothing but that, at each moment, each second, in each of our gestures and acts: survive, survive. Oscar, Jako and I made clear that our survival brooked no discussion. It was obvious. At all times, anything liable to undermine that conviction had to be rejected without pity[77]."

For that, they had to follow certain rules, which they laid down in their intimate "conferences," when they had a moment to speak to each other briefly.

Rule one: forget the world outside. "We must forget all those we love, who love us. We must imperatively do so … We banish from our memory all mentions of the past, all recollections of those dear to us, living or dead.

---

77. *Ibid.*

There can be no question of suffering at the thought of our Papa's death or that of Ida. Reliving our happiness in Bulgaria, with our family, thinking of scenes from our teenage years in France: that too is forbidden[78]."

Rule two: wash your body daily, regardless of the freezing winter temperatures in Upper Silesia.

Rule three: look like you're working without wearing yourself out (while at the same time sabotaging the enemy's war effort).

Rule four: keep your head down to avoid unwanted attention.

Rule five: whatever you can eat, eat it right away.

That is how the eternity of Hell passes. Seconds. Minutes. Hours. Days. Weeks. Months. Year. Seconds. Minutes. Hours. Days. Weeks. Months.

The life of a deportee hangs in the balance with each "selection."

"The selection: you are naked in winter, and you run for your life, elbows hugging the body, poor skeleton-like bodies.

"It all happens the moment we show them our back. Those whose muscles and buttocks have vanished to the point where the bones at the base of the spine are sticking out, those are the ones the SS point out, shouting 'Muslim!'

"Muslim… that word spells death.

"Destination: the gas chamber, then the cremation ovens."

For Oscar and Léon, the mystery of the chimney and its thick black smoke was now a part of their everyday lives: "Central Auschwitz, and then, having removed one's pajama, the wait, naked, in a long line of people before the gas chamber, the entrance to the big shed with its cement walls, with its ceiling fitted with showerheads. The gas, the suffocation, the heap of bodies, the opening of the doors, the carrying out of the pile of rigid *Muslims* to the cremation ovens."

The other route to the gas chamber lay through the infirmary. One night in his third month there, frozen stiff as they awaited the roll-call in the camp's main square, Jako was missing. He never reappeared.

"He went to the infirmary," another deportee revealed.

"We never saw him again," writes Léon. "Never."

Gas chambers. Crematoria. The white sky of Upper Silesia.

---

78. *Ibid.*

"We could, we ought to weep. But hatred and sorrow are a luxury we cannot afford. We'll weep hereafter. We'll hate hereafter. First, we must survive"[79].

Brotherly love... The longest night

"How did you manage?"

How did they manage to stay alive from December 1943 through April 1945? How did they come through those fateful six months that no one can survive without finding an additional source of food? Because "the tiniest additional mouthful outweighed the energy expended to secure it."

The question comes up over and over. It hovered on the tips of the tongues of all of the friends in the crowd:

"How did you do it?"

They didn't dare formulate the other half of the question: "... and still keep your soul?"

How to survive? Simple answer to a simple question: by making do. The French know all about that. In exchange for a ration of soup and an occasional crust of bread, they would volunteer to sweep out the hut while the others slept. They went with the flow. The flow? The Gentiles, the Goyim. Those at the top of the camp hierarchy. They did things for the Polish red triangles, the politicos, who were allowed to receive parcels. In return for rotting food, they would look after the privileged inmates' paillasses and bedcovers, wash their underwear, polish their shoes.

When that outlet closed, Oscar identified the *Kapo* of a commando working inside the camp. When he suffered a horrific beating with a belt, the *Kapo* admired Oscar for not flinching. It was double or quits. Asking to survive could get you hanged. But the *Kapo* played along and brought Oscar "into the fold." Oscar brought his brother inside too, where it was warmer... There, those wearing stars rubbed shoulders with the "others," the POWs and forced laborers from all over the world. The polyglot brothers struck up friendships with English prisoners, who "enjoyed fab-

---

79. *Ibid.*

ulous prerogatives" and who passed on those benefits to their protégés. When those protégés disappeared, the two Ardittis took their place. A little later they befriended a Frenchman brought there under the compulsory labor plan. The latter learned Lily's Paris address by heart. Then disappeared.

Yet, the true secret of Oscar and Léon Arditti was not just their visceral will to survive, their talent for making do, or sheer luck. Their true secret, as stated in the title of Léon's book, was brotherhood. Brotherhood in mind and body. Survivors thanks to their will to live. Returnees because both returned. Two beings who loved each other in a world where love was scarcer even than bread. Alive because ten times, a hundred times, Oscar took the trouble to unbutton his younger brother's fly-buttons to let him urinate. Alive because they were capable of human warmth in this cold, cruel desert by inventing the "bear dance," which consisted of hugging each other, rubbing their bodies together, tapping each other hard on the back and massaging each other tenderly. No brazier can replace the warmth of human love.

One evening, on returning to the hut, the *Blockälteste* or block elder announced:

"A parcel for you…"

There was indeed a parcel on the wooden table, containing the remains of a kilogram of sugar in torn paper.

The sender was Lily Arditti. Lily who had organized from afar Oscar's first escape from captivity. Lily who had stood up to Brunner's questioning.

Fifteen days later, the same thing. This time, it was a can of cassoulet[80].

Imagine a short story titled "Cassoulet in Auschwitz." Thanks to Lily and a worker on the compulsory labor plan, the tale was no surrealist fiction in poor taste, but fact.

January 1945. Oscar and Léon had survived for a little more than a year. Roughly six months after the Allied landings in Normandy. Around four months after the Liberation of Paris. Monowitz camp was evacuated, along with those of Birkenau and central Auschwitz. Now began the

---

80. A typical dish from southwestern France [Translator].

Death Marches. Perhaps the most terrible moment in all this ghastly experience. Especially as the humans subjected to it were close to exhaustion. The Arctic cold of the Polish and German winter. Neither pause nor food. "We progressed ever more slowly, shedding corpses as we went."

But... But Oscar supported his brother to enable him to sleep as he walked... But... Léon found in his mouth the remains of a gold crown. He traded it with an SS guard for a crust of bread, which he shared with his brother.

They reached Gleiwitz, where the selection and elimination of "Muslims" began over again. Then they boarded a train, where hunger and thirst gripped their entrails; where they urinated and defecated in their pants. A train overloaded with the dying, who were done to death and their bodies thrown overboard; take their place; stretch one's legs; claw back a little living space.

In the death train, writes Léon, "one person's missing... and all is dehumanized. Amid all these men suffering the same ordeal as I was, only my brother truly exists. The others are merely parts of a vast cohort... fleshless silhouettes, unseeing eyes, beings walled-up within themselves as I would be too, totally, as would Oscar, if we had not had the unbelievable good fortune to confront this nightmare together."

And so, in that death train Oscar sings:

"I lived through that woe
With my brother
For me and for him it was
A reason we survived
Nothing is stronger, more natural
Than a brother's helping hand.
Alone, we would have perished assuredly"[81].

Seven days and seven nights before a quarter of the new convoy reached Dora concentration camp.

Dora: Oh miracle! A labor camp with no gas chambers! But it was overcrowded, and the damned were made to march again. Direction Osterode. There, they worked on electric drills, the toughest work they had ever done,

---

81. *Ibid.*

and cleared stones. Then they were taken to Günzerode, a big farm under Nazi management, surrounded by barbed wire. They hid in a wooden conduit that led from the ground floor ceiling to an outlet in the roof. The Nazis, meanwhile, evacuated the other deportees, then eliminated them by machine-gun. The brothers barely escaped the villagers of Günzerode, who wanted to kill them. They stayed in a house serving as a prison.

Then they were back to square one, at Dora, which the SS had just fled.

Dora. At ten in the morning on April 11, 1945, Oscar and Léon Arditti encountered the First Soldier Liberator: "Twenty or so pajamas who had escaped from the infirmary were gesticulating, yelling, shouting. They had clustered around a man, a man they were touching, fingering to convince themselves they weren't dreaming, that he existed: an AMERICAN."

In the streets of this little German village, the inhabitants "stepped off the sidewalk to make way for these two *Juden*, ghosts in striped pajamas. Men doffed their hats, women made a discreet gesture, all very polite. Then went about their business."

Oscar and Léon Arditti had emerged from the worst disaster to strike the Jewish people in their thousands of years of existence.

Too weak to hate
I let them lead me
Defeated, exhausted, docile
Leaving behind in sinister Silesia
Not only the author of my days but
A teenage nephew, a sister.
Of my pre-war family
I rejoined my wife, my daughter, my niece, my mother
Miracle of human beings
We thought only of tomorrow[82].

They talked, Oscar and Léon. Léon and Oscar. To their family, to their friends. They talked all through the night.

The whole "crowd" was there: Lily, Betty, Jacques Franck, Lidia, Edgar, Henri, Joya, Robert, Yolande, Doudou, Jacques, Jenny, and all the others. The two talked. The others listened. Like they'd never listened before. One

---

82. *Ibid.*

of them was Jacques, my father. What was he thinking of? Whom does one think of when one's childhood friends from far away Bulgaria describe in sober, brutal terms what they have personally lived through and witnessed?

Jacques had received no news of his parents since his return to Paris and the Liberation of France. Neither postcard nor message of any kind since that letter from Argegno, dated July 1944.

Until then, though, he had reassured himself, thinking the war wasn't over and communications were still cut.

Jenny, for her part, listened to what Oscar and Léon had to say about the people from Salonika in Auschwitz, the cousins, uncles, and aunts close to the Amons and the Benvenistes, the children she used to play with when a little girl in the Jerusalem of the Balkans. "We came across a fellow of twenty-five from Salonika who spoke and wept in Ladino, like us," said Léon. "His whole family had been wiped out! There had been seventy-seven in the freight car. All relatives of his: his father, his mother, his sisters, uncles, aunts, cousins. He was the sole survivor."

Jenny discovered that ninety-five percent of her fellow Salonicians had been rounded up by Aloïs Brunner, the very man who had later arrested the Ardittis in Nice. When the latter arrived in the camp in December 1943, the surviving deportees from Salonika had been there since August. They stood out, Oscar said, for their capacity to resist. Knowing little or no Yiddish, some had been sent to Warsaw to clear the ruins of the ghetto. A few had managed to escape and join the Polish resistance. Other Salonicians had later been incorporated into the *Sonderkommandos* at Auschwitz, those deportees forced to escort victims into the gas chambers, then to remove and dispose of the corpses. They had revolted, taking the crematory ovens by assault, and throwing a bomb into the oven, destroying the building. They sang the "Greek partisans" song as they were slaughtered.

Long after the dawn that marked the end of that long Night, and as the Returnees fell silent once more, Jenny and Jacques were still listening to them. But, true to their promise, Oscar and Léon fell silent. Like millions of others. They fell silent like the *Kapos* who, having terrorized the camp, fell silent; like the green triangles, the common criminals who had reigned over the camp, fell silent; like the political deportees, who had enjoyed privileges withheld from the others, fell silent. They fell silent like the thousands of victims who never lived to tell their children what they had endured.

From that time on the old world of the Sephardi Youth, of which the "crowd" had once been part, was split into three groups. Jacques and Jenny numbered among the Survivors. Oscar and Léon numbered among the Returnees. Ida and Jako numbered among the Lost. The Returnees no longer spoke to the Survivors, who no longer spoke of the Lost. And the Lost became shadows, obscured behind the dead from the now-ended official war.

I now leave Jacques and Jenny alone in Silence, divided for the first time against each other. One could no longer think of anything but the dead, the other of the living. Jenny secretly devised strategies to deliver her daughter from the camp of the "star-wearers." Upon discovering that those he once loved above all else had been swept away for all time, Jacques plunged into a black hole.

No way back… A tale of two undesirables

"And Marc? Marc Amon, the person to notify when Marcel was arrested?"

"Marc Amon? Oh! He was taken," Jenny told me. "In the summer of '44. Before Paris was liberated."

Marc was the son of one of Saby's brothers, Jenny's first cousin. He had been Marcel's brother in the Resistance in 1942.

On their return to Paris in fall 1944, Jenny and Marcel learned that Marc had been arrested shortly beforehand, on July 22. He'd been interrogated by the Gestapo. Transferred to Drancy. Then brought to a destination all too well-known by that time.

"He was taken." From that long Night on, Jenny regularly interrupts her tale with this brief aside, sealing the end of a biography. "He was taken," less and less commonly associated with the two words linked to the Arditti brothers: "They returned."

Marc Amon never returned.

Oscar and Léon had seen. They had been able to tell. Marc Amon had not been able to tell. His tale remains untold. Even less so than that of the German resistant Marianne Cohn. Yet hers too is a hero's tale.

And that's just it: the postwar literary scene has little appreciation for heroes. It has tended to focus on their contrary, the antihero, the coward, the traitor, the shifty, the bastard, the evil *collabo*. We have all learned that fine sentiments do not make for good literature. Torturers and brutes make for good novels and movies. Anyway, we all have the potential for evil, we are told. Yet, dyed-in-the-wool evil is not banal, any more than goodness is, as witnessed by the story of Marc, which also comes with a poem, one by Marianne Cohn.

Jenny didn't really know Marc's story, as it is buried in the archives of the Yad Vashem Museum in Jerusalem. To impart flesh and blood to it, I shall punctuate it with excerpts from the magnificent poem *I shall betray tomorrow* by Marianne Cohn, who cared for children as a member of the Éclaireurs Israélites de France, the Jewish girl scouts.

Marc Amon was active in the Occupied Zone, Marianne Cohn in the Free Zone. She was first arrested in Nice in 1943, when the "free" (unoccupied) zone had ceased to exist. It was then that she wrote her famous poem.

I shall betray tomorrow, not today.
Today, pull out my fingernails,
I shall not betray.

Marc was only a year older than Marcel. And he was born in Salonika. He was not yet seventeen at the outbreak of the war. A brilliant physicist, he graduated top of his class from the School of Physics and Chemistry. Unlike his cousins, he did not acquire French nationality. He had remained a Greek citizen and thus was not required to wear the baleful star. Yet he would not seek to wriggle out of the common fate. He had been a Boy Scout. In March 1942, two months after Marcel's first arrest at the Lycée Buffon, he joined the boys' section of the *Éclaireurs Israélites de France*, the French Jewish Boy Scout movement, and became leader of the Joshua Troop, part of the Shema Israel Group. On July 16, 1942, he became co-head of the children's home set up in the hostel on 18 Rue Lamarck, in the 18th arrondissement of Paris, providing shelter for those who had escaped the great Vel d'Hiv roundup.

Marianne Cohn took care of the children before they left for Switzerland.
You do not know the limits of my courage,

I, I do.
You are five hands, harsh and full of rings,
Wearing hob-nailed boots on your feet.

In March 1943, Marc Amon went underground while still involved in his scouting activities, He was a member of the sixth section of the Jewish Boy Scouts, which was in turn part of the fourth division of the *Union Générale des Israélites de France* or UGIF (the legally authorized General Union of Israelites of France). His section was known familiarly as the "Sixth." Working closely with the *Organisation de Secours aux Enfants* or OSE (Children's Aid Organization), the "Sixth" found ways to conceal children aged under fifteen, obtained forged papers, provided them with the means of daily existence and, for those brutally torn from their parents, to maintain ties of affection. Marc was put in charge of the "Sixth" in the Occupied Zone, taking the name Marc Albouis, with a Penguin for a totem. He handled "cases in need of assistance: false papers, finance, cash management." According to his file, this activity made him especially vulnerable, and it was this "public action" that led to his arrest.

In January 1944, Marianne Cohn joined the team conveying groups of children from the southern zone, organizing clandestine frontier crossings, after going through Lyon and Annecy. She was arrested near Annemasse with a group of twenty-eight children on May 31.

I shall betray tomorrow, not today.
I need the night to make up my mind.
I need at least one night,
To disown, to abjure, to betray.

Marc Amon's final act of bravura was a rescue operation. The Gestapo surprised him on clandestine premises passing on instructions and equipment to his female comrade. After a tense exchange he secured the woman's immediate release … in exchange for himself.

Marianne Cohn did not talk under torture. Her network offered to arrange for her escape. She refused, fearing reprisals against the children.

To deny my friends,
To forswear bread and wine,
To betray life,
To die.

I shall betray tomorrow, not today,
The rasp is under the tile,
The rasp is not for the bar,
The rasp is not for the executioner,
The rasp is for my wrist.

In the night of July 7-8, 1944, the Gestapo in Lyon sent a team to Annemasse to take six prisoners, Marianne Cohn among them, from their cells. They were murdered, kicked, then clubbed to death with shovels. But all the children were saved.

Marc Amon was arrested by the Militia on July 22 and interrogated at the Commissariat for Jewish Questions and by the Gestapo. He was then transferred directly to his cell at Drancy. Then deported in the last convoy, on July 31, in a "disciplinary" railcar containing—according to the file—"those whom the Nazis considered to be their most dangerous enemies."

Today I have nothing to say,
Tomorrow I shall betray.[83]

To understand the significance of that "today" and of that "tomorrow," one needs to know that people under torture needed to be able to resist for twenty-four hours to give their comrades time to make their getaway. Beyond that… tomorrow… one can yield. The danger to the others will have abated by then. Like Marianne Cohn, Marc Amon was one of those tortured under questioning by the Gestapo. Very likely he managed to hold out till the next day. When one knows what "ordinary" armored railcars were like, where millions of human beings agonized in the utterly barbarous conditions, one can imagine what the "disciplinary" cars must have been like.

The Yad Vashem file contains excerpts from Marc's letters. They are undated. They were sent between his arrest and his deportation. The first was addressed to his mother: "Dear Mama, a letter for you alone, the first because I received paper with the parcel. I thought of you today and was a little upset when I imagined the moment when you heard what I would call the 'sad news.' I hope you were brave. I've never concealed from you that

---

83. Marianne Cohn, *Je trahirai demain* (I shall betray tomorrow), from *Résistez. Poèmes pour la liberté*, Seghers Jeunesse, 2014.

I was doing my duty, and the risks. It's happened. It's unimportant... Don't fret for me, this will be just a brief incident... For a while (soon I hope). I send you a big kiss. Marc."

The second seems to have been addressed to his entire family, including his sister Renée: "She must know that life is long and that sooner or later it will reward her work. So, she must do what she thinks she ought to do, the result will come eventually, provided she does not act from fear... Do not worry needlessly; being concerned is pointless and I would be much easier in my mind if I knew that you are taking it all philosophically, as something that just had to happen to someone who was doing what he knew was his duty, regardless of the risks. (It's rather grandiloquent, but that's how it is...). For all our friends, they must know that *I was thinking first and foremost of them.* I hope they weren't too worried for me, nor for themselves. They too must be strong and see clearly into the future. It is absolutely essential that they be more lucid and not let themselves be carried away by their imagination. May they be men always."

Tomorrow I shall betray.

Marc Amon and Marianne Cohn. Marianne Cohn: foreign. Ashkenazi Jewess. Resister. Undesirable. Marc Amon: foreign. Sephardi Jew. Resister. Undesirable.

Their paths might have crossed... They might have met... They were working for the same cause. She was born in Mannheim, Germany, on September 17, 1922. He was born in Salonika, Greece, on March 9, 1923. Their combined ages were less than forty in 1944.

Sixty years later, Marc's sister Renée remembers: "He knew he was going to be arrested. He told me: 'I'm going to be picked up. But it's my duty.' 'Yes, It's your duty.' I was thirteen. An adult would have said, 'Go into hiding!'... My mother, Luna, who knew nothing, had this dream: 'I saw Marc. He was in the flames.' After the war, everyone went their own way. I got married. I had three children. I didn't want to rake over all that... [One's] got to cover those who are dead with soil... But his mother, our mother, she waited fifteen years for him to come back. She never wanted to accept it. As for our father, he had psychiatric problems. That's how he escaped... by going crazy... You know.... the train that took him to Auschwitz, it was the last one ..."

Accident or suicide?

Officially, the great butchery ended on May 8, 1945, with the unconditional surrender of the Third Reich, and then on September 2, 1945, with the unconditional surrender of the Japanese Empire. The French had been liberated since the previous summer. But the other war, the one Oscar had revealed to Jacques in his hideout on the Rue de Rivoli, the unequal war to annihilate a whole people, that war continued, for that was the war Hitler was most interested in. You ask for proof? He used his last trains to take children and old folk to their death rather than supply his exhausted troops.

The war was over, but not its consequences. Most of the deported had disappeared, but the survivors had to go on living. For four years, they had had to draw on their savings—such as they had—till there was nothing left in order to hide, they had sold their silverware and jewelry, if they had any. Now, they were once again able to work as full citizens. But others had made off with the tools of their trade.

"Jacques' first outing on our return to Paris," relates Jenny, "was to go back to the store. The Italian "managing commissioner" hadn't caused us too much trouble. He was too terrified. But the once-flourishing store had been stripped of all its stock."

The store of fabric that Jacques, then Moïse, had successively been obliged to abandon had vanished into thin air too. Luckily, Jenny had retained her store of memories though; like prisoners in the Gulag, her memory became her travel bag. When I pressed her in the 2000s to testify to the Working Party on the Spoliation of Jews in France, she recalled all the lost items of textile, down to the tiniest detail, and the price per meter of each.

Says Jenny: "Jacques was unable to reopen the store till January '45. Officially, we couldn't buy anything. Which meant we couldn't sell anything. At the time, the only choice for small storekeepers was either the black market or to just give up. We were caught between Scylla and Charybdis. Jacques hesitated. He had too much integrity for the kind of underground dealing where you had to pay the wholesaler bribes that couldn't show up on the official invoice, then figure out your profit on the real retail price. But by then, I didn't give a fig whether it was legal or not. We'd had to hide for years just to go on living. Illegality had become our territory. For us, just *being* was illegal.

"So, seeing what thousands of Aryan sellers of dairy products and small traders had been doing all along to earn a livelihood, we could perfectly well copy them to survive ourselves. Only, Jacques was honest through and through, like his father. He had to force himself. He never got used to it. Still, we had to eat, and we didn't have a penny. After those dreadful years of shortages, we had come in at the end of the party: other peoples' party. All we got were the crumbs from the table. Early on, we relied for our supplies on my father Saby, who had sent a lot of the stock to Lyon from Paris in '43. But he drove a hard bargain, making us pay top black-market rates.

"They were hard times, and the State took steps to protect itself from profiteers of every stripe, introducing economic controls. That was the last straw for Jacques."

Since the Ardittis' return and the night of revelations, Jacques had ceased sleeping or eating, writing all over the place for news of his parents. To the Red Cross, to the Jewish community in Milan, to the inn in Argegno, to the Argegno city hall.

Little by little, he came to believe that the persecution he and his family had endured was ever-present and menacing. Little by little, the specter of the economic inspectors combined in his mind with the Gestapo, the Vichy militia, and even with the French police who'd come to arrest him at the start of the war. He distrusted everything, everyone.

"One day," Jenny recalls, "two women customers came in wanting some velvet. And he had velvet. At black market prices. Unsuspecting, he measured out and cut the cloth; they paid cash. Then, five minutes later, they returned. Less friendly this time. With their ID cards 'Economic Inspectors.' 'Your invoices!' Obviously, he had the official invoices. But there had been under-the-counter payments, which appeared nowhere, yet he had well and truly paid them to obtain the goods, and he had included them in the price so as not to sell at a loss. As a result, his profit margin looked huge. So, Jacques was summoned to the chief inspector. I tried to convince him that this little incident was nothing compared to what we had experienced, that we would pull through, as we always had. He began ranting. He thought they were going to send us to Drancy. He wanted to pack his bags. Then he went on saying there was no point in packing a bag. He said goodbye to me. He hugged you effusively. He refused to go to work in the store, fearing the Gestapo would come back to arrest him. That's when I decided to take him to our family doctor, Doctor Cazès, who'd been with us since Salonika."

That day, Jacques threw himself head-first into the void from the doctor's office on the fifth floor, on Rue Lafayette. Aroused by Jenny's screaming, the third-floor tenant rushed out and had the presence of mind to catch him and cushion his fall. Jacques didn't kill himself. He escaped with a broken leg and six months in bed. He was no longer the same when he got up. He put on 44 pounds. And he lost his faith.

"Do you remember Doctor's Cazès' office?" Jenny asks me. "We took you there regularly when you were little. There was an elevator on the side and opposite the stairwell, which was protected by a railing. Jacques bounded from the elevator, and before I could get out, he leaped backward. He tumbled in free fall, heading straight for the tiled floor at the bottom."

"Did he do it on purpose?"

"Of course not, it was an accident. I must say, the railing was very low."

"Did he do it on purpose?"

"Not at all. I'm telling you. It was an accident!"

I look at Jenny, incredulous, but on she goes: "It was nearly two in the afternoon and the person living on the third floor was leaving to go to work. He heard my scream and saw this man falling before his eyes. He instinctively reached out and grabbed your father's jacket, gripping him by the shoulders. He was unable to pull him up but—I don't know how he did it—he straightened him up. As a result, Jacques landed on his feet, breaking a leg in the process. I rang Cazès' doorbell. He was finishing his lunch. He gave him an injection. I told the Ardittis. We had just had lunch with them. Getting to the hospital was quite a business. I had to hail a cab, go to the police precinct. A disaster."

"Wasn't there an ambulance?"

"Are you kidding? In 1945! Finally, we got him to the Marmottan hospital. Late in the evening, Cazès visited him in the hospital, and he came out of the room saying he was absolutely *compos mentis* and that the sleeping pills he'd been taking even before the consultation scheduled that day had played a part in his unfortunate fall."

"So, according to him it could have been an attempted…"

"Certainly not, how many times do I have to tell you? It was an accident. At Marmottan Oscar came across a specialist, Doctor B. Oscar did ask him if he thought Jacques might have 'tried something.' And he answered: 'If he did try something, he didn't succeed. But it's going to take a very long time.'"

"You see. He didn't succeed because the guy on the third floor saved his hide. If..."

"It was an accident, I tell you. It's just that he was worn out by all he'd been through... And then, you understand, there was our return to Paris after the Liberation. We had been so absorbed in our own troubles and ordeals. We thought everyone had experienced difficulties of one kind or another. We couldn't get over the fact that people, our neighbors, old acquaintances, were still there, solely preoccupied with their work and their pleasures. Utterly oblivious to the persecution we'd suffered; they'd no idea. The food shortage was all they were a little concerned about. 'We too had difficulty finding butter!' But they always had relatives and friends living in the country who sent them parcels, not to mention the black market, from which they profited more than we did."

"That's just it! Don't you think ... he got to the point where he'd had it up to there, and that he decided... to end it all?"

"No, no, he'd never have done that! In any case, he never mentioned it after that!"

Jenny never said: "He'd never have done that to *me*." She didn't even say he was "depressed" or suffering from burn out, a little-used word at the time. She said, and repeated, that he was "tired." Which gives to that term, so overworked in its sheer banality, a somewhat pejorative sense: it sounds hollow against this background of misfortunes.

I did not belabor the point, as Jenny wanted to close the discussion on this "accident," to move on and talk with not a little pride about how she had pulled through. Singlehandedly, since one of its two members had deserted the team.

Today I see that, at the time of the "accident," Jenny had entered on a phase of denial. She began to downplay things. Less to let her Jacques off the hook for having done *that* to *her*, than to go on living like everyone else. To be like everyone else one had to have suffered *a little*. A modest dose of affliction allowing one to blend one's own troubles with those of others, nothing out of proportion, to wail over the butter shortage so as not to feel so different, so isolated.

"The specialist, Doctor B., told me right away: 'You can't keep him in the emergency room at Marmottan.' A normal hospital cost a fortune. We had no health insurance. By a stroke of luck, the physician lived at La Motte-Picquet, not far from us. He told me: 'If you take him home, I could come to treat him. And you'd be able to feed him properly. What one eats is vital to recovery.' So, I brought him home on a gurney with his legs strapped down. It took five people to get him up to the fifth floor. I ordered a Dupont bed[84] and hired a nurse. He spent six months with his leg suspended."

"How did you manage for money?"

"Oscar took me aside at once and told me: 'You've got to open the store and manage it. We'll help you.' Oscar Arditti knew about surviving. He helped me. I hadn't the foggiest notion how to go about it. But, well, it wasn't rocket science."

The shop was on Rue du Faubourg-Poissonnière. One had to cross Paris to reach it. At home, Jenny had a badly disabled husband with a nurse, and a five-year-old daughter. Four mouths to feed, with the restrictions we had in the 1940s. She coped.

"I cooked on Sundays for the whole week. And to begin with I opened the store in the afternoon only. Jacques needed lots of dairy products and sugar, which was hard to come by in those times of shortages."

She fed him so well he rose from his bed several tens of pounds heavier, pounds he never shed.

"And what did you do about the economic inspector?"

"Well, they came back asking to see the books and I told them about Jacques' accident. Their chief even came to see Jacques on his Dupont bed. He took pity on me, summoned me to his office. In the end, nothing happened. A tiny fine. Peanuts. And he arranged everything. The hardest part was paying off our debts, the under-the-counter payments for the velvet that your father still hadn't paid to the wholesaler, the father of a friend of

---

84. A hospital-style bed [Translator].

mine. I remember, we owed him eighteen thousand francs. For us it was a fortune. This gentleman, a coreligionist, didn't lift a finger to extend me some credit, at least for long enough for me to get back on my feet."

"But it was illegal, so you didn't have to pay!"

Jenny stares at me. "Jacques would never have allowed it. Already, his father had ruined himself repaying an Italian debt in non-devalued liras."

Trust in business dealings down the centuries and in the face of persecution has allowed Jewish families to forge networks and prosper in trade, since they had no right to engage in anything else. Doing things with a flourish in the midst of misery is all that remains after so much humiliation.

"Oscar found a beige carpet under the other brown one in our apartment on Rue César-Franck. The quality was good. He pulled it up and got a good price for it, so I was able to repay the debt. I worked hard. After a while, Jacques recovered. He advised me. We pulled through."

But Jenny felt bitter about the "fellow in religion" who had demanded repayment of the illicit debt. She felt bitter about her parents who had done little to help her, and who offered nothing without a kickback. She felt bitter about the Ashkenazi customers, the "Polacks" as she called them, even though they were survivors of the Disaster like herself, who "drove her crazy" for the price of a coupon; her favorites were her French customers, little shop girls and clerks who didn't mind spending a little more to sew their own dresses and who talked about their love lives.

This set Jenny to thinking. She thought about all those non-Jewish French who had helped them survive, her husband and her child.

While all this was going on, Jacques lay helpless on his Dupont bed, pondering over and over the contents of a telegram from Argegno, Italy, that had arrived the day before the "accident." In his delirium, he'd burned it.

Their "sad Odyssey"

That summer, two letters from Argegno, in Italian, had arrived at 8, Rue César-Franck. They merely confirmed what Jacques already knew from the telegram, which he hadn't told Jenny about. Later, he had them translated into French—in the French of the time, by an inexperienced translator, possibly foreign.

The first was dated August 28. It was signed by two names: Rosati, the innkeeper of the Albergo Argegno, and Burati, whom Jacques could not identify.

> *Albergo Argegno*
> *Argegno (Lago di Como)*
> *Telefono 21*
>
> *Argegno, 8/28/45*
>
> *Monsieur Benrey,*
> *We hope you are in possession of the telegram that we sent you in response to your request. In the conciseness of the telegram, we said little. The facts are as follows: your good parents were living quietly in our company and that of Monsieur Burati, awaiting the end of the war, which could not be far off.*
> *But it is painful for us to communicate to you that on the morning of September 1, 1944, they were taken, with all their baggage, by the German SS and driven, together with the Tagger family from Sofia, to the neighboring district of Cernobbio. We followed them, asking for news of them in Como, then in Milan and afterward in Verona. In that locality, it was no longer possible to have the least news, to our great displeasure.*
> *We think (and this is our personal opinion) that they were deported to Germany. We would be happy if you could have news to communicate also to us. We would have liked to have informed you earlier of what happened but, hoping to see them again from one day to the next, we held off doing so.*
> *We express a sincere wish that they may return home to your family.*
> *Awaiting your news, we send you our distinguished greetings,*
> *Rosati, Burati*[85]

The second letter was signed Guadagno Vincenzo, *sindaco* (mayor) of Argegno. It is dated September 24, 1945, and refers to a letter of August 27, sent by Jacques, who had not yet received Rosati's letter sent the day before.

---

85. I have tried to reproduce the somewhat gauche flavor of the original French translation [Translator].

Comune di Argegno
Provincia di Como
Servizio annonario
Protocollo n° 2700
9/24/1945
Risposta a nota del 8/27/45
Objeti Conjugi Benrey

To Monsieur Yack Benrey
8, Rue César-Franck
Paris 15ᵉ

The above-named resided here in the Hotel Argegno until the month of August 1944. At that date they were taken by the Germans of the German SS Command at Cernobbio, where they were interned for around one month and were then taken to Verona.

Being myself a personal friend of the Benreys, I wanted to know their final destination by seeking information in Verona, but no one was able to tell me anything.

As I said before, I was a personal friend of the Benreys and I too am anxious to know their sad Odyssey and would like to see them again.

The Mayor, Guadagno Vincenzo

In the original letter, Guadagno Vincenzo had initially written "friend of the Taggers," which he had crossed out and replaced by "friend of the Benreys."

Jacques received these letters, together with the one from the Red Cross, which also referred to an internment at Cernobbio and which no longer features in the archives, while he was immobilized on his "bed of pain," as it was called politely, denoting both the horrific news and the broken leg. Jenny did not comment on the receipt of these letters, leaving them enclosed in her "forgetting box."

As for me, Michou, I was away from home in August 1945. Jenny had dispatched me to a boarding school at Chambon-sur-Ligne. I did not read these letters carefully till after her death.

Afterthoughts

Nowhere in Jenny's story is there any mention of an attempt by the family to draw conclusions from the extermination of six million of *los muestros*, including a million children. Nor does she comment on the fact that three-quarters of Jews with French nationality survived, a high figure by comparison with the nationals of other European countries.

I assume, or rather I imagine, that there must have been some moment, in many families, when the Survivors and Returnees counted their Lost. Nobody in ours has the slightest recollection of a moment like that. Presumably because there never was one, never was a moment when the assembled tribe might have drawn up a list of its dead, respecting the subtle hierarchy to which they had become accustomed in the Nazi extermination camps.

Decades later, I submit this somber assessment of our five years of persecution, as our family members might have done, had they done so, in light of the hierarchy of victimhood of the time. Of their time.

As in all French families, the Benveniste family honored its heroic dead, preferably those who died fighting, when that was so. Allegra's son Rafael Modiano, Kiko to his friends and family, was killed fighting at Petites-Armoises in 1940. His mother was presented with his *Légion d'honneur* on his behalf, at Les Invalides[86], with the whole family in attendance.

So much for the official dead, the respectable ones, formally sanctioned by death certificates and commemorated by medals. In each household of the Benveniste tribe, ours included, a photograph of Kiko in military dress stood proudly over the fireplace or on the grand piano.

The Resistance fighters Marcel and Jacques did not die, nor did they seek official recognition of their services. So, they received nothing. According to Jenny, neither of them asked for anything in that respect. Jacques sought confirmation of his involvement solely in support of his application for French nationality in 1948, and Marcel in a bid to sort out a financial mix-up.

---

86. The *Légion d'honneur*, an important French distinction; Les Invalides, major Paris monument and ceremonial venue for the French Army [Translator].

For the Lost, neither homage nor funeral, not even symbolic, and no ceremony. In the first place, because there was never any document certifying their death. There was no mourning. The deportees vanished without trace; even their photos vanished from the tribe's frames.

I have placed them on display here for the first time.

Pepo, Marie Beveniste's second brother, and his wife Ester were arrested before the Normandy landings. Lost. They left an orphan. No one ever told him anything.

Marc Amon, Marcel's cousin, and comrade in the Resistance, arrested in Paris in the last summer of the war. Lost. His parents waited decades for him without a word.

Marie Jerusalmi and Moïse Benrey, arrested in Argegno, Province of Como, Italy. Vanished. My father told me practically nothing about them, and I never questioned him.

Bereft of a sepulcher, their shades haunt the confines of those terrible years. All through the nineteen fifties, sixties, seventies, and eighties, no one ever bothered to restore their photographs to their frames or their memory to people's hearts. I was still a child when I discovered a long tress of blond hair in the attic of our house in the Brie country near Paris.

"What's this, Mama, this hair?"

"Oh, nothing! They were your grandmother Marie's. The other Marie."

Abandoned to the moths, that fine head of hair vanished in turn from our wardrobes. Even Jacques, her son, never mentioned it nor called for it. No one thought to bury it in a tomb. Or even reduce it to ashes, like its owner, to preserve it piously in a jar.

As the Nazis hoped, the deportees have vanished without trace into the Night and Fog. Names reduced to registration numbers. Numbers expunged without trace from administrative records. The negationists took their absence, the void, for proof nothing had ever happened. By dint of seeking them, these human beings, without ever finding them, people became convinced they'd never existed. Those who came through, the Returnees, were mindful of the Survivors' sensitivities, divulging the truth in homeopathic doses. They too wanted to forget. Bureaucratic absurdity came to their aid: as long as there is no certificate in black and white, a dead man is not dead. Nor is he alive, since he isn't there. He just dissolves gradually into this no man's land.

Between the vagueness of those early days, the evasive answers as to the destination of that mysterious journey and the brutal date of my paternal grandparents' individual gassing, which I discovered in 2005, sixty years elapsed. Sixty years devoid of mourning.

Not all families reacted as ours did, though. They demanded answers. Right away. Reparations. The *pretium doloris*, the price of pain. In cash, if necessary. For that one had to hire a lawyer. Which cost a lot. Some did win "compensation." The word itself scorches my pen. Pain has a price?

Jacques refused to engage in any proceedings, not even just to find out: "I refuse to make money out of my parents' death!"

Again, that panache, the arrogance of the Spanish grandees of yester-year. Too proud, Jacques Quixote lived what we now call a "precarious" existence until his premature death. He demanded neither excuses nor charity. He preferred to close his eyes to the eradication of parents he'd deeply loved and above all, above all never to capitalize on horror. He asked for nothing. Not a tear. Not a penny. He was the first to fall silent. His friends the Ardittis, who had themselves lived through a thousand deaths, did receive reparations, had children, and above all bore witness. Two temperaments. Two responses.

There were many such.

What would I have done in their place?

On January 11, 1948, a leader in the French newspaper *Le Monde* titled "The survivors of the death camps" spoke of the "two hundred and eighty thousand deportees" without mentioning the word "Jewish." Under legislation adopted the same year, the word "deportee" referred solely to French citizens or residents deported for political reasons or for resisting the occupier. No distinction was made either between the camps they were sent to or their fate on arrival. Official documents classified Jewish children sealed up in trains and sent to Auschwitz to be gassed as "political deportees." These children, most of them forcibly seized from their parents by French gendarmes, were subsequently portrayed in documents and on commemorative plaques as having "died for France."

Jewish survivors aroused scant enthusiasm, to say the least. In the 4ᵗʰ Arrondissement of Paris, hundreds of people demonstrated in April 1945 to protest when a Returnee tried to recover his occupied apartment, shouting "France for the French." There was a widespread attitude that the Israelites really were going too far in trying to get back their property. The Christian philosopher Gabriel Marcel called for a firm stand against "Jewish encroachment [...]. They must not think they are privileged creditors!"

In these early post-war years, and long afterward, it was deemed "impolite," "indecent" even, to broach the subject of deportations on racial grounds. The distinction between those arrested for what they had done and those arrested for what they were was systematically blurred.

The most sensitive and the clearest sighted found no refuge save in the great silence of suicide, during or after the war. Walter Benjamin was one of the first to do away with himself, at Portbou, in Catalonia, in the night of September 25-26, 1940. Then came Stefan Zweig, who so loved his city, Vienna; he killed himself in exile in Petropolis, Brazil, in February 1942 just as the Final Solution was getting underway in Europe. Paul Celan threw himself into the Seine from the Pont Mirabeau, on April 20, 1970. Primo Levi too fell *deliberately?* into the stairwell from the third floor of his apartment in Turin, on April 11, 1987. It was a miracle Jacques failed in 1945.

As for me, Michou, without realizing it, I benefited from the general Silence to remain in ignorance.

And what about Michou?

While Jacques and Jenny strove to survive the shipwreck—soul, body and goods—I tended to be left to my own devices. Understandably, Jenny didn't know what to do with her daughter in that joyless summer of 1945.

At Eastertime, however, still in ignorance of what had happened, Jenny resolved to send me to school. And what better school than her own Lycée Victor-Duruy, which still had a kindergarten and all the elementary school classes? At the start of the semester, Easter 1945, I was just over five. In March or April, Jenny stepped hopefully through the entrance on Boulevard des Invalides, where she had so often entered herself, first as a schoolchild, then as a high school student. She brought with her a full school record, saved from looting and stored for posterity. A distinguished record, featuring Mademoiselle Maurel's arrogant signature on her upper sixth form class report card, a glorious flourish sending her favorite pupil to the *Concours Général d'Histoire* in 1934.

There was a line snaking outside the door to the admissions office. Docile, Jenny took her place and waited patiently in line, utterly sure of herself. When at last her turn came and she loudly announced her intention to enroll her daughter after the Easter vacation, she received an indignant reply:

"But, Madame, certainly not! This line is for enrolments for this coming fall."

Jenny was not to be put out:

"Does Mademoiselle Wackeinem still take the little children's class? Can I see her?"

Without a moment's hesitation, Mademoiselle Wackeinem declared:

"If I have to add another seat in my class after the Easter vacation, it'll be for your daughter," she stated firmly, before the Principal and Assistant Principal, both left speechless.

And so, hunched up and shy, I took my place in mid-school year on the extra seat in the Victor-Duruy kindergarten on Rue de Babylone, opposite the La Pagode movie theater. Having been shuttled back and forth by the vicissitudes of the war and having already had more than one name, I could neither read nor write and was scared of everything. Three schoolteachers, first Mademoiselle Wackeinem in year one, then those in years two and three, tried in turn to bring the little urchin that I was up to scratch, accustomed as I was to hiding under beds or spending days on end there, refusing to grow up and, as my third-year teacher said, determined to remain a "baby." The class photo (still mixed at that age) shows me gap-toothed with a big bow in my hair, sitting bolt upright on my seat and clearly tense.

But, for Jenny and my teachers, it was vital that I not lose a year of schooling; I had to reach the *baccalaureate* at sixteen[87], like the girls from the Faubourg Saint-Germain, still a posh neighborhood then; like the little Christian girls who had spent the war in their cradles and baby carriages on the Avenue de Breteuil or under the greenery of the Champ-de-Mars.

Despite these pressures, and to the dismay of Jenny and Mademoiselle Wackeinem, I repeated my third year in 1947, carrying the shame until my adulthood.

Meantime, my parents had come through the trial of fire—the night with the Ardittis, Jacques' "accident," the letters from Argegno. That summer of 1945, in July, the faithful second year teacher strove to teach me to read and write, giving me private lessons at home. Jacques rested on his Dupont bed, listening on the radio to the trial of ex-Marshal Pétain, who was sentenced to death then pardoned by De Gaulle.

On August 9, while a government decree restored "republican legality," I was far from the capital. Jenny was run off her feet, and she accepted her

---

87. The normal high school graduation age is 17 or 18, as in the US. [Translator].

uncle Momo's proposal to send me to spend the summer with Aunt Soly, in the Chambon-sur-Lignon boarding school where all my young cousins had survived the darkest years protected by the unfailing devotion of a Protestant pastor and his Huguenot congregation.

Momo insisted:

"You've too much on your plate now... and you've got to toughen the little one up. She spends her time clinging to your skirts. Magda and André Trocmé are fantastic people. They've saved all our children—your cousins—not to mention hundreds of others of young and not so young children."

"But, Uncle, you had all converted to Protestantism already. Not Michou!"

"Most of the children hidden there weren't Protestants."

"And this place? Where is it?"

"Chambon-sur-Lignon is on the Vivarais-Lignon plateau in the Cévennes. It's an old Huguenot region that's experienced persecution. The pastor and his wife urged all the villagers to involve themselves in the rescue."

"But were the villagers Protestants?"

"The majority, yes. But there were Catholics too. The whole village pitched in. The inhabitants welcomed refugees into their homes and farms. When German patrols came near the villagers sang a pre-arranged song and the fugitives knew it was time to go hide in the woods."

"And... no one was deported?"

"Yes. Unfortunately. One of the pastor's cousins, Daniel Trocmé, was arrested with *all* his children and deported."

"Did they come back?"

"Not to my knowledge. But I'm sure... well, perhaps they'll return... Anyway, lots of children were saved, ours included. And don't forget, Jenny, that the war is over. Your daughter needs to be free. Now there's no danger, so let her go and get some fresh air, with other children."

"And this Aunt Soly, she's the one who runs the children's refuge?"

"It isn't a refuge for wartime orphans or camp survivors. It's a children's home that was open all through the Occupation. Its director, son of the Chief Rabbi of Lyon, had been barred from working. His wife Solange was in charge of the home."

Momo's optimism, despite his good intentions, was unjustified. Daniel Trocmé was deported to Buchenwald, then to Dora. He was part of a convoy bound for the Maïdenek camp and died during the journey, which lasted nine months.

As for me, I had lived peacefully through the German Occupation clinging to my mother's skirts; now I missed them with every passing second. Of that summer 1945 spent in the Aunt Soly's home with the youngest of the Benveniste cousins, who must have been twelve and a half, there remains a photo of a group of children on the home's terrace. I'm moping, sitting cross-legged on the ground next to other little children; one little girl, the Benveniste cousin, stands in the back row proudly sporting an Alsatian-style headdress. This girl, Momo's daughter, had spent much of her childhood at Chambon during the worst of the war, and she was put in charge of me. She bathed me and helped tie my shoelaces. She pulled my hair as she brushed it and couldn't form the two plaited buns that crowned the hair piled above my ears. She would urge me to cry less and stop calling for my mommy during the long siestas in the dormitory. Still, in these trying times she represented one last family refuge for me.

I still needed some tutelary assistance during the winter of 1946-1947, when I was sent to a children's home—probably Israelite, though I was unaware of it—in Megève with Claudine Arditti. She was Oscar's daughter, the child who had got away in Nice, and was younger than me. A very bright young Polish girl called Eva took me under her wing. She was exactly the same age as me, seven, but I lied about mine to seem vulnerable and take advantage of her protection. In return for my unswerving loyalty, she defended me against the other children, who scared me. But being apart from Jenny was a disaster. I had nightmares. I dreamed that no one came for me, that I was alone in the world, like little Rachel whose parents had disappeared and who loathed the aunt who had taken their place. I wet my bed three nights running, after which the home's staff called my parents. They didn't keep children who wet their bed.

All three of us were very happy to go home together. Jenny and Jacques solemnly promised they'd never again send me to a boarding school, and they kept their word.

Jenny had other plans for me.

The Gordian knot

After three years of headaches, rejections, bureaucracy gone mad and endless legal tussles, Jacques succeeded in persuading officials in the 9th arrondissement of Paris to agree to a *fake* death certificate in the names of Moïse Benrey and Marie Jerusalmi, allowing him to recover his parents' apartment.

Like millions of others, Marie and Moïse had vanished one autumn morning and were never heard of again. Body, soul, and goods. In their baggage were the savings they'd been counting on to survive till the end of the war, half of their silverware, some jewelry, and other items, forever unrecorded, no doubt adorning another person's home or augmenting the Nazis' war booty.

All that remains of them is we who are alive, half of the retail haberdashery, though not the premises itself, and their Paris apartment on 2 Rue Thimonier, in the 9th arrondissement of Paris. Only now it was occupied by someone else.

Regaining possession of the apartment took up much of Jacques and Jenny's energy over several years; they could think of nothing but annihilation and looting.

"Most of those close to us were less fortunate," says Jenny. "Many had installed Aryan friends in their homes to preserve them. But, when it came to settling accounts, their kindly friends proved unwilling to hand back what they had *borrowed*. True, there was a major housing crisis at the time. The authorities too still employed many former collaborators and were in no hurry to restore property to its rightful owners, prompting a wave of protracted lawsuits. Some of those who had been despoiled became so exasperated they took matters into their own hands. They changed the locks and moved back in by force.

"We had our share of troubles with my parents-in-law's apartment on Rue Thimonnier. Thimonnier, the 'Gordian knot,' as Jacques used to say. Being Jewish Italian citizens, Moïse and Marie's apartment, like the store, had acquired an Italian managing administrator, a Director of Banco di Roma. He had rented it out to a friend. The latter had sold all our furniture and personal items for a song. Then, Italian property being the property of enemy aliens, it had been placed under sequester. Moïse and Marie were at fault first for being Jewish, then for being Italian, therefore enemies, and finally for being deported, hence absent. Three cardinal sins.

"Bureaucracy didn't care that they were absent because lost, more than likely dead. We needed a certificate to prove they were dead. And we had no death certificate! We sent a furious letter to the State Prosecutor, who replied drily that he 'wasn't saying the contrary.' Full stop."

"The contrary of what?"

"Who knows? The contrary of what we had written, I suppose... What to do?" Jenny went on. "How could we prove that these lost persons, one aged seventy, the other over sixty, could never regain possession of their Paris apartment? And that their son, their sole survivor, needed it desperately?"

"Jacques had stopped sleeping again, his leg was hurting, and he limped even more when under stress. He would have liked to have put his parents' disappearance behind him once and for all. But how to forget when the paperwork sent us endlessly back to the same tragedy? We hired lawyers, attorneys, business advisors of every stripe, who charged a fortune, each more incompetent than the other. The nub of the matter was that Moïse and Marie had been deported from Italy. 'Ah! My dear sir, if your poor parents had been deported from France, there would have been no problem. But from ITALY!'

"Part of the solution came to us after three years of fighting desperately for our rights. Three years during which I thought Jacques was going out of his mind. And the architect of the miracle was a big-hearted Italian lawyer called Donati."

"Donati? Angelo Donati, the one who tried to save the Jews during the war?"

"I didn't know he was well-known. Anyway, he got us out of this very tricky situation. Signor Donati got in touch with one of his nephews, a lawyer also, who found four camp survivors. They agreed to testify that they'd seen Moïse Benrey and Marie Jerusalmi die before their eyes. The document drawn up by the Justice of Peace in Modena, countersigned by the Italian Veterans Administration, was sent to France, and translated. I have preserved this false testimony… Look how it's covered with all kinds of Italian and French rubber stamps.

"Essentially, it says that on September 26, 1947, four people of Polish origin residing in Modena, two storekeepers, a tailor and a driver, testified under oath that Moïse Benrey and Marie Jerusalmi, married name Benrey, arrested at Argegno in September 1943, *a year before their actual arrest*, died 'during their deportation to the concentration camps in Poland.'

"Meanwhile, the Italian had left, and the empty apartment had been requisitioned by the Government's Public Lands Administration to house Monsieur N., a young ex-prisoner of war, recently released and just married. We had to pay the building's common charges, with nothing in return, right from 1945, but it was only once we obtained the death certificate, in 1948, that the tenant who'd been given the apartment began paying us rent, six thousand francs a month, four thousand less than the normal rent.

"We had to wait till 1950, six years after the disappearance of Moïse and Marie, and in return for a tidy inducement of three hundred and fifty thousand francs, that Monsieur N., such a good man, agreed to leave us free to sell the apartment in exchange for his mother-in-law's house in the Brie region, which he wanted to get rid of."

Says Jenny: "I came out of it with a little garden where I was able to plant a vegetable patch… my dream!"

After five years of legal chicanery and fierce struggle, a big 1,500 square-foot Paris apartment was traded for a little cottage in a village in the Brie area, east of Paris. The apartment is surely worth five times more than the house, today. Jenny, who had never liked the Rue Thimonnier apartment and had wanted to move to the French countryside, declared herself thrilled. The Gordian knot had been untied by a fake, a bribe, and a fool's bargain. And still the thrice victims thanked this "such a good man" who had been so well-served by the system.

Thus, Jenny began her infiltration into to the heart of France, a journey with no return. Henceforward, she bent her efforts toward a single goal. That goal crystalized around her child, who was supposed to accomplish a program of total assimilation. A goal her parents, now too old and too affected by their epoch, were unable to fulfil alone.

Where is God?

"Where is God, my child?"

She had a nice smile, this nun, and I was no longer afraid of her as I had been to begin with, when I instinctively looked around me, not sure what she wanted me to do.

"Where is God?"

This time, I mischievously looked all around, bent down looking under the heavy oak table, looked up at the ceiling, peered at the window giving onto a garden with its cloistered air...

The nun glared at me stonily:

"Where is God?"

I hesitated but still wanted to play hide-and-seek, pretending... I made as if to rush under the table on all fours.

"Where is God?"

This time the nun was frowning. Till now, she had never been angry, but...

"Where is God?"

Now I had to answer, otherwise I would have to forgo one of those pious images I so loved, which I collected on my bedside table and which I used to linger over before my evening prayers.

"Where is God?"

I couldn't start over with this little game. Another nun interrupted this private catechism lesson. She leaned toward the first one and whispered in her ear.

"My child, show Sister Thérèse you know very well *where* God is."

"God is... everywhere."

"Yes, my daughter. That's the right answer.

Did I ever again hunt all over the place in the hope of at last finding Him who was everywhere, since He was everywhere? Not this time, at any rate, in front of the fearsome-looking Sister Thérèse.

Today, I wonder what these two nuns could have whispered to each other, in Notre-Dame du Cenacle, in the discreet building on 58 Avenue de Breteuil housing the congregation. Did they say this little Israelite ripe for conversion was decidedly obstinate, or was she truly a bonehead? Or was she deceitfully and deliberately failing to understand the fundamental truths of the Holy Catholic Church?

This was in the winter of 1946-1947, on my return from the boarding school in Megève. Jenny was putting my proverbial timidity to the test once again. But, once her decision was made, her determination would brook no delay. And, on learning of my new religion, which stated that after the age of three the future catechumen must be conscious of what awaits her, Jacques, who had barely been consulted and was already filled with remorse, finished by giving his reluctant assent.

"Why is He everywhere?"

"Because He preserves and governs all He has created."

I very soon learned to answer the question: "Why can we not see God?" without hesitation.

"Because He is spirit."

I knew now why God is eternal, why He is almighty, why He is all-knowing, why He is infinitely good and infinitely just, infinitely merciful, and infinitely holy. I knew why He is the master of all things.

I resolved to think of God as being everywhere, and that He could see me.

I learned to love Jesus. I knew that the word "Jesus" means "God the Savior," that the word "Christ" means "the anointed," and that our Lord Jesus was anointed First Priest and King of kings. I knew that the Son of God was conceived in the womb of the Virgin Mary on the day of the Annunciation. I learned that our Lord Jesus Christ had Himself been baptized by John the Baptist.

But I loved the Holy Virgin most of all, that Lady whom the Sisters of the Cénacle held in the highest honor. Was I not called Marie, like Her, and like my *Nonamali*, whose return I still awaited patiently? It was She who obtained Divine Grace for us. It was She whom God preferred among all women. And, unlike myself and the other little girls, who were all sinners—she was free from original sin. I understood that original sin consisted in a special propensity to do naughty things, from which I was not exempt, far from it.

I scrupulously recited all my prayers before going to bed. My favorite was the *Hail Mary*, "the most beautiful prayer to the Holy Virgin," said the nun. I kept it for the end, starting with the Lord's Prayer, then continuing with the Creed, the most complicated and most terrifying: "Our Lord Jesus Christ... suffered under Pontius Pilate, was crucified, nailed to a cross, died, was buried, descended into Hell, rose again from the dead on the third day..."

That vision of Christ resuscitated troubled me. If my *Nonamali* and my grandfather, for whom I prayed fervently, did not return, and if they were transformed into "deceased," couldn't they resuscitate too? Jenny did not answer my question, and I didn't dare ask the nun in her wimple who came from another world. Nor did I pay attention to the question-and-answer that is part of the fifteenth lesson:

"Who urged Pontius Pilate to condemn our Lord Jesus Christ to death?"

"The leaders of the Jews."

At the time, the Good Friday liturgy still called upon the Catholic faithful to pray for the "faithless Jews." And called for their conversion with these words: "Let us pray also for the faithless Jews: that Almighty God remove the veil from their hearts so that they may acknowledge Jesus Christ."

Pope John XXIII removed the words "faithless Jews" by decree in 1959 and the Vatican II Council declared: "... what happened in His (Jesus Christ's) Passion cannot be charged against all the Jews, without distinction, then alive, nor against the Jews of today." In 1970, Paul VI replaced the prayer for the "conversion of the Jews" by: "Let us pray for the Jewish people, the first to hear the word of God, that they may continue to grow in the love of his name and in faithfulness to his covenant."

But right now, we are in 1947.

The last lessons were given over to the baptism itself, the purpose of my religious instruction.

"What is baptism?"

"A sacrament."

"Alright. One of the seven sacraments. And why can it be received once only?"

There, I grew a little confused. At school, if you fail a test, you can pass it again. Why not with baptism?

"Think about it. You've just said it. Because it imprints on our soul a sacramental nature. Sacramental like sacrament. Do you understand the word 'sacramental'?"

"No, sister."

"It means that it imprints on our soul an indelible sign that makes us resemble Our Lord. Do you want to be like Jesus, my child?"

"Yes, sister."

"Then you must repent of your sins."

Mentally, I approved enthusiastically. To be like Jesus and Mary, his Holy Mother, I was ready to repent of all my sins, which I was beginning to keep track of, starting with gluttony.

"What happens, my child, to a child who dies unbaptized?"

I knew that perfectly well. He goes into Limbo and will never enter Heaven.

That part bothered me. What if I had an accident before the day of my baptism and could never enter Heaven, where my *Nonamali* was waiting for me, perhaps? That prospect forced me to give up the naughtiness holding up my preparation. I wanted to receive the sanctifying grace. I wanted to become a member of the Catholic Church. I wanted to be able to receive the other Church sacraments. I wanted to be able to live as a good Christian. I wanted to renounce Satan and all his pomp, though that last word puzzled me.

On March 9, 1947, I promised to attach myself to Jesus Christ forever. False promise! It happened in the Church of Saint François Xavier, opposite the Lycée Victor-Duruy.

"We were unable to find a godfather," Jenny recalls, "but we didn't need one and we claimed it ought to have been one of my cousins, killed in the war. My sister-in-law Rolande, now Marcel's wife and a Christian, agreed to be your godmother. My parents were very hostile and hadn't been told about it. My father Saby had stayed faithful to Judaism and its institutions. He was still a member of the B'nai B'rith, which he'd helped found, and he had joined the French Jewish Consistory. Breathing any word to him of this decision was out of the question. Also present at the ceremony were my brother Marcel, and Oscar and Léon Arditti, who had encouraged the whole thing."

As for me, Michou, the main person concerned, I have no memory of the day of my baptism. I imagine it must have been a hollow triumph for Jenny, and that Jacques, still a little lame, Jacques my father, was sadder than ever.

And yet, it was from that time onwards, which has left no tangible trace in my memory, that Jenny and I became two separate beings.

From that time on, Jenny became *my mother*.

Yes, I do believe *my mother* was crazy…

"Why did you do that?"

For years I have tried to understand the motives that drove *my mother* to want to convert me—after the war, when there was no longer any objective danger. She obviously had not been touched by grace like Paul Claudel at the foot of a pillar of Notre-Dame Cathedral, or Aaron Lustiger, future Archbishop of Paris[88], who asked for a Kaddish to be recited on the esplanade in front of Notre-Dame after his death. After the war, she exhibited no special interest in Catholicism, nor in any other religion. Her Judaism had collapsed under the weight of antisemitic propaganda and its impact on her own life and of those close to her. The horrors of persecution, whose unbearable reality became clear after the war, completed the pulverization of her religious identity, so active and alive before the catastrophe.

"Why did you do it?"

My mother hesitates, thinks a bit, then launches out… "I thought about it first when Oscar and Léon got back from the camps. We kept wondering how they'd survived. They explained they owed their salvation to the Catholic deportees, the political prisoners, and the resisters, who all helped each other out, whereas with the Jews… it was every man for himself.…"

Those who had occasionally given them a lump of bread, those that

---

88. Jean-Marie Lustiger, born Aaron Lustiger to Jewish immigrant parents in 1926, converted to Catholicism at the age of 14. He became Cardinal Archbishop of Paris, a member of the Académie Française and a leading figure in French intellectual life till his death in 2007 [Translator].

had prevented them from dying of cold or dying under the blows, those that had enabled them to work indoors, it wasn't the Jews, our fellows in religion, *los muestros*; it was the red triangles, and among them Christians who, as Oscar put it, radiated the virtues of charity. It was Christians who had tendered a helping hand. Not the Jews.

"But the other Jewish deportees didn't even have a lump of bread for themselves. How could they have given one?"

My mother ignores my remark and continues: "They even passed themselves off as Catholics in the camp."

"How so? But it was impossible, surely? Weren't they circumcised?"

"I don't know… Anyway, Oscar argued in favor of your baptism. At first, I wanted you to be Protestant. Like Momo's children. But Oscar insisted, and he won me round."

"But he himself… didn't he become Jewish again later?"

"Later? Maybe. I'm talking about 1947, the year of your baptism. Oscar was no longer called Oscar but Pierre. Both brothers had changed their names…"

"And my father?"

"Jacques wasn't keen, not keen at all. But I convinced him finally. And together we decided that our daughter ought to be able to choose her own path and beliefs once she was an adult. I managed to enroll you in the Lycée Victor-Duruy, where I had spent so many happy years. You were surrounded by little girls who were practicing Catholics, I didn't want anyone to inflict on you the humiliations I suffered when they discovered my origins…. And then above all… above all, I was so afraid it would start over. Even now… I'm never sure… there are times… I thought I was… crazy."

Yes, crazy. I do think *my mother* was crazy in that year, 1946, as my father recovered from his painful accident and worked with her in the little store, now their sole source of income, and where she plotted the path that was to lead us—her and me—to 58 Avenue de Breteuil and the sisters of Notre-Dame du Cénacle. There, she held by the hand a little seven-year-old girl who understood nothing, bewildered by her now-fanatical mother, by the sight of her mother bowing and scraping to this nun. The nun, forcing a smile in my mother's direction, wielded carrot and stick to make me learn my prayers and to cross myself and genuflect correctly.

It was very likely her denial of the nearly successful annihilation of the Jews, and the sudden realization that her own daughter had escaped it by a whisker, that drove my mother to push through the doors of the Cénacle, desperate yet fiercely determined. During the war we had gone into hiding. After the war, we would make ourselves invisible; we would become like the others: good French people, Gentiles, Goyim, Aryans, Christians by any name.

To that end, *my mother* spontaneously applied a strategy I call "three C's." C for Change: Change of name, Change of religion, Change of marital status. The French Republic allowed one to change one's surname if it sounds foreign, while the Church encouraged conversion. With that, marriage to a Gentile would merely be a matter of personal affinity, and *my mother* would see to it I married the right man.

Was this a case of a resurgence of repressed feelings or signs overlooked? People sometimes neglect one instance of the three C's. They change their name but not their religion. Or they change religion but not their name. A mixed marriage works to the girl's advantage, for once, because marriage erases their name. Boys can marry good Christian girls without letting the cat out of the bag, until, that is, their offspring, betrayed by their surname, discover the unpleasant little secret in the schoolyard.

This was madness, for sure... Madness after the event... from fear that it was going to start over. Now that she *knew* what had taken place, Jenny was haunted, obsessed: the ring on the doorbell at dawn, the yellow star on the overcoat, the last metro, the roundups, the sealed railcars, the children's cries—her child's cries—and, farther on, later, even though she had not known at the time what had happened, the ashes in the crematory ovens.

Yes, I do believe she had gone crazy, like my father, like millions of dazed survivors. Her mind, worn out by so much anguish and horror, was filled with visions of an Apocalypse whose victims were her best friend Laurette, her Uncle Pepo and Aunt Ester, my little nameless five-year-old fiancé, her cousin Marc, Moïse and Marie. Then there were all the others, relatives, close friends, former boyfriends, and companions who used to have such fun at the Sephardi Youth dances not ten years earlier. And those in Salonika, Sarika whom she had loved more than her mother, the cousins, uncles, and aunts who had stayed home yet were murdered in *tierra ajena,* a foreign land, the frozen earth of ghastly Germany, ghastly Poland. All that remained was loathing and rejection of her own people who had failed to prevent all this. A feeling more powerful still than her admiration and respect for the others, for those who had come to her aid betimes, for the privileged of this world who had merely taken the trouble to exist and yet who had stretched out a helping hand.

Against her family and her tribe there welled up the great frustrations of her childhood and youth, the vomiting induced by her Uncle Rafo, the birth of the little brother that knocked her off her throne, being forced to bow before her brother's imposture, the hunk of white bread her mother had withheld from me, her child.

Jenny convinced herself that we owed our survival exclusively to the Gentiles. When she looked back at her—our—survival, all three, she saw only them, the native-born French people of good will: Madame Chaliés the concierge, Monsieur Blois, the landlady of Fleur des Alpes, and the mayor and parish priest of Villard-de-Lans.

For in *my mother's* determination in that year 1947, there weren't only the events she had just experienced in her own flesh that, like so many others, had left her winded. There were also the experiences of her own history, of her own family, of her position within the tribe. On a scale different from that of her friends back from the camps, she felt that her people, "our people" as she still called them, had not helped her. She was forgetting Nelly's son who had flouted the curfew to warn Jacques the Bulgarians were about to be rounded up. She overlooked her uncle's outstretched hand, the apartment on Rue Rossini in Nice, the refuge afforded by her father at Fleur des Alpes, or the heroism of Marc Amon.

She fell to hating them because she had begun to hate herself. To escape that hatred, I, her daughter, had to become someone else. She had to obliterate my origins, even though I had inherited them from her. She had to wipe clean the stain; she had to wash it from her own hands.

Self-loathing is a perverse serpent that comes from without, slithers inside, clings to the walls of one's innards and lies there in wait. To understand why some people, and not the weakest, sometimes succumb, one need only to listen to the discourse prevalent in the nineteen forties, following on from the thirties, not to mention the Dreyfus saga. It was then that self-hate became distorted into hatred of one's own people. At bottom, *my mother* forgave the other Jews nothing and asked little of the Gentiles, to whom she gave her all for the rest of her life, thanking them without end for having spared hers and above all mine.

My parents felt obscurely that, somehow, some of "our people" had had it coming to them. The thought makes my flesh creep. But, when one thinks about it, it was better to feel guilty without cause than the victim of chance and pure cruelty. For to see oneself as a victim is surely an intolerable affront to one's dignity.

In her *Monologue* Jenny, now recovered from her madness many years afterward, explains her actions thus: "We decided to baptize our daughter to safeguard her future. This piece of paper had saved lots of people. I hope with all my heart she will never need it." For *my mother*, after the event, baptism was a mere bureaucratic formality designed to protect her daughter from an uncertain future. By sending me to the nuns, she forgot she was exposing me to a spiritual transformation of uncertain outcome.

"And God, where is He?" might have asked the nun at Notre-Dame du Cénacle.

Having prayed to her God in vain, my mother had finished by denying Him. She wanted no other for herself. Never again. Should I then hold it against her for trying to impose on me a God that was not hers?

Catholic years

He walked by the sea and contemplated the waves breaking on the sand and the seagulls swooping on the foam with shrieks of joy. And *He* meditated on the great, the unfathomable mystery, the mystery of the Holy Trinity. Suddenly, after walking for hours on the endless beach, *He* spied a moving dot that drew near little by little, and *He* recognized a child.

"My child! What are you doing on this deserted beach?" *He* asked.

The Child did not answer straight away, and *He* then noticed that the little child was equipped with a seashell that he was using as a spoon.

"So, what are you doing with that instrument?" *He* then asked.

And *He* saw that the Child had dug a hole in the sand on the beach and was using the spoon to transfer water from the sea to this cavity.

"I'm trying," said the Child, "to pour all of the water from the sea into this opening."

He was astonished:

"Can't you see," *He* answered the Child, "that it can't be done? The water will drain away into the sand as you pour it in. And the water in the sea is without end."

Before vanishing, the Child replied:

"And yet, it would be easier for me than for you, with your poor powers of reasoning, to reach the depths of the mystery... the Mystery of the Holy Trinity."

Abbé Lesas said nothing. The entire catechism class was spellbound. The Child was there before us with his seashell, and he went on digging his hole and inexhaustibly pouring water from the ocean into it. Before him, questioning and mysterious, was the priest. Before the priest, there was us, the little girls learning the catechism. Apparently, *He*, the character meditating, was not the priest but Saint Augustine. Apparently, the Child was not just any child but the Infant Jesus. Or perhaps an angel. Anyway, the story is imprinted in my memory. And I can see, as if I was there still, the priest with his cassock, too short and threadbare, his fine deep voice with its warm inflections, standing before the child of indeterminate sex, a child like me perhaps, digging relentlessly while the waves roll onto the sand and the seagulls swoop over the foam uttering shrieks of joy.

That's what catechism was like at the *petit lycée* Victor-Duruy in the late-nineteen forties. Chaplains representing three religions came after class to educate their future congregation. There was a Protestant pastor and—it seems to me, with hindsight at least—a rabbi, but did I have the least idea what a rabbi was? My chaplain, ours, the one for we little Catholic girls, was called Abbé Lesas. I must have been a little in love with him. I loved his voice and his threadbare cassock. I knew he had taken the vow of poverty. He told us he was preparing to evangelize in China. I imagined the difficulties and trials he would be facing, the interminable voyage, the strangeness of what lay ahead.

Between 1947, the date of my baptism, and 1951, the hoped-for date of my Holy Communion, lay my years as a Christian, marked by religious fervor fueled by the Lycée's catechism classes run by Abbé Lesas. Those years witnessed a vigorous Catholic revival in France, despite the law of 1905 separating Church and State.

To convey a still fuller picture idea of the air I breathed in those years, I want to cite my contemporary, the writer Annie Ernaux. Not only is she the same age as me but also, like me, the daughter of small storekeepers. The difference is that she is native-born French, a pure provincial from Normandy, and it is through that prism that she observes the world of our common childhood.

For her, like me, the Christianity of those times "was the official framework of life and governed time," she writes in *The Years*[89]. One ate only fish on Fridays, and every newspaper carried menus for the Lenten fast, whose different stages were indicated in the Post Office calendar. That calendar, indicating the name of the saint's feast for each day of the year, lists saints' names accepted by the registry of births and death—names not on the list were not allowed. Sunday Mass, which people attended... religiously..., was an occasion for them to wear their finest clothes, scrutinize their neighbors and be seen. Afterward came the inevitable visit to the pastry shop. One could not live in this world without being baptized, nor marry without a blessing. One could not die without the last rites, the sole authorized road to the longed-for Paradise, where one would be joined again with the dear departed. Morality sprang from the commandments of the Church and took precedence over all other laws. Atheists who claimed to be freethinkers were potential libertines. Catholicism reigned over the other religions, which were deemed false or contemptible even. Such was the spirit of the times in postwar France.

My daily life was organized and inspired by the nuns' commandments. At night I knelt to say my prayers before going to bed. I genuflected and asked—in vain—my mother for a crucifix over my bed. I learned hymns, which I incorporated into my evening concerto for my parents' benefit. I

---

89. Annie Ernaux, *The Years*, translated by Alison L, Strayer, Seven Stories Press.

belted out *Il est né, le divin enfant*[90] and the *Kyrie eleison*, spelling out the enigmatic syllables without understanding them. When I was unhappy, I would converse with the Virgin Mary or my guardian angel, who I imagined bore the features of my *Nonamali*. My mother had shown me a portrait of her at eighteen, with long blond hair like a Botticelli Madonna.

I piled up marks for good behavior, trading them for coupons rewarding me for my human and Catholic qualities. I didn't attend the magic lantern sessions on Thursday afternoons, but I borrowed books and comic books from the parish library relating edifying and thrilling stories that brought me closer to Joan of Arc, Sainte Geneviève of Paris and other martyrs who left their mark on my childhood memory.

My parents, meanwhile, lived athwart two very separate worlds.

Although Jacques and Jenny slept on the Left Bank, on Rue César-Franck, in the smart, comfortable 7th Arrondissement of Paris, they worked in their little haberdashery on the Right Bank, on Rue du Faubourg-Poissonnière close to the Rue du Sentier garment district, then a working-class area. The concierge of their building there, Madame P., was rumored to have informed on people under the Occupation. There was no school on Thursdays, so I spent the day there, sitting on a corner of the counter receiving the customers' amused homage as they laughingly commented:

"Isn't she a good little girl! Good as gold!"

I was indeed quiet because I had with me my picture books, spattered with honey and jelly stains, and above all my illustrated Catholic magazines, which I'd read through and through.

A good, quiet little girl. Who suspected nothing ... And yet.

A later anecdote, which I relate in my fictitious reimagining of the myth of Orpheus and Eurydice[91], reflects the atmosphere of those mute days. This takes place in the schoolyard, in fact the one at the Victor-Duruy junior school. The characters are my schoolmates and myself during my years as a Catholic.

---

90. "He is born, the divine child," a hymn sung in French Catholic services [Translator].

91. *Histoire d'Eurydice pendant la remontée*, Seuil, 1991.

"My godfather," Clotilde lowers her voice, aware of the extraordinary impact her revelation is about to produce, "well, the Jews have put him in jail."

She pauses to savor the amazed looks on our faces as we catch our breath. She went on as if we had managed to frame the questions about to pour from our lips:

"He didn't do anything at all, except purge France of scum. He's innocent. Well, they've put him in prison."

I was dumbfounded. "Purge France," "scum." These words were foreign to me, their meaning at least; to Clotilde too, probably. But they impressed us: even Marie-Rose, whose father was a member of a Christian Democratic political party, was lost for words. All she could ask, plaintively, was:

"What's your godfather's name?"

"Xavier Vallat," said Clotilde, delighted to have held her audience in thrall.

The name sounded good and became engraved in my memory. The guttural initial sound, the alliteration... not an ordinary name. It sounded like a magic formula, the kind I used to send to my friend Véronique for use as a password: *Gzavyéwala*.

These throwbacks to the time of Collaboration and the role played in it by Xavier Vallat, first Commissioner for Jewish Questions, were uncommon, though. As Annie Erneaux remarks, adults in the postwar era droned endlessly about the privations, the food shortages, the freezing winter of 1942, tobacco coupons, swedes, and Jerusalem artichokes, not to mention *Radio Londres*, the voice of the Free French broadcast from London, and the bombing. Most of all they talked of Marshal Pétain, or rather the Master of Vichy, already too old when they handed power to him, and "totally gaga." But, as Annie Ernaux points out, they could speak only of what they had seen and known, which they relived as they recounted it to their children over a boozy Sunday luncheon, after Mass, perhaps even without having been to Mass. There was no talk of sealed wagons filled with children headed for the slaughterhouse, nor of the large-scale roundups, the Vel d'Hiv, Marseille, Nice and elsewhere, nor of the walking dead at Drancy, Compiègne, Gurs, Beaune-la-Rolande, Les Mille, and other holding camps for Jews awaiting shipment eastward.

This explains the "two-faced war," the two distinct wars experienced by the two communities. It explains the difference between Annie Erneaux's parents and mine, the "musicians," a difference "neither documentaries nor history lessons could dispel." Not for that generation at least. For "neither the crematoria nor the atom bomb occurred in the same epoch as black-market butter, the air raid sirens and sheltering in the cellars[92]."

And so, for the little Christian I was now becoming, began the decades-long sleep made of denial, forgetting, and silence.

As those nineteen forties, which had begun so atrociously, drew to a close, like most little French girls, those "valiant souls," I waited. I waited impatiently for the ultimate accolade for my good deeds and my years of catechism. I was waiting for my First Communion. The Big One. My Holy Communion.

Excommunication

"No, you can't. It's just not possible!"

"But Mommy, why? Why?"

I sobbed. I screamed in distress, in anger. I shut myself up in my room, slammed the door. I wanted to run away, sleep under the bridges by the river. Anywhere. To die.

"No, you can't have your First Communion. It's impossible."

"But why? Mommy! Mommy! Why?"

Suddenly there was a gulf of silence between us. I sensed that *my mother* was about to reply. At the same time, I was trembling. I could sense that her answer was going to be stunning, petrifying. And it was:

"Because we're... Jewish."

At first, I couldn't understand the word. I'd heard it, of course, particularly from the lips of Clotilde. And then during the catechism classes, when they told us about the Jewish leaders who had demanded the crucifixion of Our Lord. But I couldn't pin it down. I could not recognize it coming from *my mother*. Throughout the Occupation, she and my father had talked

---

92. *Ibid.*

about "musicians" and they still avoided that accursed word. But applying that word to us… It was unbearable. Impossible. Unpronounceable. And yet, *my mother*, my mummy, the person I loved most in the world, had just spoken it.

I sobbed again. I did not want to hear it. Yet, somehow, I wanted to understand. Why? Why?

Then my mother uttered another, equally unintelligible, sentence:

"Your grandfather Saby lives across the street. He might recognize you in your communion dress. He wouldn't understand."

Incredulous, now, I looked her in the face. I'd never seen *my mother* so embarrassed.

"What do you mean, he wouldn't understand?"

Why couldn't he understand? What was there for him not to understand? What did my First Communion have to do with my grandfather, whom I'd seen only rarely in recent years even though he lived close by and talked—when he did talk—about cooking and bridge?

"But Mommy… what am I going to tell the priest? And Véronique? And my dress? Aren't we going to order it then? And my coral necklace?"

My mother seemed relieved to see me concerned over minor details. To calm me down she took a conciliatory tone:

"Don't worry, darling. You'll have your coral necklace. I've already ordered it. And as for the dress, I'll have one made for you, a lovely Sunday dress. In fact, the shop has just taken delivery of some velvet and I've kept back a few yards. Not white, but you can choose the color. And, you know, I'll take Thursday off to take you to the Théâtre du Petit-Monde. And we'll have a new trousseau made up for your doll, Bleuette, and…."

She had run out of things to invent, *my mother*, as I glared at her with the eyes of an eleven-year-old, nearly twelve, now weighing her up. She was prepared to make any concession. Except the one I was demanding with more than a hint of supplication in my voice:

"I want my communion."

"Impossible."

"In that case, … I won't be able to go to Heaven. And *Nonamali*, I'll never see her again…"

My mother drew herself up, looked down icily at little me with a stare devoid of all warmth, coolly taking upon herself all the world's cruelty and barbarity.

"Do you want to know... do you really want to know: your *Nonamali* and your grandfather Moïse ... are dead ... because they were ...*Jewish.*"

I had no answer to that. I couldn't stop sobbing.

And from that moment, which became inalterably implanted in my life story, I remember only two reactions, one of resistance, the other of spinelessness.

In a paroxysm of violence and loathing of *my mother* and of myself, I flung the coral necklace against the wall, the necklace by which she thought she could purchase my complicity in her "betrayal." Apparently, the necklace shattered into a thousand pieces, and I threw it in the trashcan.

I never dared go to see the Abbé Lesas to tell him the truth behind my twofold desertion—of his catechism classes and my preparation for Communion. I never dared utter that sentence, so simple, yet no doubt so outlandish for him: "My mother, who freely chose to have me baptized, won't let me have my communion because we're Jewish." On spotting him in the corridors of the lycée, I hid in the toilets, the most obvious place to vomit up the nausea I felt—at myself, and at her in whom I had placed my absolute trust as a child. The Nazis had done a good job: not only had they exterminated millions of human beings, but they had also put countless others in voluntary thrall to self-rejection and self-loathing.

Deep inside myself, I called *my mother's* prohibition, for want of a better word, "excommunication," since against my will it disconnected me from the community to which I then aspired.

That year I was obliged to witness in silence the other girls' First Communion. An old classmate recently showed me the photograph of her as a first communicant on the esplanade in front of the Church of Saint-François-Xavier in 1951: an unbearable reminder for the girl who had been excluded.

The girls dressed as brides in graceful, immaculate white dresses, white pumps and veils are climbing the steps to the church, missal in hand, like a flock of swallows in the gorgeous spring light. I gaze at the picture today as I must have gazed on the real thing at the time, trying virtually to add one last little girl, one looking like me. After all, the Soviets effaced their pariahs from official photographs. Why could I not do the reverse and add myself

to this one? As a form of reparation, since I never dared talk to *my mother* during her lifetime about this injury, which she could have spared me.

Jenny justified herself regarding this excommunication only once. In her *Monologue* she writes: "After all, I couldn't sit by and watch Michou become antisemitic and reject us. I had to tell her."

Yes, Mommy. But there was the way it was said.

Now that my resentment has worn off, I heed the reasonable voice of little Annie Ernaux describing without pathos her own First Communion, "the glorious harbinger of all the important things that were going to happen: periods, the school certificate or admission to lower secondary school." On the benches sat the boys in dark suits with an armband, separated from the girls by the central aisle. They look like the grooms "paired off two by two, they are likely to be in ten years' time." And the little native-born Christian concludes: "After having proclaimed with one voice at Vespers I renounce the devil and unite myself to Jesus for always, we could then dispense with religious practice, being confirmed a Christian equipped with the necessary and sufficient baggage to feel a part of the dominant community and be certain there is surely something after death[93]."

Annie Erneaux's voice convinces me today that I suffered a thousand of those deaths for what was ultimately a frivolous reason, namely the fact that my grandfather Saby lived nearby on Rue Pérignon. And that I would doubtless have developed like the Catholic girls of my generation, if *my mother* had allowed me to perform the necessary ritual of First Communion, thereby completing the baptism she had imposed on me—even if that meant vouchsafing the truth to me at some later date.

But no argument, no consolation came to the ears of the disgusted child I then was, nor to those of the tormented adult I later became. None of those balms would speed the healing of an open wound.

My mother had debased herself. She had fallen from her pedestal. Never again would I see her with the same eyes. The pain and that nagging question lingered for days, weeks, years, decades: Why? The question shifted over the years. No longer was I a little girl deprived of her communion, but an adult puzzling over the contradiction. Why? Why did she do it? Why the baptism and then the taboo? Why the conversion and then the excommunication? Why?

Then I repressed it all, the baptism, the catechism, the Catholic years and, finally, the maternal ukase that had made of me a renegade vis-à-vis two religions. I forgot Christianity. I was ignorant of Judaism. I became a traitor to both. I blanked everything out in my own eyes and in those of others. I reverted to concealment behind false papers, as in my early childhood. I applied the theory of the "Three C's" for Change. After religion came conjugality, with a change of name. I never revealed my age, skating over those years of darkness and evading questions. I abandoned Moïse and *Nonamali* to their dreadful fate without sepulcher. I became opaque. And Silence fell. The silence was to linger like a long sleep, from which I would have to awaken someday. A silence I would have to break.

Now, only now do I understand Jenny, her dilemma, and her despair. She wanted to preserve me. But she could not eternally deny *herself*, deny

---

93. *Ibid.*

her people. She had fallen into denial. She had fallen into forgetting, dragging me with her.

When I set out in search of our distant ancestors, the proud Benvenistes of Spain—the Spain of the Catholic Monarchs—half of whom had become *conversos*, New Christians hunted by the Inquisition, I came to understand how, like them, my mother had become "marranized," remaining faithful to the lost tribe in her heart.

She had, I had, become a Jewess of Silence.

Law of Return

Today, the pertinent European reference
is not baptism. It is extermination...
Holocaust recognition is our contemporary
European entry ticket.

—TONY JUDT, *POSTWAR*

As I end this tale, which the narrator opens in the middle of the Great
Fire of summer 1917 in the partly Jewish city of Salonika, Spain's Law of
Return, enacted on June 24, 2015, has just come into force.[94] Making good
on a historical debt, it allows descendants of the Alhambra Decree to apply for citizenship in the land of the Catholic kings, the land that was their
home five hundred years ago.

Will this symbol leave a lasting mark on the history of my tribe? As
early as the beginning of the last century, Maïr Benveniste held a Spanish
passport, thanks to which two of his sons escaped the Nazis. My initial
reaction, though, is to be sorry that the many ancestors who spoke Ladino—Judeo-Spanish—never knew before they died that their descendants
would one day be reinstated in their rights, that an historic injustice would
be remedied, and that the great-great-grandchildren of the banished would
receive the keys to new homes in a Sefarad restored. Like in the tales Sarika
used to tell little Janja to lull her to sleep in the soft light of the oil lamp.
Today, Jews of Iberia are becoming Spaniards once more. With a passport
valid throughout the European Union, they will, ideally, find refuge in all

---

94 A similar law had been enacted in the same year by the Portuguese government.

those countries that have at one time or other in their history expelled their own Hebrews.

Jenny's tale is testimony to a sense of belonging to her erstwhile community—until it came to an end in 1951, when she became *my mother*, when she first converted me, then excommunicated me. But her life stretched into the early years of the twenty-first century. Meantime, I broke her silence, the silence that had imprisoned us both within a contrived identity—an identity that probably no longer deceived anyone but ourselves. For Jenny had lost not only her faith and her religion. She had lost her memory also. Or rather she had mislaid it. In the shock that she and Jacques experienced—the shock they thought they had experienced, then discovered—it was as if they had become deaf-mute. Or as if they had fallen into a deep coma, into which they had dragged me through mingled love and contagion. There followed a long ellipse, in my life even more than in theirs.

I was born in France—yes, I repeat the fact here for the special pleasure of my mother, buried in a small village's cemetery in the Seine-et-Marne region. In her eyes, to be born in France was the greatest gift of good fortune she could have offered me, the gift of a fairy godmother, an authentically Celtic fairy godmother, summoned by her to my crib in the depths of Brittany. Throughout my thoroughly French childhood, every effort was made to preserve me from that murky, alien, foreign "origin" that had stigmatized my mother and my father and still did so, to underscore my own sound and glorious origins.

So steeped was my mother in the history of France, making me rehearse it over and over in my primary school years, that she wound up making it her own from start to finish. At the end of her life, in the meandering babble that preceded her final breath, with her prodigious memory but less lucid towards the end, she told the faithful aide assigned to her by the local social services that she was the daughter of Gaston (of Orleans?) and of Eleonor (of Aquitaine?), celebrated French historical figures. Light years from Sabbetai and Myriam, her biological father and mother, public knowledge of which could have cost her worse than her life not long before! One glorious genealogy simply erased the other, the one my mother wanted nothing to do with nor wanted me to know anything about.

I was not alone in my ignorance of those origins. For the generations that came after me in our family, the past was cloaked in such a thick veil of silence that some younger cousins born after World War Two wondered why their grandparents spoke with such a funny accent and pronounced their r's in a way attributable to no known region of France.

The Holocaust was the other event, or non-event, we avoided discussing, and for a long time it was designated by no known name. To refer to the unspeakable, we used metonymic labels such as "the deportation" or "the camps." The word "Holocaust" did not reach France until the American television series of that name was shown. By then I was living in the United States. Claude Lanzmann's film definitively imposed the term Shoah[95] in France. My mother never saw that film and never used the word.

As a result, my search for lost time began under inauspicious circumstances. Upon reflection, I even wonder whether all the books I have written till now were not exercises in preparation for this one, rehearsals, in various forms, for this story in particular.

It was fiction that led me to the truth. The unconscious within my own texts was first made manifest to me obliquely. It took me seven years to write *Histoire d'Eurydice pendant la remontée*: Eurydice emerging from Hades. Catharsis. Emerging from Silence. Discovering that "thing" that no one yet called either "Genocide," nor "Holocaust," nor "Shoah," nor "Destruction," nor "Annihilation," but only the "disaster," with a small *d*, so as not to awaken either the reader's or my attention too sharply, before the discovery of the Disaster with a capital *D*.

As Sophie, the little adopted Christian girl, discovered her story, which was Sarah's story, I drew on my mother's memory to nourish my own and go on writing fiction. Later, that memory was to serve again in giving a voice to *Returning from Silence*, to Jenny's story.

---

95. The French now refer more commonly to the destruction of the Jews in the World War Two as the Shoah. [Translator]

Was it chance, or was it necessity? It was in the year 2000 that I was reminded of the Benvenistes in my family tree and the place of my mother's birth. To attend a seminar at the University of Thessaloniki, I journeyed by plane in the opposite direction to the journey taking little Janja to the land of Jenny aboard the legendary Orient Express.

Inside the auditorium of the Aristotle University, I was about to begin a lecture on "Marguerite Yourcenar and the paradox of women's condition," when I was overcome with the sudden realization that there, beneath my feet, lay the tomb of Rafael Benveniste and all my ancestors. This was the sacred site of the ancient cemetery of the Sephardim, preserved in the photograph below but wiped out by the successive endeavors of the Greek and Nazi authorities. More than fifty thousand of my people, meanwhile, had been carted away to undergo medical experiments or death by gas. No sepulcher for them.

Yet, in the same flash these ghosts vanished, and the dizzy spell passed. I resumed my academic voice and did not protest when our guide for the afternoon took us on an historical tour of Thessaloniki without once mentioning the role of the Jews in the old city. But I had made up my mind to recount *Jenny's Story*, after my mother's death and thanks to what she had passed on to me: her Act of Transmission. A first Journey, a first book was to emerge from this, the one I am completing today.

My mother's Act of Transmission delivered the Living and the Survivors from Silence. That left the Lost. Their silhouettes hovered around Jenny's story but did not occupy it. Even Jacques, her husband, whom she had adored all her life and beyond, interested her only when he was with her. He was born out of their encounter. She could barely imagine him "beforehand" and, not believing in life after death, nor could she imagine him "afterward."

At about the same time, I journeyed to Spain to return to the sources of the Sephardim. The ghosts of the Benvenistes of long ago, from before the expulsion and from after, were already waiting for me in the Iberian Peninsula of medieval times, constantly obscured and confined to the unspoken, like Janja. I also encountered the figures of women and men who had faced the same trial as myself, among them my distant historical ancestor

Hannah Benveniste Mendes, née Beatriz de Luna and honored under the name of Gracia Naci, the unforgettable *señora*.

Less than three months after Jenny's death on December 19, 2005, I received an email in English from the United Jewish Social Fund:

Dear Mrs. Benrey:

I was forwarded a couple of months ago your question about additional information concerning the deportation of your grandparents. We questioned the research centre in Italy that provided the following:

Moïse Benrey was born in Bulgaria, in an unknown town. He was arrested in Argegno near Como on September 4, 1944, by the Nazis. He was taken to the prison of San Vittore in Milan, then in a transit camp in Bolzano from where he was deported to Auschwitz on October 24, 1944. The same happened to his wife.

The chief archivist says she does not believe that there was a concentration camp in Argegno, it was rather the area on the border between Switzerland and Italy. The data she has come from Mr. Edmond Tagger who provided them in 1974. She asks if she could have the birthplace of Mr. and Mrs. Benrey. You may reach her at the following e-mail address:

Her name: Liliana Picciotto.

In its dry tone, this email came as a signal, prompting everything that ensued. I took it as a prayer from beyond the tomb, as a fresh exhortation to break the Silence, to investigate, explore, inquire, research, re-forge broken links, strike out in a new direction. A new challenge. It came as a reminder of my duty to mourn and erect a sepulcher, and then of my obligation to seek out the life beneath the shroud—a shroud I will have to stitch together from scratch. As memory's surveyor, Antigone takes over from Eurydice. I have set her to work. Or rather I am journeying with her to the lands where those shadows lived their lives… Turkey, Romania, Bulgaria, Italy… Another book will emerge from it:

À la recherche de Marie J. In search of Marie J.

I am deeply grateful to Hugo Moreno, who has partnered with me in this undertaking and who has supported me unstintingly from start to finish.

I owe a debt of gratitude to Marion Dupuis, the soul and instrument of my research.

This book would not exist in this English-language version without the determination, professionalism, and talent of Rupert Swyer, who has served the original in all its dimensions. For which I thank him warmly.

Thanks are due to all those whose names follow, for their contributions to the edifice.

Nicole Abravanel, Oskar Alexander, Élie Anavi, Yvette Anavi, Claude Amon, Renée Amon, Ana Arav, Pelagia Astrinidou, François Azar, Danièle Ball, Jacky Benmayor, Marcel Benabou, Lisa Benrey, Michel Benrey, Yvetta Benrey, Annie Benveniste, Fabienne Benveniste, Guy Benveniste, Rika Benveniste, Denise Berrebi, Marie- Françoise Berthu- Courtivron, André Burguière, Évelyne Burguière, Jacqueline Biran, Yair Biran, Sylvie Blaise- Bossuet, Joseph Brami, Jean Carasso, Jean-Alain Carminati, Gérard Chaliand, Giselle Chapuzet, Manuela Cisternas, Gaëlle Collin, Isabelle de Courtivron, Teresa Cremisi, Dominique Desanti, Alain de Toledo, Élyane Dezon-Jones, Veselin Djendov, Chantal Dupuis, Vidal Eliakim, Anne-Marie Faraggi-Rychner, Carol Friedmann, Ivanka Gezenko, Nilufer Gole, Alain Guezou, Jean-Max Guieu, Ladislau Gyemant, Madeleine Hage, Sappho Haralambous, Jean-Pierre Hardy, Martin Ivanov, Martine Jeantet-Peissik, Serge Klarsfeld, Claude Klein, Eva Klein, Kostas Kotsakis, Julia Kristeva, Jean-Claude Kuperminc, Jean Laloum, Batya Landsman-Unterschatz, Jenny Laneurie, Annamaria Laserra, Jeffrey Malka, Lukia Mallah, Yannis Megas, Rena Molho, Francisco Javier Moreno, Sophie Mousset, Rumania Nedialkova, Maryline Noël, Pierre Nora, Ivan Pastoukhov, Vladimir Paunovski, Erica Peraya, Brigitte Peskine, Colette

Piault, Liliana Picciotto, Elisabeth Racine-Dognin, Nicole Renault, Claire Romi, Joëlle Roubine, David Saltiel, Michele Sarfatti, Joël Schmidt, Erwin Simsensohn, Smilena Smilkova, Ralph Tarica, Lise Tiano, Haïm Vidal Séphiha, Odette Varon, Léon Volovici, Michel Wieviorka, David Woods, Michèle Woods.

Without my editor Betty Mialet, who has accompanied this project since its inception, and without Vanessa Springora, who guided it, this novel would never have seen the light of day in its present form.

Swan Isle Press is a not-for-profit publisher
of poetry, fiction, and nonfiction.

For information on books of related interest or
for a catalog of new publications contact:
www.swanislepress.com

Returning from Silence
Designed by Marianne Jankowski
Typeset in Adobe Jensen Pro